A thousand bows thru_ _ _
the air, only to be knocl_ _ _
that most of them fell f_ _ _

The second group of _ _ _ _ _
but rather than diving toward the Fal'Borna or their horses, they swooped at the other eagles and began to attack them.

The rasping screams of the birds seemed to drown out all other sound. The second group of eagles now vastly outnumbered the first, and they attacked in packs of three or four, tearing at their victims with those enormous beaks and cruel talons. Several more of the birds dropped to the ground, dead or dying.

Tirnya could see the Fal'Borna pointing up at the eagles. A moment later, the white-hairs appeared to decide that they could turn their full attention to the approaching army. She could hear voices shouting, but she couldn't make out what they were saying.

Tirnya looked at the settlement, expecting to see Fal'Borna warriors on horseback, but at first she saw nothing.

"God save us all," she heard Enly mutter.

"What?" she said. "I don't see . . ."

But she did. And the sight of it turned her innards to water.

It looked like a breaker rolling toward the Aelean shore. But instead of the aqua waters of the Sea of Stars, this wave was made of fire. It was pale yellow, like the eyes of the angry young Fal'Borna Tinya had spoken to in the last sept. The wave grew as it approached the armies of Stelpana, until it towered over them.

‡

"The final chapter of the Blood of the Southlands series is satisfying. The characters Coe has invested so much time in continue to be the focal point, and all the loose ends are tied up neatly. . . . Fans of the series will enjoy cozying up with their favorite—and least favorite—occupants of the Southlands."
—*RT Book Reviews*

Turn the page for more rave reviews. . . .

"Coe steers his characters with considerable force, en route to a conclusion that is satisfying if not surprising."

—*Publishers Weekly*

"*The Dark-Eyes' War* is an excelllent conclusion to Blood of the Southlands, a fantasy trilogy that looks hard at the ease with which old enmities are reignited and the cost of warfare. I hope that David B. Coe will continue to write stories in this intriguing, masterfully developed world with its compelling forms of magic."   —*Bookloons*

"David B. Coe is a great example of a modern epic fantasy writer. . . . The world he created and brought to readers is vivid and detailed, the characters are three dimensional, there are multiple story lines all twisted into one, and the magic battles are of epic proportion. It's everything a fantasy reader could want and more. . . ."

—*Fantasy Book Critic*

PRAISE FOR THE
BLOOD OF THE SOUTHLANDS TRILOGY

THE HORSEMENS' GAMBIT

"Coe steps up the tension and raises the stakes, leaving readers quivering in anticipation of book three."

—*Publishers Weekly*

"Coe manages to take several serious, weighty issues, approach them from distinctly different points of view, and make you sympathetic toward characters who sometimes act selfishly or viciously. He absolutely nails the plot and sequencing. this is the best yet in the series."

—*RT Book Reviews*

"David B. Coe ties off this second episode with a knot of hope, while leaving the Southlands on the brink of bloody conflict. I can't wait for the conclusion to his excellent series, and have added him to my must-read author list."

—*Bookloons*

"David B. Coe created a richly textured, unique world in his Winds of the Forelands, and topped himself with *The Sorcerers' Plague,* his first novel set in the Southlands of the same world. Now, in *The Horsemen's Gambit,* Coe weaves together engagingly complex characters; unique, unusual magic; political intrigue; and a compelling, unpredictable story into a captivating epic that will enthrall fantasy readers. . . ."

—*Fantasy Book Critic*

THE SORCERER'S PLAGUE

"The Southlands are as highly detailed as the Forelands of Coe's five-volume Winds of the Forelands. The characters, especially the old searcher, are extremely well drawn. Those who enjoyed Coe before should like him again, and since one need not have read Winds to figure out anything in the first book of Blood of the Southlands, newcomers can jump right in."

—*Booklist*

"*The Sorcerer's Plague* satisfies with sharply drawn characters and an intense, intelligent plot. I eagerly await the next book of the Southlands."

—Kate Elliott, bestselling author of *Spirit Gate*

"Coe's new series is his best yet: appealing characters, twisty plot, and absorbing world."

—Sherwood Smith

"Coe's plotting is excellent and imaginative. His characters are well drawn and unique. . . . I can't wait to read the next one."

—*ConNotations*

TOR BOOKS BY DAVID B. COE

BLOOD OF THE SOUTHLANDS

Book 1: *The Sorcerers' Plague*
Book 2: *The Horsemen's Gambit*
Book 3: *The Dark-Eyes' War*

THE LONTOBYN CHRONICLE

Book 1: *Children of Amarid*
Book 2: *The Outlanders*
Book 3: *Eagle-Sage*

WINDS OF THE FORELANDS

Book 1: *Rules of Ascension*
Book 2: *Seeds of Betrayal*
Book 3: *Bonds of Vengeance*
Book 4: *Shapers of Darkness*
Book 5: *Weavers of War*

The Dark-Eyes' War

-+-

Book Three of Blood of the Southlands

DAVID B. COE

TOR®
fantasy

A TOM DOHERTY ASSOCIATES BOOK
NEW YORK

THE DARK-EYES' WAR

Copyright © 2010 by David B. Coe

All rights reserved.

Edited by James Frenkel

Maps by Ellisa Mitchell

A Tor Book
Published by Tom Doherty Associates, LLC
175 Fifth Avenue
New York, NY 10010

www.tor-forge.com

Tor® is a registered trademark of Tom Doherty Associates, LLC.

ISBN 978-0-7653-5552-2

First Edition: February 2010
First Mass Market Edition: December 2011

Printed in the United States of America

0 9 8 7 6 5 4 3 2 1

Once again, for Alex and Erin

Acknowledgments

As always, many thanks to all who have helped me with this book and those who have come before, including Tom Doherty, Liz Gorinsky, Megan Becker, Steven Padnick, Carol Russo and her staff, Romas Kukalis, Terry McGarry, Sara Sarver, my wonderful agent, Lucienne Diver, my fine editor and good friend, Jim Frenkel, and, finally, Nancy, Alex, and Erin.

—D.B.C.

Range

Sea of Stars

AELEA

The Companion Lakes

Lake NaaJ

Highlands River

STELPANA

Aelina

Aelean Highlands

Redcliff

Greysford

Eagle's Pass

Eagles Inlet

N'Kiel's Span

Bred's Landing

Yorl

FAL'BORNA

Central Plain

Silverwater Wash

Thamia

Ofirean City

Siraam

Ravens Wash

Tanganne Moor

Fairdale

TORDJANNE

Ofirean Sea

Medgasse

Tanganne River

Shevden

Maifor City

Strait of the Sage

QOSANTIA

Faedre's Island

Ferenham

Qosantian Lowlands

Blackrock Islands

Uplands

Demon's Claw Bay

Jolly's Strait

Grand Salt Flats

NAQBAE

Cape of Fire

The Rocklands

Ebon Peninsula

Eilidh's Twins

Jalshyre

Briny Point

The Shallows

The Southlands

Border Range

The Companion Lakes

Porcupine Lake

Bear Lake

Owl Lake

Skunk Lake

Lowna

Tivston

Turtle Lake

C'Bijor's Neck

Kirayde

STELPANA

Kunnelwicks

Sentaya

Greysford

k'Sukd River

THE HORN

Threads River

D'Ragor

S'Vralna

N'Kiel's Span

Bred's Landing

Silverwater Wash

Qalsyn

Majon's Wash

FAL'BORNA

Ravens Wash

Central Plain

Thamia

Ofirean City

J'BALANAR

Ofirean Sea

Siraam

The Companion Lakes Region

DJ 2007 Ellisa Mitchell

Characters

❖━❖

Qalsyn (an Eandi City in Stelpana)

JENOE ONJAEF, a marshal in the Qalsyn army

TIRNYA ONJAEF, Jenoe and Zira's daughter, a captain in
   the Qalsyn army

MAISAAK TOLM, lord governor of Qalsyn

ENLY TOLM, Maisaak's son, lord heir of Qalsyn and a
   captain in the Qalsyn army

STRI BALKETT, a captain in the lord governor's army

OLIBAN HERT, a lead rider in Tirnya's company

QAGAN FAWLER, a lead rider in Tirnya's company

DYN GRATHIDAR, a lead rider in Tirnya's company

CROW, a lead rider in Tirnya's company

Other Eandi Leaders

GRIES BALLIDYNE, lord heir of Fairlea and a captain in
   the Fairlea army

HENDRID CRISH, marshal in the army of Waterstone

From Kirayde (a Mettai Village in the Northern
Reaches of Stelpana)

BESH, an old Mettai man, a member of the village's
   Council of Elders

LICALDI, also Lici, an old Mettai woman, now deceased
EMA, Besh's wife, now deceased
ELICA, his daughter
SIRJ, Elica's husband
MIHAS, Sirj and Elica's elder son
ANNZE, Sirj and Elica's daughter
CAM, Sirj and Elica's younger son
SYLPA, Lici's foster mother, now deceased

On the Plains of the Fal'Borna

GRINSA JAL ARRIET, a Weaver from the Forelands
CRESENNE JA TERBA, Grinsa's wife
BRYNTELLE JA GRINSA, Grinsa and Cresenne's daughter
E'MENUA, a'laq of a Fal'Borna sept in the Central Plain
D'PERA, n'qlae of E'Menua's sept and E'Menua's wife
U'VARA, E'Menua and D'Pera's eldest daughter
Q'DAER, a Weaver in E'Menua's sept
L'NORR, a Weaver in E'Menua's sept
T'LISHA, a girl in E'Menua's sept, L'Norr's concubine
F'SOLYA, a Fal'Borna woman
I'JOLED, F'Solya's husband
F'GHARA, a'laq of a small Fal'Borna sept in the Central Plain
S'PLAED, a'laq of a Fal'Borna sept in the Northern Plain,
   now deceased
O'TAL, a'laq of a Fal'Borna sept in the Northern Plain
H'LORYN, a'laq of a Fal'Borna sept in the Northern Plain
B'VRIL, son of S'Bahn, a Fal'Borna warrior

The Merchants

TORGAN PLYE, an Eandi merchant from Tordjanne
JASHA ZIFFEL, an Eandi merchant, deceased
BRINT HEDFARREN, an Eandi merchant from Tordjanne,
   also known as Young Red
LARIQENNE GLYSE, an Eandi merchant from Stelpana,
   also known as Lark, deceased

R'SHEV, a Qirsi merchant on the plains of Stelpana
STAM CORFEJ, an Eandi merchant

Lifarsa (a Mettai Village)

FAYONNE, a Mettai woman, eldest of the village
MANDER, Fayonne's son

Lowna (a Fal'Borna Village on the Companion Lakes)

S'DORYN, a Qirsi man
N'TEVVA, S'Doryn's wife
T'NOTH, a Qirsi man, friend of S'Doryn and N'Tevva
T'KAAR, a Qirsi man, brother of T'Noth
A'VINYA, T'Kaar's wife
U'SELLE, a'laq of the village
JYNNA, an Y'Qatt girl
VETTALA, a young Y'Qatt girl
ETAN, a young Y'Qatt boy

The
Dark-Eyes'
War

Chapter 1

SOUTHERN CENTRAL PLAIN, FAL'BORNA LAND,
MEMORY MOON WANING, YEAR 1211

h e was being hunted. Somehow he had become their prey, like the rilda that grazed on this plain. Except slower. So much slower.

Stam Corfej had been peddling his wares among the Fal'Borna for the better part of eight fours, more than half a lifetime. He knew as well as anyone how hard the white-haired sorcerers of the Central Plain could be. He'd bargained with them, been threatened by them, been called a cheat and a dark-eye bastard and worse. More than once he'd considered giving up on the Qirsi and returning to his native Aclca. A peddler could do well in the Mountain Nation, perhaps not inland, but along her rocky shores, in Redcliff or Yorl.

But it had never taken him long to dismiss the idea of returning to the sovereignty. Whatever gold he might make in Eandi territory he could double and then some trading among the Fal'Borna. He knew the tastes of the golden-skinned clan. He knew their ways, and he knew how to best them in a negotiation.

And while he didn't particularly like the white-hairs, he had never felt threatened by them. At least not until now.

It was said among peddlers in the Southlands that commerce cared nothing for the color of a man's eyes. Qirsi and Eandi, white-hair and dark-eye; they had spent nearly a thousand years fighting the Blood Wars, learning from their fathers to hate the other, and passing that lesson along to their children. But when it came to trade, men and women of both races managed to put aside their enmity. Gold was gold. The Qirsi might have thought the Eandi brutish and cruel, but they loved Qosantian honey wine; Eandi nobles cursed the white-hairs and their frightening magic, but they decorated the hilts of their swords and the hands, wrists, and necks of their mistresses with gems from the Nid'Qir.

Stam had done well over the years catering to such appetites. He'd traveled the length and breadth of the Southlands searching for wares that would fetch a good price. He'd traded in the fishing villages of the D'Krad and the woodland towns of the M'Saaren, the shining cities of the H'Bel and the septs of the Fal'Borna, and he had learned a great deal about the likes and dislikes of all the Qirsi clans.

So when he saw those Mettai baskets that Brint HedFarren was selling at the bend in the wash, where he and his fellow merchants often gathered, he jumped at the chance to buy them. The Mettai were renowned for their basket weaving, and these baskets were as beautiful as any Stam had ever seen. Tightly woven, brilliantly colored, and, best of all, clearly dyed by hand, which increased their value. If Barthal Milensen and Grijed Semlor and Lark hadn't been there claiming their share, Stam might well have bought every one that Young Red was selling. As it was, he only got twelve.

Who would have guessed that twelve Mettai baskets—fewer, actually, since he still had three in his cart—could kill so many people? Who would have thought that they could destroy two good-sized septs so quickly and so completely?

That night in the first sept, Stam had no idea what was happening. At first it seemed that the pestilence had come and he assumed that he would fall ill like the Fal'Borna around him. But as the night wore on and the white-hairs began to destroy their z'kals with fire and shaping magic, he realized that whatever illness had struck at the sept was nothing like any pestilence he had ever seen. He fled the village, amazed that he had managed to survive and wanting only to put as much distance as possible between himself and the horrors he had witnessed.

Three nights later, when the same disease struck at another sept he was visiting—a sept more than eight leagues away from the first—he began to suspect that this was more than mere coincidence. He still didn't understand, but he knew that he wanted nothing more to do with white-hairs and their magic.

He decided that he'd lingered too long in the north. He resolved to turn his cart south and make his way to the warm waters of the Ofirean Sea. The Snows were coming; the plain was no place for an old merchant during the cold turns.

A few days later Stam stopped at a Fal'Borna village along the Thraedes River, intending to trade for some food and wine. This wasn't a sept, but rather a small, walled city, known as H'Nivar. It had once belonged to the Eandi, but it was taken by the white-hairs during the last of the Blood Wars. As Stam approached the north gates of the village, he saw a line of peddlers' carts stretching in his direction. He slowed, unsure of what to make of the column.

"Pardon, friend," he called to the trader at the end of the line. "Can you tell me what's going on here?"

The peddler, an old Eandi man with long grey hair and a full beard, shrugged, puffing on a pipe filled with what smelled like Tordjanni pipeweed.

"Word is, th' white-hairs are searching all peddlers' carts."

"What for?"

The man shrugged again. "Don' know."

"Baskets," came a voice from farther down the column. A young woman peered back at them, the wind making her long red hair dance. "They're looking for baskets, just like all the Fal'Borna."

Suddenly, Stam found it hard to draw breath. "Why?" he asked, barely making himself heard.

The woman frowned. "Haven't you heard about the plague?"

He felt light-headed. "What does the plague have to do with baskets?"

She waved her hand, seeming to dismiss the question.

"Probably nothing at all. But you know the Fal'Borna: They're always looking for some new reason to hate the Eandi."

"They claim it's a Mettai curse," said the merchant in line ahead of the woman. "They think that the Mettai and some merchants have conspired together to destroy them." He laughed. "As if the Mettai would trust us."

The woman said something in return. Stam didn't hear what it was. His mind was racing. Baskets? A plague? A Mettai curse? What had he done? What had HedFarren done to him? Had it been his baskets that sickened the people in those two settlements? He didn't understand how it could be possible, but then again, the blood magic of the Mettai had always been a mystery to him.

He shouldn't have left the way he did. He would have been better off waiting there on line for a while longer before pretending to grow impatient. Then he might have been able to steer his cart away from the city without drawing attention to himself, without giving anyone reason to think that he'd had anything to do with the baskets. He might even have learned more about this curse the others were talking about.

But in that moment, all he could think was that he had to get away from the Fal'Borna as quickly as possible. He knew just how brutal the Qirsi of the plain could be with their enemies.

And he was their enemy now. He hadn't intended it; he hadn't known what he was doing. But they wouldn't believe that, nor would they care even if they did believe it. He was a dead man.

He turned his cart around and started back the way he had come.

"Hey, where are you going?" asked the man who had been in front of him in line.

Stam didn't look back. "I have to go."

"It doesn't affect us, you know," the man called to him. "This pestilence. It won't make you sick. You have nothing to worry about."

Stam nodded, but he said nothing and he didn't look back. It was all he could do to keep from using his whip to make Wislo, his cart horse, go faster.

"What an idiot," he heard the man say to the others.

About the only thing Stam did right that day was turn north rather than immediately striking out eastward, toward the Silverwater Wash and the safety of Eandi land. As a lone rider heading away from the city to the east, he would have been noticed instantly by the guards at the gate. By steering Wislo to the north for a league or so, he was able to use the column of waiting peddlers' carts to conceal himself from the Fal'Borna.

Not that any of this occurred to him at the time. Instead, his mind was consumed with questions. Had Young Red known when he sold those baskets what they would do to the white-hairs? He had been awfully eager to be rid of them. At the time Stam believed that the young merchant didn't know the value of his wares, though looking back now he realized how foolish he'd been to think so. Brint HedFarren, despite his age, was already one of the most successful merchants in the Southlands, a rival for old Torgan Plye himself. Of course he would have recognized the quality of those baskets. He sold them for a bargain price because he wanted to be rid of them. It was the only explanation that made any sense.

Was HedFarren in league with the Mettai? It seemed a ridiculous question, or rather it would have only a short time before. Now, though . . .

He followed the river north from H'Nivar for several hours before realizing that he was making a mistake. He needed to get out of Fal'Borna land, and instead he was driving his cart into the heart of it. He considered his options for a moment or two, but quickly recognized that he had none. To the north lay the septs of the rilda hunters; to the south he'd find only the Ofirean and the great Fal'Borna cities along its shores. The J'Balanar held the lands west of the plain, and though the Fal'Borna and J'Balanar had fought battles in the past, both clans were Qirsi. If the Fal'Borna declared Stam their enemy, he'd be no safer among the J'Balanar than he was here.

He had to turn east and hope that he could cross the Silverwater into Stelpana before the Fal'Borna found him. As soon as he formed this thought, however, he felt his entire body sag. He'd never make it. He was at least thirty leagues from the wash, and with the moons on the wane he'd have little choice but to cross the plain by day and rest at night.

Still, Stam turned his cart, determined to reach the wash or die in the attempt. Once more, he had to resist the urge to drive Wislo too hard. It wouldn't do to kill the beast before they crossed into Eandi land, and he couldn't afford to appear to be in too much of a hurry.

He kept an eye out for Fal'Borna riders, septs, and villages. He forced himself to stop periodically so that Wislo could rest and graze and drink from the rills flowing among the grasses. And when he stopped for the night, he made do without a fire, despite the cold. Since he hadn't reached the H'Nivar marketplace, he was still short on food. But he could do nothing about that now. He would get by on a few bites of dried meat and hard cheese in the mornings and evenings. He had an ample gut; he wouldn't starve. And with the cold rains that had fallen over the past turn, he'd find plenty of water.

He continued this way for two days, and by grace of the gods, or by dint of skills he hadn't known he possessed, or thanks simply to sheer dumb luck, he encountered no Fal'Borna. At one point on the second day, he thought he spotted a sept to the north, but he turned slightly southward and drove on, glancing back over his shoulder repeatedly, expecting at any moment to see riders bearing down on him.

By the fourth day, Stam had started to convince himself that he would be all right, that the Fal'Borna weren't even looking for him. Early on he had imagined the other merchants mentioning him to the city guards at H'Nivar, describing his odd behavior and noting that he fled immediately upon hearing of the plague and the baskets. But Eandi merchants had no reason to help white-hairs at the expense of one of their own, no matter how strange they might have thought him. He might still give himself away through some chance encounter with the Qirsi, but he didn't think he had anything to fear from the merchants.

He had been at a loss as to what to do about his three remaining baskets. Just as he didn't build a fire for fear of drawing the notice of the Qirsi, he didn't dare burn the baskets out here on the open plain. Nor could he risk just leaving them in the grass. What if some innocent Fal'Borna came across them and didn't know the risk? What if it was a child? He didn't particularly like the Qirsi, but neither did he wish them harm. And he refused to be the cause of any more suffering like that he'd seen in the two septs in which he'd sold Young Red's baskets.

So he carried them with him, and deep down inside his heart he was glad. They were the only weapons he had that might give him some advantage over the Fal'Borna. He didn't want to use them this way, but if the Qirsi gave him no choice, he would. At least, that's what he told himself.

On the sixth morning after he fled the gates of H'Nivar, Stam woke later than usual, his heart pounding in his chest like a war hammer, his stomach tight and sour, his breath coming in great gasps. He'd slept poorly all night and had finally been driven from his slumber by a dream of Qirsi horsemen who pursued him across the plain, laughing harshly at his vain attempts to outrun them with his plow horse. It had been raining lightly when he went to bed, so he had slept in the cart. Now, though, the sun was shining and it was uncomfortably warm beneath the cloth covering that protected his goods from the elements. He tried to sit up, but his heart still labored and the queasy feeling in his gut seemed to be worsening by the moment.

I'm sick! he thought, fear gripping him by the throat. *I'm dying!*

He'd believed all this nonsense about a white-hair plague,

and now he was going to die of the pestilence out here alone. The bitterness of this irony actually brought tears to his eyes.

For several panic-filled moments, he tried to decide if he was truly dying or if he was just a fool. In the end, he was forced to conclude that he was a fool and that everything he was feeling could be traced to his nerves rather than some disease. He forced himself to get up and crawl out of the cart. He had trouble keeping his balance at first, but the cool air steadied and calmed him. After a few long, deep breaths he began to feel better.

He took a drink of water, which also helped. A bit of food might have been a good idea, too, but he wasn't quite ready for that.

Stam started toward Wislo, who was grazing a short distance away, and noticed immediately that the old beast looked agitated. He was switching his tail wildly. He held his head high and had his ears laid flat, and he was scraping his hoof in the dirt. Stam stopped and scanned the horizon, a different sort of fear taking hold of him.

"What is it?" he asked in a low voice. "What's got you upset?"

Wislo shook his head and whinnied.

Stam gazed westward for another few moments, but he saw nothing. He was convinced, however, that something was out there. It could have been wild dogs, which moved south out of the highlands in packs as the Snows approached. It also could have been the Fal'Borna.

He'd never been one to place much faith in his own intuition, but it seemed too great a coincidence that he should wake up feeling as he did and then find Wislo in such a state.

"They've found us, haven't they?" he said. "Or they will have soon enough."

He made his decision in that moment. If the Fal'Borna caught up with him as he was driving his cart toward the Silverwater, they'd assume the worst. But perhaps he could deceive them.

He led Wislo back to the cart, put the harness on him, and climbed into his seat. And then he started *westward*, back the way he had come. Perhaps if the Qirsi encountered an Eandi merchant making his way into their land, they'd believe that he had been in the sovereignties all this time. Surely they wouldn't be able to blame him for anything that had befallen their people during the past turn.

This was Stam's hope, anyway.

Before he and Wislo had covered even half a league, he spotted the riders. There were at least a dozen of them, and they were driving their mounts hard, heading due east on a line a bit north of the one Stam had taken. They seemed to spot him just a moment or two after he spotted them, and they turned right away, thundering toward his cart, their white hair flying like battle pennons.

They reached him in mere moments, reining their horses to a halt a short distance in front of him and brandishing spears.

"Stop right there, dark-eye," one of the men called to him.

He was broad and muscular, with golden skin and bright yellow eyes. He might have been a few years older than his fellow riders, but otherwise there was little that distinguished one of the riders from the others. For all the years Stam had spent among the Qirsi clans, learning their ways and taking their gold, he had never figured out how to tell one Fal'Borna from another, or one J'Balanar from another of his kind.

"Greetings," he said, raising a hand. He was pleased to hear how steady his voice sounded.

"What are you doing in Fal'Borna land, Eandi?"

Stam let his hand fall to his side. He thought this an odd question, but he tried to keep his tone light. "I'm a merchant."

"Do you think we're fools? Of course you're a merchant. But what are you doing here?"

He opened his mouth to answer, hesitated, then repeated, "I'm a merchant."

The Qirsi and the rider next to him shared a look.

"Where have you come from?" the second man asked.

Stam had never been a very good liar, so he thought it best to keep his answers simple. He almost said, "Aelea," but that would have put him too close to Mettai lands. Instead, he said, "Stelpana."

For some reason, this seemed to pique the Fal'Borna's interest. "Where in Stelpana?"

He felt a bead of sweat trickle from his right temple. "Nowhere in particular. I just visited a few villages along the east bank of the Silverwater."

"And how many days ago did you cross?"

Stam hesitated, chewing his lip. He wasn't exactly sure how far he'd come since leaving H'Nivar, and he didn't know how many days' travel he was from the wash.

"I . . . maybe . . . I don't know. Three days?"

Again the Fal'Borna exchanged looks.

"Three days," the first man repeated.

Stam nodded. His mouth had gone dry.

"What goods are you carrying?"

The one question he'd been dreading most.

"The usual. Blankets, blades, cloth, some jewelry, a few flasks of wine."

"Baskets?"

"A couple, yes."

Their bearing changed. Clearly they'd already been suspicious of him; now they appeared to grip their spears tighter, to regard him with open hostility.

"Where did you get them?" the first man demanded in a hard voice.

"I traded for them with another merchant."

"His name?"

"I . . . I don't remember. It wasn't someone I'd met before."

The Fal'Borna frowned. "Where was this?"

He felt as if he were sinking in mud. Every lie he told seemed to compound the last one, and he was having more and more trouble remembering what he had said a moment before.

"One of the villages," he said. "In Stelpana."

"You've had them long?"

"No. Just a few days."

"I take it these are Mettai baskets."

He nodded. "Yes."

"Why would you bring them into Fal'Borna lands now?"

"T-to trade. I'm a merchant. That's what I do. But I can leave. I can turn back, if you want me to."

The first man shook his head. "Get off your cart."

"But, I—"

"Off!" the man said, his voice like a smith's sledge.

Stam hurriedly climbed off the cart, his legs trembling. The Fal'Borna nodded to two of his riders. Immediately the men jumped off their mounts, strode over to Wislo, and unharnessed him.

"What are you doing?" Stam asked.

"We're going to burn your cart, and we don't wish to harm your animal."

"No!" Stam said. "You can't!"

The man grinned darkly. "No? Perhaps you'd prefer that we search your cart. Perhaps you'd like us to handle those baskets you're carrying. Isn't that why you brought them here?"

Did they know that he'd been in their land all this time? Did they know what had happened to the septs he'd visited?

"I . . . I don't mean your people any harm. I never have. You must believe me."

"I don't. If you've just come from Stelpana, then you know that your people and mine will soon be at war, if we're not already."

Stam's eyes widened.

"That's right, Eandi. We know about the army your people are gathering on the other side of the Silverwater. We also know about your alliance with the Mettai."

Stam had no idea what to say. He wasn't even sure that he believed the man. An army? An alliance with the Mettai? It made no sense. Why would the Eandi sovereignties attack the Fal'Borna? Why would his people risk the resumption of the Blood Wars?

The hatred that divided Qirsi from Eandi was as old as Qirsar and Ean, the gods who had created the people of this land. The two gods—who were both brothers and rivals—had instilled in the people their enmity for each other. Eandi fear of Qirsi magic was rooted in the earth, like the mountains of Aelea and the woodlands of Tordjanne. The Qirsi's contempt for the Eandi was as fundamental to life on this plain as water and air. The Blood Wars had been over for a century, but the truce that followed had done nothing to change the way white-hairs and dark-eyes regarded one another.

But during the last century of the old wars, the Qirsi had beaten the Eandi armies in battle after battle. They'd taken the fertile land of the Horn, pushing the warriors of Stelpana back across the Thraedes. And then they'd gradually taken the Central Plain as well, forcing the Eandi to cede more territory, until at last the white-hairs held everything west of the Silverwater.

Now, according to this man before him, the Eandi were planning an attack. It made no sense. Or did it?

"They've allied themselves with the Mettai?" he asked. "You're sure of this?"

The Fal'Borna bristled. "You think I'm lying?"

"No, of course not. I just . . ." He shook his head. "I don't understand why they'd do this."

"Your kind hate us. Isn't that enough?"

But it wasn't enough. Yes, the Eandi of the sovereignties hated the Qirsi, and they hated the Fal'Borna most of all. But to send thousands of men to their deaths . . .

They must have believed they had a chance to succeed. Was the magic of the Mettai that powerful? Could it win this new war for them?

"Step away from your cart, dark-eye. Unless you want to burn with your baskets and the rest of your wares."

It hit him like a fist to the stomach, stealing his wind,

nearly making him gag. Young Red's baskets. That was why the Eandi were attacking now. From the way the merchants at H'Nivar spoke of this white-hair plague, Stam gathered that it was sweeping across the land, destroying septs and villages just as it had those he visited.

"Move, dark-eye!" the Fal'Borna barked at him.

Stam staggered forward, away from his cart. After just a few steps, though, he stopped. "Wait. My gold."

"Your gold will burn along with everything else. The fires we conjure spare nothing."

"But that's all I have. How will I live?"

The man regarded him, the look in his eyes so cold it made Stam shudder. "You won't," he said.

Stam felt his legs give way. If it hadn't been for the Fal'Borna warrior beside him, who grabbed him by the arm, he would have fallen to the ground.

"I don't deserve to die," he said. "I'm just a merchant."

"You're an Eandi, and your people are about to invade our lands. You've just crossed the Silverwater carrying baskets that you know will kill us. You truly expect us to spare your life?"

"I didn't."

The man narrowed his eyes. "You didn't what?"

Stam straightened and pulled his arm free of the warrior's grip. If he was going to be executed, he'd die with his pride intact. He wouldn't let the white-hairs hold him up, and he wouldn't be killed with a lie on his lips.

"I didn't just cross the Silverwater. I lied to you."

"What do you mean?" the Fal'Borna demanded. "Why would you lie about such a thing?"

Stam actually laughed. "I thought I was saving my life."

The man stared back at him, a stony expression on his square face.

"I've been trading on the plain for nearly half the year. The last time I was in one of the sovereignties, the Growing hadn't even begun. I lied to you because I sold baskets in two villages that were then struck by the wh—" He winced at what he'd almost said. "By this pestilence that's killing your people."

The Fal'Borna glared at him. "If you're arguing for your life—"

"I'm not. I'm simply telling you the truth. I didn't know what the baskets would do. It took the second outbreak of the pestilence for me to begin to understand, and even then I needed to hear other merchants speaking of it in H'Nivar before I finally made the connection."

"When was this?"

"A few days ago. I've been trying to reach the Silverwater ever since."

The man shook his head. "But this morning—"

"This morning I sensed that you were near, so I turned around and pretended to be driving onto the plain instead of leaving it. If I had known that war was coming . . ." Stam shook his head. "I don't know what I would have done, but I wouldn't have bothered with this deception."

"You know that we still intend to kill you."

Stam nodded, taking a long, unsteady breath. He wasn't ready to die. Then again, he wasn't sure he ever would be. His had been a good life. Suddenly his eyes were filled with tears.

The Fal'Borna eyed him briefly. Then he faced Stam's cart. An instant later the cart burst into flames, the wood popping violently, the cloth that covered his wares turning black and curling like a dry leaf. Wislo had been led away from the cart, but still he reared when it caught fire.

Stam was surprised by how little smoke there was. The Fal'Borna was right: Qirsi fire burned everything.

"There are more baskets, you know," Stam said, staring at the blaze. "I wasn't the only merchant who bought them."

"We know that. We'll find the others."

"And you'll kill those merchants, too?"

"We're at war," the Qirsi said, as if the answer was obvious. "The Fal'Borna won the plain by showing no mercy to our enemies. We'll defend our land the same way."

"We're merchants, for pity's sake! We didn't intend—"

"Enough," the man said. He didn't raise his voice, but he didn't have to. "Your death will be quicker than those of the Fal'Borna you sickened with your baskets. Think of that as you go to Bian's realm."

Stam wanted to be brave, to die well, as he had heard soldiers phrase it. But he couldn't help the sob that escaped him in that moment.

Abruptly he felt pressure building on the bone in his neck. He tensed, opened his mouth to scream. But no sound passed his lips. Instead he heard, as clear as a sanctuary bell, the snapping of bone. And all was darkness.

Chapter 2

—✠—

STELPANA, ALONG THE EASTERN BANK OF THE SILVERWATER WASH

Tirnya Onjaef had done everything in her power to make certain that the army of Qalsyn reached the Silverwater Wash by this day. It had been her idea to attack the Fal'Borna. She had recognized the spread of the white-hair plague across the Central Plain for what it was: a unique opportunity to win back for the people of Stelpana the lands lost to the Qirsi during the Blood Wars, and to reclaim for her family its ancestral home of Deraqor. She had persuaded her father, Jenoe, a marshal in the Qalsyn army, to use his considerable influence to push for this invasion. And it had also been her idea to propose an alliance with the Mettai, the Eandi sorcerers of the north. This strategy finally convinced His Lordship, Maisaak Tolm, Qalsyn's lord governor, to let them march.

This was to be her war. When at last the armies of Stelpana defeated the Fal'Borna and reestablished the Central Plain as Eandi territory, the lion's share of the glory would be hers as well. She stood on the cusp of history. And never in her life had she been so bored.

They'd been camped along this shallow stretch of the wash for two days, awaiting the arrival of the army from Fairlea, the largest city in northern Stelpana. This was one of two armies Stelpana's sovereign had sent to supplement the force that marched from Qalsyn under the command of Tirnya's father. The other army, from the southern city of Waterstone, had arrived the same day as Jenoe's soldiers.

Tirnya had never been patient. Her father still told anyone who would listen the story of the first year she attended Qalsyn's famed Harvest Battle Tournament. She was three years old at the time and already headstrong. Sitting with her mother and hundreds of spectators, waiting for the first match to begin, she had finally grown so irritated that she stood on her seat and screamed as loud as she could, "When is someone going to fight?" Even His Lordship had laughed, though he was a thoroughly humorless man who despised Tirnya's father.

If anything, Tirnya found it harder to wait now than she did when she was young. She prided herself on being punctual, on following orders, and on demanding the same of those under her command. She had little tolerance for those who weren't as conscientious as she.

In this case, though, her own annoyance was the least of her concerns. The Snows were almost upon them. Already, cold winds blew out of the north. In another turn or two, these winds would strengthen and bring with them wicked storms from the lofty peaks of the Border Range. An invasion of Fal'Borna lands held tremendous risks any time of year. The Qirsi rilda hunters were fierce warriors and accomplished sorcerers. Fighting them on the plain during the Snows would have been unthinkable under any other circumstances.

But the plague was striking at the Fal'Borna now. No one knew for certain how long its effects would last. Tirnya and her father couldn't afford to wait for the warmer turns of the Planting. By that time their opportunity would have vanished, and Deraqor might be lost to the Onjaefs for another century. Every day that they waited brought the Snows that much closer, and gave the Fal'Borna another chance to find a cure for this illness that had weakened them. For now, as well, the Fal'Borna didn't know of their plans, or if they did, they hadn't yet had time to gather an army of their own and send it to the Silverwater. That advantage wouldn't last forever.

Jenoe might have been as eager as she to cross the river and begin their march toward Deraqor and the Horn, but he didn't show it. After waiting a few hours the first day they reached the wash, he suggested that they make the most of the delay by using the time to train their soldiers. Hendrid Crish, the marshal of the Waterstone army, agreed, and soon captains from both armies were leading their soldiers in drills.

The Mettai, who had marched with Jenoe's army from their village of Lifarsa near Porcupine Lake, kept to themselves but eyed the soldiers from afar.

Tirnya trained with the rest that first day, but by the middle of the second morning, she had become too agitated to do much more than watch the eastern horizon for signs of the Fairlea army. She left it to her lead riders to train her men. As darkness fell that night she went to speak to her father. She was so angry that she couldn't help raising her voice, even though Marshal Crish was there with Jenoe.

"They're going to make a mess of this, Father!" she said, raking a hand through her long hair. "We can't wait much longer."

Jenoe had merely shrugged. "There's nothing I can do. I'm sure they'll get here before long. Until then, we'll train."

He was right, of course. They couldn't do anything at all. But that only served to make her angrier. She stalked off without saying more, and bedded down before most of her men had finished eating their suppers. She lay huddled in her blankets for a long time before falling asleep, and awoke frequently during the night, thinking each time that she had heard the sounds of an approaching army.

On this, the third day since their arrival at the camp, they woke to dark skies and a heavy, wet snow. Still, Tirnya's father called for the men to train. When they complained, he said, "We may have to fight the Fal'Borna in weather like this. Best we're ready for it."

Again Tirnya kept apart from her men, gazing eastward, shivering within her riding cloak.

"You should train with them."

She turned at the sound of the voice, but quickly looked away.

Enly Tolm. He was Maisaak's son, lord heir of Qalsyn. He was also a captain in the Qalsyn army, just like her. And once, not so very long ago, he had been her lover.

Of all those in her city with whom she had discussed her plans for this invasion, he had argued against it the most vehemently. It was madness to risk a new Blood War, he said. They could never overcome the magic of the Fal'Borna; they were destined to fail. Yet, when His Lordship gave them permission to march, Enly asked that he be allowed to accompany them. He'd claimed that he wished only to help them succeed, but Tirnya suspected that he was driven primarily by his lingering affection for her.

Since leaving Qalsyn she had avoided him as much as possible. He was arrogant and an ass, and she wasn't interested in hearing him argue that they should abandon their mission and return to the city. As for any feelings she might have had for him . . . That had ended long ago.

"You look cold," he said. "You should join your men. It'll warm you up."

"You're not training," she said, still facing east.

"I was. I came to see if perhaps you wanted me to keep you warm."

She smirked and shook her head. "You'd like that, wouldn't you?"

"I should think."

"Go away, Enly."

"Maybe they're not coming," he said, standing beside her and gazing to the east as well. "They might have decided that this was folly, and that they'd be better off staying in Fairlea."

"The sovereign ordered them to march. They'll be here."

"I wouldn't be so sure. The Ballidynes have a reputation for defying authority and keeping their own counsel."

She looked at him. "Do you know them?"

"I've met Shon, the lord governor, a few times. He's been a guest in my father's palace, and we visited Fairlea several years back." He glanced at her. "If you think I'm an ass, you should meet Shon. He makes my father seem gracious. And the lord heir is even worse." Enly cringed. "Gods, you don't suppose Shon will send him, do you?"

Tirnya grinned. "I hadn't given any thought to who he might send. But if this man bothers you that much, I hope he does."

"It's not funny," he said, scowling. "Gries is condescending, smug, and ambitious to a fault. I was kidding when I said they might not come. They're probably keeping us waiting just to show us that they can, to make it clear to your father that he won't have authority over them. But they'll show up eventually. If they believe there's even the slightest chance that they can improve their standing or add to their treasury, they'll be here. It's true of Shon and doubly so of the son. He'd make a terrible commander, and a dangerous ally."

"He sounds like you."

"He's nothing like me."

Tirnya raised an eyebrow, the smile still on her lips. "Why do I get the feeling that this man—Gries? Is that his name?"

Enly nodded.

"Why do I get the feeling that he's exceedingly good-looking?"

He looked away.

Tirnya laughed. "I knew it! I bet he's an excellent swordsman, too."

"He is," Enly said, his voice flat.

"Better than you?" She leaned forward, trying to look him in the eye. "Enly, has he beaten you?"

He turned to face her. "No!" he said. "He did not beat me. We drew blood at the same time. Both of our fathers agreed that we did."

Tirnya stared at him open-mouthed. "He drew blood? Against you? I'll have to ask him how he did that."

"I'm serious, Tirnya. I know you'd do just about anything to make a fool of me, but Gries is . . . You shouldn't trust him. And if he really is in command of Fairlea's soldiers, you should warn your father to be wary of any counsel he offers. He's reckless."

She rarely saw him this way: earnest, almost pleading with her to take him seriously. Most of the time Enly used his wit and his bravado to conceal his feelings. And though usually her first impulse was to poke fun, this time she felt compelled to reassure him.

"My father's a wise man," she said. "He'll weigh carefully any advice Gries gives him, just as he does the advice he gets from you and me."

Enly nodded, but his lips were pressed thin, his brow creased.

"If you're so concerned about it, you should speak with my father yourself."

He shook his head. "The lord heir of one house can't be overheard speaking ill of his counterpart in a rival family. It would be . . . unseemly."

"You spoke ill of him to me."

Enly met her gaze, but only briefly. "Yes, I did. And I trust that when you tell your father about our conversation, you'll be discreet."

Tirnya almost made a joke of this, but again she could see that to Enly this was no laughing matter.

"Of course I will," she told him.

He still didn't look mollified.

"His father probably won't even send him," Tirnya said. "We're a long way from Fairlea, and as you've told me time and again, marching to war against the Fal'Borna is pretty dangerous."

Enly shook his head. "It doesn't matter. Gries will be leading them. I meant what I said before: He's reckless. He'd risk his life and the lives of his men if it meant a chance to bring glory to House Ballidyne."

"You really hate him, don't you? I've never heard you speak of anyone this way. I think it's a good thing I didn't beat you in this year's Harvest Tournament."

"I told you, he didn't beat me! And besides, that has nothing to do with it. I'd hate him even if we'd never fought."

"I find that hard to believe. You Tolms hate to lose at anything. You don't even like it when—"

"There they are."

Tirnya spun to look in the direction Enly was pointing. Far in the distance, cresting a small hill, she saw the army, easily a thousand men strong. They marched under two banners: the blue, white, and green of Stelpana; and a second flag of blue and black that must have been the sigil of House Ballidyne.

"I have to tell Father," she said, hurrying back toward the camp.

"Tirnya!"

She stopped, turned.

"Don't let anyone else hear what I said about Gries."

"I promise," she said, and went in search of her father.

By the time Tirnya found Jenoe, he already knew that the Fairlea army had been spotted. His cheeks were flushed and his face was covered with a fine sheen of sweat, but he was grinning. He enjoyed training, even out here in the middle of nowhere.

"You should have worked with your men," he said as soon as he saw her. "Your watching for them didn't make them get here any sooner."

"Yes, Father."

"You're humoring me," he said with a slight frown.

"Yes, Father."

He laughed.

They started walking to the east edge of the camp, where they would greet the soldiers of Fairlea.

Tirnya was eager to share with Jenoe all that Enly had told her about House Ballidyne, but Stri Balkett and several of Jenoe's other captains were walking just behind them. Instead she asked her father what he knew about the lord governor and his son.

"Not much, really. I met Shon when he came to Qalsyn. You were young at the time—I don't think you'd finished your third four. He struck me as being a rather difficult man," he went on, lowering his voice and glancing back to see that the captains wouldn't overhear. "I think that he and Maisaak got on quite well, if you follow my meaning."

She smiled. "I think I do. What about his son?"

"The older one, you mean? Gries?"

Tirnya nodded.

"I've never met him. Why?"

She felt her cheeks redden. "No reason. Enly seemed to think that he might be commanding this army."

"He might be at that," Jenoe said, apparently oblivious to her discomfort.

Enly was waiting for them at the east end of camp, and he raised a hand in salute to the marshal.

"Captain," Jenoe said. "Tirnya tells me you expect the lord heir to be at the head of the Fairlea army."

Enly shot Tirnya a quick look, but then nodded to her father. "Yes, sir. I think it's possible."

Jenoe looked out at the approaching army. "It hadn't occurred to me that the lord governor would send him, but I think you're right. That's Gries leading them, isn't it?"

"Yes," Enly said, his tone betraying little. "I believe it is."

The northern army was close enough now that Tirnya could see the man clearly. He was tall and lean, with curly yellow hair and a long, angular face. He wore a simple brown riding cloak over a surcoat of blue and black, and he had a leather baldric slung over his back. Even from this distance, even with the skies dull, Tirnya could see the jeweled hilt of his sword gleaming just above his left shoulder, within easy reach of his right hand. This weapon and his impressive white horse, which he rode with easy grace, were all that marked him as anyone more than a simple army captain.

Tirnya could see immediately why Enly would dislike this man. He was handsome, he looked like someone who had grown accustomed to success, and he didn't appear to lack for confidence. Once more she couldn't help thinking that he and Enly were probably very much alike.

The man riding just behind Ballidyne's lord heir said something that made Gries laugh. He had a good smile; strong, nothing held back. She found it hard to believe that this was the man Enly had described just a short time before. She glanced Enly's way and found that he was already watching her, frowning, probably reading her thoughts. She looked away.

Before long, Gries and his army reached the wash. The Ballidyne captain dismounted, walked to Jenoe, and dropped to one knee. The other captains and lead riders in his army had climbed off their horses as well, and now every man from Fairlea followed Gries's example and knelt before the marshal.

"Well met, Captain," Jenoe said, stepping forward.

"Marshal Onjaef," Gries said in a clear, ringing voice. "The army of Fairlea is here to give whatever aid it can. We are yours to command."

"Thank you, Captain. We're honored to march alongside the soldiers of your fine city. Please rise, all of you."

Gries stood and the two men embraced, drawing cheers from every soldier there.

"We number twelve hundred, Marshal," Gries said, his tone crisp. "One hundred or so are mounted; the rest are on foot. My father and I agreed that we'd be better off against the Fal'Borna if we had more bowmen than swordsmen. So we marched with seven hundred archers. That's why we're late in arriving. We already had the bows, but laborers worked night and day to fill our quivers. I'm sorry to have kept you waiting."

Jenoe smiled. "No apology is necessary, Captain. We're pleased to have you here." He indicated Enly with an open hand. "I believe you know Qalsyn's lord heir, Enly Tolm."

Gries grinned and extended a hand, which Enly took with obvious reluctance. "It's good to see you again, Enly. I'm sure I'll enjoy fighting alongside you a great deal more than I did fighting against you."

"And this is my daughter, Tirnya. She's one of my captains."

Gries faced her, still smiling. Gods, he was handsome.

"Captain Onjaef. It's a pleasure to meet you."

Jenoe introduced Ballidyne's lord heir to Stri and the other captains. Gries was every bit as gracious with them as he had been with Tirnya and Enly.

Tirnya caught Enly's eye while this was going on and gave a small shrug, as if to say, *I thought you told me he was a monster.*

She could see that Enly wanted to say something, probably about how she was too easily taken in by a winning smile and large, deep brown eyes. But in the end he merely shook his head and looked away.

When Jenoe had finished his introductions, he instructed Gries to have his men make camp beside the armies of Qalsyn and Waterstone.

"We're eager to cross the Silverwater and begin our march toward the Horn," the marshal said. "But you and your soldiers have come a long way. We can begin our march westward tomorrow."

"With all due respect, Marshal, that's not necessary."

Jenoe hesitated, eyeing the man doubtfully.

"We've kept you waiting long enough," Gries went on. He glanced at Tirnya and the others. "All of you. It's only midday. Even with the time it will take you and your men to break camp, we can still cross the wash and cover another league before nightfall."

Tirnya caught her father's eye and nodded.

"Very well," the marshal said. "Thank you, Captain Ballidyne." He turned to Waterstone's marshal and the other captains. "You heard him. Let's break camp. I want to be moving as soon as possible."

For the next hour, the camp was like a beehive, teeming with activity. The tents of the two marshals were dismantled and packed away, riding horses were saddled, cart horses were harnessed to the wagons that held provisions, and finally soldiers arrayed themselves in their companies. They were ready to go so quickly that already Tirnya was wondering if before darkness fell they might cover two leagues, rather than one.

Then they commenced their fording of the wash.

This section of the river, known as Enka's Shallows, had been used for crossings by Eandi armies during the Blood Wars. The Silverwater was wider here, and so its waters were slower and relatively shallow. Still, the wash was one of the major waterways of the Southlands; even during the driest turns of the Growing its waters were powerful and treacherous. And with the rains that had fallen recently, its current had strengthened.

Two dozen riders were sent across the wash with heavy rope, which they were to stake to the ground on the far bank. Those on foot would then use the ropes to resist the current as they crossed. But from the start, little went as they had intended. Three of the mounts under those first riders lost their footing and were swept downstream. All three horsemen managed to right their horses before they were lost, but clearly Tirnya and her father had underestimated the difficulty of this crossing. If horses struggled to make it, the foot soldiers would have a terrible time.

Jenoe ordered a dozen more riders across with what remained of their rope. Tirnya was to lead this second group

and, after securing her piece of rope to her saddle, she urged
Thirus, her sorrel, into the waters. The other riders followed,
all of them upstream of Tirnya. The bank of the wash was
steep, and no sooner had Thirus plunged into the river than it
was up to Tirnya's thighs. The water was frigid, and it tore a
gasp from her lungs. How could anyone hope to wade across
on foot?

She wanted to shout to her father that they needed to find
another way across, even if it meant marching south to N'Kiel's
Span, but Thirus had begun to struggle against the current
and was having trouble keeping his footing in the soft silt of
the riverbed. Twice the beast stumbled and was nearly
pulled under, but both times Tirnya managed to right him.
She spoke to him, trying to keep him calm, but she could
feel him growing more agitated by the moment.

She heard someone cry out just to the right of her. Another horse had stumbled as well, and its rider wasn't as
fortunate as Tirnya had been. The horse went under briefly,
broke the surface of the water again, and began to thrash
wildly. The rider, a young captain from Waterstone, was
unseated.

Tirnya saw him go under, his eyes wide with fear and
shock. He thrust his hand up out of the water in a desperate
attempt to grab the rope that trailed from Tirnya's saddle,
but he missed. At the same time, she leaned back as far as
she could and reached for him, brushing his fingers with her
own. Again Thirus stumbled, and Tirnya lost her grip on the
reins. She heard someone behind her shout her name—Enly,
probably. She slipped off the saddle, but managed to grab
hold of the pommel before being taken by the waters.

The river was so cold she could barely draw breath, which
was the only reason she didn't let go and swim after the young
captain. She could see him still, flailing against the current,
clearly trying to swim back to the east bank. But the stream
was too strong, the water too frigid.

And then she saw something out of the corner of her eye

that lifted her heart. A figure on horseback thundered southward along the riverbank after the captain. The horse was white, and she knew without looking that the rider must be Gries. The captain's efforts to swim to safety were growing weaker by the moment. He had to be tiring, and Tirnya didn't expect that he could even remain conscious in water this cold for very long. He was also nearing the end of the shallows. Another hundred fourspans or so, and he'd be lost to swifter waters.

Gries drove his mount hard, but for several moments Tirnya doubted that he could reach the man in time. Yet somehow he did. He drew even with the captain, passed him, and then steered his mount into the water, halting directly in the captain's path. With a great effort the captain raised a hand. Gries grasped at it, lost his grip, reached for him again. And this time he managed to hold on to the man.

Tirnya heard a mighty cheer from the men behind her, and knew a moment of profound relief. The captain had been her responsibility, and she'd nearly lost him. Only a turn before, she had lost two of her men in a skirmish with some road brigands. She had grieved for days afterward, and she still found it difficult not to blame herself for their deaths. Losing this man as well might have been more than she could bear.

Confident that the captain was safe, she tried to haul herself out of the water and back onto Thirus, to whose saddle she still clung. But the cold water had weakened her, too, and her clothes weighed her down. Her arms felt leaden; her legs were growing numb. She tried a second time to climb onto her mount, and this time succeeded in getting her leg over Thirus's back.

Just as she did, she heard splashing behind her. Looking back, she saw that Enly had ridden his bay into the wash.

"What are you doing?" she asked him, breathless from her struggle to get out of the water.

"I was coming to help you."

She pulled herself the rest of the way onto her horse and took hold of the reins again. She was shivering violently, her teeth chattering, but she was safe.

"I'm all right," she said.

"You're freezing." He reached for her reins. "Let me help you to the other bank."

"I don't need help," she told him again, her tone hardening. She exhaled and closed her eyes, then looked at him again. When next she spoke it was in a softer voice. "Thank you. But really, I'm fine."

Enly looked hurt, but he nodded and started back to shore. Tirnya continued on to the other side of the wash and upon reaching it spurred Thirus out of the water and onto solid ground. He was as exhausted as she, but he managed to gain his footing on the steep embankment. The other riders had already reached land and were driving their stakes into the ground and tying off the ropes. Tirnya did so as well.

Then she straightened and gazed back across the river. Gries had just reached the armies again. Those remaining on the opposite bank were cheering both the lord heir and the captain he had saved. Several men helped the young captain off Gries's horse and one threw a blanket around his shoulders. Jenoe was there with the others and he offered Gries his hand. The marshal grinned broadly and said something; no doubt he was complimenting the man on his quick thinking and bravery.

Enly still sat his horse a short distance from them, his britches darkened and dripping. He stared at Gries and the others, but he didn't go near them. After a moment, he gazed in Tirnya's direction. Seeing that she was watching him, he turned his mount and rode away from the water's edge.

With the ropes finally in place, the foot soldiers and the Mettai who were marching with them were able to make their way across the river. It was slow going, and by the time the men and women reached the western bank, they barely had the strength to climb up out of the riverbed and onto the grass of the plain. But no one else was carried downstream by the current, and even the carts bearing their provisions forded the wash without incident. Still, by the time everyone had crossed, the sky had begun to darken. Not that it mattered. No one had the strength to march deeper into Fal'Borna land on this day. They made camp for the night barely a hundred fourspans from where the armies of Qalsyn and Waterstone had slept the night before.

Chapter 3

✦┼✦

Since leaving their home in Lifarsa, near the Companion Lakes, Fayonne and her people had been largely ignored by the Eandi warriors with whom they marched. Not that Fayonne had expected more. As eldest of the Mettai village, she had dealt with plenty of Eandi merchants and the occasional Eandi army captain. All of them were arrogant. All of them treated her and her people with disdain.

It hadn't surprised her this day when, after crossing the Silverwater Wash, the army captains had nearly reclaimed their ropes before she and the other Mettai had a chance to cross the river. Naturally the Eandi let them cross, and Marshal Onjaef even had the courtesy to apologize to her for the oversight. But she thought it typical Eandi behavior.

Still, she didn't regret at all her decision to march to war with these people. She knew that those who had come with her from Lifarsa felt the same way. The Eandi, too, had seemed to understand their eagerness to leave the village. How could they not? The ramshackle houses, the stunted crops, the half-starved beasts grazing on wisps of grass. Probably they thought her a poor leader. Probably they were asking themselves, "How could any eldest allow her people to suffer so? How could she have done nothing while her village died?"

Let them ask. What did they know of her kind, and how they had suffered? They couldn't possibly understand what afflicted Lifarsa. Nor did they have to. The Eandi needed Mettai magic if they were to have any hope of defeating the Fal'Borna in this war of theirs. Fayonne and her people needed the land they hoped to take from the white-hairs. Nothing else mattered.

After fording the river, she and the other Mettai made camp a short distance away from the Eandi, as they always did. They remained close enough that if the marshal needed to speak with Fayonne, he or his officers could find her with relative ease. But the Eandi soldiers seemed happiest when the Mettai kept their distance, and Fayonne felt the same way.

They were close enough that they couldn't escape the aroma of roasting meat from the Eandi camp. Clearly the Eandi had no trouble killing game here on the plain.

Mander had accompanied her, as was proper, since as her son he would lead the village some day. She had sent him and his friends to hunt, hoping that perhaps the luck of the Eandi would rub off on them. He returned sometime later, looking glum and resentful.

"Nothing?" she asked as he approached.

He shook his head. "The warriors killed deer, fowl, even a few boar."

"And you?"

He laughed mirthlessly. "Rabbits. Nearly a dozen of them."

Fayonne shrugged. Rabbits were better than nothing. A dozen would be enough to give the fifty Mettai who had marched with them a taste of meat, and to put something other than boiled roots and stale bread in their bellies.

"I thought it would be better once we were away from Lifarsa," Mander said, staring at the small fire she had lit with magic.

"It may get better. Be patient."

A frown creased his brow. He was so much like his father.

Not only his looks—the dark eyes and long black hair, his long, sharp features and lanky build—but also his refusal to cling to false hope. Even as a child, Mander had preferred a hard truth to an easy lie. Just like his father. Tawno would have been proud of the man his boy had become.

"It's not going to be any better, Mama. We both know that."

"No," Fayonne said, "we don't. We have leagues to go before we settle again. Distance may be our ally in this. And who knows what a century and a half of white-hair magic has done to this land. Anything is possible. It's good that you're sensible, but you must allow for some hope."

He nodded, still grim-faced.

"The others need to believe it's possible, Mander," the eldest said, dropping her voice and looking around to see that no one was listening. "Don't take that away from them. Not so soon."

"I won't," he said. "And I won't give up. Not yet."

"Good. With all our people have been through—"

Before Fayonne could say more, Mander touched her arm lightly and pointed toward the Eandi camp, a warning in his eyes.

She saw the man a moment later. Her eyes weren't as keen as they once had been.

The Eandi walking toward them had been with the marshal and his daughter the day the army first reached Lifarsa. At the time Marshal Onjaef had given the man's name, but Fayonne had forgotten it. She did remember, however, that he was lord heir of Qalsyn and the son of the marshal's lord governor. She also recalled that of the three who had dined with them in Lifarsa that night, this man had seemed least willing to forge this alliance. He had asked Fayonne why she and her people were so eager to leave the village, and he had appeared unsatisfied by her vague answer.

Fayonne stood as the man approached. An instant later Mander rose as well.

"Good evening, Eldest," the Eandi said. "I hope I'm not disturbing you."

"Not at all, my lord."

A thin smile crossed the man's features for just a moment. "Please call me captain or Enly."

"Very well. What can I do for you, Captain?"

"May I sit?"

"Of course."

Fayonne and Mander lowered themselves to the ground once more. The captain sat opposite them, on the far side of the fire.

The man cleared his throat. "I was wondering if you might be willing to tell me a bit more about your village."

Fayonne felt that Mander was watching her, but she kept her eyes locked on those of the Eandi.

"There's little to tell," she said. "I've been eldest of Lifarsa for nearly two fours now. Before that, it was a man named Gav. He was a farmer, like me, though he also had a smithy. Before him—"

"Forgive me," the captain said. "I'm not . . ." He stopped, frowning. "I won't claim to know many Mettai. But those I've encountered have always been tied to the land around the lakes. They consider it their ancestral home. The other Mettai we spoke to refused to help us, and had no interest in leaving. But you . . ."

"You told us much the same thing the night you ate as our guests in Lifarsa."

"I remember," the man said. "And you said that not all Mettai are the same."

"If you ask me again tonight, I'll tell you the same thing." She raised an eyebrow. "You think I'm wrong?"

"I think that most Mettai are the same when it comes to their feelings about their land and about involving themselves in a new Blood War."

"Do you want our help, Captain?" Fayonne asked. "Clearly the marshal and his daughter do, but do you?"

He exhaled. "I don't know. I . . ." He stopped himself, looked away. "I don't know," he repeated.

Fayonne opened her hands. "Then I don't know what to

tell you. You want me to be just like the other Mettai you've met, few though they may be. But you're nothing like Marshal Onjaef, or his daughter, or the other Eandi captains you ride with. They want to use our magic against the Fal'Borna. They trust that we'll honor our side of the agreement we reached with you. And they're right to trust us. We will shed our blood for you. We'll draw upon our magic and do everything in our power to fight the white-hairs. What more do you need to know?"

The captain stared at her across the fire.

"I suppose you're right," he said. "That's all that matters. Tirnya and the marshal have been telling me the same thing for days." He climbed to his feet. "Forgive me. Good night." He nodded once to Mander and walked back toward the Eandi camp.

For a long time Fayonne and her son said nothing. The eldest watched the man recede into the darkness and when she couldn't see him anymore, she lowered her gaze to the fire. Eandi men sang in the distance, a song she didn't know. She heard laughter from the warriors nearest to the Mettai camp. Her people were quiet, though she could hear the murmur of a few conversations.

"He won't be content with those answers forever," Mander said so quietly that his words barely reached her.

Fayonne shook her head. "He doesn't have to be. We'll march, we'll fight, and then this will be over. Hopefully we'll live and the Eandi will win and we'll have new land to settle. But whatever happens, he only has to leave us alone for a short while."

"But—"

"Listen to me," she said, turning to face him. He looked so young in the firelight, just like Tawno when she first fell in love with him. "The Eandi don't understand us. They know nothing about our magic or our ways. It would take them several turns to figure out any of this. It will all be over well before then. Just keep this to yourself, and don't let on to the others that you're worried."

He hesitated, but only briefly. "Yes," he said, nodding. "All right."

Fayonne smiled. "Good. You'll make a good leader someday."

Tirnya wasn't certain why she had volunteered to do this. Upon setting up camp on the west bank of the wash, her father had announced his intention to invite Hendrid Crish and Gries Ballidyne to sup with him and his captains. He instructed Stri and his men to find game for their meal, and he dispatched a messenger to the camp of the Waterstone army to convey his invitation to Marshal Crish.

He was about to send a second man to speak with Gries, but Tirnya stopped him.

"I'll speak with him, Father," she said.

Her father cast a look her way. She began to blush under his gaze, but with the light failing, she didn't think he noticed.

"All right," he said, in a tone that made her want to hit him.

"I just want to thank him for saving that captain today. I felt . . . I had a chance to grab his hand, and I missed. If Gries hadn't pulled him from the wash . . ." She shuddered.

Jenoe smiled indulgently, his expression softening. "I understand." He gestured in the direction of the Fairlea camp. "By all means. Go. Talk to him."

She started toward the army of Fairlea, following a circuitous route past soldiers and small campfires. And before she was halfway there, she regretted her decision to go. She didn't know this man. From all that Enly had told her, she gathered that he couldn't be trusted. On the other hand, he had seemed genuinely good-natured when they were introduced earlier in the day, and he had saved the young captain from Waterstone seemingly without regard for his own safety.

And he's very handsome.

She grinned to herself. Once again, as she had during her conversation with Enly that morning, she wondered how much of what Qalsyn's lord heir had told her was born of his jealousy and his fear that she'd be drawn to Gries.

Was that why she had offered to deliver her father's message in person? Because she was attracted to the man? Or because she wanted to make Enly think that she was attracted to him?

She paused. She hadn't seen Enly in some time, since watching him cross the wash. Where could he have gone? The men around her were from his company, but she didn't see him anywhere.

"Have you seen Captain Tolm?" she asked a young soldier, who sat with his friends pulling feathers from three quail they had apparently just killed.

The man stood. "No, Captain."

Tirnya frowned. "Well, when you see him next, please tell him that the marshal would like him to join us for supper."

"Of course, Captain."

Tirnya nodded to the man and his companions and moved on.

Before long, she had crossed into the Fairlea camp, though had it not been for the different uniforms she might not have known. The sounds were just the same—pockets of laughter, quiet conversations, a few young voices raised in song—and in the torchlight and glow of fires the faces weren't all that different from those of the men in Qalsyn's companies.

Tirnya asked one of the soldiers where she could find Captain Ballidyne, and he pointed her to the center of the camp. She stared in the direction he indicated, straining to see in the darkness. Seeing no tent like those erected for the two marshals, she smiled weakly at the man and made her way to the heart of the northern army.

Tirnya spotted him from a distance. He stood a good deal taller than any of the men around him, and his yellow hair seemed to shine with firelight. She had to admit that her heart beat just a bit faster at the sight of him, and she chided herself, feeling more like a schoolgirl than an army captain.

Stepping past the men around him and into the glow of his campfire, she said, "Excuse me."

All of them had been laughing at something, but they fell silent at the sound of her voice, and every pair of eyes turned in her direction.

"Captain Onjaef," Gries said, a smile on his face. "Welcome."

"Thank you, Captain Ballidyne. Forgive me for intruding, but my father would like you to join him for supper."

"I'd be honored."

She nodded. "Good." She stood there for a few moments, unsure of what she ought to say next, and wishing once more that she'd let her father send a messenger.

"Perhaps I could escort you back to your camp now," Gries finally said. "If that's all right."

"Yes, of course."

He had a small white scar high on his right cheek and another on the same side of his face, just by his temple. She knew scars like that. She had several herself.

Tirnya realized she was staring at him, and glanced away.

"Jondel, you'll be in command while I'm gone," Gries said to one of the men. "Not that there should be much need, but just in case."

"Yes, Captain."

He faced Tirnya again, smiling once more. "Shall we?"

She turned and began walking back to the Qalsyn army with Gries beside her. Neither of them spoke at first, and the silence soon began to grow awkward. At last, Tirnya said the first thing that came into her head.

"You must leave yourself open to thrusts when you attack with your sword hand."

"What?"

Again she blushed, and again she was grateful for the darkness.

"The scars on your face. Those are from battle tournaments, aren't they?"

"Yes, they are."

She heard amusement in his voice.

"I thought so," she went on. "They're both on the right side of your face, so I'm guessing that you have a tendency to leave yourself unguarded when you attack."

"I did, when I was younger. Those scars are several years old. It's been some time since I was bloodied in a tournament."

Tirnya smiled inwardly. There, at least, was the arrogance Enly had warned her about. "I see," she said.

"You think I'm boasting."

"No," she said. "I know you are."

Gries laughed. "I deserved that."

"I have scars, too," she told him. "Plenty of them, including one from this year."

"Let me guess. From Enly?"

She nodded. "I'm afraid so." She glanced at him. He was looking straight ahead, his straight nose and strong chin silhouetted against the pale glow of the camp. "You and he have fought, haven't you?"

"Once, a long time ago. We fought to a draw."

"That's what he told me."

He looked at her. "And you didn't believe him?"

"It's not that," she said. "But the Tolms are . . . they're very proud. And he seemed rather defensive about your match when I asked him about it."

"Neither of us could have been more than fifteen or sixteen at the time. He was the quicker swordsman, and he was probably more skilled, too. I was stronger and had a longer reach." He shrugged slightly, a strangely small gesture for such a large man. "It made for a good match."

They walked in silence for a few moments.

Then Tirnya said, "Thank you for saving that man today."

"You're welcome. He was one of yours? I thought he was from Waterstone."

"He was. But I had a chance to grab his hand, and I missed."

Gries chuckled. "Good thing, too."

"Excuse me?"

"Forgive me, Captain, but he weighed more than you do. If he'd gotten hold of you, he would have pulled you after him, and I'd have had to save both of you."

Tirnya opened her mouth, closed it again. She didn't know what to say, although in that moment she was furious enough to say just about anything.

"I've angered you."

"You're damn right you have."

"I didn't mean to. I was just saying—"

"You were calling me weak, and implying that I was foolish to have tried to save that man."

"That's not—"

"I'm a warrior in the army of Qalsyn, and for three years running I've fought Enly in the final match of our Harvest Tournament. Yes, he's beaten me, but no one else has. I took an arrow in the chest just over a turn ago, and still I've led my company this far. Before long I'll lead them into battle. You look at me and assume that I must be weak, that I must need the protection of a man. I don't. If I'd gotten hold of that soldier, I wouldn't have let go and I wouldn't have been swept downstream with him. Believe me; don't believe me. I couldn't care less."

She quickened her pace, intending to leave him there.

"I do believe you," he called to her. "I'm sorry for what I said."

Tirnya slowed again, then stopped. She didn't look at him, not even when he halted just beside her.

"I didn't mean to offend you."

She said nothing. She wasn't ready to forgive him just yet.

"You were wounded?"

Tirnya nodded. "Road brigands. We were on patrol and we tracked them to a small clearing in the wood south of Qalsyn. Part of my company got there before I did. I rode into the middle of a skirmish and was hit almost immediately."

"Sounds like you're lucky to be alive."

"I am. Two of my men died," she said. She looked up at him. His face was bathed in the warm light of fires and torches.

"I'm a captain in the army of Stelpana, just as you are. I deserve to be spoken to in a manner that befits that rank."

"You're right. I won't do it again."

She nodded once and led him the rest of the way to the Qalsyn camp in silence.

By the time they reached Jenoe's makeshift quarters, a great fire burned before it and the two deer killed for them by Stri and his men had been mounted on large spits. The air around them was redolent with the scent of roasting venison.

In Tirnya's absence Enly had returned, and he eyed both her and Gries with suspicion and manifest jealousy. Tirnya tried to ignore him.

"Captain Ballidyne," Jenoe said when he saw them. "I'm delighted you could join us."

"Thank you, Marshal. I'm honored by your invitation."

It had grown colder since sunset, and Tirnya was still chilled from crossing the river. While Jenoe and Gries chatted, she slipped into her father's tent and threw his riding cloak over her shoulders. She emerged again just as Stri, Marshal Crish, and another captain from the Waterstone army were arriving. Her father noticed her with his cloak and grinned.

"Please, make yourselves comfortable," he said, indicating with an open hand a few large, weather-worn logs that were arrayed in a half circle before the blaze. "I had a few men bring these up from the riverbank. I daresay they'll be more comfortable than the ground would be."

Marshal Crish nodded approvingly. "I'll say. Well done, Jenoe."

Tirnya sat between her father and Stri at one end of the semicircle; Enly sat at the other end, as far from her as possible, and Gries took a spot just on the other side of Jenoe. Two of Stri's soldiers stood near the fire, tending to the cooking meat.

"I want to thank you again, Captain Ballidyne," Waterstone's marshal said. "That was quite a feat you pulled off today. You saved the life of a man I value and trust."

Gries looked down and grinned, the way someone might

if he were embarrassed by such praise. But it didn't seem to Tirnya that he looked embarrassed.

"You're too kind, Marshal. I'm sure that any man here—" He glanced quickly at Tirnya. "Any person here . . . would have done the same."

"Forgive me for not asking earlier, Captain," Jenoe said, "but how is His Lordship your father?"

Gries smiled, though it appeared forced, even pained. Tirnya thought that he looked much the way Enly did when Qalsyn's lord heir spoke of his father.

"He's well," Gries said. "Thank you for asking. He wishes you success in this endeavor, and he prays that the gods will watch over all the men under your command."

"What does he think of this . . . endeavor, as you call it?"

All of them turned to look at Enly.

"I'm not sure I know what you mean, my lord," Gries said.

"Of course you do. For better or worse, we're marching to war against the Fal'Borna. Surely he expressed some opinion on the matter."

Gries's expression hardened. "He sent twelve hundred men to fight this war, Captain. He sent officers. He sent me. I believe that's opinion enough."

"Perhaps it is. My father sent me, but I'm not sure that says anything at all." He grinned, as if to show that he was joking. No one laughed.

"Do you have an opinion you'd like to share with us, Lord Tolm?" Hendrid asked.

Enly's eyes flicked toward Tirnya. She gave a slight shake of her head.

"I asked to be here," he said, looking at the marshal again. "As Gries said, that's opinion enough."

Gries turned to Jenoe. "I would like to know more about these Mettai who are with us. Was it your idea to approach them, Marshal?"

"No," Jenoe said. "It was Tirnya's. But I think that their magic will give us a great advantage in our battles with the Fal'Borna."

Gries nodded. "I don't doubt that. But I'm surprised that they agreed to this alliance. Living in the north, I have some knowledge of the Mettai. I've never known them to want anything to do with us or with the white-hairs."

Again Tirnya found herself sharing a look with Enly. But it was Jenoe who answered.

"These Mettai are strange," he said. "I'll admit that. And the lands they inhabited were blighted. I believe they're desperate to find somewhere new to live."

Gries narrowed his eyes. "You say their lands were bad?"

"They seemed so. And even the woodlands around their village were unusually quiet. Our men tried to hunt for their suppers that night, and found little. Most of them resorted to eating their rations instead."

"What was the name of this town?"

Jenoe glanced at Tirnya, a frown on his face. "I can't remember."

"Lifarsa," Enly said.

"Yes, of course," Jenoe said. "Thank you, Captain." He turned to Gries again. "Do you know it?"

Fairlea's lord heir shook his head. "No. But it's strange that any Mettai would live on blighted lands. In addition to being sorcerers, they're farmers, trappers. Their entire way of life is rooted in the land."

Jenoe didn't appear to be bothered. "Well, as I say, this is probably why they were so eager to join us."

"No doubt," Gries said.

"Capt'n Balkett," called one of the men by the fire. "Th' meat's ready."

"Excellent," Stri said, standing.

The others stood as well, and soon all of them were eating the roasted venison, which was as good as anything Tirnya had tasted in years. She hadn't realized how hungry she was until she took the first bite. It seemed everyone else had been as starved as she, because for a long time no one said a word.

Eventually Enly made his way to her side. He didn't say

anything, but she sensed that he wanted to ask her questions, probably about what she and Gries had talked about.

Before he could, she asked him, "Where did you go off to before?"

"Missed me, did you?" he said, his mouth full.

"Not at all. But I was curious."

He shrugged, but he wouldn't meet her gaze. "I went to speak with Fayonne."

"Fayonne?" she repeated. It took her a moment. "The Mettai woman?"

Enly nodded.

"Why?"

He took another bite.

"What were you talking to her about, Enly?"

He finally looked her in the eye. "I asked her the same questions I put to her that night in Lifarsa, the same questions your friend Gries was just asking. What are they doing here? Why were they so eager to leave their homes?"

She wanted to walk away, to make it clear to him that she didn't share his suspicions or care what the woman had told him. But in truth she did want to know. When at last she said, "And what did she tell you?" it felt like a surrender.

Before he could answer, Gries walked up to them, holding two large pieces of meat.

"More for either of you?"

Enly didn't look at all pleased to see the man. But he took a piece of meat and mumbled a thank-you.

"It sounds to me like you have doubts about this war, Enly," Gries said, taking a bite, his eyes fixed on the ground.

Enly stopped chewing for a moment.

Tirnya shook her head. "No, he doesn't."

Enly swallowed. "I have the same questions you do, Gries. I want to know why, after centuries of keeping to themselves, these Mettai are suddenly willing to take sides in a new Blood War."

"Have you asked them?"

"Tirnya and I were just talking about that. I spoke to the eldest a short time ago. She really didn't tell me much."

"It doesn't matter," Tirnya said pointedly, glaring at Enly. "But it does."

She looked at Gries. "Not you, too."

"I'm sorry, Captain. But anytime you march to war with an ally, you need to be certain that you can trust them, and that you understand their motives."

"These Mettai want land. They want a new life. What more do we need to know?"

Gries shrugged. "I'd like to know more about their village."

"There isn't much to tell," Enly said. "It looked like the other Mettai villages we visited, but the houses were run down, and their livestock looked . . . unwell. The stew they served us the night we supped with them was awful."

Tirnya grimaced at the memory of the meal, knowing that she couldn't argue with Enly on this point. The stew itself had been heavily seasoned with an unpleasantly pungent spice, and the meat in the stew had been stringy and sour tasting.

"Were the houses old?" Gries asked.

Enly looked puzzled. "Old?"

"Did it look like the Mettai had been living there for a long time?"

"Yes, it did," Enly said. "Some of the houses were in disrepair, and Fayonne and her people seemed desperate to get away. I definitely had the sense that they'd been there for many years."

Gries shook his head. "That I don't understand. Like I said, the Mettai are farmers. They depend on the land, and they know how to care for it. If the soil was bad, they would have left long ago."

"So what does all this mean?" Enly asked.

"I don't know," Gries told him. He looked at Tirnya. "Watch them. I doubt they'd betray us. If they've come this far, they must be sincere in their commitment to the alliance. But much of what you've told me strikes me as odd."

It wasn't the first time one of Tirnya's companions had

forced her to acknowledge that these Mettai were strange, and that they seemed too willing to join the Eandi army. But perhaps because it came from someone she barely knew, rather than from her father or Enly, both of whom had spoken against this invasion, she took Gries's warning more seriously than she had the others.

Stri joined them before she could say more, and began to ask Gries questions about his city and the Northlands. Gries seemed happy enough to talk about his home. When he learned that Stri came from southern Stelpana, near the Ofirean, he had questions of his own. For a long time Tirnya and Enly listened politely as the two captains went back and forth with tales of their childhoods.

After some time, Enly gestured to Tirnya that he wanted to speak with her alone. Reluctantly she let him lead her a short distance from the others.

"You want to gloat?" she asked when he turned to face her.

Enly gave her a sour look. "Gloat?"

"He agrees with you about the Mettai."

"After all that I told you about Gries earlier today, why do you think I'd gloat about him agreeing with me?"

He had a point.

"So what do you want?" she asked.

Enly started to say something, but then stopped himself, his eyes locked on hers. After a brief pause, he shook his head. "Nothing. I . . . I was looking for an excuse to get away from Gries and Stri."

"That's it?"

He shrugged. "That's it."

Tirnya wasn't sure she believed him, but she also didn't care to press the matter. "Fine then," she said. She turned on her heel and strode back to where her father was speaking with Waterstone's marshal.

Enly remained where he was, alone at the fringe of their small circle. He ate what was left of his meal, and he stared at the fire, though several times Tirnya glanced his way only to find that he was already watching her.

Eventually, Jenoe announced that he was going to sleep, and he urged the rest of them to do the same.

"We begin our march toward the Horn in the morning," he said. "And now that we're in Fal'Borna land, we could meet up with Qirsi warriors anytime. I want all of you well rested."

They bade one another good night, and started back to their respective parts of the camp. Tirnya hadn't gone far, though, before she remembered that she still wore her father's cloak. Laughing at herself, she turned and walked back to the fire. As she drew near she saw that her father was talking to Enly, and that he looked angry.

After a moment's hesitation, she stepped closer, taking care to keep out of the firelight lest one of them see her.

". . . was unacceptable," her father was saying. "I understand that you're lord heir, and I'm but a marshal in your father's army. But he made it clear that for the duration of this march and whatever battles are to come, you are under my command."

"Yes, Marshal. I agreed to that as well."

"Then act like it, damnit!"

Enly shook his head. "I didn't do anything—"

Jenoe raised a finger, silencing him. "Don't! You know full well what you did. Asking Gries what his father thought of this war. What were you thinking?"

"I didn't see anything wrong with the question."

"I know you too well, Enly. I know how clever you are. Don't pretend to be a fool."

Enly looked away, the muscles in his jaw tightening.

"You think this is a bad idea," Jenoe said. "I understand that. But we're here now. That discussion is over. And trying to open it again in front of our allies is beneath you." He rubbed a hand over his face. "What I said before is true. We could find ourselves facing the Fal'Borna tomorrow, or the next day. The last thing I want is for Gries and Hendrid to doubt our commitment to this invasion. I hope you didn't mention your reservations to the Mettai."

"I didn't," Enly said, still not looking at him.

"Good." He gestured vaguely at the camp. "These soldiers must have complete confidence in us, Enly. Doubt in the mind of a warrior is fatal."

"I understand, Marshal."

Jenoe stared at him for several moments, as if weighing whether he should say more. Finally he nodded once. "All right then. Don't do it again."

"Yes, sir."

"Get some sleep."

Enly nodded and met Jenoe's gaze for an instant. Then he walked away. Jenoe watched him leave before stepping into his tent.

Tirnya stood in the darkness for some time. She should have been angry with Enly. This was why she had warned him not to respond when Hendrid asked him for his opinion of their "endeavor." She also would have expected herself to take some pleasure in seeing his ears pinned back by her father. But she couldn't bring herself to feel anything but sorry for him. She'd been on the receiving end of her father's upbraidings enough times to know how he felt.

Eventually she turned and walked back to where her company slept. She'd return her father's cloak in the morning.

Chapter 4

✦✦✦

CENTRAL PLAIN, FAL'BORNA LAND

Grinsa jal Arriet had never imagined that he would return in disgrace to the sept of E'Menua, the Fal'Borna a'laq who had made him and his family captives of the Qirsi clan. He and the men with whom he had journeyed—two Eandi merchants and Q'Daer, a young Fal'Borna Weaver of the sept—had been sent to find a Mettai witch and defeat the curse she had created, which was spreading across the land, killing Qirsi and destroying their villages. Upon completing these tasks, Grinsa, his wife, Cresenne ja Terba, and their young daughter, Bryntelle, would be free to leave. And the Eandi merchants, Jasha Ziffel and Torgan Plye, who had been condemned to die for having sold cursed Mettai baskets to the Fal'Borna, would be spared and released.

Grinsa was a Weaver himself, a Qirsi who wielded all varieties of magic, and who could bind the magic of many Qirsi into a single powerful weapon. Against great odds, he had survived a war in the Forelands, where he'd spent most of his life, and had defeated a renegade Weaver who sought to conquer the Eandi realms of that land. He had saved the life of an Eandi noble falsely accused of murder. He was not at all accustomed to failure.

But he and the rest of his company had failed miserably in this undertaking. Yes, the witch, a woman named Lici, had been killed, but not by them. Rather, it had been her own Mettai companions, Besh and Sirj, who had defeated her. Besh had also found a way to overcome the woman's curse, only barely in time to save Grinsa's life and Q'Daer's. But Jasha was dead, killed by Torgan. And Torgan had escaped with a scrap of cursed Mettai basket that might still be used to sicken unsuspecting Qirsi.

At this point, Grinsa had little hope that E'Menua would allow him and his family to go free, particularly now that war had come to the plain.

He and the others—Q'Daer, Besh, and Sirj—were still several leagues from the sept, and they were making poor progress southward. Grinsa remained weak from the plague that had nearly killed him. Q'Daer had been sicker than he, and was still suffering as well. And Besh, though spry for his age, was old to be braving the cold winds of the late Harvest.

As soon as they received word that an Eandi army was gathering on the eastern bank of the Silverwater, and that a Mettai force was marching with them, Grinsa had encouraged Besh and Sirj to leave Fal'Borna lands. They had been declared friends of the Fal'Borna by another a'laq, but the Qirsi of the plain were fierce warriors and showed little mercy for their enemies. That declaration would mean little now.

But Besh had insisted that they remain and help other Qirsi combat the plague that Lici had loosed upon the land. And Grinsa had his doubts as to whether the two Mettai could reach the safety of Eandi territory without being found and killed by the Fal'Borna. For better or worse, their fates were now tied to his.

The four of them said little as they rode, Grinsa and Q'Daer on horseback, Besh and Sirj on the cart that had once belonged to Lici. Besh had a blanket about his shoulders. Q'Daer sat wrapped in a rilda skin, and Grinsa wore a woolen riding cloak he had brought from the Forelands. He pulled it tighter now, as another gust of cold wind made the grasses bow and dance. Only Sirj seemed immune to the elements.

"It must be good to be young and never feel the cold," Besh said, as if reading Grinsa's thoughts.

Grinsa glanced their way. Both men were looking at him, wearing grins.

"I wouldn't remember," Grinsa said. "It's been too long."

Besh laughed. "If you're old, Forelander, then what am I?"

Q'Daer looked back at the rest of them, a frown on his youthful, square face, but he didn't say anything and a moment later he faced forward again.

Grinsa would have preferred to steer his mount to Besh and Sirj's cart and ride alongside them for a while. But it seemed that something was bothering the Fal'Borna Weaver. He spurred his horse to catch up with Q'Daer.

"You seem troubled," he said, pulling abreast of the man.

"They're slowing us down," Q'Daer said, staring straight ahead.

"This pace is best for all of us. You and I are just a few days removed from having almost died. We're lucky to be riding at all."

"We could go faster."

"I'm not sure—"

"We could ride faster," the man said, turning to face him. His pale yellow eyes looked almost white. "We could take short rests, but more of them. They're slowing us down, Forelander. And we need to get back to the sept."

Grinsa could have argued the point further, but he'd learned that reason rarely worked in discussions with Q'Daer. He was too young, too stubborn, too much a Fal'Borna. Better simply to get to the point.

"What would you suggest?"

"They should leave, go back to their own land."

"You know how dangerous that would be for them. We owe them our lives, and I think it's up to us to protect them until it's safe for them to return to their homes."

"They won't be welcomed in the sept. The Mettai have made themselves enemies of the Fal'Borna. They should leave us now, while they can."

"The time for that has passed," Grinsa said. "They chose to remain with us so that they could protect the Fal'Borna from Lici's plague. We've no choice now but to guard them, be it from other Fal'Borna or from E'Menua himself."

Q'Daer twisted his mouth sourly, but after a moment he appeared to acquiesce. "Then we should abandon their cart and have them ride. That at least would be quicker. We have Jasha's horse still. They can ride together, or one of them can ride with us."

Grinsa didn't think that Besh and Sirj would like this idea. He hadn't seen either of them on a horse, and from what he knew of the Mettai they didn't seem to be riders. More to the point, they might well object to leaving Lici's cart. By all rights it was theirs now, as was the horse pulling it.

"What about their animal?"

The young Weaver glanced back at the cart horse and frowned, as if he hadn't thought of this. The Fal'Borna revered horses. Q'Daer would have been more reluctant to put the beast in peril than to endanger the two men.

"She'll be able to keep up without that cart behind her," he said. "We won't be able to go as fast as I'd like, but it would still be an improvement."

"All right," Grinsa said, the words coming out as a sigh. For all the time that Torgan and Jasha had been with them, he had served as intermediary between the Fal'Borna and the merchants. Torgan and the young Weaver had hated each other, and more than once Grinsa probably had kept Q'Daer from killing the one-eyed merchant, something he'd since come to regret. Now he found himself caught between Q'Daer and the Mettai. "I'll speak with them. Maybe they can have Torgan's cart or Jasha's, assuming that the a'laq hasn't burned them yet."

"Yes, maybe."

Grinsa turned his mount once more and rode back to the Mettai. Both men eyed him with curiosity as he approached and fell in beside them.

"What's wrong?" Besh asked.

"Q'Daer thinks we're going too slowly, and he . . ."

"He thinks we're slowing you down," Besh said.

Grinsa nodded. "I'm not sure I agree with him. I'm still weak from Lici's plague. I don't know how much faster I can ride."

Besh stared ahead at the Fal'Borna, the expression on his round face revealing little. "What's his solution to this?"

"He wants you to leave your cart here. One or both of you can ride Jasha's horse, or ride with one of us."

"You want us to ride?" Sirj asked. The younger Mettai rarely said much, and when he did it was usually to the point and insightful. Grinsa couldn't remember hearing him sound this unsure of himself.

"What about our animal?" Besh said, before Grinsa could answer.

"The Fal'Borna would never do anything to harm a horse. Q'Daer said that we'd bring her with us, and maintain a pace that she could match. But I don't think you'd want to ride her."

A small grin flitted across Besh's features. "And I don't think she'd want it, either."

"I'm no rider," Sirj said. He shook his head and looked at Besh. "I don't like this."

Besh laid a hand on the other man's arm and offered a reassuring smile. Then he faced Grinsa once more. "We Mettai are not horsemen. We never have been. As for Lici's cart . . ." He trailed off, shaking his head.

"What about her cart?"

Besh shrugged. "I was going to say that it's not ours to abandon. But of course it is now. It's of no value to us except as a way of getting from one place to the next. My first point stands, though. We're not horsemen, Grinsa. Riding is . . ." He smiled weakly. "I'm sixty-four years old, and I've ridden perhaps three times in my entire life."

"I've never ridden," Sirj admitted.

"Fal'Borna horses are well trained," Grinsa said. He looked at them both, but eventually his gaze came to rest on Sirj. He sensed that if he could convince the younger man, Besh would agree. "I don't think either Torgan or Jasha were experienced riders, but these animals bore them. They'll bear you."

Sirj turned to Besh, looking like a frightened boy.

"This is your decision," Besh told him. "If you don't want to give up the cart, we won't. And if Q'Daer is in too much of a hurry to ride with us, they can leave us here."

"No," Sirj said, shaking his head. "We can't do that. We both know what the Fal'Borna would do to two Mettai out here alone on the plain." He faced Grinsa and took a long breath. "We'll ride."

Grinsa smiled. "That took some courage."

"I haven't done anything yet," Sirj said. "We'll see if I can actually bring myself to climb onto one of those beasts."

"Would you rather ride with one of us?"

The Mettai shared a look.

"No," Besh answered. "We'll share Jasha's horse."

"All right."

Grinsa called ahead to Q'Daer, who halted and turned. When Grinsa explained to him what was happening, the Fal'Borna rode back to where they were.

"You're willing to ride?" he asked, looking at both men.

"If the horse is willing to carry me," Sirj answered. He still looked deeply frightened.

Q'Daer, though, grinned at this. "Of course he'll carry you. He was trained by the Fal'Borna. He'll carry anyone."

It didn't take them long to empty the cart. Besh and Sirj had few belongings and had apparently gotten rid of Lici's things long ago. They removed the harness from the white nag, and tied their sleeping rolls to the saddle on Jasha's horse. There was little they could do with the cart. They didn't dare burn it, for fear of drawing attention to themselves. But if they left it where it was, someone would spot it eventually. In the end, with Besh's permission, Grinsa shattered it with shaping power, so that all that remained was a low pile of broken wood. Then Grinsa and Q'Daer helped them onto Jasha's mount and they resumed their journey southward.

They started out slowly, allowing Besh and Sirj to accustom themselves to riding. Besh sat in front and held the reins; Sirj gripped the back edge of the saddle so tightly that his knuckles turned white. But after a short while they seemed to grow more comfortable, as did the horse. The nag followed behind the others, her tail swinging slowly from side to side, as if she was pleased to have shed her burden.

They rested three or four times during the course of the day, and after the second stop, Sirj actually sat in front of Besh. By the time they halted for the night, both Mettai appeared at least somewhat at ease sitting their horse. Besh moved stiffly after dismounting, but that would pass in a few days. Grinsa wasn't convinced that they had gained much on this day by leaving the cart behind, but he had no doubt that they would be able to ride faster in coming days. Even Q'Daer seemed in better spirits than he had in some time.

As darkness fell, however, and the four men walked through a small copse gathering wood for a fire, Q'Daer, who was a short distance from Grinsa, suddenly looked up, alarm on his face.

"Do you hear that?" he said.

Grinsa shook his head. "What—?"

Q'Daer silenced him with a raised hand.

The Mettai were ahead of them, and a moment later Sirj called out, "Riders! From the north!"

"Damn," Grinsa muttered. "Fal'Borna?"

Q'Daer looked at him bleakly. "Or Eandi warriors."

Grinsa and the Fal'Borna started back toward their camp, where they'd left their horses. After a few strides they broke into a run.

The men were almost upon them by the time they reached their animals. Sirj got there a moment later. Besh was some distance behind him. He was jogging, and Grinsa could hear him gasping for breath.

"Besh?" Grinsa called.

"I'm all right. Worry about them, not me."

Grinsa nodded and turned to face the riders. There were two dozen of them, perhaps more, all of them with long white hair that they wore tied back from their faces. Fal'Borna. Grinsa supposed he should have been relieved that it wasn't an Eandi army, but at that moment he wasn't certain that they were much better off facing a Qirsi force.

Sirj reached for his blade, probably to cut the back of his hand and ready himself to conjure. Grinsa reached out and stopped him, drawing a nod from Q'Daer.

"He's right," the young Fal'Borna said. "Not yet. We don't want to draw attention to the fact that you're Mettai if we don't have to."

Grinsa reached forth with his magic to determine the abilities of the approaching warriors. "The man leading them is a Weaver," he said in a low voice.

"Yes," Q'Daer said. "But he's the only one."

They had several shapers in their company as well, and more than a dozen men who could wield fire magic. If this came to a fight, Grinsa and Q'Daer would be at a disadvantage.

Besh reached them at last and took his place beside Sirj. "We should have our knives out," he said.

Q'Daer looked at him as if he were a fool. "Only if you wish to convince them beyond any doubt that you're Mettai."

"Look at us," the old man said. "Look at our eyes, our skin, Sirj's hair. What else could we be but Mettai?"

"No knives yet," Q'Daer said, his tone leaving no room for argument.

A moment later the leader of the riders reined his mount to a halt a few fourspans from where they stood. His warriors spread themselves in an arcing line so that in a matter of moments Grinsa, Q'Daer, and the Mettai were nearly surrounded. The Fal'Borna held their spears ready, and Grinsa sensed that all of them were prepared to use their magic at a moment's notice.

"Who are you?" the leader demanded, eyeing each of the four men. "What are you doing here?" He was powerfully built, as all Fal'Borna men seemed to be. His face was round, his cheeks full, as if he was still more boy than man. But there was a confident look in his bright yellow eyes, and Grinsa had no doubt that he would prove a formidable foe if it came to a fight.

"My name is Q'Daer. I'm a Weaver in the sept of E'Menua, son of E'Sedt. With me is Grinsa, a Weaver from the Forelands who has joined our sept."

Grinsa wasn't sure he agreed with the characterization, but this didn't seem like the time to quibble.

"And who are you, friend?" Q'Daer asked.

"I am B'Vril. My father is S'Bahn, a'laq of my sept."

Q'Daer nodded. "I know of S'Bahn. E'Menua considers him a friend, and speaks often of his strength and the many Weavers he commands."

"And all who live on this plain know of E'Menua's wisdom and might." He looked at Besh and Sirj. "Are these men your prisoners then, Q'Daer?"

"They're our companions," Grinsa answered before the young Weaver could say anything.

B'Vril regarded him briefly. Then he faced Q'Daer again.

"You had a cart. We found the remains of it earlier today and followed your tracks to here. Why did you leave it behind?"

"It was slowing us down," Q'Daer told him. "War is coming, and I'm eager—*we* are eager—to rejoin our a'laq and ready ourselves for battle."

"I can't help noticing that your companions . . ." He paused, his eyes flicking toward Grinsa for an instant. "Look Mettai."

"They are," Q'Daer said, holding his head high. "They have been declared friends of our people by F'Ghara, a'laq of a sept to the east."

"We know F'Ghara," B'Vril said coldly. "His sept is small, and he has no Weavers other than his daughters."

"That doesn't change the fact that he gave these men his stone."

As if anticipating what Q'Daer had intended to say, Besh was already holding up the necklace that F'Ghara had given him and Sirj as a token of friendship. It was a simple necklace, much like the ones Q'Daer and B'Vril both wore at their throats. It consisted of a thin black cord from which hung a single white stone.

"So you're telling me," B'Vril said, after barely glancing at the necklace, "that you left that cart back there because you're so eager to ride into battle, and yet you ride alongside those who would make war against us and steal our lands."

"These men killed the Mettai witch responsible for the plague that's been sickening the Fal'Borna," Grinsa said. "They've done more to save your people than any Qirsi warrior on this plain."

"You mean 'our people,'" B'Vril said, glaring at him.

Grinsa winced slightly, but held the man's gaze. "Yes, you're right. That is what I meant. I've only been in the Southlands for a few turns; this is all still very new to me."

B'Vril turned back to Q'Daer. "I don't know what to believe. You tell me that you and your company are returning to your sept, that you wish to fight the invaders. And yet from all that I see, you seem more like traitors than warriors. You ride with the Mettai, and this . . ." He gestured toward Grinsa with his chin, "this Forelander."

Grinsa expected Q'Daer to bristle at being called a traitor, but to the young Weaver's credit, he kept his temper in check.

"I'd think the same thing if I were in your place," he said. "And I can't offer any proof that we're telling you the truth. You're just going to have to trust us."

B'Vril shook his head. "I don't."

Q'Daer's expression hardened. Apparently his forbearance only went so far. "Suit yourselves. But one way or another, I think it's time you and your men were leaving."

The other man's laugh was harsh and abrupt. "How do you intend to make us go, Q'Daer? Do you have an army hidden somewhere nearby?"

His soldiers laughed.

"No," Grinsa said. "But we have two Weavers to your one. And we have these two Mettai, as well. We're not your enemies, and Q'Daer is no traitor. But you'd do well to leave now."

"You have much to learn about the Fal'Borna, Forelander."

"And you have much to learn about magic." He glanced at Q'Daer. "I'll handle the Weaver," he said. "I've some experience with men like him. You control the others. Don't let them do anything."

Q'Daer nodded, tight-lipped, his eyes watchful.

"Besh," Grinsa went on, "I seem to remember you using a spell in S'Vralna that drove off some men who were trying to hurt you. Do you remember?"

"Yes, I remember. I used that spell against Lici, too."

Out of the corner of his eye, Grinsa saw both Mettai men reach for their knives. He knew that the Fal'Borna would try to shatter their blades with shaping magic; that was what he would have done in their position. But he was ready for them. B'Vril, he sensed, had already readied his magic and was aiming his shaping power at Besh's knife. Grinsa reached out with his own magic and took hold of the Weaver's power.

B'Vril's eyes snapped to his. Grinsa could feel him fighting to use his magic, to free himself from Grinsa's control. But Grinsa had done this before. While still in the Forelands he had led an army of Qirsi against the renegade Weaver who sought to rule all the seven realms. That Weaver had been stronger by far than this man. And in the end Grinsa had won.

Shaping. Fire. Mists and winds. Language of beasts. Shaping, again. Even healing and delusion. B'Vril tried every magic at his disposal. And each time he reached for a new one, Grinsa was there to stop him.

Grinsa heard Besh speaking in a low voice—he was conjuring. "Wait, Besh," he said.

He knew that the old man had turned to look at him, but Grinsa didn't look away from the Fal'Borna rider. Finally, B'Vril let out a roar of frustration.

"Do something!" he yelled at his men. "Use your magic!"

"We can't!" said one of the other warriors. "The Fal'Borna won't let us."

"Damn you!" B'Vril said, glaring at Grinsa.

But Grinsa hadn't finished with him yet. Thus far, all he'd done was keep the man from attacking them. Now, he took hold of B'Vril's shaping power and slowly began to squeeze the man's skull, as if he intended to shatter the bone.

Suddenly the Fal'Borna stopped grappling for control of his various magics and instead fought desperately to expel Grinsa from his mind.

"You feel what I'm doing to you?" Grinsa asked the man.

B'Vril nodded, wide-eyed, his mouth agape.

"You understand that I could kill you with a thought?"

He nodded a second time.

Grinsa eased the pressure on the man's head, but he didn't release his magic.

"Who are you?" the man asked, still regarding Grinsa the way he might a demon from Bian's realm.

"Just a Weaver, like you," Grinsa said. "And believe it or not, I'm a friend."

B'Vril merely stared back at him.

"If Q'Daer was a traitor—if I was in league with the Eandi who are marching against your people—we'd have killed you all by now. There's nothing stopping us."

"What was it the Mettai were going to do?"

Grinsa hesitated, but only for an instant. If it turned out that they still had to fight these men, he felt confident that Besh and Sirj could think of another way to attack them. He nodded to Besh.

Besh cut the back of his hand with his knife, caught the welling blood on the flat of the blade, and mixed it with the earth he already held. He spoke a few words as he did this, though he kept his voice so low that Grinsa couldn't make them out. The dark mud in his palm began to swirl and as it did Besh threw it straight up into the air. Before their eyes, the mud appeared to fracture into a hundred pieces. An instant later, each of those clumps of dirt had begun to buzz, so that the air around them was filled with the sound.

"Hornets?" B'Vril whispered, staring at the cloud of insects.

The insects circled over them once and streamed away toward the nearby wood.

"Hornets," Besh said, grinning.

B'Vril stared at him. After a moment he began to laugh. "You were going to attack us with hornets?"

"It would have worked," Sirj said, sounding angry.

"I don't doubt it," the Fal'Borna said, raising his hands in a placating gesture. "But I was expecting you to try to kill us. And you were going to use hornets." He looked at Grinsa again. "You can release my magic, Forelander. I believe you now."

The other warrior looked at his leader, clearly puzzled. "Weaver?" he said.

"It's all right. Lower your weapons."

"Now it's my turn," Grinsa told him. "I'm not sure I trust you."

B'Vril threw down his spear, pulled the knife from his belt, and threw that onto the ground as well.

"We both know that your weapons are meaningless in this fight."

"It doesn't matter," Q'Daer said. "If he's laid down his spear, this fight is over. That's our way."

Grinsa and Q'Daer shared a look.

"You can let go of his magic," the young Weaver told him. "There isn't a Fal'Borna alive who would drop his weapon before another Fal'Borna and then attack."

Still Grinsa hesitated. If B'Vril truly thought that Q'Daer had betrayed his people, would he still consider him Fal'Borna?

"The rest of you do the same," B'Vril called to his men. "Your spears and your blades."

The other warriors dropped their weapons on the ground beside their mounts.

Grinsa took a long breath and then, with great reluctance, eased his grip on B'Vril's magic. The man smiled with obvious relief and nodded.

"Thank you," he said. "Perhaps one day you'll show me how you did that."

Grinsa had to grin. "Perhaps."

B'Vril dismounted, walked to Q'Daer, and held out his hands. Q'Daer gripped the man's wrists from below so that B'Vril could grip his wrists from above at the same time. It was a traditional Fal'Borna greeting, one that Grinsa had seen before. When B'Vril released Q'Daer and turned to him, offering his hands in the same way, Grinsa knew just what to do.

"I see you've learned some of our customs," he said.

Grinsa nodded. "Some, yes. There's still much I don't know."

B'Vril let go of his arms and turned to the Mettai. He didn't approach them, nor did he offer the customary greeting. But he looked both men in the eye.

"Your people are marching to war against us."

"Yes," Besh said. "I don't know why. I never thought I'd see the day when we involved ourselves in your battles with the Eandi."

"Your people are also responsible for the pestilence that's been destroying Fal'Borna villages. Is it such a leap to believe they'd bring war as well as plague to our plain?"

"The plague was brought here by one person," Sirj said hotly. "And Besh killed her. We've told you that already."

Besh placed a hand on Sirj's shoulder.

"Her name was Lici," the older man said. "She's the one Sirj is talking about. She came from our village, and we followed her. Eventually we captured her, and in the end I had no choice but to kill her. You're right, though. It was a Mettai curse that killed those people and razed their villages. It was also a Mettai spell that cured Grinsa and Q'Daer of Lici's plague. I created that spell, and I can use it tonight to make you and your men immune to the plague, so that if you encounter any more of Lici's cursed baskets you'll be safe. And later, you can use your healing magic to spread my spell through your entire sept. Your people need never fear that curse again."

Clearly, this was more than B'Vril had expected. He eyed Besh with obvious curiosity, but his mistrust seemed to have vanished, and a small grin played at the corners of his mouth.

"Well, this has been a most extraordinary evening," he said at last. "I'll consider your offer, Mettai. Even before this war, I never thought that I'd allow a Mettai to use his magic on me, but I would be . . . relieved to know that I was immune to that plague."

"Let me know when you're ready," Besh said.

B'Vril nodded to him, gave Sirj a quick, uncertain look, and turned back to Q'Daer. "We should talk, Weaver to Weaver. I need to know . . ." He faltered, glancing once more at the Mettai. "I have questions for you."

"Of course," Q'Daer said. "When you arrived, we were about to build a fire and eat. We don't have enough food to feed you and your men, but you're welcome to sup with us."

"I'd like . . . I'd like to speak with you and the Forelander alone."

Q'Daer looked at Besh and Sirj.

"Yes, all right," Besh said, his voice flat. "We'll make our own fire. I'm tired anyway. Too much riding."

Grinsa caught Besh's eye. "Where I can see you," he said.

The old man nodded, casting a wary eye toward the Fal'Borna warriors. "Yes, I understand."

He and Sirj walked off a short distance, taking with them the wood they had gathered. Grinsa and Q'Daer quickly built their own fire, and soon were sitting beside it, eating a bit of dried rilda meat and cheese, while B'Vril sat across from them, also eating rilda.

"You had questions?" Q'Daer asked after some time.

"Are you sure you can trust them?" B'Vril asked immediately, as if he'd been aching to say the words the whole time. "The Mettai, I mean."

Q'Daer smiled thinly. "I knew who you meant." He looked at Grinsa briefly. "For a long time I wasn't sure. And then I got their plague and I was certain that they had cursed me. But they saved me. The Forelander, too. That spell Besh offered to use on you . . . Let him. It'll protect you."

B'Vril nodded once, but he still looked uncertain. "So, these Mettai can be trusted. But the rest . . ."

"The rest have made themselves enemies of the Fal'Borna," Q'Daer said.

"That's right," B'Vril said. "And that's why I wanted to speak with you. We know so little about their magic. At first I thought that finding you was nothing more than chance, but I realize now that it's a gift from the gods." He leaned forward. "You've seen them conjure," he went on in a lower voice. "Now, tonight, I've seen it, too. But there's so much more I need to know."

"Yes, of course."

"Q'Daer," Grinsa said, frowning.

The young Weaver looked at him, as if daring Grinsa to say more.

And really, what could Grinsa say? A group of Mettai had

joined the Eandi army that was marching toward Fal'Borna land. The Qirsi had every right to defend themselves and to speak of what they knew about blood magic.

Grinsa shook his head and stared into the fire. "Never mind," he said quietly.

"From what I've seen, there are three elements to Mettai conjurings," Q'Daer began. "Blood, which they get by cutting themselves on the back of their hands, as you saw the old man do; earth, which they can simply pick up; and the spell itself, which you heard the man speak to himself."

"Do they have to say it out loud?" B'Vril asked.

Q'Daer said nothing. Grinsa realized that both men were watching him, waiting for him to answer.

"I'm new to this land," he said, not bothering to look at them. "I don't know any more about their magic than you do."

"You talk with them," Q'Daer said. "I've seen you. I think you know a great deal about how they conjure."

Grinsa didn't answer.

"They're marching against us," the young Weaver went on, sounding angry. "And if you think that the Eandi army and their allies will spare you or your woman or your child because you're from the Forelands rather than the plain, you're a fool and worse. Your hair is white; your eyes are yellow. To them, you're the enemy regardless of where you were born."

Grinsa knew Q'Daer was right, though it made his chest ache just to admit as much to himself.

"Yes, they have to say it aloud," he finally told them. He felt as though he was betraying Besh and Sirj, and he wanted to rail at Q'Daer and B'Vril for drawing him into their war with the Eandi.

Instead he raised his eyes, meeting Q'Daer's gaze. "What else do you want to know?"

Chapter 5

"What do you think they're talking about?" Sirj asked, peering through the darkness at the other fire and the three Qirsi seated around it.

Besh kept his gaze fixed on the fire and took another bite of hard cheese. "I don't know. It doesn't matter."

"They must be talking about us. That's why the Fal'Borna didn't want us there."

He was sure Sirj was right, but he said nothing. There was no sense in troubling him further.

For Besh, the Qirsi's conversation was the least of his concerns. His entire body hurt from riding that damned horse today. He'd told Grinsa that the Mettai were not horsemen, and he'd known that he was far too old to try to become one now. His back and legs were stiff, and he'd strained muscles he didn't even know he had.

Yet he could hardly argue with the Qirsi's decision to abandon the cart and make them ride. Q'Daer's people were under attack; had Besh been in his position, he would have been desperate to return to his sept. And having been away from his own family for far too long, the old man could imagine how keen Grinsa must have been to rejoin his wife and child.

For Besh and Sirj, however, this race southward couldn't have been more perilous. In the best of times, the old man would have felt vulnerable traveling across the plain. The Fal'Borna had a reputation as a hard and dangerous people. The necklace F'Ghara had given them seemed like scant protection. But now, with war coming, and with Mettai marching alongside the men of Stelpana, Besh feared that he and Sirj were riding to their doom.

Worse, he knew now that they had no choice. He'd been ready to leave Grinsa and Q'Daer, to ride back to Mettai lands and put the clans and their Eandi enemies behind them. He knew that Sirj wanted to. But Grinsa had argued that the danger to them was too great, and this evening's encounter with the Fal'Borna war party had convinced Besh that he was right. He'd had little experience with Qirsi magic, but he knew enough to understand that only Grinsa's and Q'Daer's intervention had kept B'Vril and his men from killing them. If Sirj and he had come upon the warriors on their own, they'd be dead already.

They were helpless. There was nothing they could do but follow Grinsa and Q'Daer back to the sept and hope that the Forelander would manage to keep them alive.

"I feel like a child."

"What?" Sirj said.

Besh looked at him, surprised by the question. It took him a moment to realize that he had spoken aloud. "Nothing."

"What if this new Fal'Borna is trying to turn them against us?" Sirj asked, still watching the Qirsi.

"Grinsa trusts us more than he does the Fal'Borna. Even if that's the Fal'Borna's intent, he won't betray us."

"But the other one—"

"Stop it, Sirj! We have enough to worry about without you imagining things!"

Sirj stared at him for a moment, then looked away. Besh shook his head, cursing his temper. He and Sirj had come a long way since leaving their home village of Kirayde. Eight years before, Sirj had married Besh's daughter, Elica. At the time, and in the years since, Besh had assumed that Sirj wasn't worthy of being her husband. He mistook Sirj's reticence for simplemindedness, and he would have preferred that Elica choose a more prosperous man; a wheelwright, perhaps, or a farrier, rather than a trapper. But since being forced to journey with him, Besh had come to realize that Sirj's reserved nature masked a keen mind and a courageous heart. The man didn't deserve to be spoken to in that way.

"I'm sorry, Sirj," he said after a long silence. "I really don't think that Grinsa or Q'Daer will break faith with us. I can't think that way, because I'm convinced that they're our only hope of surviving this war."

Sirj nodded, his gaze still lowered. "I know. That's why I want to know what they're saying."

Of course. Sirj wasn't being foolish. He was already a step ahead of Besh.

"We can talk to Grinsa and Q'Daer later, after the other Fal'Borna are gone." As Besh said this, he glanced toward the Fal'Borna warriors, who had made their own fire. None of them had so much as looked toward the Mettai since he and Sirj had moved away from Grinsa and the others, but Besh continued to keep an eye on them. Grinsa had seemed concerned that the men might try to hurt them. Besh thought it possible, too.

"Do you think that this Weaver will let you use the spell on him?" Sirj asked.

"He'd be an idiot not to."

Sirj grinned. "I don't think that answers my question."

Besh laughed. Even as he did, though, he saw the Fal'Borna Weaver rise from his seat beside the other fire and start walking in their direction.

"Here comes your answer," he said.

Sirj looked up, instantly growing serious. Grinsa had stood as well, and was following the man. Clearly the Forelander had taken it upon himself to keep Besh and Sirj safe. And though Besh usually had confidence in his own ability to watch out for himself, under the circumstances, he was grateful.

B'Vril stopped a short distance from their fire and cleared his throat.

"I was wondering if I might have a word with you," he said.

Besh waved him on. "Of course. Please join us."

The Fal'Borna stepped into the firelight, and after a brief hesitation, sat down on the ground. Grinsa had halted just beyond the reach of the fire's glow, and he remained in the shadows, content, it seemed, to watch and listen.

"I want to learn more about this spell you've offered to put on me."

"Not just on you," Besh said. "You need to understand that. This is a spell that you can pass on to any Fal'Borna, simply by using your magic on them."

"I'm a Weaver," the man said. "I can wield the magic of all my warriors as a weapon. Would that pass your spell to them?"

Besh looked up at Grinsa, who nodded.

"Yes, it would," Besh said, facing the Fal'Borna once more.

B'Vril exhaled. "I see."

"You fear that I intend to harm you and your men, that I'll place this spell on you and you'll be unable to stop it from spreading."

"The thought had occurred to me."

Besh nodded. "I understand. I expect that the Forelander has tried to put your doubts to rest and has failed. So I won't even make the attempt. If he can't convince you, I certainly can't."

"This plague that's been spreading through our lands has us scared."

"Yes," Besh said. "It should. But Lici didn't intend the plague for your people. She took it to the Y'Qatt."

The man frowned. "The Y'Qatt?" Clearly he didn't believe this, and Besh understood why. The Y'Qatt were aescetics, Qirsi who eschewed all use of magic because they believed that Qirsar, the god of the Qirsi, had never intended their powers to be used.

"I know. It made no sense to us, either. But years ago, when she was just a girl, the pestilence struck her village. She crossed N'Kiel's Span in search of help, hoping to find Qirsi who could heal her family and friends. Instead she found the Y'Qatt."

"Blood and bone," B'Vril muttered.

"Everyone in her village died, and Lici blamed the Y'Qatt." Besh leaned forward, making the man look him in the eye. "You believe the Mettai are your enemy. I understand that. This plague, this war; these are tragedies. But Lici didn't want to hurt you. She lost what remained of her sanity when she learned that her cursed baskets were headed out onto the plain. And the rest of us . . ." He shook his head. "You think that Sirj and I might be different from other Mettai and that therefore you can trust us. But you have it backwards. It's the Mettai who march against you who are different. I don't know why they're doing this, but I promise you that most of my people would want no part of your war."

B'Vril didn't respond other than to nod. He didn't look at Besh.

"You don't believe me," the old Mettai said, feeling weary.

"It doesn't matter if I believe you. Even if all you're telling me is true, it can't change the fact that these Mettai have allied themselves with the Eandi. They've made all of your people enemies of all of mine. That's simply the way of things."

Only to the Fal'Borna, Besh wanted to say. But he kept this thought to himself.

"But I can see why Q'Daer and Grinsa trust you," the man went on after a moment's pause. "And I'd be grateful to you if you would use your magic to make me immune to the plague."

"All right," Besh said. "In return, I'd ask that you tell other Fal'Borna what I've told you. You don't have to believe it, and you don't have to try to convince them of anything. I ask only that you repeat what I've told you and let others judge for themselves."

He didn't answer at first, and Besh started to wonder if the Fal'Borna would refuse him. But then B'Vril nodded again. "All right."

Besh smiled. "Thank you."

He pulled out his knife. But before Besh could cut himself Grinsa stepped forward into the firelight.

"You don't have to do that, Besh."

"What do you mean?" the Mettai asked.

"I used my magic on him," Grinsa said. "Or rather, I stopped him from using his magic on me. He's already immune."

"I don't understand," B'Vril said, looking first at Grinsa and then at the Forelander. "How can I already be immune?"

"The spell I created is as contagious as Lici's plague," Besh said. "When Grinsa used his magic against you he passed on the spell."

B'Vril eyed Besh doubtfully. "How will we know if it worked?"

Besh smiled weakly. "I hope we never will. I hope that the plague has run its course and all of Lici's baskets have been destroyed. But the only way we can be certain is if you're exposed to the plague."

Even in the firelight, Besh could see the man blanch.

"The spell worked when he used it on me," Grinsa said. "It'll work for you, too."

B'Vril looked back at the Forelander. "I can pass it to my men?"

"Q'Daer already did when he held their magic. You can pass it to others the same way. Any contact with your magic should make them immune, too."

The Fal'Borna turned to Besh again. "Thank you."

Besh shrugged. "It turns out I didn't do anything, but you're welcome. I'd ask that you remember our agreement."

"I will. You have my word."

B'Vril stood, thanked Besh again, and bade him and Sirj good night. He stepped past Grinsa, nodding to the Forelander as he did, and returned to his warriors.

Grinsa sat down beside Besh.

"You were ready to help him," the Forelander said. "You would have been justified in refusing, the way he spoke to you."

"No," Besh said, putting away his blade. "I wouldn't have been. How could I have justified allowing those men to die when I have the power to save them?"

"I don't know. But other—"

"Please, Grinsa," Besh said, cutting him off. "I know that you mean well. Sirj and I are grateful for your friendship and your protection. But I'm tired, and I'm sore, and I'm in no mood to talk. I want to sleep and tomorrow I want to ride as far as we can without it killing me."

Besh grimaced at what he heard in his own voice. This was no way to speak to a friend. But Grinsa merely smiled and placed a hand on Besh's shoulder.

"Sleep sounds like an excellent idea." He stood once again. "Dream well, my friend," he said, and walked away.

"He's a good man," Sirj said, and Besh thought he heard a gentle rebuke in the younger man's tone.

"I know." What else could Besh say?

They awoke the following morning with first light. B'Vril and his men said quick farewells and rode off toward the rising sun and the war that was approaching from the east. A short time later, Besh and the others broke camp as well.

Besh's muscles had grown stiff overnight, and he could barely walk, much less climb onto his horse. He needed help from both Grinsa and Sirj; by the time he was sitting in his saddle, he was exhausted and humiliated.

The first step his mount took made him gasp with pain, and he nearly told the others to leave him there. Better to be found by another company of Fal'Borna warriors than to endure such misery. But as the morning wore on, his discomfort subsided a bit. He wasn't foolish enough to think that he wouldn't be sore again come morning, but he could feel his muscles loosening, and he decided that he could go on, at least for the moment.

The company rode farther during the course of this day than they had during any day since turning south toward E'Menua's sept. By nightfall, Besh was utterly exhausted and his muscles burned. He barely ate any supper and had no sooner lay down beside the fire than he fell into a deep, dreamless slumber.

Morning seemed to come way too soon, and upon awaking again he could barely move. But once he was sitting his horse, he began to feel better. They rode even farther this second day than they had the one before.

So it went. Each day Besh's discomfort abated a bit more quickly. Each evening they stopped after having covered more distance than they had the previous day. They encountered no more Fal'Borna war parties, and they saw no sign of the Eandi army that was said to be on the march.

Besh could see Grinsa's spirits lifting with each league they covered. Even Q'Daer's mood seemed to be improving. He and Sirj, on the other hand, could not help but dread their arrival in the sept, and, ironically, by making himself a better rider, Besh was hastening that moment.

Sirj said little about his own fears, as was his way, but Besh could tell that he was growing increasingly anxious, even as his riding improved as well.

Several days after their encounter with B'Vril's company, as they were passing a series of low, grass-covered hills, Q'Daer suddenly glanced back at Grinsa and the two Mettai, a smile on his square face.

"We're close!" he said. "Another league and we'll be there."

Grinsa nodded, but otherwise none of them spoke. The Fal'Borna's grin faded, and after another moment he faced forward again, apparently disappointed by their response.

"What does he expect us to say?" Sirj muttered, turning just enough so that Besh could hear him.

"I don't think he was taunting us," Besh answered. "He must not think we have anything to fear from his a'laq."

"Or else he just doesn't care."

That seemed as likely an explanation as any. Besh said nothing.

Grinsa steered his horse over to theirs, a look of concern in his pale yellow eyes.

"You're afraid of what will happen when we reach the sept." He offered it as a statement.

Besh merely nodded.

"I am, too," Grinsa told them. "We didn't find Lici; we allowed Torgan to get away. In the strictest terms, I failed, and E'Menua would be within his rights to insist that I remain here forever and take a Fal'Borna Weaver as my wife."

"That's hardly the same thing," Sirj said, his voice tight. "We're afraid we'll be killed."

Grinsa nodded, seemingly unaffected by what the younger man had said. Besh sometimes wondered if the Forelander ever lost his temper. Then he remembered watching him confront Torgan, hearing him threaten a Qirsi man in S'Vralna who had just used magic to shatter the bone in Besh's leg. Perhaps a man wielding as much power as Grinsa did couldn't afford to give in to rage. And thinking this, Besh had another thought as well: *We're fortunate to have such a man as our friend.*

"You're right, it's not the same thing," Grinsa said to Sirj. "My point is this: We both have cause to fear E'Menua. But we can help one another. I've sworn this to you before, and I swear it again today. I won't allow E'Menua to harm you, and if I have to I'll give my life to save yours. I owe you no less."

"We can give the same oath," Besh said. "But all three of us know that it's worth far less coming from Sirj and me."

Grinsa smiled. "I'm not as sure of that as you are. But I had something else in mind. As I said before, I've failed in nearly every task that E'Menua set before me. We did find you, however, and you not only killed Lici, you defeated her curse. If you and I make it clear to him that we're friends, and that the spell you used to defeat the plague grew out of our friendship, it might help both of us."

"You should tell the a'laq whatever you think you need to," Besh said. "The truth is, without your help I never would have come up with the spell, and you would have died. As far as I'm concerned you deserve as much credit as I for defeating the plague."

"It's not just defeating the curse, Besh," Grinsa told him.

"You killed Lici. I know you don't like to talk about it, but the Fal'Borna will want to hear the story of her death. You'd be wise to tell it as often as you can."

Besh nodded, though he could feel his stomach tightening. To this day, he didn't like to think about killing Lici, much less talk about it. He'd had no choice in the matter. She had wounded him and was on the verge of killing him with a second plague that might have proved fatal to all Mettai. Still, he'd never killed before, and he hoped never to kill again.

But he knew that Grinsa was right. The Fal'Borna wouldn't care about his misgivings, and might well take them as an affront. Lici's death was more likely to save his life and Sirj's than anything else they had done since leaving Kirayde.

"I don't know if E'Menua will arrange to have a shelter built for you," Grinsa went on a moment later. "If he doesn't, Cresenne and I will make room for you in ours."

Besh laughed and shook his head. "No, Grinsa. You haven't seen your wife in a long time. If need be, Sirj and I will sleep beside a fire. But I have no desire to share your shelter tonight."

Grinsa's face turned crimson, drawing a snort of laughter from Sirj. Q'Daer glanced back at them, scowled, and faced forward again.

"He's speechless," Sirj said.

The Forelander smiled, then laughed. "I am."

They rode on, saying nothing. Occasionally Grinsa chuckled to himself and shook his head again. Soon, they topped a small rise and looked down upon the sept. It sat in a shallow basin and looked to be little more than a loose array of small triangular structures. Thin ribbons of blue-grey smoke rose from the top of several of them, as well as from perhaps a dozen fires burning outside. A narrow stream wound past the settlement and more than two hundred horses grazed in a large paddock just to the west of the structures.

As they drew nearer, Besh saw that the structures were made of skins and wood. Nothing more.

"They live like this through the Snows?" he asked.

"The z'kals are sturdier than they look," Grinsa said. "And with a fire burning within, they're quite comfortable. At least they were the few nights I spent here."

"The Fal'Borna are a hardy people."

"Yes, they are."

Grinsa sounded distracted. Looking his way, Besh saw him scanning the sept, no doubt searching for his wife.

Several children played near the paddock and now they spotted the riders. For an instant they stared. Then, with shouts of excitement, they sprinted back toward the settlement.

Men and women began to emerge from the shelters, all of them looking northward toward Besh and the rest of the company.

Abruptly, Grinsa spurred his mount to a gallop, thundering past Q'Daer and toward the heart of the settlement. Looking once more at the sept, Besh spotted the man's wife. She was taller and leaner than the Fal'Borna and her skin was bone white, not at all like the golden color of the clanspeople. She held a child in her arms and, like the others, she gazed in their direction.

Seeing Grinsa, she began to run toward him. They met at the edge of the settlement. Grinsa dismounted in one swift, fluid motion, covered the remaining distance in two great strides, and gathered her in his arms, kissing her deeply. She clung to him with one arm, and still clutched their baby in the other.

After a moment, Besh looked away, feeling that he was intruding on their privacy, even from this distance. Glancing back at Sirj, who sat behind him, he saw that the younger man was still watching them, a tear in his eye.

Besh wanted to tell him that it wouldn't be long before they returned to Kirayde and Sirj was reunited with Elica and their children, Mihas, Annze, and Cam. But it would have been an empty promise. They were a long way from Mettai land, and war was coming to the plain.

"I miss them, too," he said quietly. "Not as much as you do, but very much, just the same."

The younger man merely nodded.

By the time they reached Grinsa and his wife, others from the sept had joined them. There were several women and children, and one young man who looked a great deal like Q'Daer, to whom Grinsa spoke. Q'Daer had already joined the cluster of people, and had warmly embraced the young man who resembled him. Besh wondered if they might be brothers.

The Forelander was holding his child now, and he still held his wife's hand. Besh had never seen him look happier. He looked up as they drew near, and beckoned them over.

"This is Besh," he said to the woman, indicating the old man with an open hand. "And this is Sirj." He regarded the other Fal'Borna standing around them. "These are the Mettai who killed the woman and defeated her curse," he told them, raising his voice. "They're the reason Q'Daer and I are alive. They're also the reason all of you are now immune to the plague that has spread across the plain."

The others there looked up at them, their expressions guarded despite Grinsa's reassurances. But the woman stepped forward, stopping beside their mount and favoring them with a dazzling smile.

"Thank you for my husband's life," she said, her voice clear and strong. "My name is Cresenne ja Terba, and for as long as I live I'll be indebted to you both."

Besh had always considered the Qirsi a strange-looking people. The Fal'Borna were odd enough, with their white hair and yellow eyes. But their skin at least had a golden hue to it that made them look a bit less odd. Other clans—and apparently Qirsi from the Forelands—had skin so white that it looked almost transparent. Even Grinsa, with whom he had spent more time than any other person of the sorcerer race, still struck him as alien in appearance. But even with her pale complexion and ghostly eyes, this woman before him was as beautiful as anyone he had ever met. Her face was oval, her features delicate and perfect. There seemed to be long white scars on her cheek and along her jawline, but they were faint and didn't detract from her beauty. Her hair, which hung loose to the middle of her back, looked so fine and soft that Besh actually had to keep himself from reaching out to touch it.

"You honor us, my friend," he said, gazing back into those pale eyes. They were the color of sand or of dried plain grass.

The woman grinned. "Well, good. That was my intention."

Besh and Sirj climbed off their horse, but stayed near it, as if the beast might protect them if the crowd of Fal'Borna turned on them.

There had been a great deal of noise coming from all the people clustered around the company, but now a hush fell over them. Cresenne turned, as did Grinsa and Q'Daer.

A man and a woman were approaching from the middle of the settlement. The woman had a piercing gaze and a handsome square face. There were lines around her mouth and eyes, but otherwise she didn't appear to be particularly old. It was the man, however, to whom Besh's eyes were drawn. He was nearly a full head shorter than Grinsa, even a bit shorter than Q'Daer. But he was broad in the chest and shoulders, so that he looked bigger and more formidable than the young Weaver. With his large round yellow eyes and narrow, tapered face he resembled a cat, predatory and keenly intelligent. Like most Fal'Borna warriors he wore his white hair tied back. A white stone, much like the one F'Ghara had given to Besh and Sirj, hung at his throat.

"The a'laq," Sirj whispered.

Besh nodded. E'Menua, Grinsa had called him. Besh noticed that Cresenne had retreated to Grinsa's side, and he sensed that she feared this man. Given the silence that now hung over the sept, it seemed that all of these people did.

Even Q'Daer was eyeing the a'laq uneasily, and Besh hadn't known the young Fal'Borna to fear anyone.

Only Grinsa didn't seem cowed by the man. He stood straight, marking the a'laq's approach, his arm around Cresenne's shoulders.

The a'laq stopped a short distance from the Forelander, and for a moment they eyed each other in silence. Then the a'laq looked around, his gaze barely lingering on Besh and Sirj.

"Where are the merchants?" he finally asked, his eyes coming to rest on Grinsa. He had a rough voice, the sound of stone grating on stone.

"I think you know," the Forelander said. "Q'Daer would have told you already. He spoke to you in a dream several days ago."

The look that flashed in E'Menua's eyes could have kindled wet wood. "I'm asking you," he said.

"Jasha is dead, killed by Torgan."

"And Torgan escaped?"

Grinsa nodded. "That's right. He nearly managed to kill Q'Daer and me before he did."

"How is that possible? The man is Eandi. He's weak and a fool. And yet he nearly bested both of you."

The Forelander said nothing. At last the a'laq turned to Q'Daer.

"I . . . I told you, A'Laq. He had a scrap of cursed basket. From one of the villages we found that had been struck by the plague."

"Ah, yes," E'Menua said. He turned those bright yellow eyes on Besh and Sirj. "The plague."

Suddenly Besh understood. Grinsa was right: E'Menua had known all of this already. But he wanted to have it repeated aloud for all the rest of the Fal'Borna to hear, so that they would see Besh and Sirj as their enemies, despite whatever Grinsa had told them.

"E'Menua, son of E'Sedt," Grinsa said, "I present to you Besh and Sirj of the Mettai village Kirayde."

"We thank you for welcoming us to your sept, A'Laq," Besh said, knowing that he was taking a chance. "Three times now, your people have honored us so. You do so today. Q'Daer did so when he welcomed us into his company." He pulled F'Ghara's necklace from his pocket. "And another a'laq, F'Ghara, who leads a sept east of here, gave us this stone as a token of his friendship and that of all your people."

E'Menua's eyes narrowed briefly. "F'Ghara gave you that?"

"Yes. After he learned that I had killed Lici, the woman who created the plague."

The a'laq regarded him for another moment. Then he turned to Grinsa again. "You were supposed to kill her."

"Yes, but Besh did. She's dead. That's what matters."

"You've made a mess of everything. And you've brought these Mettai to my sept in a time of war."

Grinsa gave no indication that the a'laq's rebuke troubled him. "I don't believe we've made a mess of anything," he said evenly. "But that's a matter you and I can discuss in private."

E'Menua glared at Grinsa, his jaw muscles bunched. After a moment he turned to Q'Daer.

"Find them a place to sleep," he said, his voice thick with anger. "Make certain they have food and wood." He cast a dark look Grinsa's way. "You, come with me."

E'Menua turned sharply and started back the way he had come.

Grinsa kissed Cresenne and smiled at her. "I'll be back soon." Then he looked at Besh.

"I'm sorry," the old Mettai said. "I've made matters worse for you."

The Forelander shook his head. "No, you haven't," he said, dropping his voice. "They were going to be difficult no matter what happened here. You said what you had to to save your life, and Sirj's. You did the right thing." He patted Besh's shoulder and turned to follow the a'laq.

"Come with me, Mettai," Q'Daer said. "We may have to build you a shelter."

Besh nodded, but still he stood there, watching Grinsa walk away, wondering what E'Menua intended to do to him.

Grinsa didn't want any part of this fight. Not now, so soon after returning to the sept. He'd been apart from Cresenne and Bryntelle for the better part of two turns, this after being apart from them for turn after turn while they were still in the Forelands. All he wanted was to hold them both, to kiss Cresenne and look into the beautiful pale eyes of his daughter. Instead he had already allowed himself to be drawn into E'Menua's foolish games. The a'laq wanted this confrontation. So be it.

Grinsa could tell how angry E'Menua was with him. He had heard it in the a'laq's voice and he could see it now in the way the a'laq stalked toward his z'kal. He had incurred the man's wrath on several occasions before leaving with Q'Daer and the merchants to search for Lici. Once, the a'laq had gone so far as to strike him. So he had some idea of what to expect when they reached E'Menua's z'kal.

E'Menua pulled back the flap of rilda skin that covered the entrance to his shelter and motioned Grinsa inside. Grinsa ducked into the z'kal and turned to face the entrance. As he had expected, as soon as the a'laq stepped into the shelter and straightened, he reared back and aimed a backhanded blow at Grinsa's face.

The last time this happened, Grinsa had anticipated the blow and allowed the man to hit him. He didn't allow it this time.

Grinsa reached up and grabbed the a'laq's wrist before E'Menua could strike him. The a'laq's eyes widened. He tried to wrench his arm out of Grinsa's grasp, but Grinsa held him firm. E'Menua was a powerful man, and in his youth he might have been able to defeat Grinsa in a battle of physical strength. But not anymore, not at his age, despite the old injury to Grinsa's shoulder that had left him slightly deformed. Grinsa sensed that E'Menua was gathering himself to use shaping magic against him, and he reached forth with his own magic to stop him, just as he had done to B'Vril.

"Let go of me!" the a'laq demanded, his voice low, menacing.

"No, not yet."

E'Menua threw a punch with the other fist, but Grinsa seized that arm, too. He felt the a'laq grappling for control of his other magics, and he blocked him. He had no doubt that the Fal'Borna were skilled warriors, but based upon his confrontation with B'Vril and now this encounter with the a'laq, he sensed that their command of Qirsi magic lacked precision. Or perhaps battling the renegade Weaver back in the Forelands had honed Grinsa's skills so well that few Qirsi anywhere could stand against him in a contest of magic. Whatever the reason, his mastery of the man's magic was even more complete than his physical advantage.

"I'll call for the others," E'Menua said. "D'Pera, Q'Daer, L'Norr. You can't defeat four Weavers."

Grinsa shook his head, though he kept his expression neutral. He didn't wish to humiliate the man. He only wanted to prove to him once and for all that he couldn't be controlled. "It's an empty threat," he said, "and we both know it. You don't want them to see you like this, and neither do I."

Still E'Menua fought him. He struggled to free himself from Grinsa's grasp. He fought for control of his magic. All to no avail.

"Damn you!" he finally said through clenched teeth. But an instant later he seemed to surrender. He stopped trying to pull his arms free, and he ceded all control of his magic to Grinsa.

Grinsa let go of the man's wrist and arm but held fast to E'Menua's magic. The a'laq continued to glare as he rubbed his wrist with the other hand. It was red where Grinsa had held him.

"You can release my magic, too."

"I don't trust you," Grinsa said. "If you'd care to throw down the blades you carry, I might consider it. Otherwise . . ." He shrugged.

E'Menua regarded him again, his eyes narrowing slightly and a faint smile touching his lips. "You'll be a Fal'Borna yet, Forelander." But he didn't pull out his weapons, and Grinsa didn't relinquish his hold on the man's magic.

The a'laq walked around the fire ring in the z'kal and sat. He gestured for Grinsa to do the same.

"What is it you want?" he asked as Grinsa lowered himself to the ground.

"You know what I want."

By Fal'Borna law, all Weavers were to be joined to other Weavers. E'Menua and his people didn't recognize Cresenne as Grinsa's wife; in the days immediately following their arrival in the sept, the Fal'Borna had referred to her again and again as Grinsa's concubine. The a'laq had demanded that Grinsa be joined to a Weaver, and of course Grinsa had refused.

"We had an arrangement," E'Menua said. "You were to find the Mettai witch who made the curse. You were to kill her and prove the innocence of those merchants. Instead, the merchants are gone and the woman was killed by the Mettai. You failed, and now you must live with the consequences of that failure. You're Fal'Borna. You're a member of this sept. That's what we agreed to. You'll marry a Fal'Borna Weaver, just as you said you would."

Grinsa shook his head and laughed. "The Mettai woman is dead. Besh and I found a way to defeat the plague, and Besh went so far as to make the cure contagious, so that soon every man and woman in your sept will be immune. You're the only man in the Southlands who could look at all this and conclude that we failed."

"What about the merchants?"

"The merchants are no longer your problem," Grinsa said. "As I told you, Jasha is dead. And Torgan is alone on the plain. You've met the man. How long do you think he can last on his own? He'll be killed by a Fal'Borna war party long before he reaches the Silverwater."

E'Menua stared at the fire ring. Whatever flames had burned there had long since burned out, but the embers still glowed faintly, and a thread of smoke rose from them, undulating each time one of them exhaled.

"I don't want those Mettai in my sept. We're at war with their kind. You shouldn't have brought them here."

"Those Mettai saved my life and Q'Daer's. And if we spread their new spell quickly enough, we can protect every Qirsi on the plain from the plague. Your sept will forever be remembered as the one that saved the Fal'Borna nation."

At that, E'Menua looked up. Grinsa felt him test his magic. He did it lightly, as if hoping that Grinsa wouldn't notice. The Forelander grinned, to show E'Menua that he had.

"You can't hold my magic forever," the man said.

"No, I can't. But I can defeat you in a battle of power any time I wish. I think we both know that."

"As I said before, you can't defeat all of my Weavers. We both know that as well."

Grinsa nodded, conceding the point.

"So we're at an impasse."

"Perhaps not," Grinsa said.

E'Menua regarded him with obvious curiosity. "What do you mean?"

"The Fal'Borna are at war. I wouldn't leave your sept now even if you let me. It would be too dangerous for Cresenne and our child. And if your people come under attack, I'll stand with you."

"Will you ride to war with us?"

Grinsa hesitated. But then he nodded. "Your people didn't start this war. The Eandi are taking advantage of the damage done by Lici's plague. There's no honor in that, no justification that I can see. I'll fight with you to drive them off the plain. But if Fal'Borna warriors cross into Eandi land, they'll do so without me."

"All right."

"But that's as far as I'll go. Cresenne is my wife. You'll treat her as such, and you'll drop your insistence that I marry a Weaver."

"How do I know you won't go back on your word?" E'Menua asked. "We had one arrangement, and I have nothing to show for it."

"I disagree. Q'Daer is alive. Your people are safe. You have much to show for it. Besides, I could easily ask you the same question. I'm still holding on to your magic because I'm convinced that as soon as I let go, you'll attack me."

"As I said: an impasse."

They stared at each other for several seconds. E'Menua's face was in shadow, but his eyes seemed to glow with the dim light cast by the embers.

At last, Grinsa relinquished his hold on the a'laq's magic, drawing a smile from the man.

"Does this mean you trust me now?" E'Menua asked.

"It's my way of saying that you can trust me. I have no desire to harm you or any of your people. And I know that you don't want to admit to any of your Weavers that you need their help to defeat me."

The a'laq's mouth twitched slightly. But he nodded again. "Very well, Forelander. You'll fight with us as a Fal'Borna warrior. And I'll accept that the woman is your wife."

"You'll acknowledge it in front of the others. Everyone in the sept is to know."

"Yes, very well," the a'laq said shortly.

Grinsa stood. "Thank you."

He turned, intending to leave, and as soon as his back was to E'Menua, he felt the power building behind him. He'd expected something like this, and had been prepared for the a'laq to attack him with shaping power. E'Menua chose fire instead, and his touch was light. It seemed the man could be trusted. He wasn't trying to kill or maim. He just wanted to make a point.

But if Grinsa, Cresenne, and Bryntelle were ever to leave

this sept, Grinsa couldn't even allow the a'laq that much. Without turning to face him again, Grinsa took hold of E'Menua's magic once more and redirected it. He also amplified the power with his own, so that flames erupted from the fire pit, blazing brilliantly. He heard the a'laq cry out.

Glancing back over his shoulder, Grinsa saw E'Menua sprawled on his back, staring up at him.

Grinsa didn't say anything. He merely grinned. Then he left the z'kal, and went in search of his family.

Chapter 6

✦➶✦

CENTRAL PLAIN, BETWEEN S'VRALNA AND N'KIEL'S SPAN

he had become a creature of the night, a man who hid in shadows and walked with wraiths at his shoulder. Not long ago Torgan Plye had been a successful merchant, renowned throughout the Southlands for the quality of his wares and his refusal to back down when bargaining. He'd been wealthy, comfortable, and respected, if not liked.

Now his gold was all but gone. His wares had been taken from him by the Fal'Borna. Every a'laq in the clan lands wanted him dead; every Qirsi warrior on the plain wanted to be the one to kill him. He himself had killed; he'd snapped Jasha's neck with his own hands, and he had exposed Q'Daer of the Fal'Borna and Grinsa, the Forelander, to the deadly plague that had taken the lives of so many white-hairs. Their deaths were on his head as well.

Torgan should have been miserable. Until the night when he killed his fellow merchant and the Qirsi, he had considered

himself a coward. The Torgan of old would have been para-
lyzed with fear, ashamed of his actions. He would have been
waiting to die.

It was enough to make this new Torgan, a man he barely
recognized, laugh out loud. For too long he had allowed
himself to be controlled by his fears and browbeaten by the
white-hairs, of whose magic he was so afraid. Two turns
ago—it seemed so much longer!—when he first realized
that he had been responsible for spreading the plague to
S'Plaed's sept, Torgan had been racked by guilt. His time as
a prisoner of the Fal'Borna had changed him, made him
bolder. He had never felt so alive, so free, so strong.

It had been several days since he left Jasha's limp form
lying on the plain—he'd lost track of the exact count. His
nose still hurt from the blow he'd received from Sirj, the
young Mettai, but the pain had dulled. He probably looked a
mess, but that was a small price to pay for his freedom. He'd
gotten away from the white-hairs and the Mettai early in the
waning. Now the waning had progressed far enough that
the moons did not rise until well after nightfall. Yet in just
these few days, Torgan, who had never been much of a
horseman before, and who had lost one eye to a coinmonger
in his youth, had grown perfectly comfortable riding by
starlight. It almost seemed that sleeping during the day and
traveling at night had improved the vision in his remaining
eye, allowing him to see in darkness, something that in the
past would have bewildered him.

On this night, by the time Panya, the white moon, appeared
on the eastern horizon, Torgan had already covered nearly a
full league. He had been navigating by the stars. Seeing the
moon rise, a bright sickle carving through the darkness, he
realized that he'd been angling slightly toward the south.
He adjusted his course a bit and rode on.

He'd been fortunate so far. He had avoided Fal'Borna
septs and had managed to steer clear of any white-hair riders. The truth was, though, he didn't know what he'd do
when he finally encountered the Qirsi. War was coming to

the plain. He'd learned that much from Q'Daer before sickening the man with the small scrap of Mettai basket that he still carried. He wanted to make his way to the safety of Eandi land as quickly as possible, but a part of him also wanted to exact some revenge on the sorcerer race. The Fal'Borna had robbed him of his wealth, humiliated him time and again, and threatened so often to kill him that Torgan had come to doubt that he'd ever see his native Tordjanne again. He wanted vengeance beyond what he'd reaped by killing Q'Daer and Grinsa. He wanted to be part of the war, to be counted among the Eandi soldiers who would soon be fanning across the plain.

So when he spotted the sept ahead and slightly to the north, he stopped, his eyes fixed on the faint glow of spent cooking fires, and the small shelters illuminated by Panya's light. Then he turned and rode toward the settlement.

It was late, and no one stirred in the sept. Still, he stopped well short of the first shelters and covered the remaining distance on foot. He'd named the horse the Qirsi had given him Trey, after a farrier he'd known as a boy. The beast, like all Fal'Borna horses, was well trained and obedient. He left it behind, confident that it would stay put and keep quiet.

Torgan wasn't entirely certain what he intended to do once he reached the village, but he'd brought the scrap of Mettai basket with him. Now, as he walked, he pulled out his knife and cut away a small piece from that scrap, and tried to decide what to do with it.

He had sickened Q'Daer by hiding the piece of basket in the Fal'Borna's sleeping roll. Clearly he wouldn't be able to get that close to any of the Fal'Borna living in this settlement. Instead, he scanned the sept for a place he could leave the cutting where it wouldn't be noticed but would infect as many as possible. As soon as he spotted the grinding stones, it came to him. The grain, of course. What better way to spread the plague than through their food supply?

He stayed clear of the paddock at the west end of the sept, fearing that if he frightened the horses they'd wake the

Fal'Borna. As it was, his mere presence in the settlement drew a few low whinnies from the beasts. Three wild dogs searching for food at the fringe of the sept growled at him. But though Torgan stopped in his tracks, his heart hammering as he watched for movement, no one awoke. After several moments, he went on toward the grinding stones and the large baskets of unground grain just beside them.

He didn't place the basket cutting in the largest of the grain baskets, but rather in the one nearest to the grinding stones. He didn't leave it where it could be seen, but neither did he bury it too deeply in the grain. The women who worked the stones would find it soon enough, and by the time they did it would be too late.

Satisfied that he had placed it as well as he could, Torgan began to retreat into the darkness. He slipped what was left of the basket scrap back into his pocket and sheathed his blade.

The dogs growled at him again as he slipped past them.

And that was when he heard the voices.

"There it is again!" one of them said. A man's voice, youthful, but strong.

"The dogs, you mean."

"Yes. Over this way. Near the grain."

"It's probably rabbits, or something of that sort."

Torgan had to resist an urge to run, knowing that they'd hear him. He slowly backed farther into the shadows and lowered himself to the ground. He could see the men now. Both of them were broad and muscular, their white hair tied back in the way of Fal'Borna warriors. They reminded him of Q'Daer.

As they approached, one of the men shouted something at the dogs and scared the animals off.

"You see anything?" the other man asked.

The first man peered into the darkness, his gaze passing right over Torgan. After a moment he shook his head. "No, nothing."

"A rabbit or two won't eat much grain," the second man

said. "We should get back to the horses in case those dogs come back."

His companion nodded, but continued to stare in Torgan's direction. A lone cloud drifted in front of Panya, darkening the plain somewhat.

"What is it?"

"I thought I saw something. Did the a'laq say anything to you about one of the horses getting loose?"

Torgan felt his mouth go dry, even as he thanked every god he could name for that stray cloud.

"Not that I remember. You see a horse?"

"I thought I did. I was probably imagining it, or looking at another dog."

One of the horses whinnied again.

"Come on. Let's get back to the paddock."

Still the first man stared Torgan's way for another second or two. Then he gave up and followed his companion in the opposite direction.

Torgan closed his eyes and took several long, deep breaths, enjoying the smell of the plain grass and the very fact that he was still alive. At last, when he was certain that the men were far enough away, he climbed to his feet. Keeping in a low crouch, he crept back to Trey. He led the beast away on foot, repeatedly glancing over his shoulder, half expecting at any moment to see a Fal'Borna war party bearing down on him.

When he could no longer see the shelters or the dim glow of the fires, he remounted and rode on.

He rested a few times, but still managed to cover another two leagues or so before the sky in front of him began to brighten with the approach of dawn. Then, as he had each of the last several nights, he began to search for a place to bed down for the day. There were few copses in the central plain, but the closer he came to the Silverwater, the more he found. On this morning he found a small, dense cluster of trees along a rill that fed into the stream he'd been following. He dismounted, walked Trey to the center of the copse, and pulled out his sleeping roll.

Before lying down, he ate a small bit of dried meat and the last of his hard cheese. He'd left the company in a rush. Grinsa and Q'Daer were sickened but alive, and the two Mettai would have used their magic against him if he'd given them the chance. So Torgan had been forced to flee without much food in his travel sack. He'd managed to salt away a bit during their journeying, but he hadn't expected that he would wind up alone on the plain. Thus far he had rationed what little he had, and supplemented it with roots that he found along the way. At this point he would have paid handsomely for some meat, if only he had some gold and somewhere to spend it. But he wasn't starving, and he actually felt himself growing leaner.

"All part of the new Torgan," he muttered to himself.

Trey shook his head and snorted.

Torgan lay down, wrapped himself in a blanket, and soon fell into a deep slumber. He awoke once to the sound of hoofbeats when the sun was high overhead. He heard no voices, though, and the footfalls sounded relatively light. He assumed that a herd of rilda had gone past. In moments he was asleep again.

When next he woke, the sky had begun to darken and a cold wind had risen from the west. Was his mind playing tricks on him, or did he smell a hint of smoke riding that wind? Torgan threw off his blankets, hurried out of the copse, and scrambled up the bank of the rill back onto the plain. Looking westward, back the way he had come, he saw several small smudges of smoke rising from the ground. The sept? Had he actually managed to spread the Mettai woman's plague to that small settlement?

He shivered, blaming it on the wind. Then he returned to the copse, packed up his sleeping roll, and ate a few more bites of dried meat. When the sun had set, and Torgan thought it was dark enough, he led Trey out of the trees and resumed his ride toward the Silverwater.

Over the course of the next two nights, Torgan encountered no more septs, and while he would have been willing to use another piece of the cursed basket against another settlement, a part of him was relieved that he didn't have to. He'd come too close to being found by the Fal'Borna sentries that night. He didn't want to take such risks again.

On the third night after his foray into the settlement, he woke in yet another copse, ate a small meal, and began to ride just as he had the previous nights. The sky had clouded over and a light snow had begun to fall. There was little wind, and the air was cold, but not frigid. Torgan's spirits were high—he liked snow, and though he knew he was still in danger, he knew as well that he'd covered much ground since leaving the company. He sensed that he was drawing nigh to the Silverwater.

With the sky clouded over, he couldn't navigate as he had in recent nights, nor could he see as well. He tried to keep Trey on a straight path toward what he thought was east. Eventually the moons would rise, and even through the clouds he'd be able to see their glow. Then he'd be certain.

"The moons won't be up tonight."

He reined Trey to a halt and looked around wildly, his pulse abruptly racing.

"Who said that?" he called.

He saw no one, and when he received no answer he started to wonder if he'd been imagining things. Maybe he'd spoken the words himself without realizing it. It did occur to him now that it must have been late in the waning. This might well be Pitch Night, the last of the turn, when neither moon would rise.

If so, the morning would bring a new turn—the Celebration Moon, the last turn of the moons of this year.

Torgan looked around for another moment before clicking his tongue at Trey. The beast started forward once more.

"If tomorrow begins the Celebration Moon, then what does that make tonight?"

Torgan stopped again, his hands shaking.

"Who's there?" he shouted. He tried to sound angry, but even he could hear the fright in his voice.

"A friend," came the reply. And then laughter. Not of one voice, but of dozens.

Had the Fal'Borna found him? Was he surrounded by warriors here in the dark of the plain?

He considered spurring his horse to a gallop in an attempt to get away. He couldn't ride as well as the Fal'Borna, but Trey was a strong animal and had been trained by the clanspeople. It might work.

"You can't escape us."

Three times the voice had done that, but only now did Torgan take note. They were reading his thoughts. Yes, it had to be the Qirsi. Who else could do that?

"Let me show you."

Suddenly the grass around him seemed to be gleaming, as if some magical mist were rising from the ground. At first the light was soft, silvery, diffuse, like Panya's glow seeping through clouds on a hazy Planting night. But it hardened quickly, growing brighter, taking form.

Wraiths. A horde of them.

And at the fore, surrounded by men and women who clearly were Qirsi, their long white hair radiant, nearly blinding, stood Jasha Ziffel. His eyes glittered like white gems and his head was tilted to the side, as if he were a child asking a question of his father.

The wraith gestured at his neck. "You did this," he said.

Torgan shook his head. "I'm dreaming. You're not real."

"You've forgotten what day it is, Torgan. You've forgotten your moon lore."

The realization stole his breath. If the turn of the Celebration Moon began with the morrow, then this was Pitch Night of the Memory Moon. Some in the north and beyond the Border Mountains in the Forelands called it Bian's Moon. The dead walked the land this night. The wronged dead. They haunted those who had caused their deaths or tormented them during their lives.

He should have expected to see Jasha, and Grinsa and Q'Daer as well. But who were these others?

"What are these people doing here with you?" Torgan narrowed his eyes. "Are they from S'Plaed's sept? Or C'Bijor's Neck? I didn't do anything wrong to them! At that point I didn't know that the baskets were cursed!"

"They're not from S'Plaed's sept or the Neck," Jasha's wraith said. "They're from Q'Rohn's sept."

Torgan frowned. "I've never—"

"Three nights ago," one of the Qirsi said, his voice like an icy wind. "You poisoned our grain, spread the plague through our village. Twenty-seven died. We're fortunate it wasn't more."

Torgan said nothing. He sat his mount, staring at the dead—at *his* dead—until at last his gaze came to rest once more on Jasha.

"Where are the two white-hairs? The Forelander and the Fal'Borna?"

Jasha shrugged. "They're not dead."

"What? That's impossible! I gave them the plague. Q'Daer was dying. Grinsa was starting to get sick. I saw them!"

"They're not dead," the wraith said again, with maddening equanimity.

It made no sense. They had to be dead. But clearly they weren't here.

"So what is it you want of me?" Torgan asked. He glanced at the Fal'Borna wraiths again, but quickly turned back to Jasha. For some reason he couldn't bring himself to look into the eyes of those other dead. For better or worse, he had known Jasha. For a brief time they might even have been friends, although he wasn't sure that the young merchant—

"We were never friends," Jasha said coldly. "I don't think you've ever had a friend."

"Stop doing that," Torgan said.

"Doing what?"

"You know full well what I mean! Stop reading my thoughts!"

A terrible grin spread across the wraith's face. "No," he said.

"I don't care what you do," Torgan said. He flicked the reins and Trey started forward again. The creature seemed perfectly calm. If the wraiths bothered him, he showed no sign of it.

"He can't see us. Only you can."

Torgan ignored him, staring straight ahead. He knew better than to think that the ghosts would leave him alone. But if they were going to haunt him throughout the night, he could at least cover some ground at the same time.

"What do you know about wraiths, Torgan?" Jasha asked him. "What do you know about this night?"

Torgan refused to answer. The young merchant seemed to be floating along with him, as did the wraiths of the Fal'Borna. They didn't appear to be moving, yet they kept pace with Trey. In fact, they appeared to be coming closer, pressing in on him.

"Do you know that if you touch us, you'll cross over into the god's realm and be lost forever to the world of the living? Do you know that you don't even have to mean to touch us? It can just be an accident. A chance encounter."

The other wraiths laughed.

"Leave me alone," Torgan said.

Their laughter grew, and immediately Torgan wished that he'd kept silent.

"Leave you alone?" Jasha repeated, sounding delighted, as if Torgan had just shared a joke. "That's the last thing we want to do! There's so much each of us wants to say to you. One night is hardly enough."

Torgan clamped his mouth shut, determined not to say anything more to any of them.

Still the glowing figures closed in on him, eyeing him hungrily. Torgan tried to ignore them, but he couldn't help but wonder if what Jasha told him was true. Would he die if he touched one of them? Could the wraiths make him touch them? Could they kill him, in effect, by giving him no choice but to touch them?

"Of course it's true," Jasha said. "The dead cannot lie,

Torgan. Bian forbids it. Isn't that ironic? The god known as the Deceiver demands the truth of all who dwell in his realm." The young merchant leered at him. "Do you know what else? Since we can read your thoughts, you can't lie to us, either. All those times you lied to me when I was alive; the way you deceived all of us at the end, when you sickened Grinsa and Q'Daer. And now that I'm dead I can finally have an honest conversation with you." He shook his head. "Don't you find that funny?"

Suddenly Jasha swung his fist at Torgan's face, making the merchant jerk away.

"I asked you if you thought that was funny," the wraith demanded, his voice so hard and cold that it could have been the god himself asking the question.

"No!" Torgan said. "I don't find any of this funny."

Jasha shook his head, grinning again. "No, I don't suppose you do. Aren't you going to beg for our forgiveness, Torgan?"

"Would it do me any good?"

Jasha laughed, a terrible sound, like boulders grinding against one another. "Now that's the Torgan Plye I know. Always looking to make that profit." He laughed again, then shook his glowing head. "No, Torgan. It wouldn't do you any good at all."

The moment he said this, two of the Fal'Borna wraiths broke away from the others, soaring up into the night sky, wheeling like hawks, and diving straight at Torgan's face.

Torgan ducked out of the way and pulled Trey's reins, making the horse veer off to the side.

Immediately two more wraiths did the same, coming directly at him again, so that once more he had to turn sharply. He'd barely recovered from that assault when a third pair swooped down at him. Soon they were diving toward him from every angle, so that he had to turn his horse repeatedly. It was as if he had stumbled upon a swarm of giant hornets. He did everything in his power to keep them from touching him, knowing that one mistake would mean his death. Torgan wasn't an accomplished rider, and he could feel the beast straining against his increasingly desperate attempts to turn. He also sensed that the horse was tiring. He tried reining the animal to a halt, but instantly the Fal'Borna wraiths altered their attacks and dove at him from the side. He had no choice but to spur his mount into motion again.

On and on it went. The wraiths, it seemed, were immune to fatigue, or perhaps by taking turns they kept themselves from growing weary. Torgan, though, could barely keep himself in the saddle. The muscles in his back, legs, and arms were on fire. His hands shook with exhaustion and terror. His breath came in great gasps and his clothes were soaked with sweat so that the cold night wind knifed through, chilling the merchant to the bone.

"You look tired, Torgan," Jasha called to him.

"Make them stop. Please."

"I could, you know," Jasha said.

"Then do. For pity's sake."

Abruptly, Jasha was beside him, matching Torgan's every movement as if the wraith were also on a horse. "Did you know that in the Deceiver's realm Eandi and white-hairs live together?"

Torgan dodged another assault, and then another.

"I hadn't known," Jasha went on, as if they were chatting over ales in some city inn. "I hadn't thought about it much, really. But if you'd asked me I would have told you that there must have been two underrealms; one for our kind and one for theirs." He shrugged. "I was wrong."

Two pairs of Fal'Borna ghosts dove at him simultaneously, one pair from the left, the other from the right. Torgan was forced to pivot first one way and then the other. Trey reared, nearly unseating him. And no sooner had Torgan righted himself than he saw another pair of ghosts streaking toward him. Again he turned the horse, and again it tried to throw him off.

"I can't help it!" he told the animal. "They're trying to kill me."

"No, we're not," Jasha said, beside him once more. "If we wanted to kill you, you'd be dead by now."

"Then what? What is it you're trying to do to me?"

Still more of the wraiths flew toward him. Torgan fought his mount, trying to make the animal respond. But apparently Trey had reached his limit. Torgan pulled hard on the reins, frantic now. Wraiths were coming at him from both sides. If he didn't move they'd surely hit him. He yanked back with all his might. Trey reared once, twice, kicking out with his front hooves.

And Torgan tumbled back, slamming into the cold ground, the force of his landing knocking the breath from his lungs. He heard Trey bolt away, but before he could raise his head to see where the beast had gone, he found himself surrounded by the wraiths once more. They pressed in around him, staring down hungrily, their pale eyes like flames, their hair gleaming as if lit by the white moon. They began to reach for him. One might have thought that they could pluck the life from his body, so eager did they seem to touch him. Torgan huddled in a ball on the ground, trembling, cold, terrified, certain that he was about to die.

"Enough."

Jasha didn't raise his voice. He didn't need to. The wraiths sighed as one. Torgan could tell without looking that they had backed away from him. He opened his eyes slowly and unfolded his body. He felt ungainly, thick, dull. The wraiths still stared at him, their hair stirring slightly, though for the moment the wind on the plain had died away. From what he saw in the ghosts' eyes he could tell that they had broken off reluctantly, that they had yet to satisfy their desire for vengeance.

"Thank you, Jasha," Torgan whispered. He sat up, and his head began to spin. He tried to look past the wraiths to see where Trey had gone, but they blocked his view.

"Don't thank me," the young merchant said.

Torgan climbed to his feet, staggered a bit, but managed to remain upright. He thought he could see Trey a short distance off to the . . . the south? Torgan turned a slow circle, peering over the heads of the ghosts. He tried to spot something— anything—that might allow him to orient himself. He looked up at the sky, but it was still covered over with clouds. What time was it? How soon until morning?

"You seem confused, Torgan."

He looked at Jasha. Had this been their purpose all along? What had he said before? *If we wanted to kill you, you'd be dead by now.*

"Where will you go?" Jasha asked him. "Which way to Eandi land?"

Torgan shook his head. "It doesn't matter. It's just a few hours. As soon as the sun starts to rise I'll know which way to go."

"And where will you sleep? You don't travel by day. We know you don't. That's very clever, by the way: resting when it's light and making your way eastward after nightfall? Very clever indeed. But where will you pass the night?"

Torgan looked around again, but could see little. The wraiths were too bright and the land beyond them too dark. He strained his ears, hoping to hear flowing water. There had to be woodlands nearby.

"What if there aren't?"

Torgan looked at Jasha again, but the wraith's face revealed nothing. He wasn't smiling anymore. He didn't appear to be gloating or mocking him. If anything, he looked slightly sad.

"You don't want the Fal'Borna to find me, Jasha." Torgan eyed the others. "None of you do. I still have more of that cursed basket."

An angry murmur rose from the wraiths.

He forced himself to look the ghosts in the eye, one by one. "If your purpose tonight was to ensure that I'll be captured by your fellow white-hairs, then you've made a terrible mistake. I would have gladly ridden the rest of the way to the Silverwater without hurting anyone else. But if I can only survive by bringing the plague to more septs, then that's what I'll do."

"Do you have the basket with you, Torgan?" Jasha asked.

"Of course I do. How do you think—?"

Jasha shook his head. "I mean with you. In your hand or in your pocket?"

"No, of course not. It's . . ." He trailed off, looking past the wraiths once more. Had he really seen Trey, or had he imagined it? What if the horse hadn't stopped a short distance off? What if it was still running even now?

"You've been very clever," Jasha said again. "But what will you do without that basket? What will you do without your horse, without your food, without a sleeping roll or a blanket? What will you do if you don't know where you are or which way you're supposed to go?"

Torgan was shaking again. And this time he couldn't blame it on exhaustion or the cold. "I'll survive," he said, his voice quavering. "That's what I've always done." He nodded. "One way or another, I'll make it to the wash."

Jasha nodded once. "We'll see."

An instant later, the wraiths were gone. Torgan blinked several times, but he couldn't see anything. He felt as if he'd been staring into a fire too long.

He whistled. Nothing. He called out Trey's name, but the only sound he heard was the distant howl of a wild dog. He opened his mouth to shout for the horse again, but then stopped himself. What if there was a sept nearby?

He took a step, stopped, looked around again. Which way was east?

"Damn you, Jasha," he whispered.

Chapter 7
✤❧✤

It had been two days since the armies of Stelpana forded the wash, and they had yet to see even a single Fal'Borna rider, much less a white-hair army. Enly, who rode at the head of the force with Tirnya, Stri, Gries, and the two marshals, had expected that he would be in no rush for their first battle. He still doubted the wisdom of starting this war, and he feared their first encounter with Qirsi magic.

But to his surprise, he felt himself growing impatient with every hour that passed. This wasn't battle lust, or some sudden change of heart. On the contrary, he realized that one way or another he just wanted to get that first fight over with. If war was coming, then let it come; Enly had waited long enough.

So on the third morning, when two of the scouts regularly sent out by Jenoe returned so soon after they'd been dispatched, Enly knew a moment of relief, even as he felt his pulse quicken. The marshal had assigned scouts to ride ahead of the army, behind it, and on either flank. These two men had been sent forward.

Upon seeing them riding back toward the army, Jenoe called a halt. Tirnya, who as usual rode between Stri and her father, glanced at Enly, her cheeks flushed. He couldn't tell if she looked eager or frightened.

"Report," Jenoe said, as the two men stopped in front of him.

They were both young soldiers from Qalsyn—Enly assumed that they came from Stri's company, or maybe Tirnya's. One of them had a wispy beard and mustache that were blond, like his hair, and barely visible. The other one appeared too young to manage even that much.

"There's a village up ahead, Marshal," the bearded one said. "Very small. But a village jes' th' same."

"It's called a sept," Gries said quietly.

The others looked at him briefly.

"Well, whatev'r i' is, 't's small. Can' be more 'n hundred people."

"All septs look small to men who come from the larger cities of the sovereignties," Gries told them. "Most of our soldiers can only compare the settlements to their homes, and it's not a helpful comparison."

"You seem to know a good deal about the Fal'Borna, Captain," Jenoe said.

"My father has taught me much, Marshal. Perhaps he knew that this war would come eventually."

"How big is the paddock?" Enly asked.

Gries looked at him and nodded approvingly at the question.

The scout appeared puzzled. "Th' what?"

"The paddock," Gries said, facing the man again. "How many horses are grazing beside the . . . the village?"

The young soldier turned to his companion and shrugged. "I don' know. D' you?"

"A lot," the other man said. "Couple o' hundred a' least. Bu' we didn' see any white-hairs. No' one."

"They're there," Gries said. "They wouldn't flee the sept and leave their horses behind. More likely they spotted these two or learned of our approach. They'll be ready for us."

"Do you have any idea how many warriors this sept might have?" Jenoe asked him.

"With that many horses, they'll have several hundred people in their sept."

Jenoe nodded. "So roughly half of them would be warriors."

"No," Gries said. "The Fal'Borna are as patriarchal as any clan in the Southlands. But you're about to attack one of their septs. Every person in that settlement who's old enough to carry a weapon is a warrior. And every one of them past his or her fourth four will be able to wield magic."

Jenoe and Tirnya exchanged a look.

The marshal faced the scouts again. "Well done," he said. "I need for one of you to go to the back of our column, find the leader of the Mettai, and bring her to me."

Before either man could respond, Enly said, "I'll get her."

Jenoe furrowed his brow. "Really, Captain, I was hoping that you'd remain here and help us devise a strategy."

"I doubt that I have much to offer, Marshal. I trust Captain Ballidyne to speak for me."

Tirnya couldn't have looked more surprised.

Jenoe, however, seemed to understand. "Very well, Captain. Please bring her to me as quickly as possible."

"Of course." Enly turned his mount and rode at a brisk canter back past the other soldiers to the small cluster of Mettai villagers. The villagers were all sitting on the ground, despite a light covering of snow from a squall the previous night. Seeing him approach, Fayonne rose. After a moment, her son did as well.

"You're looking for me, I assume," the eldest said.

"Yes. The marshal wishes a word with you. Our scouts have spotted a sept ahead. It looks as though we'll be facing the Fal'Borna before the day is through."

Fayonne didn't look formidable in any traditional sense. She was small, so thin as to be almost waiflike. The years had whitened her hair and left deep lines on her face. But at the mention of the Fal'Borna she didn't quail, or widen her dark eyes, or betray any hint of the fear that Enly himself felt. He couldn't help but admire her courage.

"I'd like to bring my son," she said in an even voice. "I believe he'll be of value in any discussion of tactics."

Mander's expression didn't change. He stared back at Enly as if daring him to refuse the eldest's request.

"Of course," Enly said. "Please follow me."

He turned Nallaj, his bay, and began to lead the two Mettai toward the front of the column. He noticed that soldiers from all the armies were watching them, their eyes seemingly drawn to the Mettai like moths to a flame. There was fear in the looks they gave the woman and her son, and hostility as well. Once again, Enly wondered if this alliance Tirnya and Jenoe had forged with the sorcerers would work. Allies were supposed to trust one another. And he saw no trust at all in the way Stelpana's soldiers regarded these two.

By the time they returned to the front of the column, Jenoe, Tirnya, and the others had dismounted and were standing in a loose circle. Seeing them approach, Jenoe stepped away from Marshal Crish and the captains, a smile fixed on his youthful face.

"Eldest," he said. "Thank you for joining us. Did Captain Tolm tell you why we stopped?"

She nodded. "He said there's a sept ahead."

"That's right. We believe it's a large one, with several hundred Fal'Borna warriors. Their paddock is full, but our scouts saw no people at all."

Fayonne made a sour face. "You gave yourselves away."

The marshal bristled, and Enly wondered if he'd reply in anger. After a moment, though, he merely said in a tight voice, "So it would seem."

"That's unfortunate," Fayonne went on. "It will make this more difficult. They'll raise a mist and I'd imagine they'll try to unnerve your horses with their magic. And when you're close enough, they'll use shaping power against you."

"What would you suggest we do?" Jenoe asked.

She looked at her son, who was staring at the ground, seemingly oblivious to their conversation.

But to Enly's surprise, he was the one who answered.

"There are about fifty of us," he said, "and I think we'd be best off dividing ourselves into three or four groups. One group can use fire against their shelters. Another can use a finding spell. And still—"

Enly held up a hand. "Wait. What's a finding spell?"

Mander grinned, clearly pleased with himself. "It's magic that seeks out other magic. We can spread it over the village and if the white-hairs are hiding, it will show where they are."

"Can it be used to find a specific kind of magic?" Gries asked.

Mander and his mother exchanged looks.

"I don't know," the man said. "What did you have in mind?"

"Can it find Weavers?" Gries turned to Jenoe. "If we could identify the Weavers by sight, it would make fighting them much easier. We could have our bowmen concentrate all of their fire on the leaders. If we kill them, defeating the rest would be easy."

"Can you do this?" Jenoe asked the Mettai.

Mander looked uncertain. "We can try."

"There was more," Tirnya said. "You weren't done telling us which magics you'd use."

He nodded. "Right. The last thing we should do is conjure wolves, and send them in along with the army."

Jenoe frowned. "Wolves?"

The smile returned to Mander's face. "Not just any wolves. B—"

Fayonne touched his arm and shook her head.

"Enchanted wolves," Mander went on a moment later, still eyeing her. "Intelligent, powerful, and immune to language of beasts. The white-hairs wouldn't be able to confuse them with their magic."

"You've done this?" Gries asked.

"We know how to do it," Fayonne said. "Some spells have been passed down for generations. This is one of them. It was used long ago, early in the Blood Wars."

Fairlea's captain shook his head. "I've never heard of such a thing." He looked at Enly. "Have you?"

"It doesn't matter if you've heard of it," Tirnya said before Enly could answer. "This is just what we've been hoping for. We've known all along that early in the Blood Wars things were different. The Eandi did well against Qirsi magic. Now we know that some of the spells used back then survive to this day. We should use them all."

They turned to Jenoe, who gazed toward the western horizon, as if he could already see the sept. He didn't look pleased.

"Father?" Tirnya said, ending a lengthy silence.

The marshal shook his head slowly. "I don't like this. Forgive me, Eldest," he added with a glance at Fayonne. "We brought you here to wield your magic, and wield it you will. But I have to say that I'm uncomfortable fighting this way. I've never had to rely on any form of sorcery, and I never thought I would."

"You can't defeat them without us," Fayonne said, her tone as blunt as her words. "We both know that. So I'd suggest you put your qualms aside and let us fight the way we know how."

Once again, Enly expected the marshal to react angrily. Instead, he laughed.

"I suppose I deserved that. You're right, Eldest. We need your magic, and we'll be grateful to you and your people for shedding your blood on our behalf."

Fayonne nodded solemnly. "Get the others," she said, turning to her son once more. She looked back at Jenoe. "I'm sure you understand, Marshal, that we can be most effective at the head of your army."

"Yes, of course." Jenoe looked at Enly, Tirnya, and the others. "Our archers will begin the assault; we should bring them forward also."

"Yes, Marshal," Enly said, speaking for the others before they all returned to their companies.

Enly found his lead riders in a tight cluster, talking quietly among themselves as his soldiers milled about. Seeing Enly approach, they turned to face him. Aldir Canithal, the senior man among his riders, barked a command to the rest of the company that instantly had them scrambling to muster themselves back into formation.

"It's all right," Enly called.

The soldiers slowed, though they still returned to their positions.

"What's happened?" Aldir asked in his usual clipped tone.

"The scouts have spotted a sept ahead. The marshal wants us to bring the bowmen forward. We're about to have our first battle."

Several of the other riders blanched at these tidings, but not Aldir. He was actually several years older than Enly, and might well have made captain already had Enly not requested that the man remain under his command. He'd explained as much to Aldir, who had dismissed his apologies with a wave of his hand.

"I'm a soldier," he'd said at the time. "I'm in no hurry t' be a captain. You boys never get yar uniforms dirty."

Enly had laughed, thinking at the time that the man was right: He was a warrior to the very core. He definitely looked the part. He had a high forehead and a broad, homely face. His nose had been broken so many times in battle tournaments and training sessions that it always looked swollen and bent. His eyes, clear blue like lake waters during the Snows, were small and widely spaced. He wasn't particularly tall or broad, but he moved with an efficient grace, like a wolf on the prowl. There was no one else with whom Enly would have felt more at ease going into battle, except perhaps—and Enly never would have admitted this to his father—for Jenoe.

"We saw ya go past with th' Mettai," Aldir said now. "We suspected th' scouts had found somethin'."

"What are th' Mettai goin' t' be doin'?" asked Jinqled Savlek.

"Magic," Enly said. "Which is just what we brought them to do."

Jinq looked away, but nodded, his lips pressed in a flat line. He was, in many ways, as different from Aldir as any man could be. Tall, handsome, with red hair, green eyes, and a smile that had charmed many a barmaid into his bed, he was the youngest of Enly's lead riders. He was a good soldier. Someday he'd be a great one, but for now he was too reckless, too prone to mistakes. He'd made clear to Enly on several occasions that he didn't like the Mettai and had no interest in riding into battle beside them.

"There are other ways t'—"

Aldir silenced Jinq by laying a hand on the younger man's shoulder. "Let it be, lad."

Jinq looked away again.

Enly stepped closer to them. "If it makes you feel any better, Jinq," he said, dropping his voice to a whisper, "the marshal isn't too sure about this, either."

"Then why are we doin' it?"

"Because as much as we don't feel comfortable with sorcerers, we're going to war against them, and having magic on our side balances things a bit. Do you really want to face the Fal'Borna with nothing more than arrows and steel?"

Jinq gave a grudging shake of the head.

"Divide the men—archers and swordsmen. Aldir, you'll command the archers, and I expect you'll answer directly to the marshal. Ilyan, you'll lead the swordsmen. The rest of you go as your talents dictate. If you've any skill with a bow, follow Aldir. Archers will be most helpful against this enemy." He looked at Aldir again. "The Mettai will be performing what they call a finding spell. It'll enable us to identify their Weavers. Listen for the marshal's command and concentrate your volleys where he tells you. The Weavers are the key to all of this. If they can be defeated, the rest of the Qirsi army won't have a chance."

Aldir and the other riders nodded to him and Enly started away, intending to walk among his men.

"What kind o' spells will they be doin', Captain?" Jinq asked, stopping him. "Th' Mettai, I mean. Aside from this findin' spell."

Enly turned to face him. He'd evaded Jinq's question the first time; he didn't feel right doing so again. "They'll be using fire on the shelters." He hesitated, but only for a moment. "And they'll be conjuring wolves."

"Wolves?" Jinq repeated, the blood draining from his face.

"Apparently the Mettai who marched with our people during the early years of the Blood Wars did this, to great effect."

The young rider nodded, but he looked even more unsettled than he had before. Enly left him, knowing there was nothing he could say that would ease his mind.

It didn't take the soldiers of the three armies long to rearrange themselves, and soon they were ready to march again. The Mettai villagers now walked at the van beside Jenoe, Hendrid, and their captains. They were followed by nearly fifteen hundred bowmen. The balance of the army, some twenty-five hundred swordsmen, brought up the rear. For all his doubts about this war, Enly couldn't deny that his father and the other lord governors had put together an impressive force. The Fal'Borna might have been prepared for an attack, but he found it hard to believe that they were ready for an army of this size.

They hadn't gone far when they topped a gentle rise and looked down upon the sept, which sat on a large, wedge-shaped piece of land at the confluence of two small streams. As the scouts had said, the paddock at the far end of the settlement was crowded with horses—greys, blacks, sorrels, bays, and whites. Enly couldn't remember seeing so many horses in one place.

But while the paddock was full, the sept looked to have been deserted. Except for a few narrow plumes of pale smoke rising from shelters, Enly saw nothing to indicate that there were any people in the settlement. In fact, several of the shelters appeared to have been destroyed. Some of them were blackened, as if by fire, while others simply looked like they had been crushed.

"What do you make of it?" Jenoe asked, his voice low.

Enly turned to answer, but then realized that the marshal had been speaking to Tirnya. She was eyeing the sept through narrowed eyes, her brow creased.

"If I didn't know better, I'd say they'd already been attacked," she said.

Enly shook his head. "Not attacked. Struck by the plague."

Tirnya looked at him quickly, then faced her father again. "Of course. He's right. This is what the plague does. It robs them of control over their magic before it kills them. They destroyed their village themselves."

"So are all of them dead?" asked Marshal Crish.

"No," Gries said. "There are fires burning in the shelters that remain. Some survived. I think the eldest was right. They know we're coming and they're prepared to fight us."

"Then we'll hold to our plan," Jenoe told them. "Eldest, you and your people can begin at any time."

Fayonne shook her head. "Not from this distance. We need to be closer for our magic to work."

A look of annoyance crossed the marshal's face. "Very well." He raised a hand and indicated that the army was to resume its advance. A moment later they were marching again.

When they had covered perhaps half the remaining distance to the sept, many of the horses, including Enly's, began to act strangely. Nallaj swished his tail and began to fight against Enly's efforts to steer him toward the sept. Several of the others, Tirnya's sorrel among them, actually reared.

"They're using language of beasts!" Gries called out. "We need to leave the horses here!"

The marshals and captains riding up front dismounted, and word began to spread back through the ranks that other captains and lead riders should do the same.

"Will your magic work now?" Jenoe asked.

Fayonne offered a noncommittal shrug. "I'd like to be closer."

The marshal, it seemed, had reached the limits of his patience. "Yes, Eldest, and I'd like to be on my horse still. But this is war, and we can't always have things just as we'd like. Can your magic be effective from this distance?"

"Not very," the woman said in a flat voice.

Jenoe cast a look at Tirnya that seemed to say, *What's the use of having these people with us?* But he held his tongue, and they started forward once more, all of them now on foot.

They hadn't gone far when thin tendrils of white mist began to emerge from the ground around the shelters, spidery and ghostlike. The mist coalesced slowly into a dense fog that would soon obscure the Fal'Borna shelters.

"Will the finding spell work through this mist?" Gries asked.

"The spell will work, but naturally it will be harder to see the results."

"Then what good is it?" Jenoe asked, his voice rising.

"I told you all of this would happen, Marshal," Fayonne said. "I predicted that they would go for your horses first. I predicted that they would call forth a mist."

"Yes, and you also made it sound as if your magic could overcome these things. Now it seems that it can't. We don't know for certain, of course, because you haven't shown us any magic yet!"

The eldest smiled thinly. "Very well. Blades!" she called to her people. "Start with the finding spell. Use the wording Mander taught you."

The Mettai pulled their knives from their belts and stooped to grab handfuls of dirt. Then they sliced open the backs of their hands. Even knowing that these people wielded blood magic, Enly couldn't help but wince at the sight. He wanted to ask them if it hurt, but like the others from Stelpana, he kept silent and watched. The sorcerers deftly gathered the blood from their wounds on the flat sides of their blades, turned over their bleeding hands to reveal the earth they had gathered, and tipped the blades so that the blood mingled with the soil. Enly heard them begin to mumble to themselves. They all seemed to begin with the words "Blood to earth, life to power," but after that he had difficulty making out what they said. Too many people were speaking at once.

When they finished, though, they all heaved the bloody mixture they held in their hands toward the sept. He never would have believed that they could throw the dark mud so far, and as soon as the stuff left their hands, it appeared to transform itself into fine golden sand, which should have billowed like smoke in the wind and fallen uselessly to the grass. But it didn't.

It seemed to be propelled by some unseen force, which, Enly realized, it had been: magic. It soared through the air, shimmering faintly as it went, and spread over the settlement before seeming to sprinkle down on the shelters like a light rain. At first nothing happened. Soon, though, a few of the shelters that hadn't yet vanished within the Qirsi mist began to glow faintly.

No one from the army said a word. The marshals and most of the captains standing up front stared open-mouthed at the sept. Thinking this, Enly realized that his own mouth was open.

"That was remarkable, Eldest," Jenoe finally said.

"It was a difficult spell," she said, as if answering a question no one had asked. "Twelve parts, which is a lot for any Mettai. We needed to make it so in order to reveal not only magic, but Weaver magic. And also to make it reach the settlement from here."

Jenoe nodded. "Well, I apologize for doubting you."

She shrugged and licked her blade clean. The other Mettai cleaned the blood from their knives the same way. Tirnya looked away, frowning slightly.

Noticing Tirnya's expression, Fayonne said, "The Mettai never waste blood." She turned back to Jenoe. "The Weavers will have a yellow glow. All the others will be white."

Enly scanned the mist that had now enveloped the settlement. He could see several places that seemed to gleam faintly with a pale light, but he saw no yellow.

Jenoe turned to the captains. "Tell the archers to aim for those light areas when we're close enough."

"What about the fire magic?" Gries asked Fayonne. "And those wolves you spoke of?"

"For those we should wait until we're closer."

"All right, then," the marshal said.

He pulled his sword free and held it aloft so that all in his army could see. Then he waved it forward twice, and once again the army began to march. They still saw no sign of any Qirsi other than those pale areas of light within the mist. Nor did they hear any voices.

"This is all very odd," Enly muttered. "We're marching on a Fal'Borna village, and all we've had to face so far is a mist and some agitated horses."

Jenoe nodded. "I agree. Call the archers forward now. I want them ready as soon as we're within range."

The captains turned and called to their lead riders, who in turn called for their archers to advance. The bowmen ran forward even as the rest of the army continued their march. Soon three broad lines of archers took positions at the front of the army, spreading to the left and right so that they could launch their arrows from a variety of angles.

As soon as they were close enough, Jenoe shouted an order, making the army halt. He raised his sword again and this time waved it sideways. Those in command of the bowmen barked their commands, hundreds of bows thrummed, and a volley of arrows leaped into the sky, arcing high over the plain and then descending into that magical mist.

Screams went up from the sept. Some of them sounded like the death cries of men, but many others seemed to come from women or perhaps even children.

An instant later, a pale yellow light appeared in the fog, like a candle on a misty night.

"There!" Jenoe called. "Aim for that yellow light!" He looked at the Mettai. "The rest of your magic! Now!"

Again Enly heard the dull thud of the bows, and a second volley climbed toward the clouds.

"Not the fire," Fayonne said. "Flames in that mist will make you lose track of the Weaver."

"The wolves then! Hurry!"

Once more the Mettai gathered handfuls of earth, cut themselves, mixed the blood and soil, and began to speak their spells. As before, Enly couldn't understand much of what they said. But he could make out a bit more of it. There seemed to be a pattern, linkages between the phrases: "Life to power, power to thought, thought to . . ." He lost track after that.

And then the sorcerers threw their clumps of blood and earth, and Enly stopped caring what they had said.

Watching that golden powder fly toward the settlement had been as remarkable as anything he had ever seen. But what they conjured this time stole his breath, and left him frightened as well as awed. As soon as the mud left the Mettai's hands it began to change and grow. It happened so quickly that the shapes he saw appeared to be writhing. And by the time they hit the ground, the balls of mud had taken the form of great wolves. They landed lightly, gracefully, as if rather than being created by magic they had jumped down from some unseen crag. They were a good deal larger than wolves Enly had seen while hunting with his father in the Aelean Highlands. Their heads came almost to his shoulder. Their fur was black, with just a streak of silver-grey on their snouts or foreheads, and their eyes were bright yellow. Several of them bared their teeth and snarled at the Eandi soldiers. But then one of them turned and started loping toward the sept, and the others followed. In moments, they had broken into a full run, as if they had caught the scent of their prey.

The archers released another swarm of arrows, which curved across the sky toward that yellow glow of the Fal'Borna Weaver. Enly felt a wind rise out of the west, and knew immediately that the arrows would fall short. But the mist summoned by the Qirsi had started to grow thin. He could make out some shelters once again, and he wondered if this meant that the magic of the Weaver was failing.

Jenoe shouted with some urgency for the bowmen to loose their darts again. As soon as they did, Enly understood what the marshal hoped to do. The arrows reached their zenith and began to descend, just as the Mettai's black wolves splashed through the stream that fronted the sept. They would reach the Weaver just moments after the arrows did. The Fal'Borna had to choose which threat to combat with his magic.

The mist was vanishing, and now Enly felt the wind die away as well. He heard several of the leading wolves yelp in pain, and saw them collapse a short distance in front of the man. Shaping power, no doubt. But the others leaped over the fallen animals and converged on him. The arrows struck, several burying themselves in the Weaver's chest and shoulders. And as he went down, the wolves pounced.

A cheer went up from Stelpana's army.

"Advance!" Jenoe cried.

The Eandi swordsmen let out a deafening war cry and started forward past the bowmen, who held their ground. The archers launched one last salvo at the village, but from what Enly could see, few sorcerers remained alive.

A small number of Fal'Borna warriors emerged from the shelters, all of them glowing white, some bearing blades, others spears.

Many of the wolves seemed intent on devouring the Weaver, but more than a dozen of them broke off from the pack and began to advance on the sorcerers who remained. Enly thought it likely that the battle would be won before he and the other swordsmen crossed the stream.

He looked over at Tirnya and found that she was already gazing his way. She looked pleased, her cheeks flushed. Enly couldn't blame her. It was just as she had predicted back in Qalsyn when she first proposed that they attack the Qirsi and attempt to retake D'Raqor. These Fal'Borna had been weakened by the plague that had ravaged their land, as

Tirnya had foreseen. Fayonne and the other Mettai had proven themselves formidable allies, as Tirnya had said they would. Amazingly, they had conquered a Fal'Borna settlement without shedding any Eandi blood.

The first battle was theirs.

And then it all began to go horribly wrong.

Chapter 8

◆┼◆

R ealizing that the battle was theirs, that her efforts to persuade her father and Enly and the lord governor to go ahead with this invasion had been vindicated, Tirnya knew a moment of pure and profound relief. She would never have admitted it to anyone, but she had spent the last turn doubting that this day would ever come. She didn't need Enly to tell her how strange these Mettai were, nor did she need her father to tell her how difficult it would be to defeat the Fal'Borna if it turned out they hadn't been weakened by this so-called white-hair plague. She had spent day and night afraid that in her rush to reclaim Deraqor, her family's ancestral home, she was leading thousands of soldiers to their doom.

Now, though, seeing how easily they had conquered this first Fal'Borna settlement, her worries vanished. It seemed that a terrible burden had been lifted from her shoulders. She strode toward the sept beside her father, struggling to keep a satisfied grin from spreading across her face. This was warfare. Even now, with the last few Fal'Borna warriors scattering before the onslaught of Fayonne's wolves, it would have been wrong of her to take too much pleasure in their victory. Her father would have told her so if he had known how pleased she was. He would have warned her that this was just one battle in what still promised to be a difficult and dangerous war. And of course he would have been right.

But wasn't she allowed a few moments to enjoy this feeling? Could she be faulted for wanting to gloat just a little the next time she found herself alone with Enly? Thinking this, she looked over at the lord governor's son. A second later, he turned to face her, almost as if he felt her gaze upon him. They shared a quick look. Then Enly looked away.

"All right, Eldest," Jenoe said as they continued to advance on the settlement. "You can call back your wolves now. The day is ours."

As he said this, three of the wolves were closing in on a Fal'Borna woman who was backing away from the creatures, gripping a spear with both hands. As Tirnya watched, fire appeared to burst from the ground just in front of the middle wolf, but the animal leaped over the flames and charged the woman. At the same time, its two companions attacked her from either side. The woman managed to impale one of them with her spear, but she could do nothing about the other two. One of them clamped onto her arm with its mighty jaws. She screamed. The other wolf tore at her leg. Tirnya saw her go down, but looked away rather than watch what followed. The woman continued to howl for several seconds. Then she fell silent, which was even worse.

"Eldest!" Jenoe said, sounding frantic.

"There's nothing I can do, Marshal. I have no way of calling them back."

"What? You created them! You have to be able to stop them!"

Another pair of wolves had begun to stalk a young man. He held a spear in one hand and a blade in the other. But rather than fight the creatures, he turned and ran. This proved no better than facing them. The wolves raced after the man, quickly closing on him. They took him down from behind, as if he were a rilda.

"They're wild creatures," Fayonne said, clearly unnerved by what she was seeing. "They may be born of magic, but they're alive now. I can't control them any more than I can control you."

"Can't you use some other magic against them?"

She glanced at her son. "We can try. But I'd suggest you have your archers take aim at them. That may be our best hope."

Jenoe nodded once. He turned to one of his soldiers and ordered the man to hurry back and bring the bowmen forward.

A moment later, though, matters turned far, far worse. The large pack of wolves that attacked the Fal'Borna Weaver had moved on, leaving little more than a bloody carcass where the man had been. They made their way through the settlement, snarling at any movement, snapping their jaws. Several broke off in pairs and threesomes to pursue stray warriors. But the bulk of the pack seemed headed for the horse paddock.

Before they reached it, two large groups of Fal'Borna children, who apparently had been hiding in shelters near the far end of the sept, burst into the open. There were at least thirty of them in all. Several of them looked nearly old enough to be warriors, but most were far younger. As soon as they appeared, the wolves turned and started after them.

"Gods!" Jenoe whispered. "They'll be slaughtered!"

"We have to do something, Father," Tirnya said, finally finding her voice.

He nodded. "To the wolves!" he shouted, raising his sword and breaking into a run. "Kill the wolves!"

The rest of the army raised their blades as well and followed. But Tirnya knew that they wouldn't get there nearly in time. The wolves closed in on the children even faster than they had on the fleeing warriors. She saw the great animals drag down several of the young Fal'Borna. They didn't even bother hunting in teams; the children were easy prey. She heard snarls and the horrible shrieks of the children. She felt her stomach heave and clamped her teeth shut to keep from being ill.

Along with her father and the other captains, she was among the first to wade through the frigid waters of the stream and enter the settlement. Tirnya could see the beasts clearly now. Many of them had blood on their snouts; others were feeding on the bodies of children, and still others were closing in on those children who had escaped their first attack. The Eandi army was still too far from them to help, and the archers couldn't aim a salvo at the wolves without killing the young Fal'Borna as well. Jenoe shouted at the wolves and waved his arms over his head, trying to draw the beasts' attention, but most of the animals barely took notice. A few broke off and turned to face the advancing soldiers, but the others remained intent on the children.

"Ideas?" Jenoe asked, slowing to a walk and then stopping.

No one spoke. Tirnya didn't know what to suggest. She stopped beside Jenoe, knowing that he couldn't fight the wolves alone. The other captains halted as well. Eight of the great animals stood before them. It almost seemed that they'd been chosen to fight the soldiers and thus give their brethren time to hunt the children.

The creatures started forward slowly, growling, their ears laid back, their teeth bared. Tirnya and her father crouched low and readied their blades. Other captains and soldiers on either side of them did the same.

Tirnya heard a cry go up behind her. Glancing back quickly she saw something soaring toward them. She squinted. Whatever it was looked like a series of small, thin clouds. It took her a moment to realize that they resembled the odd, sparkling powder sent forth by the Mettai when they cast their spell against the Fal'Borna. Was this more magic? She wasn't sure whether to rejoice or shudder. She watched it pass overhead and then rain down upon the wolves and children at the far end of the settlement.

But she had no time to see what this newest spell had done.

As if responding to some silent signal, all eight wolves suddenly charged the soldiers. Tirnya had never seen a normal wolf in the wild, though she'd once seen a captive one that came to Qalsyn with a traveling festival. But that animal had been timid and gentle. These magical creatures were something else entirely. Not only were they large and unnaturally swift, they were also canny. They didn't fight like wild dogs; they fought like warriors.

The one in front of Tirnya and Jenoe broke off its charge at the last moment, darted to the side so that it had a clearer path to Tirnya, and then sprang at her. She tried to stab the creature with her sword, but it managed to evade her thrust with a twist of its body. Its snapping jaws just narrowly missed her shoulder. The animal landed behind her, turned with blurring speed, and attacked again, this time leaping for her neck. Tirnya slashed at it with her blade and was certain that she drew blood. But the wolf crashed into her, knocking her to the ground. She landed on her back, losing her grip on her weapon.

The wolf struggled to get to its feet again, its claws scraping her chest and neck. An instant later its face was just next to hers, its hot breath stinking of blood. Tirnya gagged.

She heard her father shout something, and then felt the full weight of the beast sag onto her body. Its blood, slick and warm, soaked into her coat of mail. She tried to push the beast off of her, but couldn't. After a moment, though, it rolled away.

Her father stood over her, his sword stained red, his chest rising and falling.

"Are you all right?" he asked.

Tirnya nodded, and struggled to her feet. She bent to retrieve her sword, and as soon as she straightened again, she swayed. Her father put out a hand to steady her. Looking at the carnage around her, she saw that the other seven wolves were also dead. Five men, including one of her father's captains, had been wounded.

Her father, though, had his head turned away from the wolves and injured men. Following the direction of his gaze, Tirnya saw that he was looking toward the Fal'Borna children. She'd forgotten momentarily, but it all came back to her now, and she hurried toward them. After only a few steps, she halted. From what she could see, all of the children appeared to be dead, as did all the wolves.

Tears streamed down her face and once more she feared that she'd be ill.

"What did you do?" she screamed, turning to look for the Mettai. "What did you do to them?"

Fayonne was just emerging from the stream, her son and the other Mettai with her.

"We put them to sleep," she answered, striding purposefully in Tirnya's direction. "It was all we could think to do."

"To sleep?" Tirnya turned again and looked a second time at the children and magical beasts. She took a tentative step forward, and then another. Clearly many of the children were dead. Some had been mauled so violently that it was hard to say where one body's blood ended and the next began. There were at least a dozen like this. But beyond them, scattered among the prone bodies of perhaps twenty wolves, were many more young Fal'Borna. All of them appeared whole and unhurt, save for the fact that they were unconscious.

"They put them to sleep," she whispered. She faced Fayonne again. "How long?"

The eldest had stopped next to Jenoe. She shook her head. "I don't know. Not long. Especially for the wolves. They're bigger; the magic will have less effect on them."

Right. Tirnya still held her sword in her hand, and now she walked to the first of the sleeping wolves. Once more she was amazed by how large the creatures were. This wolf's paws were as large as her hand; its jaws appeared capable of biting through the limbs of an oak. In other ways, though— the glossy black fur, the peaceful rise and fall of its flanks with each breath—the animal looked for the moment like any domesticated dog. That is, except for the smear of blood on its muzzle.

Tirnya raised her blade and plunged it into the creature's chest. The wolf spasmed, rolled onto its back, its paws clawing at the air. She pulled the sword out and stabbed the wolf a second time, and then a third. She drew back the weapon for a fourth thrust, but the animal was dead.

She looked up at her father, who regarded her, grim-faced.

"Kill the rest of them," Jenoe called to his soldiers, without taking his eyes off of Tirnya.

She walked over to the nearest of the children. It was a small girl; she couldn't have been more than five or six years old. Her face was smeared with dirt and tears, and her long white hair was in tangles, but Tirnya could see that she was beautiful. She had a small rounded nose and eyelashes that were fine and long and pale, as if made of spun silver.

Yes, she was a white-hair, but in that moment Tirnya would have given up everything she owned to spare this child the horrors and anguish to which she would awake.

She heard a footfall behind her, but didn't bother to turn.

"We should do something for them," she said.

"There isn't much we can do," her father told her, as she had expected he would. "You know we can't take them with us, not even as prisoners."

"Yes, I know." She looked back at him. "What about food? Could we leave them some of . . . ?"

She trailed off. He was shaking his head.

"We can't start giving away our provisions, Tirnya. If this war goes as I expect it will, these aren't the last children we'll be leaving behind as orphans. It's not our responsibility to feed them all. This is war. Even the Fal'Borna would tell you that."

Tirnya nodded, knowing that he was right. There were older children lying nearby. No doubt the Fal'Borna had food stored somewhere in the sept, and if the children needed to leave this place, they could take some of the horses. This little girl and the others around her would survive.

Jenoe looked like he might say more to her, but Enly, Gries, Marshal Crish, and several of the other captains were coming toward them. So, too, were Fayonne and her son.

"The rest of the wolves are dead, Marshal," Gries said, casting a dark look sidelong at the eldest. "The men who were wounded will be all right. None of the adult Fal'Borna survived. Fourteen children were killed."

Jenoe's mouth twitched. "Damn."

"I'm sorry, Marshal," the eldest said. "We didn't know that this would happen."

"Of course you didn't, Eldest. How could you?"

She glanced at her son, but quickly faced the marshal again. "This was an ancient magic, and we thought it would help us win the battle. The next time we—"

"There won't be a next time," Tirnya said.

Her father frowned. "Tirnya."

"No more of those . . . creatures. I want you to promise me."

He looked at her with obvious concern, his eyes straying to the drying wolf blood on her mail. But then he took a breath and shook his head. "I can't promise that," he said, keeping his voice low. "We'll have to be more careful next time. But the wolves the eldest and her people created for us did what we wanted them to do. We defeated a Fal'Borna settlement today. Not a single Eandi soldier was killed. Only five were hurt. I'd be mad to promise that we won't use that magic again."

"There are other creatures we can conjure," Fayonne said. "It doesn't have to be wolves."

Tirnya eyed the woman for a moment before turning and starting the long walk back to where they'd left the horses. She brushed past Enly and Gries, and continued past men from all the armies, including her own soldiers and lead riders, but she said nothing. Reaching the stream, she paused long enough to wash the blood from her blade and sheath it. Wading through the water chilled her, but though she was shivering she stopped again halfway across to splash away the blood on her coat of mail. The other captains had followed her, and several walked past now. No one spoke to her, though, or even made eye contact.

The foot soldiers had remained behind, and Tirnya could see a column of dark smoke rising from the settlement and twisting in the wind.

"What are they doing?" she demanded of no one in particular.

"They're burning the dead. Men and wolves."

She turned. Gries stood waist deep in the stream a short distance away.

"The dead children, too?"

He nodded. "Your father had his men move the survivors so that they wouldn't awaken to all that blood."

Tirnya continued to stare at the billowing smoke.

"Come on, Captain," Gries said, starting toward the far shore. "You'll freeze in this water."

Reluctantly, she walked after him. When they reached the bank, he held out a hand to her and helped her up the slope to the plain.

They found the horses just where they had left them, and soon the captains were riding back to where the rest of the armies waited for them. Tirnya had tethered her father's mount to her saddle, so that he trotted alongside Thirus. Gries had done the same with Hendrid's horse.

By the time they crossed the stream again and found the two marshals, several of the Fal'Borna children were awake. They sat in a tight cluster, watching the Eandi soldiers. The youngest among them looked frightened, but a few of the older boys and girls wore expressions of pure hatred. Jenoe and Hendrid stood a short distance off, speaking in low voices and glancing occasionally at the children.

Tirnya and Gries steered their horses to the marshals. Tirnya dismounted and approached her father.

"How long have they been awake?" she asked.

He shook his head and began to untether his mount. "Not long. Fayonne thinks the others will be awake soon. It would have been easier if we'd been able to leave while they were still sleeping."

"Have they said anything?"

"Not a lot." Jenoe pointed to a long-limbed boy who wore his hair tied back. "That one threatened me. He said that he'd follow our army and cut my throat while we slept."

Tirnya stared at the boy. He had a narrow, bony face and he sat with his knees drawn up to his chest, his muscular forearms wrapped around his shins. Tirnya had heard that Qirsi came into their power around the age of sixteen; this boy couldn't have been more than a year or two away. She noticed that he had an empty sheath strapped to his side.

"Is that why you took his knife?" she asked.

"You should have heard the way he said it," Jenoe said, sounding defensive. "You would have done the same."

"I don't doubt it."

After watching the children for another few moments, Tirnya approached the angry boy her father had disarmed. His eyes flicked in her direction, but he seemed determined not to look at her.

"My name is Captain Onjaef," she said. "You can call me Tirnya."

No response.

"It looks like you'll be in charge here now. Do you know where your people stored your food? Will you be able to feed the others?"

He continued to ignore her, but a few of the other children were watching. Tirnya approached one of them, a girl who looked to be nearly as old as the boy. She had a dark wound on her neck—an old burn, from the look of it, perhaps from when the plague struck—and a cut high on her cheek that appeared to be healing well.

"What's your name?" Tirnya asked.

She didn't answer.

"Is there food here? Do you know where to find it?"

The girl hesitated before nodding once.

Tirnya smiled. "Good. Thank you for telling me that." The beautiful young girl Tirnya had seen earlier was still asleep beside this older child. Tirnya pointed to the young one now and asked, "What's her name?"

"Don't answer," the boy said. He scrambled to his feet and crossed to where Tirnya was standing. Looking down at the older girl, he said, "Don't tell her anything more. Do you hear me?"

He was half a head shorter than Tirnya. From all that she

had heard about the Fal'Borna, she gathered that he wouldn't grow much taller, but would wind up broad in the shoulders and chest. Right now, though, he looked terribly young, even more so than he had when he'd been sitting. Still he didn't flinch from her gaze.

"I was speaking to her," Tirnya said. "You had your chance to answer my questions."

"As you said, dark-eye, I'm a'laq now. This sept is mine. And I'll decide who you speak to."

She had no desire to humiliate him. "Very well. Then you'll answer my questions."

"I'll speak to a man. Not to you."

On second thought, maybe she did want to humiliate him. "You threatened the marshal. You won't be speaking with him again. You've got me now. And I want to know if you can take care of these children."

His eyes widened and he suddenly looked terribly sad. "No, I can't. Won't you stay and be our mother? Won't you cook our food and smooth our blankets at night?" He grinned harshly.

Tirnya drew her blade and had it leveled at his eye so quickly that the boy actually staggered back a step. His grin had vanished.

"I think this girl here can lead the others just as well as you can," Tirnya said, gesturing vaguely at the girl who had answered her question. "They won't miss you at all if I kill you."

To the boy's credit, he recovered quickly from his surprise and stood unbowed before her.

"A Fal'Borna warrior doesn't fear death," he said.

"What about a Fal'Borna child?"

His cheeks reddened, and he glowered at her. "Go ahead and kill me, dark-eye. If that's what it takes to make you feel like a real soldier, then do it."

"Where is the closest sept?" she demanded.

"Why? So you can destroy them, too? So you can send your plague and your wolves and your arrows into their z'kals?"

Tirnya shifted her stance so that her blade still menaced the boy, but she could look the girl in the eye.

"Tell me where the nearest sept is," she said.

The girl swallowed and shook her head. "I-I don't know. South, I think."

"Z'Maara!" the boy said.

"She'll kill you otherwise!"

"Actually, I wouldn't have," Tirnya said, not certain why it mattered to her that they know this. "But thank you for telling me." She faced the boy again. "We're not going south. That sept will be safe for you. Take the others there."

"I don't take orders from you."

Tirnya ran her hand through her hair. She wanted to scream at him, but she could imagine an Eandi boy his age speaking the same way to an enemy. She and her army had conquered his village, killed his family. For all he knew, she was about to kill him, too. Where was the boundary between bravery and folly?

"You're going to follow this order," she told him, speaking with as much patience as she could muster. "You can't stay here. There may be food enough to keep you alive, and shelter for when the Snows begin in earnest. But you're still just children. You have those horses. Use them. Ride south to the next sept. They'll care for you there."

The boy stared back at her. The look of defiance had fled his face, leaving him looking like a child once more. He appeared confused, as if he didn't know how to respond to what she'd said. Finally, Tirnya glanced at the girl again.

"Did you hear what I said?"

Z'Maara nodded.

"Sleep here tonight," Tirnya went on. "Leave in the morning. The little ones will be scared; it'll be up to the two of you to reassure them and keep them safe. The wolves that attacked you are all dead. I promise. Any wolves you hear tonight will be the wild ones you're used to."

"I told the old man that I'd follow you, and kill him when he sleeps," the boy said. "I won't ride south, like a coward."

"You think it's brave to get yourself killed taking on an entire army by yourself?"

He bristled.

"I won't pretend to know a lot about your people. But I do know that an a'laq takes care of those in his sept who can't take care of themselves. You can try to kill the marshal and leave these children without a leader, or you can take them south to the next sept and make sure that every one of them is safe."

For a moment she saw doubt in his pale eyes. And she thought she saw acquiescence as well. He'd take them south. A moment later, though, his expression hardened again, and this she understood, too. He was Fal'Borna, an a'laq. He couldn't appear weak in front of the other children.

"What does a dark-eye woman know about being an a'laq? What does she know about bravery?"

She held his gaze, refusing to let him provoke her; refusing as well to let him believe he had shamed her. After a few seconds she turned and walked away, sheathing her weapon as she did.

"Is it brave to destroy a sept that's already lost most of its warriors to the plague?" the boy called after her. "Is this how the Eandi fight their wars?"

Tirnya didn't look back. When she reached Thirus, she swung into her saddle. Her father was already sitting his horse, waiting for her. He looked like he might say something. Before he could, though, she spurred Thirus into motion.

She continued to look straight ahead, but as she rode past her father she slowed just long enough to say, "Give the boy back his knife. He won't be following us."

Eventually the armies resumed their march westward, leaving behind the Fal'Borna settlement and its orphaned children. Once more Fayonne and the other Mettai took their place at the back of the vast column. Mander walked beside the eldest, silent and clearly disturbed by what had happened this day. Fayonne knew that he would want to speak of it, but she didn't press him. He'd talk when he was ready.

For her part, the eldest wasn't certain that any of it could have been helped. Of course she'd been troubled by the deaths of so many children. But to declare that they were never to conjure the blood wolves again struck her as an overreaction. The marshal's daughter was young. She'd never seen what Fal'Borna magic could do. That was why she had spoken so rashly. Let her face a full, healthy sept. Let her see Eandi soldiers cut down by shaping magic and Qirsi fire. Then she would understand the value of Mettai conjurings. All of them would.

She would need to speak with the marshal. He'd been angry with her, as had several of the captains. Fayonne noticed how the young man from Fairlea looked at her, and she knew what he was thinking. Perhaps during the next battle they would be better off using gentler magic. The sleep spell had worked well against both the wolves and the children. They would be better off using such magic again. She'd heard her grandmother speak of poison spells used during the earliest of the Blood Wars. Mettai sorcerers had wiped out entire settlements with a simple conjuring. Fayonne thought that she could teach herself a similar spell, but she wasn't certain that Mander and the others would let her use it. The Mettai of old had forsworn all such spells after withdrawing from the wars and retreating into the Northlands around the Companion Lakes. They decided that earth magic shouldn't be used to kill indiscriminately.

Fayonne understood, of course. That kind of magic led to evil. But for years she and her people had known that other Mettai had begun to dabble once more in the darker powers. How else could they explain all that had befallen the families of Lifarsa for so many generations? How else could they explain the plague that had killed so many Fal'Borna over the past few turns? Teaching themselves the blood wolf spell had been a violation of the old Mettai laws, but the people of Lifarsa were hardly the first Mettai to cross that line. And if this invasion really did mark the return of the Blood Wars, they wouldn't be the last.

"We nearly made a mess of things, didn't we?" Mander said suddenly, his voice low.

Fayonne shrugged. "I suppose. The Eandi soldiers who were hurt will recover. The Fal'Borna children . . ." She shrugged. "Marshal Jenoe and the rest will forget about them soon enough."

"It had to have been the curse."

She hissed and quickly looked forward to see that none of the soldiers had heard. "Keep your voice down!" she said.

He regarded her sullenly, but when next he spoke it was in a whisper. "They'll figure it out eventually."

"There's nothing to figure out," Fayonne told him. "You don't know that what happened today had anything to do with . . . with anything else. You're assuming it did, but you *don't know.*"

"Don't I, Mama? It's been following our people around for more than a century. We were fools to believe that it would remain in Lifarsa while we came out here onto the plain."

She started to argue, but thought better of it. The truth was, Mander might well be right. This was precisely the way the Curse of Rhcyle worked. They conjured; their spells did most everything she and her people wanted them to do. But at the end they turned out . . . wrong, somehow. It almost seemed that Qirsar reached down at the last moment and twisted their magic into something dark, something far from what they had intended.

Conjuring had been like this for Fayonne all her life. It had been this way for every man and woman in Lifarsa.

She still remembered watching her father use a simple fire spell to light a cooking fire in their home one stormy night. Most nights they lit their fires without magic, but on this evening they'd started the meal too late. Fayonne didn't remember why. She did recall watching her father as he took every precaution he could think of—moving the wood pile outside; having Fayonne, her older brothers, and younger sister stand outside as well. Families in Lifarsa had burned their homes nearly to the ground with such spells. But he didn't, and for a few sweet moments all of them—her parents, her siblings, and she—thought that for this one night they had escaped the village's unhappy fate. Her mother cooked the meal, and they sat down to eat.

When the fire popped, they thought nothing of it. All fires popped; this one had several times already. But then they smelled the burning cloth and hair, and Traisa began to scream. By the time they put out the flames, she had burns on her back and neck. Fayonne's mother said that they were fortunate Traisa hadn't died, and she made their father promise never to use a fire spell in the house again.

Mander smiled grimly. "You know I'm right, don't you?"

"I'll admit it's possible that the curse had something to do with what happened today." She paused, glancing at the Eandi soldiers again. The nearest of them appeared to be absorbed in their own conversations. "But that's as far as I'll go. We were using ancient, powerful magic. We'd talked of using the blood wolf spell, and a few of us thought we'd figured out how to make it work. But we'd never actually tried it before. Even without the curse we might have had trouble controlling those wolves."

Her son shook his head and laughed bitterly. "Believe what you will, Mama. But we'd best take care with the next set of spells we conjure for the Eandi. Because if we have another day like this one, they're going to start asking questions."

She nearly said the first thing that came to her mind: *They already are.* Qalsyn's lord heir had already made it clear that he didn't trust them and didn't like relying on their magic. If this occurred to Mander as well, he kept it to himself.

"We should never have left the village," he murmured after a lengthy silence.

They'd had this discussion before, and Fayonne wanted no part of it today.

She didn't want to be out here on the plain any more than he did. Mander knew this, but still he blamed her. And maybe it was her fault. But she still believed that they might find a way to escape the curse, and as eldest it was her responsibility to give the people of Lifarsa an opportunity to live as other Mettai did.

Once, little more than a hundred years ago, their ancestors had been among the most prosperous of Stelpana's Mettai. They lived farther south then, in a village called Rheyle at the southern tip of Bear Lake. They were farmers, cloth weavers, trappers, basketmakers. Merchants—Eandi and Qirsi alike—came from every corner of the Southlands to trade with them.

From what Fayonne's father and grandfather had told her, she knew that other Mettai villages came to resent the people of Rheyle, and perhaps with good reason. It wasn't just that they were so successful, or that they lured peddlers and their gold away from neighboring villages. Rheyle's leaders grew more aggressive as time went on and for a brief time—nearly two years—they engaged in small raids on these other villages. They took fertile farming lands from one, and a bountiful woodland from another. By the end of the second year, the men and women of Rheyle had established four small hamlets as protectorates of the main village. Even Fayonne's grandfather once admitted to her that they were wrong to have done so. He also stated his belief that they would have continued to expand had the other settlements in the Bear Lake region not banded together to stop them.

When Rheyle's soldiers next attempted to take land from Gavdyre, a fishing village on the lake's southeastern shore, warriors from other villages came to Gavdyre's defense. In a bloody skirmish known to the Mettai as the Battle of Seven Villages, the new alliance drove off the men from Rheyle.

Emboldened by their success, they then attacked Rheyle's other protectorates, defeating each of them in turn. When all of the outpost villages had been conquered, they turned their attention to Rheyle itself. They didn't attack this time, but rather used magic fueled by blood taken forcibly from Rheyle prisoners captured in the preceding battles.

They placed a curse—the Curse of Rheyle—on the village's people and their descendants. It laid waste to their once-fertile lands. Suddenly their soil seemed poisoned; crops that had thrived for years before now barely managed to stay alive. Game animals, both large and small, forsook the woodlands surrounding the village. Rheyle's hunters and trappers had to range farther and farther from home in order to find their prey. Much the same thing happened to the lake waters near the village. Schools of fish seemed to vanish overnight.

But the curse did more than that. It touched their magic as well. Spells that Rheyle's people had conjured with ease for centuries abruptly stopped working. Or if they did work, they turned dark, as had this day's conjuring of the blood wolves.

After suffering under the curse for several years, the people of Rheyle finally made a difficult and painful decision. They abandoned their village, moved northward away from their enemies, and established a new settlement on the northwestern shore of Bear Lake, which they called New Rheyle. When they found their new home they thought the lands as rich as any they had ever seen.

Within a year, however, New Rheyle was no better than their blighted first home had been. The curse had followed them. A year later, they fled New Rheyle and built yet another settlement, which they called Dranig, as if by abandoning the name "Rheyle" they might confound the spell and thus escape it.

Three years after that they left Dranig, and settled in what became known as Lifarsa. Lifarsa proved no more immune to the curse than the other settlements had been, but the village's leaders concluded that there was nowhere they could go to escape the magic of their enemies. So they remained in their newest home and did their best to make a life for themselves there, regardless of the curse.

In the hundred years since, none of Lifarsa's eldests had tried to find a new home for their people. Until now.

It wasn't that matters had grown any worse in recent years. But Fayonne could see how the curse wore on her people; she herself knew how great a burden it was. So when

Jenoe and his soldiers came to Lifarsa offering them an opportunity to make a new home for themselves far away from the Companion Lakes, she leaped at the chance. How could she not?

Mander was probably right in thinking that the curse would follow them no matter where they went. But what kind of a leader would she have been if she refused even to try?

"Maybe we shouldn't have left," Fayonne finally said, drawing her son's gaze. "Maybe we can never escape the curse. It was placed on our ancestors and they've passed it to us, and it's possible that no matter how far we go, we'll always carry it in our blood and in our magic. But no spell is perfect. We're far from the Companion Lakes, and we increase that distance every day. Mettai magic is blood magic, but it's also earth magic. Look around you, Mander."

He did, taking in the great expanse of the plain.

"Our blood may be the same, but this is different earth. Maybe the curse will be weaker here. Maybe that's why the Eandi soldiers were only wounded by the wolves."

The look on Mander's face told her that he hadn't considered this before. He nodded thoughtfully.

"We'll still have to be careful," he said.

Fayonne managed a smile. "Of course. But perhaps it can work to our advantage. The wolves killed those poor children, but they also killed white-hair warriors, even after the marshal told us to call them back. Without meaning to, we've brought the Curse of Rheyle to the Fal'Borna. Maybe it's a weapon we can use."

Clearly Mander hadn't considered this, either.

Chapter 9

I should be tanning rilda skins," Cresenne said lazily, making no effort to leave the warmth of their blankets.

Grinsa had his arm around her, and her head rested on his shoulder. Their fingers were laced together.

"Maybe you should go then," he said, in the same languid tone.

"Hmmm."

They kissed and then Grinsa lay back once more and closed his eyes. They had made love for much of the night, until their pent-up passion for each other was finally sated. They'd dozed off, awakened before dawn and made love once more, and then had fallen asleep again. Grinsa felt quite certain that the a'laq would be looking for him soon enough, but until then he had no intention of going anywhere.

Bryntelle was awake on her small pallet, chattering to herself. Occasionally she glanced Grinsa's way and let out a small laugh, as if she couldn't believe that her father was actually there.

Grinsa couldn't believe it, either.

He could hear voices outside the z'kal. Others had been up and about for some time now. And with war coming, he knew that the haven he and Cresenne had carved out for themselves over these few precious hours wouldn't last much longer.

He'd said as much to Cresenne the night before, when he told her that E'Menua had agreed to recognize the legitimacy of their joining, and that he had pledged himself to fighting alongside the Fal'Borna.

"I know that we're not part of their clan," he had said. "Not really, at least. But I couldn't—"

She held a finger to his lips, then kissed him. "I know," she whispered. "I expected no less. I don't want to stay here, and I don't like E'Menua, but if the Eandi attack these people, I'll fight, too." Suddenly her brow furrowed and a slight smile touched her lips. "He's willing to accept that I'm your wife?" she asked, as if finally realizing what Grinsa had said moments before.

He smiled. "Yes."

"How did you get him to agree to that? I thought he'd go to Bian's realm thinking of me as your concubine."

"Well, he might. But he understands now that he can't control me with magic or threats. And he knows that I'm capable of humiliating him in front of all his people if he tries."

"Grinsa, you don't want to make him afraid of you," she said, clearly unnerved by this. "That's every bit as dangerous as making him angry. If he thinks you're a threat to him, he'll find a way to kill you."

"It'll be all right. He's not going to kill me. He's not even going to make the attempt."

"You don't know what he's capable of doing. He's . . . cruel. He likes to control people, just for the fun of it, just for the satisfaction of knowing that he can. If you defy him . . ." She shook her head. "You need to be careful."

Grinsa narrowed his eyes. "What did he do to you?"

But Cresenne shook her head. "Not now." She kissed him again. "I'll tell you tomorrow, but I don't want to talk about him tonight."

Neither did Grinsa, of course, and he gladly gave himself over to his hunger for her. Now, though, as the sept awoke, and the sounds of morning beckoned to them, he asked her about it again.

This time Cresenne didn't put him off, though her expression darkened, as if just thinking about it made her angry.

"He didn't really do anything to me," she said. "Remember when we first arrived in the sept, and every morning the Fal'Borna brought us food and firewood?"

Grinsa nodded.

"Well, they didn't do that for us so much as they did it for you, because you're a Weaver." She shrugged. "That's how they treat their Weavers."

He understood immediately. "So once I was gone, they stopped bringing you food and wood."

"The wood I could find on my own," she said. "I had to gather it each day after I finished tanning, but I didn't mind so much. The food, though; we didn't come here early enough to plant crops or hunt rilda. We had nothing."

"Why didn't you tell me any of this?" Grinsa asked. He rolled onto his side so that he could look her in the eye.

"I knew how angry you'd be. And there was nothing you could do. You were looking for the cursed baskets and the woman who made them." A smile lit her face. "Besides, I handled it."

He smiled in turn. "How?"

"F'Solya convinced me to go to E'Menua and ask for his help."

"F'Solya is your friend who tans the skins with you, right?"

She nodded. "She's been a good friend. But of course E'Menua saw this as an opportunity to split you and me apart. He wouldn't let me buy food from the sept. Instead he made L'Norr share his food with me; I was to go to his z'kal for my evening meals."

"L'Norr?" Grinsa repeated. For a moment he couldn't imagine why the a'laq would send her to the young Weaver. He didn't know L'Norr well. The man was Q'Daer's closest friend, and as one of the sept's Weavers he wielded some influence in the settlement. But he hardly struck Grinsa as someone who would willingly take advantage of Cresenne's misfortune. But then it occurred to him why E'Menua would have chosen this man to share his food with Cresenne. L'Norr was young, handsome, and he had not yet been joined to a

Weaver. By forcing the two of them together in the middle of Grinsa's lengthy absence from the sept, the a'laq hoped to foster a romance between them. E'Menua was as clever as he was devious.

"I guess the a'laq wasn't satisfied with you being only my concubine," he said, grinning. "He wants you to be L'Norr's, too."

She didn't look amused. "It's not funny. L'Norr has a concubine already, and she accused me of trying to steal her man. For a while there everyone in the sept believed her. Even F'Solya."

"I'm sorry," he said, brushing a strand of hair from her forehead. "What did you do?"

"I convinced her that she was wrong," she told him, clearly pleased with herself, "and that L'Norr was in love with her."

Grinsa laughed, drawing a delighted shriek from Bryntelle. "And was he?"

She shrugged. "I'm not sure. I think he is now. But I convinced her that she had nothing to fear from me. That's all that mattered to me."

He shook his head, still laughing. "I think that you're more dangerous than E'Menua."

But thinking this, he looked toward the entrance to the z'kal, his laughter fading. After a moment, he stood, pulled on his britches, and walked to the flap that covered the entryway. Peering outside, he saw that the ground around the z'kal was bare. No wood; no food.

He turned to face Cresenne, who was pulling on a shirt.

"It seems I did make him angry," Grinsa told her.

"Still no food?"

"No wood, either. Being a Weaver doesn't mean what it used to around here."

He meant it as a joke, but neither of them smiled.

"What should we do?" Cresenne asked.

"I'll talk to Q'Daer. He might be able to help us. If worst comes to worst, you and Bryntelle will go back to L'Norr and I'll find another source of food." He pulled a pouch of food from his travel sack and threw it onto the blankets. "In the meantime, we have enough there to last us a few days."

She nodded, but Grinsa could see the disappointment on her face.

"I'm sorry," he said.

"It's not your fault. I just assumed that everything would be all right once you were back."

"We'll leave here as soon as we can. I swear it."

Cresenne nodded once more and they finished dressing in silence.

When Cresenne went to the tanning circle as she did every day, Grinsa sought out Q'Daer. He found the young Weaver sitting with L'Norr outside the a'laq's shelter. Seeing him approach, Q'Daer averted his eyes and wouldn't look at Grinsa even when he offered a greeting.

Grinsa stopped in front of the two men and, rather than forcing a conversation with Q'Daer, turned to L'Norr.

"I want to thank you," he said.

L'Norr shifted uncomfortably. "For what?"

"For feeding my wife, of course. You were most generous to share your food with her. I'm in your debt."

"It was nothing. I was just doing what the a'laq . . ." He swallowed, suddenly as reluctant as Q'Daer to meet Grinsa's gaze. "It was nothing," he said again.

And abruptly Grinsa understood. E'Menua had anticipated what he and Cresenne intended to do next.

"He ordered you both not to share any more with us, didn't he?"

He had expected that neither man would respond. It seemed, however, that the time he had spent journeying with Q'Daer had built some small rapport between them. Q'Daer glanced back quickly at the z'kal. Then he looked up at Grinsa and nodded.

"I don't know what you did, Forelander," he whispered. "But the a'laq is determined to punish you."

"Is he in there?" Grinsa asked, indicating the z'kal.

Q'Daer nodded again and started to stand. Grinsa raised a hand, stopping him.

"I don't need you to announce me."

The young Weaver shook his head, the familiar scowl on his square face. "You're just making matters worse," he said.

"I'll take that chance."

He stepped past the two men, pushed the flap covering the entrance aside, and entered the z'kal. E'Menua sat in his usual spot on the far side of his fire pit, facing the entry. He regarded Grinsa mildly, as if he'd been expecting him.

"You intend to starve us?" Grinsa asked, not bothering with any of the formalities E'Menua usually demanded of his people.

"Not at all," the a'laq said, his voice even. "But I don't intend to feed you, either."

"You're angry with me, so you're punishing my wife and my child." He sneered. "What a great leader you are."

The embers in the a'laq's fire pit and the small open circle at the top of the shelter offered scant light, but still Grinsa saw the man bristle. "Watch your tongue, Forelander! Q'Daer and L'Norr are just outside. If I wanted to, I could order them to kill you, and for all your might and your bluster, you'd be powerless to stop them."

He'd been back for less than a day, and already Grinsa had grown weary of this man. He nearly responded with a threat of his own, something that would have made it clear to the a'laq that Grinsa could kill him before he ever had a chance to call for the young Weavers. But Q'Daer had been right a moment ago, and so had Cresenne. Threats and defiance would only make matters worse, and for now at least, with war coming and Besh and Sirj at the mercy of this man, Grinsa had little choice but to remain here.

"I don't want to fight you, A'Laq," he said, addressing E'Menua by his title for the first time since his return. "And I don't think that you want to have me killed. I don't even think you really want to starve us."

E'Menua said nothing.

"So what is it you do want?"

"You seem to think you know me quite well," the a'laq said. "Answer the question yourself."

"I've already told you that I won't marry a Weaver."

The a'laq dismissed the idea with a disdainful wave of his hand. "You flatter yourself, Forelander. And anyway, aside from the n'qlae there are no female Weavers in the sept. My daughter will come into her power soon, but trust me when I tell you that I have no desire to see her joined to you."

Grinsa chuckled. "No, I don't suppose you do. But if not that, then what?"

E'Menua merely gazed back at him.

"I've already told you that I'll march to war with you and your people, that I'll fight to protect Fal'Borna lands. Do you want me to promise that we'll stay here, even after the war is over?"

"Take some time to think about it, Forelander. Perhaps you'll figure it out eventually."

"And in the meantime, we'll have to forage for our own food, is that right?"

No response. It occurred to Grinsa that perhaps Cresenne was right in saying that he'd been handling this the wrong way.

"We'd be most grateful, A'Laq, if you would consider helping us through the Snows. We have no stores of roots or rilda meat. We came to you late in the year and now we have little choice but to ask for your help."

A slight smile touched the a'laq's lips and was gone. "You speak to me like that in private, where no one else can hear, but in front of the others you treat me with contempt. Why should I honor your request? Why should I listen when you tell me that these two Mettai you've brought to my sept aren't threats to us?"

Grinsa considered this briefly. Then he shook his head, smiling at his own stupidity. "You shouldn't," he said. "While we were searching the plain for the Mettai woman, Q'Daer said something similar to me. He wondered why I'd refuse to submit to your authority and would show so little regard for Fal'Borna ways, and then turn around and risk my life trying to save your people from the Mettai woman's plague."

"Were you able to explain this to him?"

"Not well," Grinsa said. He rubbed a hand over his face. "You and I have been fighting since the moment I arrived here. The same is true of Q'Daer and me. Cresenne and I were looking for a new home, a place where we could raise our daughter—"

"We've given you that, and more! And yet you still act as if we're your enemies!"

"It's not enough to give us a home and tell us we have to live here! You've tried to control us with threats. You've tried to force us to adopt your ways, regardless of what they would do to our family. Is it any wonder that I've fought you?"

E'Menua looked away, his jaw set. "You are a most diffi-cult man, Forelander. I'm still not sure why I haven't had you killed yet. Most a'laqs would have by now."

"Well, that speaks well of your wisdom, A'Laq."

The Fal'Borna cast a quick look his way, as if to deter-mine whether Grinsa was mocking him. Grinsa allowed himself a small smile to show that he wasn't.

After a moment, the a'laq actually smiled as well. "I'm not sure it does." As quickly as it had come, his smile vanished. "You've made your share of threats, too. You spoke of killing me the very first time you set foot in this z'kal. And you've shown little regard for me or my people. The Fal'Borna clan is as strong as any in the Southlands. We're feared by the dark-eyes and respected by every Qirsi nation, even the J'Balanar. We honored you by welcoming you into our sept, and you've done nothing since but reject our ways and make it clear that you intend to leave as soon as possible."

Grinsa nodded, his lips pursed. "You're right."

E'Menua stared at him, seeming to expect more. When Grinsa didn't say anything else, he frowned. "That's all? I'm right? No arguments? No insults?"

Grinsa shrugged. "I can tell you that Cresenne and I never meant to give offense. We were looking for a home and found you first. I'm still not sure that we belong among the Fal'Borna. But that wasn't really your point. And looking at it as you would, I can see that you're right. You made us part of your sept, and we told you that we wanted to leave. If I were in your position, I'd be angry, too."

The frown lingered on E'Menua's thin, tapered face. Clearly he hadn't expected Grinsa to say any of this.

"And I suppose I can understand that you didn't want to give up your woman," he finally said.

"Thank you for that, A'Laq."

E'Menua nodded, though he still looked unnerved by their exchange.

It seemed to Grinsa, though, that something had shifted between them. He remained wary of the man—he didn't think that he could ever be around E'Menua without keeping at least a light hold on his magic, just in case. But despite his pledge to fight on behalf of the Fal'Borna, only now did he begin to think that perhaps they could work together and face the Eandi as allies, if it came to that.

"You mentioned the Mettai before," he said after a lengthy silence. "Regardless of what other Mettai have done, I'm certain that we can trust Besh and Sirj. They want to help us. They believe that the witch's plague is to blame for this war, and so rather than returning to the safety of Mettai lands, they chose to come here with Q'Daer and me."

"They also found a way to defeat the plague and make us all immune," E'Menua said, surprising him. "Isn't that so?"

"Yes, it is."

"Doesn't that strike you as odd?"

Grinsa's heart sank. He'd actually allowed himself to believe that he and the a'laq had reached an understanding of a sort, that he might be able to reason with the man.

"You believe that this is all part of a Mettai plan to win your trust?" he asked wearily.

"Or yours. They've already succeeded at that."

"I don't believe that they're capable of anything so . . . insidious, A'Laq. But I'd suggest that if you're suspicious of them, you speak to them yourself. I have no doubt that they'd be willing to answer any questions you ask them. I can arrange such an audience, if you'd like."

E'Menua appeared disappointed, as if he'd hoped that Grinsa would respond in anger to his doubts about the Mettai. "Yes, all right," he said, sounding bored with their conversation.

Grinsa rose. "Thank you, A'Laq."

He turned, intending to leave, and immediately sensed that E'Menua was drawing upon his magic, as he had the day before. Instantly, Grinsa reached out with his own power and took control of the a'laq's. He wasn't convinced that E'Menua actually intended to harm him—the a'laq made no attempt to free himself from Grinsa's hold on his power. But the Forelander knew that he could never show any signs of weakness in his dealings with this man.

Grinsa glanced back over his shoulder, his eyebrows raised.

"Before, when you spoke of the two Mettai, you said that 'we' could trust them, that they wanted to help 'us.' Do you consider yourself Fal'Borna now?"

"There's a war coming," Grinsa said with a grin. "Do you think I'd choose this day to count myself as part of any other clan?"

E'Menua laughed. "If you'd been born in the Southlands, you would have been Fal'Borna. I'm sure of it."

"I'll take that as a compliment, A'Laq."

"There will be food for you by midday. Enough for two. And wood, as well."

Grinsa inclined his head. "Thank you." He released E'Menua's magic and left the z'kal.

Cresenne's late arrival at the tanning circle drew the notice of several of the Fal'Borna women, though none of them said anything to her. Even before Cresenne started eating her meals with L'Norr, she had been an outcast in the village. Many of the women who tanned with her had believed T'Lisha, L'Norr's concubine, when she told them that Cresenne was trying to steal L'Norr from her. T'Lisha no longer believed this, but several of the women still eyed Cresenne with open hostility. *You may have been innocent this time*, they seemed to be telling her with their glares, *but that doesn't mean we trust you.*

Through all of this, though, F'Solya remained her good friend. As usual, the woman had saved Cresenne a space beside her, and seeing Cresenne approach, she smiled slyly.

"I didn't think I'd see you here at all," she said, as Cresenne lowered herself to the ground and pulled out the skin she'd scraped clean the day before.

"I'm not that late," Cresenne said, smiling.

"I know! That's what I mean. If I'Joled had been away as long as your man has been, I'd still be beneath a blanket." She grinned. "And so would he."

Cresenne felt her cheeks coloring, though if anything her smile broadened.

"I don't think I've ever seen you look so happy," F'Solya said. "I'm glad for you."

"Thank you."

Cresenne reached for the foul tannin that the Fal'Borna used to soften and preserve their rilda hides, and for some time the two women worked without speaking.

"What do you know about the Mettai your man brought back with him?" F'Solya asked, abruptly breaking the silence.

Cresenne paused in her work to look at the woman, surprised by the question. "Not a lot. Grinsa said that they killed the witch who first spread the plague. And he also said that they found a way to defeat the curse; if they hadn't, Grinsa and Q'Daer would both be dead, and none of us would be safe."

F'Solya nodded thoughtfully, but she wore a frown on her pretty face. "I'Joled says it's dangerous to have them here."

Cresenne felt herself tense, knowing that they had crossed into hazardous terrain. I'Joled, F'Solya's husband, struck her as a decent man. From what she'd seen of the two of them together, she had no doubt that he loved his wife and boys. But she didn't like him, and she had the sense that he didn't like her, either. They had met only once—the night F'Solya invited her and Bryntelle to eat with them at their z'kal. At the time, she hadn't yet spoken to E'Menua about her need for food. F'Solya and I'Joled generously shared their meal with her—she had no right to think ill of him.

But she believed he was a typical Fal'Borna man: proud, stubborn, distrustful of outsiders, and disdainful of women who didn't behave the way Fal'Borna women were expected to behave. It didn't surprise her to learn that he was suspicious of the Mettai. This was how a Fal'Borna warrior thought: If one group of Mettai had declared themselves enemies of the Fal'Borna, then every Mettai in the Southlands was an enemy. Never mind all the good that Besh and Sirj had done.

Clearly Cresenne couldn't say any of this without angering her friend.

"Why does he think it's dangerous?" she asked instead, hoping her voice wouldn't betray her thoughts.

F'Solya let out a small, breathless laugh, though she didn't look at all amused. "Well, because we're going to war against the Mettai, of course."

"Right. Of course. I just . . ." She shook her head, wishing she hadn't spoken at all. "I don't know if Besh and Sirj know the Mettai who are marching with the Eandi."

"That doesn't matter," F'Solya said. "They're Mettai."

Cresenne thought it best not to answer.

If only it had been that easy.

Her friend looked at her for a long time, the skin she was working lying forgotten in her lap. Cresenne tried to keep working, but in the end she had little choice but to look F'Solya in the eye.

"You disagree," the woman said.

"I'm not sure we should talk about this, F'Solya."

"I believe we should. You've lived among the Fal'Borna for more than two turns now. You're learning our ways, you speak of being our friends. You also know that we're under attack by the Eandi and the Mettai." Her voice rose as she spoke, and her cheeks were flushed. "You've known these two Mettai men for a day. And yet you're willing to trust them. You're willing to discount our fears of them. I want to know why."

No matter how Cresenne answered, she knew that she risked losing this friendship, the only one of any meaning she had formed since arriving in the sept. She knew as well, though, that if she lied or tried to soften the truth, she'd only make matters worse. F'Solya had never been anything but honest with her; she deserved the same in return.

"Because," Cresenne began, "when I lived in the Forelands, I was once part of a Qirsi conspiracy that aimed to destroy the Eandi courts. Eventually, I came to see that the man leading the conspiracy was evil and brutal and intent on destroying the land, not saving it. I left the movement, and thanks to Grinsa and the compassion of an Eandi king who had no reason to believe that I was anything more than a white-hair traitor, I'm still alive today. They could have assumed that I was just like all the others; they would have been within their rights to execute me."

F'Solya didn't look convinced. If anything, her expression appeared to have hardened.

"I'm not from a clan, F'Solya. Maybe that's why we look at this so differently. You've grown up believing that the world is divided into Fal'Borna and J'Balanar and Talm'Orast, and also Mettai and Eandi. My world was . . . different. There were Qirsi and Eandi. And there were different realms—Eibithar, Sanbira, Wethyrn. But someone could be both Qirsi and Aneiran, Eandi and Caerissan. It was more complicated."

"So you think we're simple?" F'Solya demanded.

Cresenne winced. She wasn't handling this well. "Of course not. It's just . . ." She stopped, shaking her head again.

"You want to know the real reason I trust these men?" She didn't wait for a reply. "They saved Grinsa's life. They cast a spell that defeated the curse, and then they made it so that Grinsa could pass that spell on to Bryntelle and me."

"That's what they tell us," F'Solya said, in a voice that chilled Cresenne's blood.

"You don't believe them?"

"We have no proof that they made us immune. We can only take their word for it and hope that it's true. But if we trust them, and then it turns out that they've lied to us, thousands could die. And maybe that's what they have in mind. Maybe the Eandi put them up to this."

"They saved Grinsa and Q'Daer! Surely you believe that!"

"Saving two to kill thousands? That's a trade any warrior would make."

"F'Solya—" Again Cresenne stopped herself. She had intended to say that Besh and Sirj wouldn't do this. But her friend would surely ask how Cresenne could be so certain, and she had no good answer. She was trusting all to Grinsa's judgment, and though she believed that he was right, she knew that F'Solya wouldn't share her faith in him.

A small, satisfied smile touched the woman's lips and was gone. "Think about it," she said. "Your man trusts them. And perhaps if they had saved I'Joled, he and I would feel the same way. But they didn't. They saved the life of a Forelander. Perhaps they knew that your husband would be easier to convince than a Fal'Borna. Perhaps this was part of their plan."

"Q'Daer trusts them, too!" Cresenne said.

F'Solya raised an eyebrow. "Does he?"

Another question she couldn't answer. Cresenne had assumed that the young Weaver and Grinsa were of one mind with regard to the Mettai. But did she know this for certain? For that matter, did Grinsa?

"How many others feel this way?" she asked after some time.

F'Solya shrugged. "I'Joled didn't say. Many, I'm sure. As

I said, we're at war with the Mettai. We'd be wary of these men no matter who brought them here." As soon as she said this she smiled again, though her brow creased.

Cresenne knew what she was thinking. "No one else would have brought them here, though. Isn't that right?"

The woman hesitated, then nodded. "I can't imagine that Q'Daer wanted to. He would have tried to send them away long ago."

Cresenne put down the skin she was working on and stood. "Excuse me," she said. "I have to find Grinsa."

The words sounded oddly formal to her own ears. She sensed that her friendship with F'Solya had changed, perhaps forever. But that was the least of her concerns. She left the tanning ring without waiting for her friend's reply.

Chapter 10

◆━┼━◆

Besh couldn't remember the last time he had slept so soundly. The Qirsi shelter, this z'kal, as the Fal'Borna called it, was remarkably effective in keeping out the cold and wind of the plain, and the pallet on which he lay was as comfortable as his bed back in Kirayde. For the first time in a turn, he had slept through the entire night, untroubled by visions of Lici and her plague. He would gladly have slumbered for another several hours, but Sirj had already left the shelter, and Besh could hear that others in the sept were up and about.

Reluctantly he threw off his blankets, pulled on his britches and shirt, and stepped out into the brisk morning air. Sirj sat on a stump of wood beside the shelter looking out over the sept.

"How long have you been up?" Besh asked, inhaling deeply and stretching his back.

"Not long. An hour, maybe."

Besh nodded. "Have you seen the Forelander?"

Sirj merely shook his head. Looking at him again, Besh realized that the younger man wasn't merely gazing out at the settlement. His eyes were alert and he wore a grim expression.

"What's the matter?" Besh asked.

"I'm not entirely sure," Sirj said. "Try not to appear alarmed. But take a casual look around. It seems to me that we're being guarded, but they don't want us to know."

Besh nodded again. His pulse now was racing, and his stomach began to knot. He glanced about, trying to appear relaxed. It didn't take him long to see what Sirj meant. There were at least a dozen Fal'Borna warriors nearby, all of them with blades on their belts, several of them holding spears as well. Some of them were standing; others sat. But they had formed a loose ring around Besh and Sirj's shelter. There was no way for the Mettai to leave the area without encountering at least one of them.

The Qirsi didn't seem to be watching the two men, but there was something a bit too studied in their demeanor.

"Damn," Besh said under his breath. "You say that you haven't seen Grinsa?"

Sirj gave a quick shake of his head. "Not yet."

"What about Q'Daer?"

"Not him, either."

"Have any of them said anything to you?"

"They've barely even looked at me. I think they were told to keep watch on us, and that's all. But I don't like it. If they're watching us, that means they don't trust us. They're halfway to deciding that we're the enemy."

"Grinsa won't let that happen. We healed him, and Q'Daer, too. We made them immune to the plague."

"Yes. You killed Lici, too. They don't seem to care about any of that. And I don't think that Grinsa can help us much. He's not Fal'Borna."

"He's a Weaver," Besh said. But he knew that Sirj was

right. From all he'd heard about the Fal'Borna, it seemed that they were distrustful of Qirsi from every other clan in the Southlands. He could only assume that they would be even more wary of outlanders. "All right," he said a moment later. "Let's assume Grinsa can't help us. What do we do?"

Sirj shook his head. "There's not much we can do. Even if Mettai magic was a match for Qirsi magic, we're only two against an entire sept." He looked up at Besh. "If they decide to make us their prisoners, or worse, if they decide to kill us, there's nothing we can do to stop them."

"Well, then," Besh said, taking a long breath, "we need to find out what their intentions are."

Sirj looked at him with alarm. "What are you going to do?"

"Nothing I hadn't been planning to do anyway," Besh told him, starting toward the heart of the settlement. He glanced back over his shoulder. "It's morning and I'm ready for my breakfast."

There were two Qirsi in front of him, both of them standing, both of them bearing spears. As soon as they saw him coming, they planted themselves in his path. They held their spears ready, but they didn't actually point the weapons at him.

Besh didn't break stride, but rather walked right up to the two men and stopped in front of them. He heard Sirj hurrying to catch up with him.

"Where are you going, Mettai?" one of the Fal'Borna asked him.

They were both young men, powerfully built, with golden eyes, long white hair, and bronze skin. Strange as they appeared to him, they were also beautiful and forbidding. It almost seemed to Besh that all Fal'Borna warriors resembled these two. Looking closer, he could see that the man who had spoken had a rounder, softer face than the other, and that his eyes were more widely spaced. But the differences were subtle. It was as if Qirsar himself had reached down and created these people in his own image.

"I was on my way to speak with my friend Grinsa," Besh told the men, offering his most disarming smile. "He and I have matters to discuss. And I have to admit that I'm also hoping he'll have a bit for me to eat."

The two men exchanged glances.

"Is there a problem?" Besh asked, looking from one of them to the other, as Sirj stopped beside him.

"You're to stay here," said the first man. "Both of you. We can have food brought to you."

Besh's smile faded. "I was led to believe that we're guests of your a'laq. Was I wrong? Are we in fact prisoners?"

"You're Mettai," the man said, as if that answered the question. "We're at war with your people. You are guests of the a'laq. If you weren't, you'd be dead by now."

"We were declared friends of the Fal'Borna by an a'laq named F'Ghara," Sirj said. "That must count for something."

Besh still carried F'Ghara's white stone in his pocket. He pulled it out now and held it up for the man to see.

The Fal'Borna cast a quick look at the necklace, but his expression didn't change at all. "I don't know anything about that," he said. "I was ordered to watch you, and to keep you here. The rest is up to the a'laq."

Besh turned to Sirj, who stared back at him bleakly. After a moment the younger man shrugged and shook his head.

The old man faced the warrior again. "I'd like to speak with your a'laq."

"The a'laq decides who he'll speak to. If he chooses to see you, you'll be summoned."

Besh felt himself growing angry. If this was what it meant to be a guest of the Fal'Borna, he would have hated to be their prisoner. But he knew that railing at this man would do no good, and that defying him might well get him killed, and Sirj, too.

"Food, then," he said thickly. "We'd like to eat. Please. And we'd like to speak with the Forelander."

The warrior nodded, then looked at his comrade, who turned and started toward a cluster of shelters. There was nothing for the two Mettai to do but make their way back to their shelter.

"This isn't going to end well," Sirj said under his breath as they walked.

Besh merely nodded, knowing the younger man was right.

They think Besh and Sirj made it up?" Grinsa asked, hardly believing what Cresenne was telling him.

She nodded, watching him. She looked pale and frightened and lovely.

She had found him wandering the empty grounds of the marketplace, where he'd gone after his conversation with E'Menua. Bryntelle was with the young Fal'Borna women who cared for the sept's children, and Cresenne had been at the tanning circle where she usually spent her days. He'd been surprised and pleased to see her, but that had quickly given way to alarm when she began to tell him what she'd heard. They had walked beyond the horse paddock, where they were unlikely to be disturbed. They gazed out over the plain as they spoke, holding hands once more. Even now, angry and afraid for the two Mettai, he couldn't be with Cresenne without touching her. They'd been apart for too long. It was almost as if he needed to assure himself that she was real, rather than a dream or some conjured illusion.

"Is it possible?" she asked after a lengthy silence. "I know you trust them, but you have no proof that their spell will protect us from the plague, do you?"

He looked at her, pained by the question. She shook her head and lifted his hand to her lips.

"I'm sorry," she said. "But F'Solya . . . she sounded so sure of herself. And she said that the only way to test the spell was to put our lives at risk, which is true."

"I'm alive," he said. "So is Q'Daer. That's my proof."

"Don't be mad at me. I was just . . . I don't know anything about these men except what you've told me. And most of what I've heard about the Mettai—the plague, their alliance with the Eandi—doesn't lead me to trust them. I know that they saved you, and for that I'll forever be in their debt, but if F'Solya can make *me* wonder about them, imagine how easy it will be for I'Joled and the others to convince the rest of the sept that they're our enemies."

She had a point. E'Menua had made it clear that he wasn't ready to trust them; what F'Solya had said to Cresenne was quite similar to what E'Menua had told him. And he had to admit that he had doubts of his own. None of them had anything to do with Besh's and Sirj's motives. He trusted the two men completely. But Cresenne was right: How did they know that the spell had made Grinsa immune to another onset of Lici's plague? How did they know that he was able to pass that protection on to Cresenne and Bryntelle and the others?

"Grinsa?" she said, her forehead furrowed with concern. "Say something."

"There's not much I can say, except to admit that you're right. E'Menua voiced similar suspicions. Once the Fal'Borna have made up their minds about an enemy, there's very little chance of convincing them otherwise."

"But we have to try," she said. "Don't we?"

He looked her in the eye and smiled. "Yes. So let's start by convincing you."

"What do you mean?"

"Come with me. We'll go and speak with Besh and Sirj. Once you're convinced, maybe the four of us can think of some way to win over the others."

She smiled in return and they started back toward the settlement. As they neared the shelters, Grinsa changed directions, drawing a puzzled look from Cresenne.

"Where are we going?" she asked.

"If we're going to have any chance of changing E'Menua's mind, we'll need Q'Daer's help. He should be part of this conversation."

She frowned deeply.

"You disagree?" Grinsa asked.

"No. But this sounded much more pleasant when it was just going to be the four of us."

Grinsa laughed. "Well, I can't argue with that."

Q'Daer and L'Norr were still outside the a'laq's shelter. L'Norr's face colored slightly at the sight of Cresenne, but he said nothing.

"Can we have a word with you?" Grinsa asked Q'Daer, taking care to keep his voice low.

Q'Daer looked sidelong at the entrance to E'Menua's z'kal, as if the a'laq were standing right there. After a moment, he nodded. He climbed to his feet and followed them a short distance from the shelter.

Before Grinsa could say anything, Q'Daer told him, "The Mettai wish to speak with you."

"Did they tell you what it was about?"

Q'Daer shook his head. "I didn't see them. One of their guards came to me and asked where he might find you."

A chill went through Grinsa's body. "One of their guards?" he repeated. "They're being held prisoner?"

Q'Daer's expression soured. "They're being watched, Forelander. And before you say anything more, you should ask yourself if you have any reason to be surprised by this. I tried to tell you that the Mettai didn't belong here. We should have sent them back to their lands when we had the chance. Now . . ." He looked away, shaking his head.

"Now, what?" Grinsa demanded.

"It doesn't matter. What is it you want to discuss with me?"

"This!" Grinsa said. "We came to you to talk about the Mettai. There are people saying that they can't be trusted, that their spell hasn't done anything to protect us, and that they're the enemy."

Q'Daer didn't look at him, and for a moment Grinsa thought he'd refuse to talk to them and walk away. But then the young Weaver nodded once. "I've heard talk of this."

"And have you told people that they're wrong? Have you explained that Besh and Sirj saved our lives?"

At that Q'Daer met his gaze. "No, I haven't."

"Why not?"

"Because I'm not exactly sure what happened that night. I know how it seemed at the time. To both of us. But those who say that it all worked out too well for them may have a point."

Grinsa wanted to scream. Could Fal'Borna distrust of all Eandi truly run so deep? But he held his temper in check. Q'Daer hadn't said that he agreed with I'Joled and the others. He had merely admitted to having his doubts. So Grinsa started with the simplest elements of the events on the plain that led to their illness.

"Do you believe that they sickened us?"

The Fal'Borna twisted his mouth, looking like a small boy. "No," he finally said. "I believe Torgan did that, just as I believe that he killed the other merchant."

"Do you believe that Torgan was working with them?"

He shook his head. "No, I don't believe that, either."

"Then you don't believe that Besh and Sirj meant to do us harm."

"I suppose not," he said, grudgingly.

"And you can't deny that they healed us."

"I said only that the others had a point!" Q'Daer told him. "You don't need to speak to me like I'm a fool."

"That's not what I'm doing, Q'Daer. I'm trying to figure out what you believe and what you don't. And it sounds to me like you don't think the Mettai are enemies of . . . of our people, but you're also not certain their spell actually has made us immune to the witch's curse. Is that right?"

The Fal'Borna was scowling again. It seemed to Grinsa that his face didn't relax into a smile as most people's did, but that this was his most natural look. He nodded once more. "Yes, that's about right."

"Come with us, then. Cresenne and I were on our way to

speak with Besh and Sirj. The three of us are their only friends right now."

"I'm not their friend," Q'Daer said quickly.

Grinsa took Cresenne's hand and the two of them started walking in the direction of the Mettai's z'kal.

"You don't believe they want to kill us," he said over his shoulder. "Right now, that makes you as good a friend as they have among the Fal'Borna."

He hoped that Q'Daer would follow, but wasn't certain he would until he looked back and saw the young Weaver walking behind them, muttering to himself, his eyes trained on the ground.

Grinsa noticed the guards well before they reached Besh and Sirj. At first he saw only the two directly in front of them. But as he started looking for them, he spotted several more. They were keeping their distance from the Mettai, but they were there just the same, and he had no doubt that Besh and Sirj had noticed them.

The two Mettai were sitting on the ground in front of their shelter, eating. Besh saw Grinsa first and quickly got to his feet. Sirj did the same.

"Are you both all right?" Grinsa asked as he, Cresenne, and Q'Daer drew near to the two men.

"We're prisoners," Besh said flatly.

"You're guests of the a'laq," Q'Daer told him, before Grinsa could respond.

Besh glared at him. "I don't know what that means. We're being watched by armed guards. We're surrounded by them. *That* I understand."

"Do you understand as well that your people and mine are at war? Do you understand that we're under attack by Eandi and Mettai alike? How do you expect to be treated?"

"Like the men who saved your life," Besh said, his voice as cold and hard as Grinsa had ever heard it.

The last thing Grinsa wanted was for Q'Daer to express his doubts about whether the Mettai really had saved them.

"This isn't helping any of us," he said, before Q'Daer could answer. He turned to Besh and Sirj. "We need to find some way to convince E'Menua that the two of you aren't threats to the sept."

"I would have thought that the spell we cast protecting all of you from Lici's plague had done that already."

Perhaps there was no way to avoid this conversation.

Grinsa looked at Cresenne. "Tell them."

She gazed back at him, clearly reluctant.

He took her hand again. "It has to be you. Coming from Q'Daer, it'll sound too belligerent. And I'm not the one who spoke to F'Solya."

Cresenne nodded and raked her free hand through her hair. Grinsa couldn't help but smile at the gesture—it was so familiar, and yet it had been so long since he'd last seen her do it.

"What is it you want her to tell us?" Besh asked.

"Many in the sept don't believe that your spell will protect them," Cresenne answered, facing the two Mettai. "Some think that the magic simply won't work. Others . . ." She took a breath, her eyes flicking briefly in Grinsa's direction. "Others wonder if you're trying to trick them into risking their lives. They think you want them to believe that the spell will protect them, but—"

"I understand," Besh said, despair in his dark eyes.

He stared off to the side. It took Grinsa a moment to realize that he was looking at one of the guards.

"So the fact that I killed Lici means nothing?" the old man asked after a lengthy silence. He faced Grinsa again. "The necklace given to us by F'Ghara means nothing?" His voice rose as he spoke. "The spell we cast to cure you and Q'Daer of the plague means nothing?"

"You were given the necklace before we knew of the coming war," Q'Daer said, surprising Grinsa with his tone, which was as gentle as Besh's had been harsh. "And there are those who would believe that you sickened us and then cured us to win our trust."

Besh let out a bark of laughter, high-pitched and abrupt.

"Whose mind works that way? Who would do such a thing?"

"Lici," Sirj said in a low voice. "She would have done it."

This was met with another silence, though after a moment Besh gave a small nod, as if conceding the point.

After some time Besh raised his eyes to look at Cresenne. "The person who voiced these doubts to you, does he wield much influence with the a'laq?"

"It was a woman," she said. "And no, neither she nor her husband has much influence with E'Menua. But I believe that the doubts she voiced to me are fairly typical. They've been kinder to me than have most people in this settlement, but in other ways they're very much like the rest of the sept."

Besh nodded again, looking from Cresenne to Grinsa and finally to Q'Daer. "So," he began. "Do you think that we cursed you with the plague and then healed you so that you'd trust us?"

"I'm certain that you didn't," Q'Daer told him. "It was Torgan."

"Have you said as much to your a'laq?"

Q'Daer hesitated, then shook his head.

"Why not?" Sirj asked.

The Fal'Borna cast a dark look at Grinsa before answering. "Because while I'm sure that Torgan made me sick," he said, "I'm not entirely convinced that you hadn't intended to do the same thing."

Grinsa gaped at him. "What?"

"Don't look so surprised, Forelander. I told you again and again that they might band together against us. The Mettai may wield magic, but their eyes are dark. Their blood is Eandi."

This was true. Several times after Besh and Sirj joined their company on the plain, Q'Daer voiced concerns about the Mettai or the merchants striking at them, or even joining forces against them. At the time, Grinsa had dismissed the Fal'Borna's suspicions. He believed then, as he did now, that Besh and Sirj were sincerely interested in stopping Lici and

her curse. But with an army of Eandi warriors and Mettai
sorcerers now advancing across the plain, he could see why
Q'Daer would be even less inclined to trust these two men.

He'd urged Besh and Sirj to leave the plain while they still
could. Now he wished that he'd insisted.

"I'm sorry," Q'Daer said to the Mettai, frowning deeply.
"I didn't want to say any of this, but the Forelander wanted
me to come here with him, and I didn't feel that I should lie
to you."

"I didn't make you sick," Besh said, sounding angry. "Neither of us did. We've left our home, our family, just so that
we could keep Lici's plague from killing any more of your
people. And now you think—" He looked away, his lips pressed
thin, his chest rising and falling. "We never wanted to hurt
anyone."

Q'Daer shrugged. "Our people are at war."

"Sirj and I aren't."

The Fal'Borna started to reply, but then stopped himself.
Grinsa thought he could guess what he'd intended to say. To
the Fal'Borna, clan was everything. Q'Daer could no more
imagine these two Mettai refusing to follow their people
to war than he could imagine himself marrying an Eandi
woman.

"So what happens now?" Grinsa asked, looking at Q'Daer.

"What do you mean, what happens? We'll be riding to
war before long. The Mettai will remain here."

"As guests," Besh said, a bitter smile on his lips. "How
fortunate for us. How long will it be before your a'laq decides to execute us as enemies of your people?"

Q'Daer's mouth twitched. "I don't know."

"But you think it's possible that he will?" Grinsa demanded.

The Fal'Borna exhaled, then nodded. "Yes."

Grinsa glanced at Besh, who was already regarding him,
looking grim. "I tried to tell you to go home," Grinsa said.

"If we'd gone when you told us to, you'd be dead." Besh
looked sidelong at Q'Daer. "Both of you would be."

"What can we do?" Grinsa asked the Fal'Borna.

"Nothing. If the a'laq decides that the Mettai are to be killed, they'll die."

"Right. And I'm asking you what we can do to convince him not to make that decision."

Q'Daer's expression hardened. "Have you listened to anything I've said? I don't trust these men!"

"Mind-bending."

Grinsa and Q'Daer both looked at Cresenne.

"What?" Grinsa asked.

"One of you could use mind-bending magic on them. Force them to tell you the truth about what they did and what their intentions are."

"I've had mind-bending used on me before," Sirj said, looking doubtful. "By F'Ghara. I wouldn't be eager to have it done again. It's . . . unnerving."

Besh laid a hand on the younger man's arm. "I'll do it," he said.

Grinsa turned to Q'Daer. "Would that convince you?"

The man frowned. "I've . . . I've never used that magic. I wouldn't know how, and I don't want to . . . to damage him."

Besh paled.

"Then I can do it," Grinsa told him.

"You could make him say anything."

Grinsa threw up his hands. "So you don't trust yourself to do it, but you don't trust me, either."

"I trust the a'laq."

"No," Grinsa said, shaking his head. "I don't trust him. He'll bend Besh's words just to spite me."

"D'Pera, then," Cresenne said. "The n'qlae."

"I haven't had many dealings with her," Grinsa said, discomfited by the suggestion. "Do you trust her?"

"I think so. I don't like her, but I think she'd be fair. And E'Menua is far more likely to be convinced if she wields the magic."

Grinsa couldn't argue with that. He turned back to Besh. "What do you think?"

"I'd rather the Fal'Borna simply let us go," the Mettai man said. "But if my choice is between subjecting myself to this magic and being executed as an enemy of the clan, I'll take my chances with the magic."

"The a'laq will never agree to this," Q'Daer said, shaking his head. "You can't go to him and suggest that the n'qlae use her magic on the Mettai because you don't trust him to deal with you honestly. I'm offended by the idea of it. He'll be outraged."

"He'll agree," Grinsa said. "And he'll have no right to be angry, since he will have insulted me first."

early on, when he and Cresenne first arrived in the sept, Grinsa had felt that the a'laq was always one step ahead of him, anticipating his every attempt to win their freedom. He'd allowed himself to be drawn into the demon's bargain that had almost forced him to remain with the Fal'Borna when his search for Lici failed. A few turns later, he and Cresenne had yet to find a way to leave the sept, but at least now he knew what to expect from E'Menua.

He started their discussion with an earnest appeal to the a'laq to trust Besh and Sirj. "They saved my life," he told the man, again. "They saved Q'Daer. Why don't you believe they're our allies?"

"Because," E'Menua said, so predictable it was almost funny, "their kind have marched to war against us. They are no better than the dark-eyes with whom they've allied themselves."

"With all due respect, A'Laq, I believe you're wrong about them," Grinsa told him. "These other Mettai might have cast their lot with the Eandi, but Besh and Sirj are different. They're our friends. F'Ghara acknowledged as much when he gave them his stone."

"F'Ghara is a fool. He leads a sept with no Weavers. And even the Mettai admit that he gave them his stone before the war began. The war changes everything."

"I can prove to you that they can be trusted," Grinsa said.

"Let me use mind-bending magic on them. We can ask them whatever you want; they'll have no choice but to tell us the truth."

E'Menua frowned. Apparently he hadn't expected this. All the better.

"No," he said.

"Why not, A'Laq?"

"This is a waste of time. I need to be preparing my warriors for battle, not arguing with you about these two dark-eye sorcerers."

"All the more reason to do what I'm asking of you. Right now you have a dozen warriors posted around their z'kal. Those men should be readying themselves for war. We can settle this in just a few moments, if you'll let me do this."

E'Menua shook his head.

Come on! Grinsa pleaded silently. *Say it! You know you want to.* He kept silent, though, watching the a'laq, an expectant look on his face.

When E'Menua didn't say anything more, Grinsa tried to give him one last push.

"Suit yourself then," he finally said, turning as if to leave E'Menua's shelter. "I'll question the men myself. I'll have Q'Daer with me. He can tell you what they said."

"It won't mean anything," the a'laq told him.

"Why not?" Grinsa asked, his back still to the man.

"Because there's nothing to stop you from twisting their words."

There it was. Grinsa smiled, then quickly schooled his features and faced him again.

"You think I'd lie to you about this?"

"Not lie," E'Menua said, seeming to choose his words with care. "But you'll be controlling them. You can make them say whatever suits your needs. You want to save their lives, and you might be inclined to keep them from saying anything that would lead me to execute them."

"Then what would you suggest?"

The a'laq grinned, as if he already knew what Grinsa would say. "I could question them using my magic."

"And how can I be sure that you wouldn't make them say what you want to hear?"

"What would that be?" E'Menua asked.

"Whatever it would take to give you an excuse to kill them."

The a'laq gave a small shrug. "I don't suppose you can be sure. As I said, this is a waste of time."

He didn't rush to it; he didn't want to give E'Menua any indication that he'd been thinking along these lines from the start. Once more he made as if to leave, going so far as to push aside the piece of rilda skin covering the entrance to the z'kal. But then he stopped himself.

"What about another Weaver?" he asked, looking at E'Menua again. "What about the n'qlae?"

The Fal'Borna narrowed his eyes. Clearly he hadn't expected this, either. "D'Pera?"

"We both trust her. She wields the magic. Why not?"

"When would we do this?" E'Menua asked, suddenly wary.

Grinsa didn't want to give him time to discuss any of this with the n'qlae. He trusted the woman to a point, but there could be no denying where her loyalties lay. If E'Menua had the opportunity to turn her to his purposes, he would.

"Now," Grinsa said. "Besh and Sirj are being treated like prisoners and they deserve better. They might even be convinced to help us in this war, but first we have to win their trust."

E'Menua stared back at him, seeming to have recognized too late that he'd been manipulated. For a moment Grinsa feared that the a'laq would refuse to allow D'Pera to question the men. But then E'Menua stood and nodded once.

"Very well. We'll find her now."

Grinsa had been expecting more of a fight, and now he wondered if the a'laq intended to deceive him somehow.

But E'Menua stepped past Grinsa and led him out of the

z'kal. Q'Daer and Cresenne were waiting for them outside the shelter. Seeing them both, the a'laq faltered briefly and shot a dark look back at Grinsa. But he said nothing and started across the sept. Grinsa and the others followed.

"What happened?" Cresenne asked in a whisper as they walked.

"The n'qlae will question the Mettai."

Cresenne looked like she might say more, but Grinsa shook his head.

They found the n'qlae near the tanning circle, where she was overseeing the shaping of spears. Grinsa had met D'Pera before, but once again he was struck by her appearance. She was beautiful, with thick, long white hair that she wore unbound, and a hard, hawklike gaze that seemed to miss nothing.

Seeing her husband approach, she stood.

"Has something happened?" she asked.

E'Menua shook his head. "No. I need you to speak with the Mettai. I want you to use mind-bending magic on them. Find out what they intend to do to us." He glanced quickly at Grinsa. "I believe this is the only way we're likely to know if they can be trusted."

D'Pera looked from her husband to Grinsa to Cresenne, and finally back to E'Menua. "All right," she said. "You wish to do this now?"

The a'laq nodded. "Yes, now."

D'Pera looked around, seeming unsure as to whether she could just leave what she'd been doing. After a moment, though, she appeared to decide that she could. She and E'Menua began walking in the direction of Besh and Sirj's shelter. Once more, Grinsa, Cresenne, and Q'Daer could only follow.

"This is too easy," Cresenne said under her breath.

She was right. E'Menua had agreed to all of this too quickly; he'd been too willing to enlist D'Pera's help and approach the Mettai right away. But Grinsa was at a loss as to what they could do about it.

"You may be right," he whispered in reply. "But I started this. We have to see it through to the end."

She nodded, looking tense.

As they neared Besh and Sirj's shelter, Grinsa saw that the two Mettai were sitting outside, just as they had been earlier. Two of the Fal'Borna guards stood nearby, watching the men. The guards bowed to E'Menua when they saw him approaching. Besh and Sirj stood.

"Leave us," the a'laq told the two warriors without breaking stride.

"Yes, A'Laq."

The guards bowed again and started to walk toward two of their comrades who stood some distance from the shelter.

Before they'd gone far, though, E'Menua appeared to reconsider. "Actually, I want you to remain here," he called to the men.

They stopped, looking confused, but then quickly reassumed the positions they'd been in before.

E'Menua stopped in front of Besh and Sirj, regarding the two Mettai with obvious mistrust.

"You know why I'm here?" he asked.

Besh's eyes flicked toward Grinsa.

"Don't look at him!" the a'laq said sharply. "When I speak, you look at me!"

"Yes, A'Laq," Besh said evenly, meeting the Fal'Borna's gaze. "I know why you're here. You want to use magic to determine if we're telling you the truth."

E'Menua nodded. "Yes, that's right. The n'qlae will be using her magic on you." It was his turn to glance in Grinsa's direction, a thin smile on his feline face. "The Forelander and I don't trust each other enough to do it ourselves."

"I've never had this magic done to me before," Besh said. He looked pale and small next to the a'laq. The two men were about the same height, but E'Menua was by far the broader and more powerful of the two.

"You have nothing to fear," D'Pera told him. Grinsa heard

nothing comforting in her tone. The woman's expression remained deadly serious. "The a'laq will ask you questions. I'll simply use my magic to ensure that you answer truthfully."

Besh didn't appear reassured. "I've heard some say that this magic can . . . can damage a person, leave them permanently addled."

"That's very rare," Grinsa told him. "And it's most likely to happen when the magic is forced upon a person and he or she tries to resist. You're allowing us to do this, and I'm sure the n'qlae's touch will be gentle. You shouldn't be in any danger."

The Mettai man nodded and smiled weakly.

"Are you ready?" D'Pera asked him.

"Yes."

There was a brief silence, and then D'Pera looked at her husband and nodded once. Grinsa had never watched another Qirsi use mind-bending magic on someone. He'd done it himself several times, but that was different. He now realized that his perceptions of what the magic did to people had been colored by what he sensed in their thoughts. As far as he could tell, nothing had happened to Besh. He looked exactly the same; his expression hadn't changed at all. Granted, D'Pera wasn't attempting to control him, as some Qirsi did with this power; she was merely making certain that he didn't lie. Nevertheless, seeing the magic in this way reminded him of why mind-bending was viewed by many in the Forelands as the most dangerous and insidious of Qirsi magics. A cunning sorcerer could exert control over the unsuspecting with no one realizing it. A merchant could be coerced into parting with gold; a noble could be tricked into condemning an innocent man; a king could be compelled to lead his people to war.

"Where do you come from?" E'Menua asked Besh.

"Kirayde, near the Companion Lakes."

"Why did you leave your village?"

"Lici had gone, and then people started getting sick. I

believed that she was responsible for the plague and I wanted to stop her before more people died."

"Where is this Lici now?"

"I killed her. She attacked me and I had no choice."

E'Menua glanced at Grinsa, looking slightly disappointed.

"So you killed this woman," the a'laq went on. "But you stayed here on the plain after she was dead. Why?"

"To find her baskets. They were cursed and I knew that they'd spread the plague."

Grinsa chanced a quick look at Q'Daer, who was already eyeing him. The young Weaver held Grinsa's gaze for a moment, and then gave a quick, small nod. Grinsa had to smile. Q'Daer at least was convinced.

"How did Q'Daer and the Forelander get sick?"

"The merchant—Torgan—he exposed them to the plague. He used a scrap of basket that we'd found in another sept, one that had been destroyed already."

"And you were working with him, is that right?"

"Yes. Sirj and I were going to sicken them ourselves if Torgan hadn't. Then we could heal them and win their trust."

Grinsa felt like he'd been punched in the stomach. He stared at Besh, who looked panicked, his eyes wide and darting from face to face. E'Menua had a harsh, triumphant grin on his face. D'Pera was watching her husband. Grinsa couldn't be certain, but she appeared unnerved.

"And this spell you created that was supposed to shield us from the plague," the a'laq said. "Will it work?"

"No. That was a lie. If you're exposed to the plague, all of you will die."

"Of course. That was part of your plan as well, wasn't it?"

"Yes," Besh said, even as the look in his dark eyes screamed, *No!*

Chapter 11

✦✛✦

At first the sensation had merely been odd. As soon as the n'qlae reached forth with her magic, Besh was aware of her presence in his mind. It wasn't intrusive; as Grinsa had promised, her touch was light. But there could be no mistaking the fact that something alien had stepped into his thoughts. When the a'laq asked him the first question, Besh answered without thinking, without fully intending to speak. One moment he was listening and the next, words were coming out of his mouth. It felt strange, even a bit frightening. But he could hear what he was saying, and he knew that it was the truth, and so he didn't resist.

So it went for several moments: a question and then his answer. He didn't have to think or struggle to find the right word. Almost as soon as the thoughts formed in his head, he gave them voice. There was something quite comfortable about it; he could see how easy it might be for a Qirsi to take control of another person's thoughts.

Then, abruptly, it all changed. At first, for just an instant, he thought that the n'qlae had tightened her control over him. Suddenly her touch wasn't light anymore. It felt like a powerful hand had taken hold of his head and thrust him underwater, intent on drowning him. He tried to fight, to shake off the hand. And that was when he realized that it wasn't the woman after all. He still felt her presence. He even sensed her emotions. Confusion, anger, and something else that he couldn't name. But her touch remained as gentle as ever.

It had to be the a'laq. Or perhaps Q'Daer. He refused to believe that Grinsa would do this to him; he didn't think that the Forelander's wife could. And he thought it unlikely that the guards would dare to interfere.

All of this occurred to him in the span of a single heart-beat, the time it took him to realize that another had control of his thoughts. Then he heard the things this second sorcerer was making him say, and terror gripped his heart.

Sirj and I were going to sicken them ourselves. . . . If you're exposed to the plague, all of you will die. . . .

He'd heard Grinsa's warnings about not fighting the magic, but he didn't care. What did it matter whether his mind remained sound if the Fal'Borna were going to execute him and Sirj? He fought with all his might, though he had no idea how to throw off such magic. He tried to reach for his knife so that he might conjure a spell—any spell—to win his freedom. He tried to scream that these weren't his words.

But he was utterly helpless. He could no more lift a hand in his own defense than he could fly to the sun.

He looked from face to face, seeking help from any of them. The guards eyed him with contempt, and perhaps a hint of fear. The a'laq grinned back at him, seeming to relish what he saw on Besh's face. The n'qlae wasn't looking at him at all, but instead had her eyes fixed on her husband. Grinsa, Cresenne, and Sirj appeared horrified, as if they knew just what had happened, but didn't know how to make matters right again.

And Q'Daer. To Besh's surprise, the young Fal'Borna looked both troubled and confused, as if he didn't want to believe what he'd heard Besh say, but knew he had no choice but to believe it.

The a'laq had done this for the young Weaver. In that moment Besh was as certain of this as he was of his own name. Neither Grinsa nor Cresenne would ever be convinced that he and Sirj were murderers. But Q'Daer was more than willing to believe this of them. And now he would be certain. He'd tell others in the sept what Besh had said here, and they would share his certainty.

"Let him go," Grinsa said, stepping forward to stand beside Besh and glaring at E'Menua. It seemed that the Forelander understood exactly what had happened.

An instant later, that firm hand was gone from his mind. And then the n'qlae withdrew her magic as well.

Freed from their control, Besh actually staggered forward. Then, righting himself with Grinsa's aid, he fixed the a'laq with as cold a look as he could muster.

"You bastard!" he said.

The guards started forward, brandishing their spears. Q'Daer pulled his knife from his belt, and E'Menua practically launched himself at Besh, a wild look on his face.

But Grinsa put himself between Besh and the a'laq.

"Out of my way, Forelander!" E'Menua said, the words coming out like a growl. "No one speaks to me like that! Especially not a dark-eye sorcerer!"

Grinsa held his ground.

"I said, get out of my way!"

The a'laq reared back, his fist clenched. Besh was certain he was going to hit the Forelander, who didn't raise a hand in his own defense.

Cresenne shouted the Forelander's name in warning.

But suddenly E'Menua froze, his eyes widening.

"Step back," Grinsa said calmly, though his eyes glittered dangerously.

E'Menua didn't move. He just continued to stare at Grinsa, his hand still raised.

"I'll do it if I have to, A'Laq. Don't make me."

Slowly the a'laq lowered his hand and straightened. "You heard what he said. He as much as admitted that they're enemies of our people. And still you protect him?"

"He said what you made him say."

"I didn't make him say anything!" the a'laq shot back. But the denial sounded hollow and forced.

"I think you did."

E'Menua narrowed his eyes. "Tread carefully, Forelander. You're coming very close to calling me a liar."

"Am I?" Grinsa said, sounding unconcerned. "Perhaps we should ask the n'qlae what happened."

E'Menua smiled. "Yes, let's." He turned to his wife. "Did the Mettai speak truthfully?" he asked.

She regarded her husband for just a moment before lowering her gaze. "Yes, A'Laq. He answered questions truthfully."

"All of them?" Grinsa demanded.

Her eyes flicked toward him, then returned to E'Menua. "As long as my magic held him, he couldn't tell a lie."

Grinsa opened his mouth, as if to question her further. Before he could, however, she turned and hurried away, back toward the z'kal she shared with E'Menua.

"You see?" the a'laq said, looking pleased with himself. "It's just as I told you. These men want to destroy us. They used you and Q'Daer to win our trust, but they're enemies of the Fal'Borna, just like those Mettai who march against us with the Eandi army."

"I felt your magic on my mind," Besh said. "I felt the n'qlae's and I felt yours as well. You made me say those things at the end. I'd been telling the truth until then."

"I'd expect you to say as much," E'Menua told him coldly. "You'll say anything now to save your life." He beckoned to the guards with a wave of his hand.

Immediately the two men strode forward, eager, it seemed, to exact revenge for the evils to which Besh had been forced to confess.

"Take their knives," E'Menua said, indicating Besh and Sirj. "I don't want them using their magic against us anymore. We'll keep them here for now. They're to remain in their z'kal." He looked at Grinsa. "And they're not to speak with anyone."

"Try to stop me from speaking to them," Grinsa said.

E'Menua glowered at him, but appeared to think better of challenging the man. "Fine," the a'laq said after a brief, uneasy silence. "No one else, though." He waved disdainfully at Grinsa and Cresenne. "Just these two."

"Yes, A'Laq," one of the warriors said, scowling at Grinsa.

E'Menua turned to Q'Daer. "You'll come with me."

He started away, not even bothering to look at Grinsa again. Q'Daer hesitated, staring first at Besh and Sirj, and then at the Forelander. After a moment he turned and fell in step behind the a'laq.

"In the z'kal," the first guard said, indicating the shelter with a wave of his spear.

"They're going to talk to us out here," Grinsa said, his voice seeming to grow more taut by the moment.

The Fal'Borna shook his head. "The a'laq just said—"

"I don't care what he said! We'll see to it that they don't escape. But you're not going to make the four of us crowd into that shelter."

"The a'laq—"

Before the man could finish what he was going to say, he suddenly gave a strangled cry and let go of his spear so quickly one might have thought the weapon's shaft had grown too hot to touch. The spear hit the ground and immediately shattered. Actually, Besh realized, shattered wasn't the right word. The wood exploded, fracturing into thousands of tiny splinters.

The guard stared down at it, wide-eyed, mouth agape.

Grinsa nodded with grim satisfaction. "I'll do that to every spear in the sept if I have to. Now get away from us so we can talk."

The Fal'Borna looked up at the Forelander, saying nothing, fear and rage mingling on his square face and making him look young. After a few moments he and the other guard turned and strode toward the nearest of their comrades.

"You're just giving E'Menua more reason to be angry," Cresenne said, her voice so low that Besh wasn't certain he had heard her correctly.

Grinsa scowled at her.

She didn't flinch from that look. Besh doubted that he could have been so brave. "You know it's true," she went on. "He's been looking for reasons to condemn these two and make you an outcast in the sept. And you just keep giving them to him."

The Forelander exhaled sharply and looked away, his expression softening into something more akin to a grimace. "You're right," he said. He looked at Besh and Sirj. "Forgive me. I haven't handled any of this very well."

Sirj shook his head. "I'm not sure it's your fault."

"I think most of it is," Grinsa said. "I was so certain that we could use the n'qlae to keep E'Menua from doing any harm. I was wrong. And what Cresenne said is true: I've been provoking the a'laq at every turn. I can't seem to stop myself."

"So is there anything we can do?" Besh asked.

"There has to be," Grinsa said. "I'm not going to let these people execute you. I'll fight off every one of them if I have to."

"You've been trying that," Cresenne told him, softening the words with a smile. "Maybe we should try something different."

Besh wondered if the Forelander would grow angry again. But the man smiled and took her hand.

"Point taken," he said. "You have something in mind?"

The woman shrugged. "You could try talking to Q'Daer."

"Yes!" Besh said quickly, drawing the gazes of all three of them. "When they were using their magic on me, and E'Menua was making me say those things, I had the distinct impression that he was doing it for Q'Daer."

"Of course," Grinsa agreed. "He was with us on the plain. We've been claiming all along that you saved his life as well as mine. If E'Menua can convince him that this isn't true, he can convince every Fal'Borna in the sept."

"Will he listen to you?" Cresenne asked.

"I don't know. I get along with him only slightly better than I do with E'Menua. But I'll try."

Cresenne nodded, then faced Besh again. "Did the n'qlae do what she promised she would?"

Besh frowned. "What do you mean?"

"Did she let you tell the truth? Are you sure it was E'Menua and not she who made you say those things at the end?"

He nodded. "I'm sure. She had a light touch. She compelled me to speak, but that was all. The magic that forced me to lie came from someone else."

"All right, then," she said, gazing off in the direction the n'qlae had gone when she left them.

"You're going to speak with her?" Grinsa asked.

"I'm going to try. She probably won't listen to me. The last time we spoke she basically accused me of trying to steal her husband."

Grinsa raised an eyebrow. "You never told me that."

"It wasn't worth telling." She looked at the two Mettai. "It was my idea to use mind-bending magic, which makes me as responsible as Grinsa for what happened here. I'll find some way to undo the damage we've done."

"This isn't good."

Besh looked at Sirj, who had spoken, and then turned in the direction the younger man was looking. The two guards Grinsa had sent away were returning with four more warriors.

"They can't hurt you while I'm here," Grinsa said.

"No," Cresenne said. "But they can once we're gone. Don't provoke them."

Besh heard Grinsa exhale through his teeth.

"Again, she's right," the Forelander said, looking at Besh. "You should go into the shelter. We'll do what we can."

Just a few hours before, Besh had marveled at the comfort of the z'kal and had been more than happy to call the structure his home for a few days. Now that it had become a prison rather than a shelter, he was loath to step foot in it. He knew, though, that they had no choice.

"We don't blame you for any of this," he said quickly. "It was the a'laq's doing. We know that. But we'll be grateful for any help you can give us."

Grinsa nodded. "We won't rest until you're free."

"Come on," Sirj said, pulling aside the flap of rilda skin

that covered the entrance to the shelter and motioning Besh inside.

Besh glanced back at the approaching warriors one more time and then slipped into the shelter. Sirj followed him. It was dark within, and it felt far smaller than it had when he awoke that morning.

"They're in the z'kal," Besh heard Grinsa say. "And I understand that you've been ordered to guard them. But if I hear that any of you has put so much as a toe inside that shelter, if I hear that you've threatened or abused those men in any way, I'll kill every one of you. You understand me?"

Besh didn't hear any reply from the Fal'Borna, nor did he hear Grinsa or Cresenne say anything more. After some time he assumed that the two of them had moved off, she to find the n'qlae, he to find Q'Daer. He looked at Sirj again, feeling that he should offer some word of reassurance. But nothing came to him. He lay down on his pallet and closed his eyes.

Cresenne looked for D'Pera in the same place they had found her earlier, but the woman wasn't there. She knew better than to go to the shelter D'Pera and E'Menua shared. Even if the n'qlae was there, Cresenne couldn't approach her for fear of letting the a'laq know what she was doing. She walked to the tanning circle, but didn't find D'Pera there, either. She was about to give up her search when she spotted a lone figure walking near the horse paddock.

She set out in that direction, but before she had gone far, one of the young Fal'Borna girls who cared for Bryntelle intercepted her, telling her that Bryntelle was crying and appeared to be hungry.

Cursing her foolishness and feeling somewhat ashamed for having forgotten her child, Cresenne followed the girl. As the young Fal'Borna had surmised, Bryntelle was ravenous and nursed greedily for far longer than she usually did. By the time Cresenne had finished feeding her and had changed her swaddling, she felt certain that whomever it was who had been out near the paddock would be gone. To her surprise, though, that lone figure was still there. It almost seemed that he or she hadn't moved at all.

Cresenne hurried toward the figure. A bank of low dark clouds had rolled in over the plain, and a cold wind now flattened the grass that surrounded the sept. Before she had gone far, Cresenne could see that it was in fact the n'qlae she'd seen. The woman stood with her back to the sept, her wrap pulled tight around her shoulders, her long white hair dancing fitfully in the gale.

Cresenne knew that the n'qlae wouldn't hear her approach over the wind, which hissed in the grass and whistled in the wood of the paddock. So when she was a short distance from the woman, she cleared her throat.

D'Pera turned quickly, saw who had come, and turned her back again, though not before giving Cresenne a sour look.

"I don't wish to be disturbed right now," she said, the words barely reaching Cresenne.

"No," Cresenne said. "I don't imagine you do."

D'Pera faced her again, a hard expression on her handsome face. "Meaning what?"

"I think you know exactly what I mean, N'Qlae."

The woman glared at her for several seconds. "I think you should go," she said at last, "before you get yourself in more trouble than you can handle."

Cresenne made herself hold the woman's gaze. She was trembling. She knew that she had already crossed a line with the woman, and that if D'Pera were to kill her where she stood, E'Menua and every other Fal'Borna in the sept would think her justified in doing so.

But back in the Forelands Cresenne had been victimized time and again by the renegade Weaver and his servants. She had been raped, stabbed, and poisoned, and yet she had survived. She'd vowed that she would never allow herself to be treated that way again, and she refused to allow this woman to intimidate her.

Cresenne also sensed that D'Pera had been disturbed

by what E'Menua had done to Besh. She intended to make the woman admit as much; she just hoped that she could do this without getting herself killed in the process.

"You think you're brave," D'Pera said icily. "You stand there, brazen, showing me no respect at all, and you think that I won't hurt you because your man is a Weaver. You and he are exactly alike. You show contempt for all Fal'Borna. You do your best to humiliate my husband. I should kill you. You deserve no less."

"You're wrong about us," Cresenne said, struggling to keep her voice steady. "All we've ever wanted is to be free, to come and go as we please. The a'laq has made us feel like prisoners since the day we arrived here." She could hear that her voice was rising, but now that she had started down this path, she couldn't stop herself. "He's done his best to drive a wedge between Grinsa and me. And the one time you and I spoke, you practically called me a whore! So before you accuse us of showing contempt for the Fal'Borna, you might want to consider how we've been treated!"

She stopped, breathing hard. Just a short while before, she had warned Grinsa about provoking the a'laq. Now she'd done much the same thing with his wife. What was it about these two that brought out the worst in them?

Cresenne drew breath, intending to apologize for her outburst. But before she could form the words, she felt a sudden sharp pressure on her throat. She couldn't speak; she couldn't exhale. It seemed that someone had wrapped a powerful hand around her neck, though the n'qlae hadn't moved. Cresenne began to panic. She even reached up with a hand, as if she might pry those invisible fingers away from her neck. Then she let the hand drop to her side. She closed her eyes and tried to calm herself. She still couldn't breathe, but she didn't think that the woman had it in mind to do anything more than scare her. D'Pera was a Weaver. If she'd truly wanted Cresenne dead, she could have snapped her neck with a thought.

After a few more harrowing seconds, the pressure on her

throat vanished. Cresenne took a long shuddering breath and opened her eyes again, swaying slightly as her vision swam. When she could focus again, she saw that the n'qlae was regarding her with obvious curiosity.

"You may have some courage after all," the woman said.

"Thank you, N'Qlae."

"What did you think would happen here today?" D'Pera asked. "Did you think I'd . . . ?" She pressed her lips in a thin line, looking away briefly before facing Cresenne once more. "What did you think I'd say?"

Cresenne shrugged. "I don't know. I believe that you did just what Grinsa and I hoped you would. You allowed Besh to tell us the truth. But I also think that something else happened back there, something that you weren't expecting. Something that troubled you."

D'Pera looked away. "You're wrong." She kept her voice low. Cresenne heard no anger in her denial.

"Besh felt a second presence in his mind. Someone forced him to say those things about making Grinsa and Q'Daer sick, and about the protective spell not being real."

"Of course he'd say that," the n'qlae said, still not looking at her. The words were just what Cresenne would have expected, but D'Pera's voice sounded flat, passionless. "He'd probably say anything to save his life and that of the other man."

"I was struck by what you said before, when Grinsa asked you if Besh had responded truthfully to every question. You said that as long as your magic controlled him he couldn't tell a lie."

"Yes. That's right."

"But as soon as the a'laq began to use his magic on Besh, you weren't controlling him anymore, were you?"

"The a'laq did no such thing."

Cresenne said nothing. She couldn't challenge this statement without calling the n'qlae a liar, and thus putting her own life at risk, but she refused to accept the woman's denials. So she merely stood there, staring at the n'qlae, waiting for her to say more.

For a long time D'Pera kept silent as well. She began to fidget, clearly uncomfortable under Cresenne's gaze. Finally she looked away again.

"What is it you want from me?" she asked.

"I want you to tell me what really happened."

"Why? You can't save them, you know. The Mettai have made themselves enemies of the Fal'Borna."

"Not these Mettai. These men have done nothing wrong. They saved my husband's life, and Q'Daer's, too. They created a spell that will save us all. You know this is true, regardless of what E'Menua made Besh say."

"You don't understand the Southlands. You haven't been here long enough. You haven't grown up in the shadow of the Blood Wars."

"I understand it better than you think. The Forelands had its share of trouble before Grinsa and I left. And if the Eandi king who decided my fate had thought as you do, I'd be dead."

D'Pera shook her head and stared off toward the western horizon, where a smudge of rain had appeared just below the dark clouds.

"You can't save them," she said quietly. "No one can. E'Menua has made up his mind, and that's the end of it."

"You can save them, N'Qlae. You may be the only one who has that power now. The a'laq is your husband and you love him. I understand that, as well. But he used you, and you let him. And unless you do something to stop him, two innocent men are going to die."

The n'qlae looked at her, her expression bleak. Cresenne hoped that D'Pera would say more, at least to admit that E'Menua had used his magic on Besh. But the woman remained silent. For her part, Cresenne had said all that she could. If she went on, she risked angering D'Pera further, and she knew that she'd already made her point. Either the n'qlae would heed her words or she wouldn't. So after staring back at the woman for a moment or two, she turned and started toward the sept.

Thoughts swarmed through Q'Daer's mind like flies in the middle of the Growing. He should have been pleased. The Mettai had admitted that he was an enemy of the Fal'Borna, proving that Q'Daer had been right to doubt him, and that Grinsa had been a fool to place his trust in the dark-eye sorcerers. The rift between the Forelander and E'Menua had never been greater, which meant that Q'Daer's status as the a'laq's most trusted Weaver, aside from D'Pera of course, was secure. In every way, the day had been a good one for him.

Yet he felt sick to his stomach. He hadn't realized it until the moment when E'Menua began questioning the old Mettai man, but he wanted to believe that the dark-eye sorcerers had saved his life. He wanted to go to sleep at night secure in the knowledge that their spell would protect every Fal'Borna on the plain from the curse of the Mettai witch, which remained a threat to them even though the woman herself was dead. Most of all, he wanted to believe that the a'laq had allowed the Mettai man to speak the truth. He wanted to be certain that the leader of his sept hadn't used his magic to make the man lie. And he wasn't sure of this. Not at all.

"Something is troubling you," the a'laq said, as they made their way past the z'kals of his people toward E'Menua's shelter. The a'laq offered this quietly, as a statement rather than as a question. But Q'Daer felt as though he had demanded the truth. He felt as though E'Menua was holding a knife to his throat.

"It's . . . it's nothing, A'Laq."

E'Menua looked at him, raising an eyebrow.

"I . . . I had hoped the Mettai's spell would protect us. I'm disappointed. That's all."

"Ah, of course," E'Menua said, nodding. "I understand. You journeyed with the Mettai for many leagues. You'd come to believe that they might be our friends."

"Yes, A'Laq. I had hoped it was so."

"No doubt the Forelander tried to convince you of this."

"He trusts them, yes."

"But do you trust him?"

Q'Daer stared at the ground. He could feel the a'laq's eyes upon him, but at that moment he didn't dare meet the man's gaze.

All of this should have been so simple. He was Fal'Borna. Nothing else mattered. Hadn't he said as much to Grinsa a hundred times as they traveled across the plain together? The Forelander had refused to submit to the a'laq's authority. He had spent every moment of the last several turns trying to leave the sept, making it clear that he wanted nothing to do with the Fal'Borna or their traditions. Q'Daer had no reason to trust him. Faced with a conflict between the Forelander and the Mettai on one hand, and the a'laq and his people on the other, there should have been no question as to where his loyalties lay.

But on this day nothing seemed as clear as it should. If he was to be honest with himself, he had to admit that he didn't just want to believe the Mettai. He *did* believe him. He didn't merely wish that Grinsa had been right about all of this. He felt certain that the Forelander was right.

And that meant that the a'laq had deceived them.

He did it to protect the sept, said a voice inside his mind. *We're at war! Nothing matters more than the safety of our people.*

But what threat did these Mettai pose? They had saved his life, and Grinsa's, too. They had cast that spell.

You heard Besh! There was no spell. It was a trick. Nothing more.

Yes, he had heard what the Mettai said. But he had seen the look on the old man's face. More, he had seen the look on D'Pera's face. He had seen how she stared at the a'laq, an accusation in her pale eyes. E'Menua had betrayed her. He had betrayed all of them.

"I asked you a question, Q'Daer. Do you trust the Forelander?"

But that really wasn't the question he had asked, or was asking now. E'Menua wanted to know what kind of man he was. He wanted to know if Q'Daer was willing to sacrifice a pair of dark-eye sorcerers for the good of the sept. He wanted to make certain that Q'Daer would remain true to his a'laq no matter what.

Are you Fal'Borna? That was what E'Menua had asked him.

He shouldn't have needed even to think about it.

"I don't believe the Forelander means to harm us, A'Laq. I think he'll fight beside us when it comes time to face the dark-eyes."

"That's not what I meant."

Q'Daer knew this. He hadn't intended to avoid the real question. His mind had taken him there, as if of its own free will. He needed time to think. He needed to be alone.

"I'm sorry, A'Laq. What did you mean?"

He chanced a look at E'Menua and saw that the a'laq wore a slight frown, as if he were searching for the right words.

"You say that the Forelander trusts these two Mettai. But you just heard the old one admit that they meant to harm you, that they meant to harm us all."

"Yes, I did hear that." This time Q'Daer couldn't keep the edge from his voice.

E'Menua cast a quick look his way, his eyes narrowed. "I don't like your tone."

"Forgive me, A'Laq."

The a'laq started to say something more, still looking angry, but then stopped himself, as if thinking better of it. They were still walking, and had gone beyond the bounds of the sept to follow the small rill that ran by the settlement.

Q'Daer tried to keep his eyes fixed on the ground in front of them, but he couldn't keep himself from glancing repeatedly at E'Menua. He had never been good with people. L'Norr had a much easier time reading the moods of others and getting along with them. He could have used his friend's insights now. What did the a'laq expect of him? What should he have said? This was a man he had known and respected all his life. Before today, he'd rarely had cause to question the a'laq's decisions. He knew that E'Menua had his reasons for doing what he had. But he didn't know what those reasons could be, and he didn't expect the a'laq to explain himself.

He was surprised.

"You're wondering why I did it, aren't you?"

Q'Daer swallowed, still unsure of what to say.

"It's all right, Q'Daer. You're a Weaver. You could be a'laq of your own sept someday. We're leaders. We understand each other."

"Yes, A'Laq."

"These Mettai, they can't be trusted. You understand this, right?"

"I . . ." He licked his lips. "Yes, A'Laq."

He could feel E'Menua's eyes on him. "They're Eandi, Q'Daer. They may wield magic, but their eyes are dark."

Q'Daer nodded, still not looking at the a'laq.

"We're about to ride to war against a dark-eye army," E'Menua went on. "There are Mettai in that army. We can't have our warriors wondering if those people are truly our enemies. They have to be certain. And these two men—they confuse things. If we let them live, if we give our warriors reason to think that the Mettai are our friends, that they have saved your life and protected us, we put doubt in their minds as they go to war. I can't allow that."

This he could understand. The Forelander seemed to make things so complicated all the time. But what the a'laq had told him made sense. This was how a Fal'Borna thought. Perhaps north of the Border Range, where Grinsa came from, a Qirsi could afford to look for the good in his dark-eye enemies. But out here on the plain, in a land that had seen nearly a thousand years of war between the races, a warrior didn't have that luxury.

"Are you with me, Q'Daer?"

"Yes, A'Laq," he said, finally facing E'Menua.

The a'laq grinned. "Good." He placed a hand on Q'Daer's shoulder and both of them stopped walking. "You know that the Forelander will talk to you about this. He'll try to convince you that the Mettai are being treated unjustly."

Q'Daer nodded solemnly. "I know that, A'Laq. I can handle Gr—" He stopped, his cheeks growing hot. "I can handle the Forelander."

E'Menua patted his shoulder and started to walk back to the sept. "That's what I hoped you'd say," he called back over his shoulder.

Chapter 12

◆‑I‑◆

Grinsa spotted E'Menua and Q'Daer together and knew immediately that he'd already lost this battle. He had hoped that Q'Daer might understand what the a'laq had done, and that he might be angry enough about it to stand with him in protecting the Mettai. But seeing them now, E'Menua's arm resting easily on the younger man's shoulder, a smile on his bronze, tapered face, Grinsa felt his hopes vanish. He actually considered turning and walking away without even speaking to Q'Daer. He dismissed the idea in the next moment, but only because he couldn't imagine facing Besh and Sirj again and having to admit that he hadn't even tried to sway the man.

E'Menua turned away from the young Weaver and started walking in Grinsa's direction, looking far too pleased with himself. Grinsa ducked back out of sight in the shadow of a z'kal, though he thought that the a'laq had probably spotted him.

As he suspected, a short time later he heard the man call out in a low voice, "I know you're there, Forelander."

Slowly, Grinsa stepped out from behind the shelter.

"You're too late, you know," E'Menua told him. "You'll never get him to help you."

"Why did you do it?" Grinsa asked him. "Why do you hate those men so? They've risked their lives to save ours, and yet you remain determined to put them to death."

"Ask Q'Daer. He can explain it to you."

E'Menua smiled again and started to walk past him.

Grinsa reached out and grabbed the a'laq's arm, forcing him to stop. "I'm asking you."

The a'laq wrenched his arm free and glowered at him. "You'd better watch yourself, Forelander. You keep pushing me, as if I'm no one of consequence. You seem to think that I'm powerless to defend myself. You're wrong. And if you're not careful, you'll feel the full weight of my wrath. Trust me when I tell you that you don't want that."

He stalked off, leaving Grinsa to rail at himself for his foolishness. Cresenne had warned him about this, and yet he'd been unable to keep himself from provoking the man. He had already come to the realization that he had little chance of winning Q'Daer over to his side in this conflict. E'Menua held the lives of the two Mettai in his hand, and Grinsa was giving him every reason to kill the men, if for no other reason than to spite him.

Still angry with himself, Grinsa started walking toward Q'Daer, who was making his way back to the sept. Seeing him approach, the young Weaver halted. Grinsa had expected that Q'Daer would try to avoid him, but the Fal'Borna made no attempt to wave him away. He wasn't even scowling. Rather than take comfort in this, Grinsa swore silently. *You're too late, you know.* What had E'Menua said to the young Weaver?

"You're wasting your time," Q'Daer said.

Grinsa opened his hands and forced a smile. "I haven't even said anything yet."

"You don't need to. I know why you're here, and there's nothing you can say that will make me turn against the a'laq."

"Can I ask you why?"

At that, Q'Daer frowned. "You wouldn't understand. You're not Fal'Borna."

"No, I'm not. But your reasons must be quite compelling. These men saved our lives. They cast a spell to protect all Qirsi from Lici's plague. The only way the a'laq could convince his own people to turn against them was to use magic to make Besh lie. Surely if what the a'laq told you can convince a Fal'Borna to betray a friend, it should be enough to sway a man as simple as—"

"That's enough!"

The familiar scowl was back on Q'Daer's face, and for some reason Grinsa found this reassuring.

He kept silent, waiting for the Fal'Borna to say more, knowing that if he waited long enough the man would feel compelled to explain himself.

"We're about to ride to war," Q'Daer told him at last. "That may not mean much in the Forelands, but here it does. The Mettai are allied with our enemies. And our warriors have to be clear about that as they ride into battle."

He drew himself up, as if readying himself for Grinsa's retort.

But Grinsa nodded. It was more than merely clever. It actually made sense. He'd known soldiers back in the Forelands—a man named Gershon Trasker came to mind immediately—who would have seen the value in seeking such clarity for the men under their command.

"So accepting that Besh and Sirj are friends might weaken the resolve of our warriors if they face a Mettai army. Is that right?"

Q'Daer made no effort to mask his surprise. "Yes. That's exactly right."

"Did E'Menua admit that he'd forced Besh to say those things?"

The Fal'Borna didn't answer.

"Never mind," Grinsa said. "It doesn't really matter if he did. You and I both know the truth. The n'qlae does, too." He smiled bitterly. "And it doesn't make a damn bit of difference, does it?"

Grinsa didn't expect a response to this, either, but after a moment the young Weaver shook his head.

"No, it doesn't."

"Does he intend to execute them?"

"I would imagine."

"Do you know when?"

"No."

Grinsa continued to eye him.

"Truly, Forelander, I don't know. He didn't say much about this. He told me . . . why it would be dangerous to let these Mettai live. But he said nothing about their executions."

"Do you think it would be possible to convince the a'laq to spare them?"

Q'Daer exhaled loudly. "I thought you understood. I don't want their lives spared!"

"I do understand, Q'Daer. But you have to understand that in my mind this is wrong. You're not talking about executing enemies of the Fal'Borna."

The man started to say something, but Grinsa raised a hand, silencing him.

"E'Menua can force Besh to say that he started the very first Blood War, but that doesn't make it true. And you and the a'laq can convince yourselves that you're justified in killing them, but that doesn't change the fact that this is murder, plain and simple."

Q'Daer regarded him with contempt. "For just a moment,

I thought that perhaps you were finally starting to think like a Fal'Borna. I should have known better."

"No, Q'Daer, I am starting to think like a Fal'Borna. But I'm still a Forelander in my heart."

The young Weaver shook his head and started away from him.

"Wait," Grinsa said. "I'm not fool enough to think that I can change E'Menua's mind about Besh and Sirj. Not yet at least. But do you think that he would allow them to live as prisoners if he thought that he could learn something from them about Mettai magic?"

When the man didn't answer, Grinsa went on. "Think about it, Q'Daer. They'd be prisoners. That would be clear to your warriors. But we wouldn't be killing innocent men, men who saved your life and mine. Wouldn't you prefer that?"

Q'Daer faced him again. "I won't speak on their behalf."

"I'm not asking you to," Grinsa said. "I'm simply asking you if you think it's possible that E'Menua would agree to it."

"I don't."

"No, of course not," Grinsa said, shaking his head. He could only hope that Cresenne had more success with D'Pera. He looked the young Weaver in the eye. "You may not believe this now, but if Besh and Sirj are executed, their wraiths will hover at your shoulder for the rest of your days. You'll carry them with you to Bian's realm."

He didn't wait for Q'Daer to say more. Instead, he turned and hurried back to his shelter.

Cresenne was already there, gathering firewood from a sizable pile that had been left for them beside the z'kal. Bryntelle sat nearby, amusing herself by scraping the dirt with a small stick.

Cresenne looked up at his approach and smiled weakly. "There's food, too. That's something at least."

Grinsa felt himself sag. "Your conversation with the n'qlae didn't go well?"

She straightened. "Not really," she said, lowering her voice. "She's not happy with what E'Menua did, but he's her husband and the a'laq. She's not going to do anything to humiliate him."

He nodded, knowing that he should have expected this. "Maybe she doesn't have to." He asked Cresenne much the same question he'd asked Q'Daer.

"Prisoners?" she said, frowning. "Besh and Sirj won't like that idea at all."

"I don't like it, either," Grinsa told her. "But at least they'd be alive. We'd still have a chance to save them."

"A chance, yes," she said. "But do you know how we'd do it?"

"I have an idea," he said, lowering his voice. "It's something I urged E'Menua to do as soon as we arrived back in the sept, but he ignored me. Maybe it's time I did it myself."

She looked puzzled, and even after he explained to her what he had in mind, she still looked doubtful.

"You'd be taking a great risk . . ." She shook her head. "There's so much that could go wrong."

"I know. But at least they'd still be alive. If this doesn't work, we can try something else. But for now, the important thing is that we convince the n'qlae to help us. Do you think we can?"

Cresenne nodded: "I don't know, but we should try. You should also speak with Besh and Sirj, to prepare them. As I said, they're not going to like this."

"I will," he said. "Tomorrow."

"What if E'Menua executes them tonight?"

"He won't," Grinsa said. "He'll want to make a spectacle of it. He'll want to use their deaths to humiliate me."

She nodded. "You're probably right."

They stood looking at each other. After a moment, she took his hand and gave it a squeeze.

"It wasn't supposed to be this complicated," she said.

He smiled sadly. "No, it wasn't."

Bryntelle gave a small squeal at something she'd done

with the stick. This time Grinsa's smile was full and genuine. He bent down and scooped the child into his arms. She squealed again, and he kissed her cheek.

"We have smoked rilda meat," Cresenne said. "And silverroot. Let's have supper like any other Fal'Borna family, and pretend none of this is happening. At least for a little while."

"That sounds nice," Grinsa said. "Doesn't it, Bryntelle?"

Bryntelle brushed his nose with her hand and laughed.

"She thinks so, too," Grinsa said, turning to Cresenne.

She was smiling. "It's nice to see the two of you together again. I'd like to see more of that."

"Me, too."

Grinsa carried an armful of firewood into the z'kal. Before long the silverroot was boiling on a low fire, and the aroma of watermint and thyme filled the shelter. He and Cresenne ate a quiet dinner and after putting Bryntelle to sleep, they slipped out of their clothes and lay together on the small pallet, surrendering to their passion once more. He had missed everything about her—the taste of her lips, the feel of her skin, the softness of her hair.

"This concubine thing has its advantages," Cresenne said after, her head resting on his chest, her eyes closed.

"I was thinking the same thing."

She smiled, but said nothing. A few moments later, she started slightly, seeming to rouse herself.

"I'm falling asleep," she murmured.

"You should," he told her. "There's no reason why both of us need to stay up all night."

"I should be up with you, though."

"No. Sleep. I'll be all right. And you'll need to get up with Bryntelle in the morning."

She took a breath, then raised her head to look him in the eye. "All right," she said, sounding more awake. She kissed him softly on the lips, rolled off of him, and lay beside him, her eyes open and reflecting the faint firelight. "You think this will work?"

"I don't know," he admitted. "But I'm running out of ideas."

Cresenne nodded. "Wake me if you need me."

"I will."

Grinsa rose from the pallet, pulled on his clothes again, and stepped out into the cold night air. Clouds hung low over the sept, obscuring the stars but glowing slightly with the light of Panya and Ilias, the two moons. The sept was quiet save for the occasional whinny of a horse and a low thread of laughter coming from a nearby shelter. He pulled his over-shirt tight around his shoulders and sat on a log by the z'kal.

Closing his eyes, he reached forth with his magic, seeking out the magic of the Weavers nearest to him. He sensed Q'Daer immediately, and then a second similar presence who must have been L'Norr. E'Menua and D'Pera were to-gether, of course. He hesitated, deeply conscious of the risk he was taking. Then he stepped into the n'qlae's dreams, as a Weaver could.

Whenever he had used this magic to speak with Cresenne or his sister, Keziah, he had used the same setting: a stretch of the Caerissan Steppe near where he grew up in the kingdom of Eibithar in the Forelands. It was familiar to him, just as it had been to Kezi, and it was similar enough to the lands in Wethyrn, where Cresenne spent her youth, to be familiar to her as well. But it would have been utterly alien to the n'qlae, and that would make what was bound to be an un-nerving encounter for her even more difficult. Instead, he summoned an image of the Central Plain here in the South-lands. It was an imperfect image; he didn't know this land well enough to get the setting just right. But it would serve his purpose.

As soon as he reached into the n'qlae's mind with his magic, he saw her in the dream landscape he had conjured. She stood before him wrapped in a blanket and nothing more. She turned a quick circle, looking to see who had entered her dreams. When she spotted him, her pale eyes blazed.

"How dare you!" she said. "Leave me at once!"

"I'm sorry, N'Qlae," he answered, keeping his voice low and even. "I can't do that. I need to speak with you, and I don't want the a'laq overhearing our conversation or seeing us together."

"And you think I won't tell him as soon as I wake up?"

"No, I don't."

"Then you're a fool."

"You don't want those men killed. And you don't want the magic you used to get Besh to tell the truth to be the reason he dies."

She looked away, her lips pressed so thin that they had whitened. "I don't know what your woman told you, but if you think that I'll defy my husband, that I'll let you disgrace him in front of the entire sept, you're wrong."

"That's exactly what Cresenne told me you'd say. She knows how much you love E'Menua, and I know that he's revered by every man and woman in the sept." He smiled. "Don't you see? That's why I've come to you this way. I don't want to embarrass him, and I don't want another open conflict with him."

She appeared to consider this. "What is it you do want?" she asked at last. "You know that he can't turn around and declare the Mettai our friends," she went on before Grinsa could respond. "Not after what the older one said."

"You mean what the a'laq made him say."

D'Pera stared back at him.

"You're right," he said after a brief silence. "I do know that he can't pretend none of this ever happened. For better or worse, the warriors guarding the Mettai heard Besh say those things. But you and I both know that Besh wouldn't have said any of it without E'Menua's interference."

Again she didn't answer.

"You'd let him get away with this, wouldn't you? You'd let these two men die, even though you know them to be innocent of any crime against your people. And you'd do this simply because E'Menua wants it. He's like a willful child whose parents would rather coddle than discipline."

"That's my a'laq you're talking about!" D'Pera said, her voice rising.

Grinsa let out a short, sharp laugh. "Yes, I know. Q'Daer has said the same thing to me a few times now. It seems I'm not as impressed by that as the rest of you."

"You're not Fal'Borna. You can't possibly understand what an a'laq means to his people."

"No, I don't suppose I can. But coming from the Forelands I know that it's possible for Eandi and Qirsi to live together, to build friendships." He faltered, but only briefly. "Aside from Cresenne, no one in the Southlands knows this about me, but I was once married to an Eandi woman."

She looked at him with a mix of disgust and horror. "Why are you telling me this?"

"Because I want you to understand why I'm fighting for these men. I actually understand what it means to be Fal'Borna better than you think. I've learned a lot in the past few turns. But your people seem to think that this is the only way to live, and it's not. Besh and Sirj have risked their lives time and again to protect the Y'Qatt and the Fal'Borna from the curse that the Mettai witch set upon you. Despite the color of their eyes and color of your hair, despite the Blood Wars, they gave up everything to save the lives of complete strangers who they've been taught to hate since they were children.

"The reason E'Menua was able to get away with what he did today is that their actions are so alien to the Fal'Borna, no one in the sept really believes they could have done it. But they did. I'm alive because they did. And unlike everyone else, you know it's true. You used mind-bending on Besh today. You read his thoughts. You know the truth. That makes you different from every other Fal'Borna here."

"Your point?" she asked warily.

"Isn't it clear? Knowing what you do, you have a responsibility to try to save them."

"I've already told you—"

"Yes, I know. E'Menua won't admit what he did. For now he doesn't have to. All I'm asking is that you prevail upon him to spare their lives. Tell him they'd be more valuable as prisoners, that they might be able to teach us something about Mettai magic. Think of something. But don't let these men die."

"What if he won't listen to me?"

"Make it clear to him that you didn't like what he did today." He held her gaze. "You didn't like it, did you?"

"That's not your concern."

Grinsa smiled. "You're right. It's not. I have a long night ahead of me, N'Qlae. So I'll leave you now. I do apologize for coming to you this way. It was presumptuous of me, but I couldn't think of any other way to approach you without the a'laq's knowledge."

"What do you mean, you have a long night ahead of you?" D'Pera asked. "You intend to speak with others this way?"

"I intend to do what E'Menua should have done long ago, when Q'Daer first told him that Besh had healed us. I'm going to contact other a'laqs on the plain and pass the spell to them. I'm going to save as many lives as I can."

She eyed him with curiosity, as if looking at him for the first time. "I'm not sure I understand everything you've said to me tonight. The Forelands sound . . . strange. But I'll do what you ask." She started to say more but then stopped herself. "Now leave me so I can sleep." She softened the words with a faint smile.

"Thank you, N'Qlae. Dream well."

He broke the magical connection linking his thoughts to hers and opened his eyes. He knew a moment of dizziness, but it was gone as quickly as it had come. All was quiet in the sept. He got up and peered into the z'kal and saw that Cresenne and Bryntelle were both sleeping.

Returning to his seat outside the shelter, he closed his eyes once more and again reached out with his magic. This time, he reached far beyond the sept, directing his thoughts northward, toward the Horn, where so many Fal'Borna lived and where so many merchants ventured this time of year, perhaps including those who still carried some of Lici's baskets.

Before the night was through, he intended to reach to the south as well, toward Thamia and other Fal'Borna settlements near the Ofirean Sea. From all that Jasha had told him before he died, it seemed that merchants often passed the colder turns on the warm shores of the inland sea. And in the nights to come, he'd attempt to speak with a'laqs in settlements near the Silverwater. He felt certain that Torgan would be headed that way with his small scrap of cursed basket, and though he thought it likely that the one-eyed merchant would try to avoid any septs he spotted, Grinsa couldn't ignore the danger.

Reaching across the plain with his magic, the first sept he found appeared to him as a small cluster of light amidst a vast darkness. Sifting through those lights he could sense the type of magic wielded by each person, and so could pick out Weavers from among the others. And when he found two Weavers sharing a z'kal, he knew that he had found the a'laq and n'qlae. Reaching into the mind of the man in this first sept, he summoned that image of the plain once more and stepped into the a'laq's dreams.

He was an older man, his back slightly stooped and his face deeply lined, but his pale yellow eyes were still bright and alert. They narrowed as he looked at Grinsa across the expanse of plain grass.

"Who are you?" he asked. "What clan are you from?"

"My name is Grinsa jal Arriet, A'Laq, and though I come from the Forelands, I'm living now among the Fal'Borna in the sept of E'Menua, son of E'Sedt."

"You're with E'Menua's sept?" the man asked, sounding doubtful.

"I am, A'Laq. You've heard of the plague making its way across the plain?"

"Yes, of course."

"I've had that plague and I've survived, thanks to two men named Besh and Sirj. These men are Mettai and they have been traveling through Fal'Borna lands, risking their lives so that they might stop this plague from spreading farther. They killed the Mettai witch who first conjured the plague, and they've found a way to make all Qirsi immune to it. By entering your dream and touching your magic, I've spread their spell to you. You're now immune to the plague, and you can make every man and woman in your sept immune by using your magic on them. Touch them with healing, enter their dreams, use your power to augment theirs. Whatever you choose, it will have the same effect."

The a'laq gaped at Grinsa as if the Forelander had told him he could now hold Morna's Ocean in the palm of his hand.

"You're certain of this?" he asked breathlessly. "You truly had the plague yourself?"

Grinsa smiled. "Yes, A'Laq. This is a gift to you from E'Menua. All he asks in return is that if you encounter the plague, you contact him immediately to let him know that the spell worked and saved your people."

"Yes! Yes, of course!"

"Thank you, A'Laq. I have to leave you now. I have many more a'laqs to contact."

"I'm sure you do. Thank you, Grinsa of the Forelands. May Qirsar smile upon E'Menua and his sept."

"I'll convey your kind words to the a'laq."

He stepped out of the man's dreams and immediately began searching for the next sept farther to the north. Before long he found it, and reached down with his magic for the a'laq.

Chapter 13
✦✦✦

Upper Central Plain

Two days after their attack on the first sept, the Eandi army encountered their second Fal'Borna settlement. This one was larger than the first and it didn't appear to have been damaged by the plague. It also was situated in a part of the plain that had fewer rises and dales. The army had no hope of taking these Fal'Borna by surprise. In fact, Tirnya and her father were quite certain that the Qirsi spotted their army only a short time after their forward scouts caught sight of the sept.

"Now our planning will be tested," Jenoe muttered, eyeing the terrain around the settlement, seeming to search for any advantage the land might offer them.

To Tirnya's untrained eye, the landscape appeared to offer little.

"We should do this without the Mettai, Marshal," Gries said, looking regal on his white stallion.

Jenoe shook his head, still surveying the plain. "I'm not convinced that we can, Captain Ballidyne. These Fal'Borna are at full strength, and they know we're here. Fighting the white-hairs on such terms is what led to our loss of these lands in the first place."

"Wolves, then?" Tirnya asked.

Her father glanced at her. Then he turned to one of the scouts who had first brought word of the settlement. "Bring the eldest. Quickly."

The man bowed in his saddle, and then rode back toward the Mettai.

"We'll have to ride closer," Gries said. "That's what the eldest will say. Last time, the white-hairs went for our mounts and raised a mist. If this is a full sept, they may well have several Weavers. They could attack us with shaping and fire as well as the rest."

"What would you suggest then, Captain?" asked Marshal Crish.

"If they've seen us, there's nothing we can do," Enly said, before Gries could answer. "This has been the risk all along, hasn't it? We based our strategy on the assumption that the Fal'Borna have been weakened by the plague. The first settlement had been. But it seems that the plague spared some septs and now we have to fight our way through." He hesitated, his eyes flicking toward Tirnya. "Or we have to turn back right now."

Tirnya hoped that others—her father? Gries? Hendrid?—would rush to gainsay him, but no one said a word.

"We're not leaving," she finally said.

Enly nodded once, as if he'd expected her to say as much. "Then I'd suggest we prepare for battle. And I'd also suggest that we give free rein to the Mettai."

Gries frowned. "Free rein? You can't be serious."

"I am. I don't know about you, Captain, but I'd like to survive this war. We're facing a Fal'Borna army; a true one this time. None of us has ever done that before. This is no time to get squeamish about resorting to magic of any sort. Given the choice between a couple of Fal'Borna Weavers and those wolves we saw the other day, I'll take the wolves in a heartbeat."

"That may not be the only choice," Jenoe said in a tone seemingly intended to end their discussion. "Here comes the eldest."

They all turned. Fayonne and her son were striding purposefully in their direction, following the mounted scout. The rest of the Mettai were behind them.

"I brought all of my people, Marshal," the eldest said,

stopping in front of Jenoe. "I hope you don't mind. I assumed that you'd have me send for them soon enough."

A faint smile flickered on Jenoe's face. "Thank you, Eldest. I appreciate your foresight."

She inclined her head, then looked past him toward the sept. "We've found another settlement, I see."

"Yes. There's no evidence that the plague has struck this one. We'll be facing a full Fal'Borna sept this time."

Her eyebrows went up, but otherwise she offered no response.

Jenoe glanced at Tirnya, uncertainty in his deep blue eyes. "We're wondering what kind of magic you think might work against such a force," he continued after a moment.

Fayonne turned to her son. "The sleeping spell worked well last time, as did the finding spell."

"Yes," Mander said. "Either of those."

"But don't we have to be close to the sept for you to use that kind of magic?" Gries asked.

"Yes, Captain," Fayonne said. "We'll have to be far closer to the sept for just about any of our spells to work. That's the nature of Mettai magic."

"Can you do anything to help with their horses?" Tirnya asked.

Fayonne looked puzzled. "Their horses?"

"Well, last time the Fal'Borna used language of beasts against our mounts and we had to advance on foot. I assume that these Fal'Borna will do the same. But they'll be on horses, which gives them an advantage if it comes to close fighting."

"The blood wolves," the eldest said plainly. "They can attack their horses. Their mere presence will unnerve the animals." She shrugged. "But you've made it clear that you don't want us to conjure any more of them."

Tirnya took a breath, holding the woman's gaze. "Well, I may have to accept that we have no choice in the matter."

The woman shrugged again, her bearing maddeningly calm.

"Pardon me, Eldest," Enly said. "You said a moment ago that we had to be closer for *just about* any of your magic to work. Are there spells you can use from this distance?"

"There may be one or two," Fayonne said. "But if you didn't like the blood wolves, you might not like these conjurings, either."

"Why not?" Jenoe asked. "What are they?"

"Early in the Blood Wars, when we first fought alongside your people, we had many sorts of creatures that served our armies. The wolves were one. There were also blood eagles, great birds of prey that could attack an enemy from the sky. They could be sent forth from farther away. Of course, the Qirsi could fight them off with shaping magic, but the eagles were said to be deft fliers. Some of them might be able to avoid the conjurings of the Fal'Borna."

Gries wore a troubled expression. "I take it you can't control them any more than you could the wolves."

"That's right. But like the wolves, they can be slain with arrows or put to sleep with a spell."

"But until they are, they'll be killing indiscriminately. They won't distinguish between us and the Fal'Borna."

Fayonne regarded the Fairlea captain coldly. "No, they won't. On the other hand, I can assure you that the Qirsi will be quite precise with their killing. Have you heard tales of the Blood Wars, Captain?"

"Yes," Gries said thickly.

"Then you have some idea of what Qirsi shaping magic can do to an army when directed by a Weaver."

"What other creatures did your people use in those early battles?" Jenoe asked, drawing the woman's gaze once more.

"Serpents, bears, hornets."

The marshal's eyebrows went up. "Hornets?"

"As long as a knife blade and with enough venom to bring an Aelean soldier to his knees."

Tirnya felt herself blanch. Suddenly the blood wolves didn't seem so terrible.

"And you can conjure all of these creatures today?" Enly asked.

Fayonne shook her head. "Not all of them, no. I can conjure hornets, but not the kind that my ancestors used against the white-hairs. But the wolves and eagles I can summon are much the same as those used in the Blood Wars."

Jenoe was gazing at the sept again. Tirnya looked that way as well, but saw no evidence that the Fal'Borna were headed toward them. Was it possible that they hadn't spotted the army yet? Or had the white-hairs decided that they wanted to defend their settlement rather than face the Eandi on the open plain?

"Send the eagles," Jenoe said after a brief pause. "You can direct them toward the sept, can't you? They won't turn on us immediately."

"We'll move a bit closer to the settlement," Fayonne told him. "And we'll do everything in our power to send them to the Fal'Borna."

Tirnya's father didn't look satisfied with this reply, but he nodded, perhaps sensing that this was the most assurance he was likely to get.

One thing about the Mettai: Once they were given an order, they didn't waste time in carrying it out. No sooner had the eldest answered Jenoe's concerns than she led her people away from the army and toward the sept.

"I want archers ready to march as soon as these magical eagles are flying," Jenoe said. "And I want swordsmen just behind them. This will work best if the Fal'Borna have to fight off eagles and arrows at the same time."

"Yes, Marshal," Enly said.

He started shouting orders to the men of Qalsyn. Gries and two other captains from Fairlea hurried off to ready their army, and Hendrid's captains started back toward the men of Waterstone.

The Mettai, in the meantime, halted after walking about a hundred fourspans. They pulled their knives free, stooped to pick up handfuls of dirt, cut themselves, and finally gathered blood on the flat edges of their blades and mixed it with the earth in their hands. Tirnya couldn't hear them speaking, but she knew that the next step in this odd process was for all of them to mutter their spells. A moment later, acting in near perfect unison, they flung their clods of bloody mud into the air.

When the Mettai conjured the great wolves during their last encounter with the Fal'Borna, Tirnya had been disturbed by the way the dirt in their hands contorted and grew in those moments before the animals took form. This magic was no different. If anything, it seemed more alien to watch those small clumps of dirt sprout enormous wings and talons and heads. But in just a few seconds, nearly fifty eagles were soaring above the army.

They were larger by far than any bird Tirnya had ever seen. Even from far below, their hooked beaks and sicklelike talons appeared large and sharp enough to rend a full-grown rilda in two. The creatures circled once over the army, and when their shadows passed overhead Tirnya shuddered, feeling as a rabbit must when it finds itself under the gaze of a hawk. But whatever intelligence the Mettai had imparted to the great birds seemed enough to allow them to distinguish between friend and foe, or Eandi and Qirsi. After completing one turn above the soldiers of Stelpana, the birds wheeled toward the sept. They flew in a series of loose columns, like airborne warriors in formation. They gave only one or two flaps of their great wings, and then glided, their tails twisting slightly this way or that to keep them in line.

Fayonne and the Mettai watched them pass back overhead, and then the eldest turned to face Jenoe, as if to say, *Now it's your turn.*

Tirnya's father looked back at the captains. "Are we ready?" he asked.

"Qalsyn's archers are in place," Enly said. "So are Fairlea's. The men of Waterstone were a bit farther off. And the swordsmen aren't in formation yet."

Jenoe frowned, clearly displeased. "Well, we'll make do with what we have. Have the swordsmen mustered forward as quickly as possible."

"Yes, Marshal."

"Archers, advance!" Jenoe called to the men behind him, gesturing with a raised arm and at the same time spurring his mount to a canter.

A great shout rose from the men, and the bowmen of Qalsyn and Fairlea started toward the sept, their bows ready. Tirnya and the other captains followed the marshal on horseback. When they reached the Mettai, Fayonne and her people began to jog alongside the riders.

Somehow Enly had positioned himself beside Tirnya, though he said nothing to her. For her part, Tirnya barely allowed herself a glance in his direction. Instead, she divided her attention between the great eagles soaring toward the sept and the settlement itself. She still saw no sign that the Fal'Borna were making ready for battle; she saw no white-hairs at all.

"Something's not right," Enly said. "Where are they?"

"Could they have fled?" she asked. "They would have gotten word that we were coming. They may have abandoned the sept or joined forces with another settlement."

Enly shook his head. "There are still horses in the paddock. They're here. They're just waiting for something."

"You should stop here, Marshal," Fayonne called to Jenoe. "Language of beasts. They'll be able to reach you soon."

A moment later, Jenoe reined his horse to a stop and dismounted, though this, too, seemed to darken his mood. Hendrid, the captains, and the lead riders also halted and swung themselves off their mounts. They wasted little time in resuming their advance on foot.

By now the eagles were over the sept and were circling like great buzzards, each turn bringing them lower.

"Are you close enough for a finding spell?" Jenoe asked.

"Not quite," Fayonne said.

Tirnya's father nodded curtly. "They're too close," he said

a moment later. "I wanted our archers to be in position before the eagles reached the sept. Now they'll—"

Before he could finish the thought, a harsh, piercing screech split the air, followed by another and another. Several of the lowest eagles suddenly began to thrash violently, their wings bent at odd angles, their talons clenched in tight balls. They struggled for an instant or two and then plunged to the ground. As soon as they landed, men swarmed around them, spears in their hands, their white hair gleaming in the sun.

"Damn!" Fayonne said. "They're using shaping magic."

"Can you send more eagles?" Jenoe asked.

The eldest looked at him and blinked once. "More?" she said, sounding simple.

"Yes! You conjured these eagles. Conjure another flock and send them—"

He broke off as more of the eagles screamed. All of them looked up into the sky in time to see several of the giant birds fall to the earth, their wings broken.

Jenoe faced the eldest again, appearing more desperate by the moment. "Send more of the birds to attack the sept. Perhaps that will allow us to get close enough for your spells and our archers to have some effect."

Fayonne abruptly seemed unsure of herself, as if Jenoe's request was the last thing she had expected.

"You can do that, can't you?"

"I— I think so," she said. "I've never heard of it being done, but I can't see any reason why it can't."

Jenoe nodded once. "Good. Then do it. Now, quickly!"

The eldest still seemed hesitant. She turned to the other Mettai and held up her knife for them to see.

"More eagles," she said, her voice barely more than a whisper.

The other Mettai didn't appear to be fazed by this at all. Except for the eldest's son, whose face went white. He said nothing, though, and a moment later all of the Mettai had soil in their hands, blood on their blades, and the softly spoken words of the spell on their lips.

Still more eagles screamed out in pain and tumbled to the ground.

"Hurry, Eldest," Jenoe said. "There'll be none left before long."

The muttering of the spell seemed to go on for a long time, but at last the Mettai hurled their fistfuls of mud at the sky, and several dozen more eagles began to rise into the air and soar toward the settlement.

"Forward!" Jenoe shouted to the army.

Again the warriors started off at a run toward the Fal'Borna settlement. The white-hairs' assault on the eagles continued. The second group of birds glided toward the few remaining eagles first conjured by the Mettai.

When at last the soldiers of Stelpana were close enough to the sept, Jenoe called for a halt, his breath coming in great gasps and his face shining with sweat.

Tirnya was winded as well, but she felt fresher than her father looked. "Are you all right, Father?" she asked.

"Yes, of course," Jenoe said impatiently. "Archers!" he called.

It almost seemed that the Fal'Borna had been waiting for Jenoe's signal, so suddenly did the wind rise from the west.

Jenoe scowled. "Damn them!" He turned to Fayonne. "Find me their Weavers, Eldest."

"Yes, Marshal."

Once more, the Mettai began to conjure, and this time when they threw their mud in the direction of the sept, it turned into that silvery dust Tirnya remembered from their last encounter with the Fal'Borna. The white-hairs' wind didn't seem to slow the conjuring. It flew straight at the sept before settling over the shelters and garden plots like a fine mist. Almost instantly the entire settlement appeared to glow, as if the white moon had fallen to the ground with the latest group of slain eagles. Tirnya could see at least three faint glimmerings of yellow in the sea of white light.

"You see them?" Jenoe called to no one in particular. "Those are the Weavers! Concentrate your volleys on them! Fire!"

A thousand bows thrummed; a swarm of arrows rose into the air, only to be knocked back by the white-hairs' wind so that most of them fell far short of the village.

The second group of eagles was over the settlement now, but rather than diving toward the Fal'Borna or their horses, they swooped at the other eagles and began to attack them.

"No!" Fayonne whispered.

"Eldest!" Jenoe called to the woman. "What are they doing?"

"I don't know, Marshal. I wasn't really sure what they'd do, but I didn't expect this."

The rasping screams of the birds seemed to drown out all other sound. The second group of eagles now vastly outnumbered the first, and they attacked in packs of three and four, tearing at their victims with those enormous beaks and cruel talons. Several more of the birds dropped to the ground, dead or dying.

Tirnya could see the Fal'Borna pointing up at the eagles. A moment later, the white-hairs appeared to decide that they could turn their full attention to the approaching army. She could hear voices shouting, but she couldn't make out what they were saying.

"Try putting them to sleep," Jenoe said. "That seems our best chance at this point."

Fayonne looked at him. "The eagles?"

"No, the Fal'Borna. Your finding spell worked. This one works the same way, doesn't it?"

"Yes," Fayonne said. "If you mean the way it gets to them."

Jenoe didn't have a chance to answer. At that moment, several of the Waterstone captains shouted a warning. They were pointing in the direction of the sept. Dozens of the men behind them had broken ranks to flee.

Tirnya looked at the settlement, expecting to see Fal'Borna warriors on horseback, but at first she saw nothing.

"Gods save us all," she heard Enly mutter.

"What?" she said. "I don't see . . ."

But she did. Finally. And the sight of it turned her innards to water.

It looked like a breaker rolling toward the Aelean shore. But instead of the aqua waters of the Sea of Stars, this wave was made of fire. It was pale yellow, like the eyes of the angry young Fal'Borna Tirnya had spoken to in the last sept. That was why she'd had trouble seeing it at first. Now she could see nothing else. The wave grew as it approached the armies of Stelpana, until it towered over them.

Jenoe stared at the wave as if it were an army of wraiths, his eyes wide, his mouth agape. "Eldest!" he finally managed to say. "Can you do anything?"

"We can try" was all the eldest said.

She and the other Mettai were already bending to pick up dirt, their blades ready. They had spread themselves in a single broad row so that they stood in front of a good portion of the army.

The Mettai cut their hands, mixed the blood with the earth, and began to chant their spell. For once, Tirnya heard them distinctly. "Blood to earth," they said. "Life to power, power to thought . . ."

That was all. They stood utterly still, watching that rolling wave of flame. A strange silence settled over the plain. Everyone seemed to be waiting to see what that wave would do to them, and what the Mettai might be able to conjure to protect them.

"Eldest?" Tirnya's father said.

Fayonne raised her blade hand, as if to silence him, but she didn't say a word or take her eyes off the Fal'Borna's fire.

Tirnya could feel the heat of it on her face and hands. The air was growing hot enough to make it uncomfortable to inhale. She could hear the flame hissing, although as far as she could tell it had done nothing to burn the grass over which it passed.

Her father was watching the Mettai, clearly unnerved. She could tell that he wanted to say something—to demand to know what they were going to do, or to implore them to do whatever it was quickly. But she could see as well that he didn't dare. He was treading on unfamiliar ground, watching a battle of magic against magic. She had never seen him look more helpless.

And still the wave bore down on them, the heat striking at the Eandi armies like a war hammer. Tirnya thought that her clothes and hair and skin would burst into flame at any moment, and she felt certain that Fayonne and her people had waited too long.

But when at last the eldest called out "Now!," her voice sounded surprisingly calm.

"Earth to water!" the Mettai said in almost perfect unison.

At the same time, they hurled the dirt at that wall of flame, the small clods of mud looking pitiful against the Fal'Borna's fire. But instantly the mud turned to water; great torrents of water that appeared to surge toward that magical wave like Ravens Wash during the rains of the Planting. Tirnya didn't know how it was possible for the Mettai to conjure so much water from so little earth. But they did. And when that magical fire met the conjured flood of water, they produced an explosion of white steam that scalded Tirnya's face and knocked her, her father, and many of the captains standing with them onto their backs. The Mettai were thrown back as well, and the steam rose into the air in a huge billowing cloud.

Tirnya could hear screams coming from the right and left, and she assumed that the Mettai had not been able to block entirely the Fal'Borna fire magic.

"Report!" Jenoe called, climbing to his feet. "I want to know numbers of wounded and dead!"

He turned to the eldest, who was being helped to her feet by her son. "The sleeping spell, Eldest! Please! Before they can attack us again!"

"We're lucky that wasn't shaping," Gries said, his face red from the heat of the fire and steam. "We'd all be dead."

Enly shook his head. "It wasn't luck. The shapers were still fighting off the eagles."

Tirnya looked toward the sept again, and saw that with the first group of eagles all dead or maimed, the second flock had begun to attack the Fal'Borna, and the white-hairs had resumed their magical assaults on the birds.

The Mettai were conjuring again, and as with the finding spell, when they threw this magic it turned to a fine glittering powder and streaked over the plain to the settlement, where it fell like a light snow on the sept. Immediately Tirnya saw the white-hairs go down, as if struck by unseen warriors. A cheer went up from the Eandi soldiers behind her.

Seeing their prey rendered helpless, the great eagles that still circled over the sept pounced, digging their talons into the prone bodies and tearing at them with their massive beaks.

"We should finish it," Jenoe said grimly. He turned to Tirnya and the other captains. "I want the children spared. But every adult is to be killed."

Tirnya and Enly shared a look.

"Forgive me, Marshal," Gries said. "But am I to understand that you want us to slaughter the Fal'Borna while they sleep? The men and the women?"

Jenoe drew himself up and took a breath. "That's right, Captain."

"But—"

Tirnya's father held up a hand to stop him. Several soldiers were approaching from both ends of the army.

"Report," Jenoe said.

A man in a Qalsyn uniform sketched a quick bow. "We los' one hundr'd an' twelve, sir."

"One hundred and twelve dead?" Stri said, incredulous.

The soldier nodded. "Anoth'r two hundr'd or so were burned an' need healin'."

Jenoe turned to a soldier wearing the colors of Fairlea. "What about your men?"

"Ninety-six dead, sir. More'n a hundr'd hurt."

"And yours?" Jenoe said to a soldier from Waterstone.

"We don' know yet, sir. A' least one hundr'd an' fifty dead. More than tha' probably. An' two hundr'd hurt."

Jenoe nodded. "I'm sorry for your losses, Marshal, Captain," he said to Hendrid and Gries, both of whom appeared shocked by what they had heard. "But to answer your question, Captain Ballidyne: Yes, I want them killed while they sleep. That was just one attack, and thanks to the Mettai we were spared the worst of it. And still we had hundreds of soldiers wounded or killed. We can't trifle with this enemy. They're at our mercy now, and I don't dare show them any." He gazed toward the sept as the eagles continued their bloody feast. "Please carry out my orders. Take archers with you and kill those eagles, too. I don't want to lose any more men today."

"Yes, Marshal," Enly said quietly.

The other captains led their men into the sept, but Tirnya hung back for a moment.

"Father?"

Jenoe didn't seem to have noticed that she was there. He started at the sound of her voice and frowned upon seeing her.

"You have orders to carry out, Tirnya. Please see to them."

He turned his back on her before she could say more. She wasn't used to hearing him speak to her so, but she couldn't bring herself to be angry with him. After a moment, she followed the others.

She walked quickly and soon had caught up with her men. Oliban and Dyn, two of her lead riders, were walking together. When they saw her they made room between them.

"Capt'n," Oliban said by way of greeting, his voice low.

Tirnya merely nodded. The men around them were so subdued one might have thought that they had lost this battle.

She heard the thrum of bows once more and looked up in time to see two eagles laboring to keep aloft, both with several arrows jutting from their breasts.

"I've never had t' kill an enemy like this before," Dyn said.

Tirnya pulled her sword free. "None of us has."

Already she could see soldiers thrusting their blades into the chests of sleeping Fal'Borna. Some of the soldiers were from Qalsyn; others were from Fairlea or Waterstone. All of them seemed disturbed by what they were being made to do.

"We should check the shelters," she said. "There'll be warriors in many of them."

She approached the nearest of the structures, which had been fashioned out of wooden poles and rilda skins. Pushing aside a flap that covered the entrance and stepping into the shelter, she found half a dozen sleeping children and two women, both of them holding spears.

"Damn," she whispered.

"Capt'n?" Oliban called to her from outside the shelter.

"It's all right," she said, her teeth clenched against a sudden sick feeling in her stomach.

She considered ordering Oliban into the shelter and telling him to do this. But she quickly dismissed the idea. Then she wondered if she and her men should drag the women out of the shelter, so that the children wouldn't awake to find themselves with two corpses. But would they be any better off leaving the shelter and finding the bodies out there? And did she want anyone else to see her do this?

In the end she decided that she didn't. She stood over the first woman and pulled her sword back, intending to stab her through the heart. These women were white-hairs. Their people had taken Deraqor from the Onjaefs and had killed thousands upon thousands of Eandi over the centuries. This should have been easy for her.

Her sword hand dropped to her side. She opened her mouth to call for Oliban, knowing that she wouldn't be able to carry out her orders.

But at that moment, the woman before her stirred and her eyes fluttered open. Golden yellow they were, and for just an instant, she stared up at Tirnya.

Her heart abruptly pounding, Tirnya jumped forward and plunged her blade into the woman's chest. The Fal'Borna cried out, flailed briefly, and then was still, blood staining her shirt.

The piece of rilda skin covering the shelter's entrance was thrown back.

"Capt'n!" Oliban said. "Are you all right?"

"Yes," Tirnya said, breathing hard. "One of them . . . one of them woke up."

Oliban looked down at the woman Tirnya had slaughtered. After a moment, he drew his blade, walked to the other woman, and killed her as well.

Then they left the shelter and made their way to the next one.

It was slow, grim work. At one point, Tirnya heard shouting and screams from the far end of the sept. She later learned that several Fal'Borna, including at least two shapers, had awakened before any of the Eandi soldiers reached them and had put up quite a fight before being killed by Stelpana's archers. Several more Eandi soldiers had died, most with snapped necks.

But by late in the day, all the adult Fal'Borna had been slain, as had the remaining eagles. Tirnya had rarely seen such carnage. The sept was littered with bodies, the earth stained crimson in many places. Jenoe ordered his men to pile the bodies and burn them, which meant that all of the Fal'Borna children were awake long before the Eandi army left the sept. Most of the younger ones cried piteously, while the oldest among them stared stony-faced at the pyres and the Eandi soldiers.

Tirnya had learned her lesson from her encounter with the boy in the last settlement; this time she made no effort to speak with any of the children. She stood at the edge of the village nearest to the horse paddock, staring off across the plain, hoping that the wind wouldn't shift and send the stench of burning corpses her way.

She hadn't been alone long when she heard a footfall behind her. Knowing that it had to be Enly, she turned, the words on her tongue intended to send him away and let him know in no uncertain terms that she didn't need comforting or sympathy. But it wasn't Enly who stood before her, nor was it Gries, or Stri, or her father, any of whom she also might have expected. Instead, she found herself facing her lead riders, Oliban, Qagan, Dyn, and Crow.

"What's happened?" she asked.

Oliban looked at the other three, but they were all eyeing him. For a long time he had spoken for all of them. It seemed that the others expected him to do so now, too.

"Oliban?" Tirnya said.

"We . . ." He shook his head. "Th' men are . . . troubled by wha' happened t'day, Capt'n. They wasn't happy abou' goin' t' war alongside th' Mettai, bu' they knew tha' we'd be better off with a bit o' magic on our side. Bu' this . . ." He shook his head. "Killin' white-hairs is one thing. Don' ge' me wrong. None of us has any problem with that. Bu' killin' them while they sleep? What are we doin', Capt'n?"

Before she could answer, Crow said, "There's some who are sayin' now tha' they'd rather face th' Fal'Borna with no magic at all than use any more o' this blood magic."

"Is that what you say, Crow?" Tirnya asked.

He hesitated, but only for an instant. "Yes, Capt'n, I guess it is."

Tirnya wasn't sure what to say to them. A part of her felt that she should have been angry. They were questioning her judgment as well as her father's. But she also understood. The first time the Mettai used magic on their behalf, their monstrous wolves nearly killed several soldiers. This time the eagles seemed more intent on each other than on the Fal'Borna, and the sleeping spell, while effective, made what should have been a battle into something more akin to a massacre. She didn't want anything to do with magic anymore, regardless of whether the conjurings were done by Mettai or Fal'Borna. Then again, had it not been for Mettai magic, most of them would be dead. She reminded the men of this.

"Ye're right," Oliban told her. "Tha' spell saved hundr'ds, if no' thousands." He glanced at Crow. "T' be honest, some don' hold with those who'd go on without any Mettai magic at all. I don' much like th' Mettai, bu' I don' think we can win this war without 'em. What we did t'day, though; tha' was . . . it was wrong, Capt'n. There's no other word for it. It was wrong."

"Do you think we could have won the battle any other way?" she asked, looking at each of the men in turn.

For some time none of them answered.

Finally, Oliban said, "Probably not."

She thought to ask if they were suggesting then that this war wasn't worth fighting, but she wasn't sure she wanted to hear their answer to that.

"I don't think so, either," she said instead. "This is war. You do what you have to in order to win. Today we did something that none of us felt good about. But at the end of the day, we're alive and our army is largely intact. Given what that Fal'Borna fire did to our lines, despite the Mettai spell, I think it's clear that matters could have been far worse."

Crow looked like he might argue the point further, but Oliban cut him off with a sharp look.

"Thank you, Capt'n," Oliban said.

The others muttered thank-yous as well, and they left her there. She watched them walk back into the sept and rejoin the rest of her company. Then she started back herself. She spotted Enly from afar and steered clear of him, but wound up face-to-face with her father.

"I just had a meeting with the captains and Hendrid," he said. "Where were you?"

"I'm sorry, Father. I was . . . my lead riders needed to speak with me. I was with them."

"Is there a problem?"

She shook her head. "They were asking about rations. That's all."

He eyed her doubtfully.

"What did you tell the other captains?" she asked, hoping to forestall more questions.

"I didn't like the way today's battle went. We were poorly prepared and took too long to develop a strategy for attack. Out here on the plain, an army as large as ours can easily be spotted from a distance. The Fal'Borna will be ready for our attack, and the next sept might ride to meet us. So we're going to alter our marching formations. I want archers and the Mettai at the front of our lines at all times. And I want the archers mustered into companies of one hundred each. These companies will march together, eat together, and make camp together. They should be able to respond to commands instantly. Each of you will have command of one of them. Enly will tell you which is yours."

"Enly?" she said.

"You weren't there; he was."

She heard the rebuke in his voice and didn't dare argue. "All right. What about the swordsmen?"

Her father shook his head, glancing around the sept at his army. "I almost wish I hadn't brought any. This war will be won with magic and arrows. We lost more than two hundred bowmen today. I've already ordered as many swordsmen to take the places of those who fell. If I had more bows, I'd order more into the arrow companies."

Tirnya nodded. *Magic and arrows.* "What about the Mettai?" she asked.

"What do you mean?"

"Some of the men were disturbed by the way today's battle went. To be honest, I was, too."

Jenoe's eyes narrowed. "Disturbed in what way?" he demanded.

Tirnya threw her arms wide. "You have to ask? We killed them in their sleep, Father! I had to kill a woman who lay in her shelter beside children!"

His face reddened and the muscles in his jaw tightened. He rarely lost his temper, but Tirnya had seen him go on tirades in the past, and she expected he would now. When he spoke, though, his voice was low and controlled. In many ways this was worse.

"You wanted this war, Tirnya. You wanted the Mettai with us. You got both. This is the magic we have, and distasteful though you may find it, this is the only way we can win. If you prefer to watch the Fal'Borna slaughter our army, then I'll tell Fayonne to take her people and go home. Otherwise, I'd suggest you keep quiet and follow my orders."

She felt as though he had slapped her.

Jenoe walked off before she could speak, leaving Tirnya to stare at the ground and try not to cry.

When at last she had composed herself, she looked up and caught sight of Enly and Gries, who were together and walking her way. Her first thought was that for two rivals who were supposed to hate each other, they agreed a lot and spent a good deal of time together. Her next thought was that she really wanted nothing to do with either of them just then.

She turned and started to walk away.

"Tirnya!" Enly's voice.

She stopped, exhaled, and turned back to them.

"What?" she said, making no effort to mask her annoyance.

Enly stopped in front of her, seemingly unaffected by her tone. "I thought you'd want to know that I put you in charge of the archers from your company and Stri's. Stri agreed to take command of a company from Fairlea."

Tirnya nodded. "Very well. Thank you."

"Are you all right?" he asked, stepping closer to her and lowering his voice.

"Why wouldn't I be?" she said, turning and walking away from him again. "We won today, didn't we?"

Chapter 14

✦✦

U'Selle had spent much of her life living at the fringe of her own clan, upending traditions she'd never intended to challenge. She had been born in Lowna, an established town along the Silverwater, rather than in the impermanent septs of the Central Plain. She and her people had made their gold by trading in the marketplace rather than by tracking rilda. She knew that some on the plain considered towns like hers to be Fal'Borna in name only. In most ways that mattered, these people believed, the people of Lowna were more like the Talm'Orast or H'Bel, the prosperous merchant clans that inhabited the lands west of the Ofirean.

It didn't help that U'Selle was one of the few female a'laqs in all the land. Rather than earning her a modicum of respect from other sept leaders, her position served only to isolate her further. Most of the other a'laqs seemed to think her undeserving of the title. And perhaps she was. Yes, she was a Weaver. But if there had been another male Weaver living in Lowna when her beloved F'Jai died ten years before, she would gladly have allowed him to become a'laq.

As it was, she had been so grief-stricken those first few turns after he died that she barely understood that the clan council of the village had chosen her to lead them. When at last she realized that everyone seemed to be calling her A'Laq, it was too late to do anything.

Over the years, she had come to enjoy leading the village, and though the other a'laqs seldom showed her the respect she thought she deserved, her own people never seemed to question the choice they had made all those years ago.

Now she was dying of consumption, and though she fought the illness as best she could, she had to admit to herself that she was ready to die. She wished that there was a Weaver in her village who might take her place as a'laq, but there was nothing to be done about that. All in all, she'd had a good life, despite losing F'Jai too soon. And she had fully expected these last turns of her life to be peaceful.

The gods, it seemed, had something else in mind for her. First, they brought Jynna, a young Y'Qatt girl who came to Lowna with a wild story of a Mettai witch and cursed baskets and a white-hair plague. The tale turned out to be true, and in the end Jynna was joined by several more Y'Qatt children, orphans all, who now lived among them, almost as if they had been born Fal'Borna. Not content with this, the gods then sent to Lowna a merchant named R'Shev, who told a remarkable story of his own. An Eandi army had been seen along the Silverwater making ready for an attack on the Fal'Borna. And amazingly, they marched with Mettai sorcerers.

There would be no peace for her in the last days of her life. Instead, U'Selle had been the one to warn the rest of the clan that war was coming to the plain. Less than a turn before, she had used her magic to enter the dreams of other a'laqs and tell them of the approaching Eandi warriors and their Mettai allies. This once, they had treated her with courtesy and gratitude. It almost seemed that they finally recognized what U'Selle had known all along: Regardless of how her people made their gold, or how she had come to lead her village, she was Fal'Borna. Nothing else mattered. If there was to be a war, her people would fight in it. They would spill their blood in defense of the clan lands; they would kill or be killed, just like every other Fal'Borna on the plain.

Ever since giving this warning to her fellow a'laqs, U'Selle had waited for some word as to what would happen next. By now, she was certain, the Eandi had crossed into Fal'Borna land and were attacking septs. But she heard nothing. No Weavers walked in her dreams to tell her how the war was going or what other a'laqs on the plain expected her and her people to do. Had they forgotten Lowna? Had they been defeated? Impossible! Had they already destroyed the invaders? She thought this unlikely as well.

Night after night, U'Selle slept fitfully, waiting for dreams that never came, waking in the morning to frustration and a vague fear that she tried to ignore.

On this night, though, the ninth of the waxing, all that finally changed. Or so she thought.

Her dream began as had others in which Weavers walked. There was a clarity to such dreams that U'Selle had learned to recognize long ago, when F'Jai first courted her without the knowledge of her parents. He had visited her in her dreams, where they could share kisses and speak of their future life together in private. Always these visions had seemed more real, more solid, than any other dreams she'd ever had. And even now, with F'Jai long dead and Weavers disturbing her sleep for far less pleasant reasons, that solid feeling remained.

So as soon as the dream began she knew to look for a Weaver. Whoever had come had conjured for her a bland stretch of plain that she didn't recognize, a cloudless blue sky, and a gentle, cool wind. She turned, searching for the a'laq.

Her first thought upon seeing the man was that her senses had betrayed her and this wasn't real, after all. This Weaver didn't look at all Fal'Borna. He didn't look like any Qirsi she'd ever seen. He was as broad in the chest and shoulders as one of her own people, but he was nearly a full head taller than any Fal'Borna she knew, and his skin was ghostly pale.

He must have sensed her doubts, because he said immediately, "It's all right, N'Qlae. I'm a friend. I intend you no harm."

She looked around again. It felt the way Weaver dreams

always did. The setting, his voice—it had to be real. And yet . . .

"What clan are you from?" she asked. "Who are you?"

"My name is Grinsa jal Arriet. I'm from the Forelands, though right now I'm living among the Fal'Borna. I'm in the sept of E'Menua, son of E'Sedt."

U'Selle nodded. She had no trouble believing that this strange, handsome man came from the Northlands. And she'd heard of E'Menua. "Why have you come to me this way?"

"You've heard of the plague that's been spreading across the plain?" he asked. "The one conjured by the Mettai?"

U'Selle smiled thinly. "Yes, I've heard of it. Are there any among our—" She frowned. "Among my people who haven't?"

A small smile touched his lips and he inclined his head, seeming to concede the point. "Probably not, N'Qlae."

"I'm properly addressed as A'Laq."

The man frowned at this, clearly puzzled. "I've never . . . I thought . . ."

"It's rare for a woman to become a'laq, but it does happen. My husband was a'laq. When he died, there were no other Weavers in the village, so I took the title."

"Forgive me, A'Laq."

"Tell me, Forelander, how did this plague become your concern?"

"I told you, A'Laq: I'm living now among the Fal'Borna. It's the concern of every Qirsi on the plain. But more than that, I've had the plague, and I very nearly died of it."

"What?" she said. Then she shook her head. "I don't believe you. I haven't heard of anyone surviving this illness."

"I had help. I was saved by two Mettai men. Their names are Besh and Sirj, and they come from the village—"

U'Selle shook her head and held up a finger, stopping him. "You're telling me that you were healed by Mettai? The same people who conjured this plague in the first place, who now march against us with the dark-eyes; you want me to believe that they healed you?"

"It's the truth," he said simply. "This plague wasn't spread by all Mettai people. It was created by one twisted old woman from the same village these men come from. They tracked her, killed her, and sought to keep the plague from spreading. Eventually another Fal'Borna and I wound up journeying with them, and when we fell ill, these men created a new spell that cured us."

"That's a most remarkable tale, Forelander," the a'laq said in a voice intended to make clear that she still didn't believe him.

"It gets more remarkable, A'Laq."

She raised an eyebrow.

"The spell these men created did more than heal. It protects us from ever getting the plague again. Like the plague, it's spread by magic. So by walking in your dreams, I've passed their spell to you and made you immune to the plague."

"You're sure of this?" she asked, not yet daring to hope that it was true.

"I am, A'Laq. As I say, I had the plague. I offer as proof the fact that I'm alive. But there's still more. You can pass this spell on to the others in your sept, simply by touching them with your magic. Any magic will do. This is a gift to your people from E'Menua. All he asks is that if you encounter this plague, you let him know immediately that the spell worked and saved your people."

She regarded the man through narrowed eyes. "This is all very strange," she said. "I haven't met E'Menua, but from all I've heard about him, he doesn't seem like the kind of a'laq who would send gifts freely to other septs."

The Forelander appeared amused by this.

"And why would he have you tell me this? He has other Weavers—Fal'Borna Weavers—who could do this for him."

For a long time the man just looked back at her, a faint smile on his face. Finally he shook his head and laughed.

"I've been doing this for several nights," he said. "And you're the first a'laq to challenge me on any of it. You're also the first woman I've spoken to. My wife would tell me there's a lesson to be learned from that."

U'Selle didn't respond.

"Everything I've told you is true," the Forelander said. "Except for the part about this being a gift from E'Menua. He doesn't know that I've been doing this." He faltered, but only briefly. "And he wouldn't be happy if he did."

"As an a'laq, I'm obligated to tell him."

"I understand," he said evenly.

"This doesn't frighten you?" U'Selle asked.

"I don't frighten easily, A'Laq. And I believe that what I'm doing is necessary. I knew there was a risk when I began. If E'Menua finds out, so be it."

U'Selle eyed the man for several moments, tapping a finger to her lips. "You're a most unusual man, Grinsa of the Forelands. Did you really have the plague?"

"Yes, I did."

"And these Mettai cured you of it?"

"That's right."

She considered this. "But E'Menua doesn't believe you, does he?"

The man smiled. "No, he doesn't."

U'Selle nodded, though she continued to stare at him. "Why should this matter to you so much? I understand that if you're living in his sept he's your a'laq, and you don't want him doubting your word. But you've gone to a great deal of trouble to tell me all of this. There must be more to it than that."

He said nothing.

"Explain this to me, Forelander. You don't seem to fear E'Menua, but I can't imagine you want him to know about this conversation. Tell me the truth, and perhaps I'll keep all this to myself."

"All right. We can prevent this plague from spreading. We can stop it from killing. And because he doesn't believe me, the a'laq does nothing."

U'Selle waited, expecting him to say more. When he didn't, she said, "Is that all?"

"Isn't that enough?"

She narrowed her eyes again. "No, I don't think it is."

He gazed back at her for several moments, as if testing his will against hers. At last he looked away, gave another small shake of his head, and laughed again. "Your people are fortunate to have such a wise leader, A'Laq." He took a breath. "You're right: That's not all. E'Menua is holding the two Mettai men as prisoners. These men killed the woman responsible for the plague, cured me, and created this spell to protect all Qirsi. And E'Menua intends to execute them as enemies of the Fal'Borna."

U'Selle shrugged. "We're at war with the Mettai."

The man's expression turned to stone. "And here I'd started to believe that you were different."

"I'm not saying E'Menua is justified, Forelander. But even if you've only lived among the Fal'Borna for a short time, you should understand that this is how my people think. The Mettai have declared themselves enemies of the Fal'Borna; therefore, these two men are enemies as well. It's our way."

"Well, in this case, your way is leading E'Menua down a dark and dangerous path."

She nodded. "Yes, I suppose it is."

He looked frustrated, discouraged.

"Well, A'Laq, I should leave you to sleep. I have more Weavers to contact before this night is over."

"I hope all your effort is rewarded, Grinsa of the Forelands. I can't say that I'm hoping to encounter this plague— I've heard too much about it, and I've seen what it does to those it leaves behind. But if we should be exposed to it, and if we survive the encounter, I'll be sure to thank E'Menua for his generous gift."

That made the man smile. "Thank you, A'Laq."

"Go," she said. "I'd like a few hours of peace before dawn."

He bowed to her. "May the gods smile on you and your people."

"They usually do," she said, and woke up.

Jynna was sick again, the pain in her stomach so sharp that she could do nothing more than lie on her side, her knees drawn up to her chest. She could hear her brothers and parents calling for her, and she wanted to answer them, to tell them that she was here, that she needed their help. But she had her teeth clenched against the illness in her gut; she couldn't bring herself even to open her mouth.

And then she saw the old woman. She was walking in Jynna's direction, her eyes fixed on the girl, a broad grin on her wizened face. She carried a basket in each hand, and within the baskets were smaller baskets, which in turn held even tinier baskets. The back of her left hand was bloody, and Jynna saw that the knife on her belt dripped blood as well.

"You aren't supposed to be alive," the woman said. "It was supposed to kill all of you."

She wanted to shout back at the woman to leave her alone. She wanted to tell the woman that this plague she had brought to her people wouldn't kill her.

But the woman began to cackle, as if she could read Jynna's thoughts.

"You're right," she said.

And though the woman was still a few strides away, her voice seemed to come from just beside her. It seemed to Jynna that she could feel the woman's foul breath on her neck.

"You're right, child," she said again. "It won't kill you. But I will."

She pulled the knife free, and then pulled a second from behind her. This time Jynna did open her mouth to scream. If only her father or mother could hear her. If only her brothers could.

"They're dead," the woman said, laughing again.

But Jynna screamed anyway.

"Jynna!"

She felt a hand on her arm and struggled to get away.

"Jynna, wake up, love."

She opened her eyes, saw S'Doryn sitting on the edge of her bed looking down at her, his brow furrowed with concern.

Closing her eyes again, she took a long breath.

"It was the same dream."

"It sounded like it."

Jynna looked at him. "Why? What did I say?"

He looked away.

"Was I calling for Mama and Papa again?" she asked, her eyes stinging.

S'Doryn nodded. "And your brothers, too."

She wiped a tear from her cheek and made herself smile. "Well, it was just a dream."

He tried to return her smile, but his forehead was still creased and there was concern in his golden yellow eyes. She sat up and looked around the small chamber.

"Where's Vettala?" she asked.

"She woke up some time ago. She and N'Tevva went to the marketplace. Not that they'll find much there, but Vettala wanted to go."

Vettala, like Jynna, had come to Lowna from Tivston, the Y'Qatt village where they had been raised. A few turns before, Tivston had been destroyed by the plague loosed upon the land by the old Mettai woman she'd seen in her nightmare. Nearly everyone in the village had died, including Jynna's parents and her older brothers, Delon and Blayne. There were a few other survivors of that horrible night who had come to Lowna with Jynna and Vettala. Etan and Hev, Pelda and Sebbi—all of them children.

For a long time, Vettala had been unwilling to speak to anyone or stray from Jynna's side. But S'Doryn and N'Tevva had welcomed Jynna and Vettala into their home and now were as close to a father and mother as the girls would ever have. And with time, Vettala had come to love and trust N'Tevva, just as Jynna loved and trusted S'Doryn.

"So they've gone to the market," Jynna said with false brightness. She threw off her blanket and swung herself out of bed. "What are we going to do?"

She'd had this dream enough times to know that the images she'd seen would be with her for most of the day. Her stomach still felt sour, and would for a few hours, until she was hungry enough to force down some food. But she knew as well that she'd be better off getting out of the house and doing something—anything—that would distract her.

"What do you want to do?" S'Doryn asked.

She gave him a sly look. "The last time we went fishing you caught one more than I did—"

He shook his head. "Two."

"That small one didn't count. That's why you threw it back. You caught one more than I did and I want a chance to beat you."

He grinned, and this time it appeared genuine. "All right. Fishing it is." He stood and crossed to the door. "Get dressed and I'll . . . I'll pack some food to take with us, in case you get hungry."

Jynna nodded. After he left the chamber she closed the door and pulled on her breeches and a shirt that N'Tevva had made for her. It was soft and heavy and very comfortable, particularly now that the Snows were nearly upon them. She pulled on a pair of hose and reached for her shoes. As she was putting them on her feet, she heard voices coming from the common room. N'Tevva and Vettala, no doubt.

But when she stepped out of the small room she shared with Vettala, she saw S'Doryn speaking with U'Selle, Lowna's a'laq.

"Good morning, Jynna," the old woman said. Immediately she was taken with a fit of coughing.

This happened to her quite often. Jynna gathered that the a'laq was dying, though few in the village ever said as much or even spoke of her being sick. In fact, the only person whom Jynna had heard say anything about it was U'Selle herself, who often joked about how odd it was that she was still alive. Jynna thought that U'Selle had to be very brave to laugh about her own impending death. It was one of the reasons Jynna liked the a'laq so much.

"I understand you're going fishing," U'Selle said when she could speak again. Her cheeks were red and she seemed to struggle merely to draw breath.

"Yes, A'Laq."

"Jynna's under the mistaken impression that she can catch more fish than I can," S'Doryn said, winking at Jynna. "I intend to disabuse her of the notion."

"He sounds a bit too confident to me, Jynna. I think he's in for a surprise."

Jynna smiled. "I think so, too, A'Laq."

"Before you go, though, my dear, I need a word with S'Doryn in private. I hope you don't mind."

The a'laq said this with a smile, but Jynna could tell that she took seriously whatever matters she'd come to discuss. Suddenly Jynna felt cold. Had the plague come back? Was the Eandi army headed toward Lowna?

"The fishing poles are around back," S'Doryn said, forcing a smile as well. "Why don't you fetch them and the bucket and that net we used last time? I'll be out shortly."

Jynna nodded and crossed to the door. She could feel them watching her, and she knew they'd say nothing of consequence until they were certain she was out of earshot.

She tried to do just what S'Doryn had asked of her. She retrieved the poles from where she and S'Doryn had left them after their last visit to the lake. She found the bucket and net right beside them, and though she struggled a bit, she managed to bring all of it around to the front of the house in one trip.

The problem was that this left her with nothing to do. She checked the poles for tangles in the line. She made certain the net had no holes.

But her mind kept returning to the same question: What were S'Doryn and the a'laq talking about? Most likely, it was nothing that concerned her. S'Doryn was a member of the clan council, and he and U'Selle had been friends for a long time. The a'laq often came to him to discuss things that Jynna thought were terribly boring: disputes between traders in the marketplace, or between villagers who wished to work the same plot of land; provisions for the coming Snows; requests from young couples who wished to build a new house in one part of the village or another. Once they'd spent half the day talking about a fight between two men who claimed to have caught the same fish. Jynna had thought that one especially funny. She could hardly believe they were talking about adults.

Other times, though, they talked about Jynna and Vettala and the other children who had come to Lowna from Tivston. Or they spoke of the plague that had claimed Jynna's family, or of the coming war. These conversations fascinated Jynna. Often after U'Selle left, she would ask S'Doryn so many questions about what they had said that he would finally tell her to leave him alone, something he never did under any other circumstance.

After standing there for several moments, looking at the net, and the bucket, and the poles with their untangled lines, she sidled closer to the house. She knew it was wrong; she knew that S'Doryn would be angry with her if he found her trying to listen. But she couldn't help herself.

At first she couldn't hear much of anything. A small flock of finches chose that moment to alight on the branches of the spruce tree just beside the house, and for several moments their chattering drowned out everything else.

Then they moved on, and Jynna stepped closer to the house, even going so far as to press her ear against the wood. She heard S'Doryn's voice first.

". . . peculiar that a man from the Forelands would be doing all this?"

"Yes, I do," U'Selle answered. She began to cough and for several moments said nothing more. "It seems he's living on the plain now," she went on at last, her voice sounding strained.

"So it's not surprising that he should be concerned about the plague. But I gather that he and E'Menua are at odds. I'm not sure what that means."

"And these Mettai he mentioned; do you know where they came from?"

"I don't know the name of their village, if that's what you mean. But he said they came from the same village as the witch."

Jynna could scarcely believe what she was hearing. They had to be talking about that woman! Licaldi! The one who killed her family; the one who had haunted her sleep this past night. What other Mettai witch could they have been referring to?

"This could all have been a lie," S'Doryn said. "He might have intended to kill you rather than help you."

"Why would a Weaver from the Forelands—" She broke off, taken by another coughing fit. "Why would he want to kill me?" she continued eventually. "I'm practically dead already. And as Fal'Borna septs and villages go, Lowna isn't important to anyone other than us."

"So you believe him," S'Doryn said.

"Yes," U'Selle told him, "I suppose I do. I came to you to gauge your reaction. If you don't want me to pass this spell on to you, then I won't, nor will I take it to any of the others. But if you believe we should trust this man, then I want to spread the spell as quickly as possible. The plague is still out there. Just because it's spread westward doesn't mean it can't come back this way."

For several moments neither of them spoke, until finally S'Doryn broke the silence.

"You've put me in a difficult position, A'Laq."

"Yes, I have. Would you have preferred that I go to one of the others?"

"You know I wouldn't. Since Jynna first came here," he went on, dropping his voice lower, so that Jynna had to press her ear more tightly to the wood, "I've tried to tell her that she shouldn't hate all Mettai for what befell her family. But the truth is, I've never trusted the Mettai. I've tried to avoid having dealings with them in the marketplace. And now you want me to accept this spell of theirs. I don't know if I can do it."

"I understand. But this can save lives, S'Doryn. This can protect all of us from the plague."

"If it's true."

"Yes. For whatever it's worth," the a'laq said, after another brief silence, "I feel well today. Or at least as well as I ever do. The spell hasn't affected me at all."

"Maybe it doesn't work, then. Maybe the Mettai and this Forelander are hoping to make us overconfident. If we no longer fear the plague, we might grow complacent, careless. They could kill us that way."

U'Selle offered no reply, and finally S'Doryn said, "You don't believe that, either."

"No," the a'laq said. "I don't."

"Very well, then. What is it you'd have to do?"

"I just need to touch your magic with my own."

"Jynna!"

Jynna jumped so violently that she scraped her ear on the side of the house. N'Tevva was striding toward her, with Vettala following at a run.

"What are you doing?" N'Tevva demanded, though she already seemed to know, judging from the angry expression on her face.

Jynna stared back at her, wide-eyed with fright. Back in Tivston, before the plague came, her own mother and father had grown angry with her at times, just as they did with her older brothers. She knew that all parents yelled at their children.

But this was the first time either N'Tevva or S'Doryn had been so angry with her. And yet, her thoughts were focused elsewhere.

I just need to touch your magic with my own.

"Jynna, answer me!" N'Tevva said, stopping a short distance from where the girl stood. "What were you doing?"

Vettala had stopped just behind N'Tevva and was gaping at Jynna, looking even more frightened than Jynna felt.

Jynna bolted past N'Tevva, ran up the small steps at the front of the house, and pushed open the door.

"Jynna!" S'Doryn said, obviously startled by her entrance. "Did I just hear N'Tevva?"

"You can't do it!" Jynna said. "You can't let her touch you with that spell!"

S'Doryn's expression hardened. "You were listening?"

"Yes. I'm sorry. I shouldn't have been. But you can't let that magic touch you!" She felt tears on her cheeks and she swiped at them angrily.

"Jynna, you know better than that!" S'Doryn said. "I told you to wait for me outside! That didn't mean go outside and then put your ear to the wall!"

She felt her cheeks color. A shadow darkened the common room, and glancing back, Jynna saw N'Tevva standing in the doorway.

"Come with me, Jynna," N'Tevva said severely. "We need to have a little talk."

"No!" Jynna said. "Not until—"

"Why shouldn't he let me pass the spell to him?" U'Selle asked in a voice that silenced them all. The a'laq didn't appear angry, but she looked deadly serious. "If you were listening, you understand that this spell could save lives. It could keep the plague from spreading to our people. Surely, you of all people would want that. You know what this spell does, Jynna. Don't you want N'Tevva and S'Doryn to be protected from it?"

"It's Mettai magic!" she said.

Suddenly she was bawling as she hadn't in years. She cried so hard she could hardly draw breath and couldn't see for her tears. She felt hands on her—S'Doryn's hands—and she jerked away, not wanting to be held or even touched.

"Jynna—" S'Doryn began in a soothing voice.

"No! You can't do this! You know what the Mettai did to us! You know that they hate us, that they want us dead!"

"We know what one Mettai did, Jynna," the a'laq said. "That's all."

"What about the Mettai who are with the army?" Jynna knew she wasn't being clear, but she assumed U'Selle would know what she meant.

"These Mettai aren't with the army. And they didn't make the plague. In fact, they killed the woman who did."

"That's what the Forelander says. How do you know it's true?"

Through her tears, she saw the a'laq smile sadly.

"I don't," U'Selle said. "I wish I could tell you that I know beyond doubt these men can be trusted, but I'd be lying. At some point, Jynna, a leader must trust her instincts. Mine tell me that this Forelander is telling the truth, and that these two Mettai have done what they can to help us, regardless of what others of their kind might be doing."

Jynna didn't know what to say to the a'laq. U'Selle had always been honest with her, and had always spoken to her as if Jynna were an adult. Even S'Doryn didn't do that. She understood what the a'laq was telling her. She could even see the sense in it. If this spell could protect the people of Lowna from Licaldi's plague, U'Selle would have been mad not to pass it on. And yet, Jynna couldn't get past her hatred of the Mettai and her rage at what their magic had done to her family.

"I don't want the magic to touch me," she finally said, knowing as she did that it made little sense. She was too young to have come into her power, which was why she had survived the plague when it destroyed Tivston. This spell must have been intended for grown-ups, not for children. Still, she wanted them all to understand that she didn't approve of this.

For a moment she feared that U'Selle would laugh at her, that all of them would. But the a'laq regarded her solemnly.

"That seems fair," she said. "But I will pass the spell on to N'Tevva and S'Doryn. Is that all right?"

She looked back at N'Tevva, and then at S'Doryn. Like the a'laq, both of them appeared to be taking her seriously.

"Yes," Jynna said. "But I don't want to be here when you do it."

U'Selle nodded.

Jynna turned to leave the house, but before she could, S'Doryn said, "We still need to talk about what you did, Jynna. I don't care about the reason. Listening to other people's private conversations is wrong."

"All right," Jynna said, her voice low. She looked at the a'laq once more. "What about the other Mettai?" she asked. "You're willing to trust these two men, but what about the others?"

U'Selle straightened. "The other Mettai are enemies of all Fal'Borna people. Like the dark-eye army with which they've allied themselves, they'll be crushed. If I have the chance, I'll destroy them myself."

Jynna nodded once. "Good." And she walked out of the house.

Chapter 15

E'MENUA'S SEPT, CENTRAL PLAIN

It happened without much fanfare, just as Grinsa had hoped and expected it would. The morning after he walked in the n'qlae's dreams, he heard from Q'Daer that the a'laq had decided that the Mettai were to be spared for the time being. When Grinsa asked the young Weaver why E'Menua had chosen to keep the men alive, Q'Daer shrugged as if the decision were of little consequence, and said, "We're preparing for war. Right now nothing else matters. And I think he believes we can learn something of Mettai magic from them."

If the young Fal'Borna knew more than he was letting on, he did a good job of concealing it. After ending his conversation with Q'Daer, Grinsa hurried to the Mettai's z'kal. Besh and Sirj were inside, both of them looking grim.

"They're not letting us out of here," Besh said, as soon as Grinsa stepped into the shelter. "They say that we're prisoners and we're not to set foot outside."

"I'll see what I can do about that," Grinsa told him. "Believe it or not, you're better off than you might have been. E'Menua had every intention of executing you both. I've seen to it that he won't, but for now you are prisoners. There was nothing I could do about that. I'm sorry."

Besh shook his head, looking sad and old. "It's not your doing."

"They're going to want you to tell them about Mettai magic," Grinsa said.

Sirj looked up sharply. "What about it?"

"How it works. How to combat it."

"And if we refuse?" the younger man asked.

Grinsa shrugged. "I don't know what they'll do. I'm not telling you this because I think you should answer their questions. I just thought you should know that they'll be asking you about your magic."

Sirj nodded but said nothing more.

Grinsa didn't stay with the Mettai for long. The entire sept had begun preparations for the coming war, and though E'Menua and the other Weavers had made it clear to him that Weavers weren't to labor with other Fal'Borna, he felt that he should do something. Men and women were shaping spear shafts while children sharpened the heads. Others were gathering food for the sept's warriors, and still others were collecting blankets for the warriors to carry with them on the journey. Surely there was work enough that all needed to contribute.

But Grinsa soon learned that it wasn't just the Weavers who felt he shouldn't stoop to menial work. Nearly all the Fal'Borna seemed uncomfortable with the idea of a Weaver helping them. Mostly he sat outside his z'kal playing with Bryntelle while Cresenne worked. Twice a day he carried his daughter to the tanning circle and let Cresenne nurse her before taking her back home. He occasionally went to check on Besh and Sirj, to see if they needed anything and to make certain they were being treated well. But his conversations with the Mettai remained strained.

That was where he was on the third day after his conversation with the n'qlae, when a young warrior found him and informed him that the a'laq wished to speak with him. Immediately, he took Bryntelle to the older Fal'Borna girls who usually cared for the young children of the sept. Then he made his way to E'Menua's z'kal.

He found the a'laq sitting outside the shelter with D'Pera, Q'Daer, and L'Norr. At least two dozen younger warriors, most of whom Grinsa didn't know, stood around their small circle, clearly listening to their conversation. He guessed that these men were a'jeis, leaders of small hunting parties who answered to the a'laq's Weavers. It seemed logical that in times of war the a'jeis would take on responsibilities similar to those of captains in an Eandi army.

"At last," E'Menua said, not bothering to hide his annoyance.

"Forgive me, A'Laq. I was—"

"I know where you were," E'Menua said coldly. He indicated a space next to Q'Daer at his right. "Sit down."

Grinsa sat. The other Weavers hardly spared him a glance, but the young warriors stared at him, some merely with curiosity, others with open hostility.

"I've spoken with other a'laqs on the plain," E'Menua began, casting a quick look Grinsa's way. "All are preparing to drive back the Eandi invaders. Our warriors are to meet those of the other septs east of S'Vralna. We have enough spears to arm every man and woman in the sept, and we have horses for every able warrior. Even now, U'Vara . . ." He glanced at Grinsa again. "My daughter. She is directing the children of the sept as they pack sacks of dried rilda meat and raw silverroot. We have skins for water, and plenty of blankets."

"You've prepared well, A'Laq," Grinsa said, and he meant it. He'd seen Eandi lords in the Forelands task their quarter-masters with readying an army for battle, only to have those preparations take days and days. Yes, E'Menua's army was small compared to those of Eibitharian dukedoms, but still, Grinsa thought, many Eandi nobles could learn a thing or two from the Fal'Borna about readying their people for war.

"You expected less of us?" E'Menua asked testily.

"I didn't know what to expect. I'm very impressed."

E'Menua frowned, as if disconcerted by the compliment. "Each of you will be leading a party of riders, aided by six or seven a'jeis. L'Norr and Q'Daer, you'll take those with fire magic. I intend to take the shapers." He turned to Grinsa. "You have experience with mists and winds?"

Grinsa smiled, remembering his and Cresenne's sea voyage to the Southlands, when he had used the power of winds to steer their ship through a violent storm. "Yes, A'Laq. I'll guard our men from the arrows of the Eandi bowmen."

It was E'Menua's turn to sound surprised. "You've done this before?" the a'laq asked.

"Yes. A war was fought in the Forelands just before we left. On more than one occasion I had to summon winds to defeat the arrows of Eandi attackers."

"Very well then," the a'laq said.

Several of the warriors appeared to regard Grinsa with even more enmity. He wondered if these were men with magic of mists and winds who would have to take orders from him.

"There will be many septs on the plain, and many a'laqs. You'll take orders from me, and no one else."

Grinsa stared at the ground, refusing to be the one to ask the obvious question. Eventually Q'Daer found the courage to ask it.

"And . . . and if you should fall, A'Laq?"

"Then you'll be in command," E'Menua told him. "And upon completing our victory, you'll become a'laq."

"Thank you, A'Laq," Q'Daer said, his voice dropping to a whisper.

"How soon do we ride?" Grinsa asked.

"Tomorrow, at first light. We'll be pushing the horses hard. We want to reach the other septs in no more than three days."

Grinsa nodded.

"What can you tell us about Mettai magic, Forelander?" E'Menua asked. He wore a sly smile on his lips. It seemed to Grinsa that the a'laq thought he'd refuse to answer.

"I can't tell you much," he said. "Just a turn or two ago I didn't even know that Mettai still existed. All of you probably know far more than I do." He paused, eyeing the a'laq, who merely stared back at him, silent, waiting. "They use blood and earth," he went on eventually. "And they have to recite their spells, either out loud or to themselves. So they can't attack with their magic as quickly as we can. On the other hand, they can do things we can't."

"Like what?" one of the young warriors asked.

"Well, I saw Besh, the old Mettai man, conjure a living fox from blood and dirt. I've also seen him create a swarm of hornets. When was the last time you saw a Qirsi do anything like that?"

"You expect them to attack us with foxes?" E'Menua asked, laughing, and drawing chuckles from the others. "Do you think that a swarm of bees will be enough to defeat the combined might of a dozen Fal'Borna septs?"

"Of course not, A'Laq," Grinsa said evenly. "You asked me about Mettai magic and I'm telling you what I've seen. If they can conjure foxes and hornets, they can summon other creatures as well."

E'Menua's mirth faded slowly. "Yes," he finally said. "All right. What else?"

"What else do you want to know?"

"Can they combine their magic as we can?" L'Norr asked.

Grinsa shook his head. "I don't see how they could. But I may be wrong."

"They can't," E'Menua said, sounding sure of himself. "That's our greatest advantage. That's why, even with the Mettai on their side, the dark-eyes can't defeat us."

E'Menua stood and the other Weavers scrambled to do the same, even the n'qlae.

"I want every a'jei to prepare his riders," the a'laq said. "Tell them what I've told you here today. We ride at dawn. I'll expect all of you to be ready. That's all."

The warriors bowed to E'Menua and said, "Yes, A'Laq," in near unison. Then they moved off, leaving the Weavers still standing in a loose circle.

E'Menua turned to Grinsa. "I want a word with you."

Grinsa nodded, having expected this as soon as the man told them that he had been speaking with other a'laqs.

"Leave us," E'Menua said to Q'Daer and L'Norr.

The two young Weavers glanced at Grinsa before walking off. By now, he was sure, they were used to the a'laq sending them away so that he and Grinsa could continue their running feud. E'Menua and D'Pera shared a quick look. A moment later she ducked into their z'kal. E'Menua began to walk, and Grinsa followed.

"I take it I've angered you again," Grinsa said.

"You walk in the dreams of my fellow a'laqs, offering gifts in my name that I never intended to give. You dare to walk in D'Pera's dreams in order to turn her against me. Why should I be angry?"

"I didn't try to turn the n'qlae against you. I asked her to intervene on behalf of Besh and Sirj. What you did to them the other day was wrong. I was determined that you wouldn't use the words you coerced out of Besh to justify killing them."

"That doesn't excuse it!" E'Menua said, his voice rising.

They were still in the sept, and several people stopped what they were doing and looked at the two men as they walked by.

"She is my wife," the a'laq went on, his voice dropping once more. "You had no right to approach her in that way. You had no right to come betw—" He stopped, pressing his lips in a thin line.

Grinsa knew better than to point out what E'Menua had so clearly recognized himself. He kept his gaze lowered and said, "You're right, A'Laq. I had no right trying to come between you. I did what I thought was necessary, but I was wrong to do it. I'm sorry."

For several moments neither of them said anything.

Finally, E'Menua said, "As for speaking to the other a'laqs . . ." He broke off and shook his head. "You were surprisingly clever."

Grinsa grinned. "Was I?"

"Yes," E'Menua said, looking at him. "They were all so grateful to me. At first I didn't know why, but then one of them said something and I began to piece it together." He faced forward again. "D'Pera told me why you did it. You may well be right. Whatever my doubts about the Mettai, their spell might save Fal'Borna lives. I should have passed it on to the other septs, or at least to their a'laqs so that they could decide for themselves what to do with the dark-eye magic."

"Thank you, A'Laq."

"How many a'laqs have you contacted?"

"Perhaps twenty," Grinsa said.

E'Menua looked at him again, his eyes wide. "Twenty?"

"I haven't been sleeping much," Grinsa said, smiling sheepishly.

The a'laq didn't appear amused. "You'd better sleep tonight," he said. "We'll be riding hard come morning, and I don't know how close the Eandi are. You'll be of no use to me if you're half asleep."

"Yes, A'Laq."

They walked in silence for several moments, until Grinsa began to wonder if E'Menua wanted him to go away.

But abruptly the a'laq asked, "What creatures?"

Grinsa blinked, not understanding the question. "I'm sorry?"

"You said before that if the Mettai could conjure foxes and hornets, they could conjure other creatures, too. What kind?"

"I don't know. Anything, I would think. I assume it would have to be something real, something that actually exists in our world. But I don't even know that for certain."

E'Menua halted, as did Grinsa.

"Are you saying that they could summon creatures from legend?"

"I'm saying that I don't know what they can do. You laughed when I mentioned the fox and hornets. I wanted you to understand that this power they possess is no trifle."

The a'laq rubbed a hand over his face, looking deeply troubled. "There are tales of monsters—creatures of myth, demons from Bian's realm. Our magic would be powerless against them."

Grinsa wasn't sure what to say. "It may be that they can't do this, A'Laq. I just don't know."

"I want to speak with them," E'Menua said, starting back toward Besh and Sirj's z'kal. "I want to speak with the Mettai immediately."

Grinsa hurried after him. He didn't expect that Besh and Sirj would have any interest in speaking with the a'laq, but he knew better than to argue. And he knew that he had to be there when the a'laq questioned the two men, if for no other reason than to protect them when they refused to answer.

For the past few days, Besh had spent most of his time sleeping or fighting off the interminable boredom. In the best of times, Sirj was not one for idle conversation. Since discovering that they were prisoners of the Fal'Borna, the younger man had retreated into a sullen, brooding silence. Besh could hardly blame him, but it did make for long, tedious days.

At first, just after the a'laq's betrayal, Besh had been too angry to sit still. He'd paced around the tiny shelter, seething, trying to think of some way to retaliate. Soon, though, he came to realize that there was no way. He and Sirj were powerless here. It wasn't that the Fal'Borna had taken his blade. As Lici had shown him all too clearly while she was still alive, a Mettai needed only a bit of malice and sharp fingernails in order to conjure. But it didn't matter whether he and Sirj could draw upon their own blood; whatever magic they might have been able to do was nothing next to the power of the Fal'Borna. They were being held by a foe they could not defeat, menaced constantly by magic that could overwhelm their own.

After three days, he had surrendered to despair. Even his faith in Grinsa and the Forelander's ability to protect him, which had led him to this sept in the first place, had now vanished. He knew that Grinsa wanted to help them, that he was trying still to win their freedom. But he no longer believed Grinsa could succeed.

So it was that he was asleep again when the flap covering the shelter's entrance suddenly was thrown back, flooding the small structure with light.

Besh sat up so quickly that his head began to spin. His heart was racing and he felt disoriented.

"Come out here!" a voice commanded. "I want a word with both of you."

"It's the a'laq," Sirj said quietly. "Do you think he means to kill us?"

"I'm here, too."

That voice Besh recognized. "Grinsa?" he called.

"It's all right," the Forelander said. "You're in no danger."

Besh and Sirj shared a look.

"All right," Besh called.

Sirj stood and pulled Besh to his feet. Then both men stepped out into the daylight.

It was just the two of them: Grinsa and the a'laq. The Forelander appeared calm, which Besh found reassuring. E'Menua, on the other hand, looked unnerved and agitated. Besh was pleased by this, too.

"I want to know more about your magic," E'Menua said. "I want to know what it can do."

"You mean," Sirj said, "you want us to help you defeat the Mettai who are marching against you."

"That's right," the a'laq answered. "You claim that you mean my people no harm. They may be harmed by the magic these other Mettai use against us."

Besh laughed, drawing a hot glare from the Fal'Borna.

"Forgive me," Besh said. "But I have to ask: What would you call a Fal'Borna prisoner who helped his captors in a fight against you? A traitor? A demon? Or would you dispense with name-calling and simply kill him?"

The a'laq looked so angry that for a moment Besh thought the man might strike him. Instead, he showed the first true sign of weakness Besh had seen in him.

"I . . . I could free you. If you answer my questions, I can release you, send you back to your people."

Something had the man deeply frightened.

"That would be even more of a betrayal," Sirj said. "I won't buy my freedom with the blood of other Mettai."

"I can use my magic against you!" the a'laq said. "I can make you answer!"

Besh smiled bitterly. "You can make me say a lot of things. You've already proven that."

The a'laq's face colored.

"If I was in your position, I wouldn't answer, either," Grinsa said. "But I don't think any good can come of a defeat for the Fal'Borna, or a defeat of the Eandi for that matter. We need to find some way to drive this army back across the Silverwater without too many people being killed. Any information you can give us might help with that."

Sirj let out a sharp laugh. "So you count yourself as one of them now?"

"Sirj," Besh said, laying a hand on the man's arm.

"It's all right," Grinsa told him. He looked at Sirj. "I deserved that. I promised that I'd keep you safe, and I've failed. I'm sorry." He took a breath. "Yes. In this war, I consider myself Fal'Borna. If the Eandi and the Mettai reach this sept, they won't stop to ask where I come from or how long I've lived on the plain. They'll see my white hair and my yellow eyes, and they'll kill me. And then they'll do the same to Cresenne and our daughter."

Sirj dropped his gaze.

"You think you can prevent this war?" Besh asked.

Grinsa shook his head. "The war's probably started already. But I'm hoping that we can find a way to end it before too much damage is done. And as I see it, the only way to stop the war is to drive the Eandi back. If they manage to retake any of these lands, it could mean another century of warfare. The Fal'Borna won't waste any time in trying to take back the cities and lands they've lost. More Eandi will come, and before long fighting will spread all across the Southlands."

"So you do want us to help them," Besh said, unable to keep the despair from his voice. He understood the Forelander's reasoning, and he could hardly argue with the progression of events Grinsa had laid out. The history of the Southlands was littered with battles and failed campaigns that began much the way this latest invasion had. But he couldn't help feeling that Grinsa had betrayed them in some small way.

"I want you to help me. The a'laq will leave us, and we can—"

"I will not!" E'Menua said, glaring at the Forelander. "They're my prisoners! I'll stay here and question them for as long as I see fit!"

"You just offered to free them," Grinsa said.

"If they were to tell me what I want to know!"

"And Sirj has already said no to that," Grinsa said. "I'm offering a compromise. They'll talk to me, and I'll carry the information they give me into battle. If any of what they tell me can save Fal'Borna lives, I'll share it with you. But other than that, what the three of us discuss here will remain secret." He turned to Besh and Sirj. "Is that acceptable?"

"It's not acceptable to me!" the a'laq said.

Grinsa regarded him placidly. "Then you'll learn nothing from them at all."

"There are other ways!"

"None that I'll allow you to use."

The two Qirsi stood staring at one another, the a'laq clearly enraged, Grinsa calm, but resolute.

"You tricked me," the a'laq finally said. "You planned this all along."

"It was your idea to come here, A'Laq. I simply followed, and I planned nothing. But I won't apologize for turning your choice to my advantage. You tricked all of us the other day. You deserved this."

"I should have known better than to trust you."

"You *can* trust me," Grinsa said. "I meant what I said a moment ago. If any of what I learn from these men can help me save even one Fal'Borna life, I'll tell you immediately."

E'Menua didn't look mollified. "I won't free them."

"It wouldn't be safe for them to leave the sept right now anyway. Let them remain here as your guests. Allow them to leave their z'kal and wander freely throughout the settlement."

"Another compromise," the a'laq said, contempt in his voice. "You talk like an Eandi."

"I talk like a man of the Forelands, as I always have." He looked at Besh again. "Will you agree to this? Will you answer my questions?"

Besh glanced at E'Menua. "Will he allow us to leave our shelter?"

Grinsa looked at the a'laq, too, raising an eyebrow.

E'Menua nodded reluctantly. "I want to know what their kind can do," he said. "I want to know what they can conjure."

"I understand, A'Laq. I want to know those things, too."

Still the a'laq eyed him, finally shaking his head and saying, almost under his breath, "You're a most difficult man." He cast a dark look at Besh and Sirj and then stalked off.

"I'm still not sure we should help you," Sirj told Grinsa, once E'Menua was out of earshot. "I don't like the idea of working to defeat other Mettai."

"They deserve defeating," Besh said.

Sirj looked at him, clearly surprised.

"We have no business in this war. Our people haven't fought against the Qirsi since the earliest days of the Blood Wars. What kind of fool would choose to start fighting again now?" Besh could see that Sirj had no answer for him, so he turned to Grinsa. "What is it you want to know?"

"You conjured a fox," the Forelander said. "I'll never forget it. And I saw you conjure hornets as well. What other creatures can you summon in that way?"

Besh nodded. "A good question. I'm not sure I can answer. There were spells that our people did long ago, back in the days when we fought. Many of them have been lost to time, though tales of them remain."

"E'Menua fears that you can conjure creatures from myth and legend."

"Of course he does. No one wants to face a creyvnal in battle, much less a score of them."

Grinsa frowned. "A creyvnal?"

"A beast from the ancient stories. It has the body of a lion and the head of a wolf."

"Can you conjure such a thing?"

Besh smiled, but quickly grew serious again. "No, I can't, but you're asking if our people can. And that's a more difficult question."

He rubbed the back of his neck, staring at the ground. As a rule, his people were reluctant to speak with outsiders about their history, their magic, or their traditions. This was one of the many reasons he thought it so odd that Mettai had chosen to fight alongside the Eandi army. It wasn't just that his people valued peace; over the centuries they had also come to embrace their isolation.

There were stories of the early Blood Wars that had been passed down by generations of Mettai. These weren't the tales that parents told their children at bedtime, or that had been turned into songs sung around fires on cold nights during the Snows. These stories were told in hushed voices and were intended as warnings. Many people doubted that they were true, either because they couldn't believe that Mettai magic had once been so powerful, or because they didn't want to believe that Mettai men and women could be so evil.

Besh had been among those who thought the stories more fanciful than accurate. But he had also seen that the stories served a purpose. Magic had its place, these tales cautioned, but those who wielded it were responsible for its consequences. A Mettai did not conjure carelessly or without good reason. Blood and earth were not to be wasted on trifles, nor were they to be taken up in anger except as a last resort. These were the lessons passed on to children as they came into their power. And the tales of ancient evils gave weight to those lessons.

Now, though, he could see that there was a darker side to these stories. For those Mettai looking for glory or gold or land, the old tales might actually encourage them to march to war. Because it was told that once, centuries before, Mettai magic had been a mighty weapon. Qirsi had trembled at the mere thought of some Mettai spells. Eandi had come to see Besh's people as one of their greatest assets when they marched to battle. If it hadn't been for the Mettai, some of the tales said, the Blood Wars might have ended hundreds of years earlier; they might never have been fought at all.

It was so hard to credit. And yet, hadn't Lici found a way to kill hundreds with her magic? Back in the warm, hazy days of the late Planting, before Lici left Kirayde and began spreading her plague across the land, Besh had never imagined that

Mettai magic could harm so many. He never thought that it would start another war. But it had. Was it such a stretch, then, to believe that these old stories were true? If Lici could conjure her pestilence, couldn't the ancient Mettai have created evil creatures and bound them to their service?

"There may have been spells that could do such things," Besh finally said. "But if they existed at all, most of them would have passed out of memory long ago."

"You don't even know if they were real?" Grinsa asked.

"No. I want to believe that they weren't. They were . . . they could do terrible things."

"What kind of things?"

"It was said that the Mettai of old could kill hundreds at a time with a single conjuring. They could send poison at their enemies. They could conjure animals, birds, even dragons."

"Dragons?" Grinsa repeated. "But surely . . ." He stopped himself.

Besh had some idea of what he was thinking. He'd asked about the creyvnal, and Besh had said, in essence, that he didn't know if the beast could be conjured. But if it was even possible, then so was a dragon, or any of the demons and beasts said to live in Bian's realm.

"You've never believed those tales," Sirj said.

"No," Besh said. "I haven't. But I never thought that a Mettai could conjure a killing plague, or, for that matter, that I could create a spell that would defeat such a plague."

"You say that these spells have been lost to time," Grinsa said. "But are you certain of that? Is it possible that some Mettai still remember them?"

Some Mettai. The Mettai who had joined with the army of Stelpana.

"I suppose it's possible," Besh said. "Like the Qirsi clans and the Eandi sovereignties, different Mettai villages have different traditions. We may well remember different things."

Grinsa frowned. "But the way your magic works, can't you simply come up with an incantation and summon that beast you mentioned before?"

"The creyvnal, you mean?"

"Yes. Couldn't any Mettai do that?"

Besh shook his head. "It's not that easy. Not nearly. The phrases have to be right, and they have to be spoken in the correct order, but that's the least of it. I can't create something that I can't picture in my mind. When I conjured that fox for you when we first met, I knew exactly what it would look like. I've seen hundreds of them. I have some idea of how a creyvnal should look; at least, I think I do. I've heard the legends. I can imagine a wolf's head on a lion's body. But that's not the same as knowing how the creature would move and sound."

"What about the blood wolves?" Sirj asked. "Or one of the other battle creatures?"

Grinsa looked from one of them to the other. "Blood wolves?"

Besh glanced at Sirj, wishing the younger man hadn't mentioned battle creatures.

"There are stories—the same ones that speak of the poisoning spells. They tell of creatures conjured by the Mettai during the early years of the Blood Wars. Great wolves, unnaturally quick and canny. Other beasts as well. Snakes, falcons, wild cats. Blood creatures, they were called." He took a breath and exhaled through his teeth. "These creatures might be easier to conjure than that poisoning spell. I might even be able to do it. I haven't seen them, but I've seen wild wolves. I know how they behave. I could create something like them, but bigger, stronger, smarter. They might not be exactly like the blood wolves of old, but they'd be close enough."

"Do you think these Mettai who have joined the Eandi army would use them?" Grinsa asked.

Besh nodded. "I think that once this war begins, and the full power of Fal'Borna magic is unleashed against this army, they'll use every spell they can think of. Wolves might well be the least of it."

Chapter 16

"She really is quite beautiful. I can understand why you can't take your eyes off of her."

Enly looked sharply at Gries, who was watching him, a faintly mocking smile on his handsome face. Enly hadn't fully realized that he was staring at Tirnya until the captain spoke, but now he felt his face reddening.

He didn't answer, and after a moment he faced forward, making an effort not to look at her or at Gries.

They were riding west again. Their forward scouts scanned the horizon for the next Fal'Borna settlement, while their rearguard watched for an assault from the east. The sky was leaden, and Enly could see rain falling in the distance to the north. But the wind blew from the south, warmer than usual and heavy with the scent of storms.

"Is she as taken with you as you are with her?"

"Of course she is," Enly said drily. "Haven't you noticed how she dotes on me?"

Gries laughed. "Good for you, Enly. I've always thought that there was more to you than that serious, spoiled lord heir who seemed so intent on beating me in the ring."

Enly glanced at the man. "Is that right?"

"You and I could be great friends, you know. It won't be too long before we lead our cities." He looked around, as if to be sure that no one else could hear. "Neither of us will ever be sovereign, of course," he continued, dropping his voice. "But Ankyr is weak, not to mention a fool. House Ballidyne and House Tolm could be the most powerful of allies. Together we could present a united northern front to the Kasathas. We could make Stelpana the supreme sovereignty in the land."

"Our fathers might still have a bit to say about that," Enly said.

"Yes, of course," Gries said with impatience. "You get my point, though, don't you? It might not happen today or tomorrow. But the day is coming when we will rule this land in fact, if not in name. Think of all we could accomplish working together!"

Enly had to laugh. "It's an interesting idea, Gries, but I think you're forgetting something. You and I don't like each other. We never have."

"Nonsense!" Fairlea's lord heir said, waving off the suggestion. "We didn't like each other before because we were too young to know better. You were spoiled and arrogant and I was even worse. But we're men now. We're captains, we're statesmen. We understand the world."

Enly laughed again. Understand the world? He didn't even understand Tirnya. He was barely capable of speaking in civil tones to his own father. And Gries was ready to join him in ruling the world.

"What's so funny?" Gries asked, sounding irked by Enly's laughter.

"It's nothing. What is it you want from me, Gries?"

The man shrugged. "Who says I want anything? We're riding to war on this desolate plain. We're comrades in a great struggle. Isn't that enough for now?"

Enly wasn't sure what the man was up to. Maybe this was nothing more than idle thoughts born of boredom and a long ride and a grey sky.

"Yes, all right," he said. "That's enough."

"Splendid!" Gries said.

They rode in silence for a short while. Then Gries turned to him again. "So if she doesn't dote on you, as you say, why do you persist in pursuing her?"

This was not a discussion Enly cared to have with anyone, Gries least of all. "Who says I'm pursuing her?"

Gries merely stared at him, his eyebrows up.

"Tirnya and I have known each other for a long time—since we were children. Any chance there was that we might be anything more than fellow soldiers in the Qalsyn army vanished years ago."

"Really?" Gries said. "Then perhaps you wouldn't mind if I were to court her."

"You?" Enly knew he shouldn't have been surprised. He'd seen the two of them together on a number of occasions, and though he didn't care to believe that Tirnya had any interest in Fairlea's lord heir, he wasn't at all surprised to learn that Gries was attracted to her.

"Why not?" Gries said. "She's beautiful, she's smart. And as I've said, I'd like to forge a bond between Fairlea and Qalsyn. What better way than for my city's lord heir to wed the daughter of Qalsyn's most renowned soldier?"

"Of course," Enly said, resisting a sudden urge to pull his sword free and hack off the man's head. "You might find, though, that she's not really the marrying kind. She cares more for swords and battles than for more . . . wifely things."

Gries smiled in a way that made Enly's sword hand itch. "Leave that to me," the Fairlea captain said. "I've thawed colder hearts than hers, albeit for a night rather than for a lifetime. But still, I think I can coax the sword from her hand."

"Well, good luck to you, then," Enly said, spurring his mount ahead of the man.

Gries caught up with him almost immediately. "Enly?" He leaned forward so he could look Enly in the eye. "You're sure you're all right with this?"

"Absolutely," Enly told him, a brittle smile on his lips. "As I say, I wish you all good fortune in your . . . pursuit."

He rode ahead once more, and this time Gries let him go.

Enly hadn't been riding on his own for more than a few moments, however, when he heard a shout go up from the army's right flank. Fearing that they were under attack, he wheeled his horse sharply and pulled his blade free. What he saw stopped him cold.

A lone horseman, flanked on either side by Qalsyn scouts, was riding toward the army. The man had an arm raised in greeting, and a broad smile on his homely face. He was a large man, both tall and heavy, and he was Eandi. He wore travel-stained clothes and a torn blanket around his shoulders. A black patch covered his left eye, giving him the look of a brigand.

Gries had halted his mount beside Enly. He, too, had his sword drawn, but his blade arm had dropped to his side.

"What is he doing here?" he whispered.

"You know him?" Enly asked.

Gries looked at him. "Of course. Don't you?"

Enly shook his head.

"That's Torgan Plye."

Enly stared at the stranger again. "The merchant? You're sure?"

"Absolutely. I've spent enough gold on his wares over the years. I'd know him anywhere."

Jenoe and Tirnya rode out to meet the man, and after a moment's hesitation, Gries joined them. Enly followed.

"I'd heard there was an Eandi army marching on the plain," Torgan called to them, beaming. "I never would have guessed that it would be so grand and impressive a force. I take it you're their commander," he said to Jenoe.

"That's right. Jenoe Onjaef, marshal of—"

"The Qalsyn army," the man broke in. "Of course. I should have recognized the uniforms. Your name is known throughout the land, Marshal."

"And you are, sir?" Tirnya's father asked, still sounding wary.

"Torgan Plye. I once was a merchant of some renown. More recently I've been a prisoner of the Fal'Borna."

"What?" the marshal said, his blue eyes widening.

"I was taken hostage by the Fal'Borna after I sold baskets

to a sept near the Companion Lakes. The baskets were cursed with a plague that killed the white-hairs and destroyed their village. They thought I was to blame and they threatened to kill me. They took another merchant hostage as well. A younger man; a friend of mine. I managed to escape with my life. He didn't."

Jenoe was gaping at the man. "You're telling me that this plague was . . . was caused by magic?"

"Yes. A Mettai spell."

"Impossible!"

Everyone turned toward Fayonne, who stood a short distance off, her face pale, her white hair shifting in the wind. Her fists were clenched, her back rigid.

"There are no Mettai who would conjure such an illness!" she said.

"Forgive me, good woman," Torgan said, his tone less courteous than his words. "But it's the truth. I saw the Mettai woman who sold the baskets, and I saw what these baskets did. I even met two Mettai men who came from her village, and who claimed to have killed her in order to keep her from spreading her plague."

"Where are these men now?" Jenoe asked.

"I don't know, Marshal. Last I knew, they had been taken by the Fal'Borna as well. I assume they're dead."

Jenoe nodded, then asked, "How long has it been since you won your freedom, Torgan?"

"A long time. I . . . I lost my way. I've been traveling by night and sleeping by day, hoping that the Fal'Borna wouldn't be able to track me. But with the moons rising later and later, and then not at all a few nights ago . . . As I say, I got lost."

"Well, you should be on your way now," the marshal told him. "This is no place for an Eandi merchant."

"No!" Torgan said. "I can help you! I can be of more use to you than you could possibly know. And all I ask in return is a bit of food and your protection."

"Do you have a cart nearby, sir?" Enly asked. "Or have you stored your wares someplace close?"

Torgan frowned. "No. The Fal'Borna took all of my goods and destroyed my cart."

"So you're an Eandi merchant in Fal'Borna lands, and you have no goods to sell, no cart to carry supplies." Enly glanced briefly at Gries, who was grinning. "Forgive me for saying so, but you don't appear to be a swordsman, and I doubt very much that you'd be an effective lookout. What use do you think you can be to us?"

Jenoe cast a disapproving look Enly's way, but one of the Waterstone captains snickered.

The man's frown deepened. "I'll be glad to tell you, Captain. But not in front of all these men." Facing Jenoe once more he straightened, as if trying to reclaim a scrap of his dignity. "I request a word with you in private, Marshal. If after we're done you still wish to send me away, I'll go, though I would be grateful for one small meal before I do. It's been days since I ate well."

For a moment Enly thought that Jenoe would refuse. The marshal seemed to begrudge even this small delay, and though he might have thought Enly discourteous for speaking to the man as he had, he clearly was as skeptical of Torgan's claims as Enly had been. After some hesitation, however, he relented.

"The men need a break," he said, as if explaining himself to his captains and Marshal Crish. "I'll give you a few moments, sir, and then we have to be moving again. This enemy doesn't rest."

Torgan nodded.

At a barked command from Stri Balkett, the soldiers broke formation. Some sat on the grass; others remained standing but pulled out food or waterskins. Jenoe, Hendrid, and several of the captains, including Enly, Gries, and Tirnya, clustered around the merchant.

"Now, what is it you believe you can do for us, Torgan?" Jenoe asked. "Quickly."

"As I told you," the man said, his voice low, "this plague was spread by cursed Mettai baskets. At one point the white-hairs who held me prisoner found a sept that had been destroyed by the plague. Apparently when the Qirsi are sickened they lose control over their magic and it destroys everything in sight. It's something to behold, I'll tell you. Fire magic, shaping: those white-hairs—"

"Is there a point to this?" the marshal demanded.

Torgan licked his lips. "Yes, of course. Forgive me, Marshal. The point is this: While we were in that ruined village, I found a piece of one of those baskets. I still have it with me."

At first, no one said a word. They just stared at the merchant, who stared right back at them, waiting for some sort of response, an expectant smile on his scarred face. As the moments passed, and no response came, the smile faded.

"Let me see if I understand this," Jenoe said at last. "There are cursed baskets out there that have spread this white-hair plague across the plain. And you have one of them? With you?"

"Not a basket," Torgan said. "Just a scrap. A piece of one of the baskets that brought the plague to this village we found."

"A scrap," Jenoe repeated, clearly skeptical. "And what do you propose we do with it?"

Torgan opened his mouth, closed it again. He eyed them with unconcealed consternation. "Isn't it clear?" he said. "Do you really need me to explain this to you?"

"You want us to use the plague as a weapon," Tirnya said. "You think that this scrap of basket can spread the illness to more settlements."

"I know it can," Torgan said. "That's how I got away from the Fal'Borna in the first place. I sickened the white-hairs who held me prisoner and then I left them. Whatever curse the Mettai first put on this basket is still there. It still works."

Tirnya looked at her father, clearly troubled. Enly was relieved to see this. Over the past few turns, as she pushed for this invasion and then for the alliance with Fayonne and her people, Tirnya had seemed to transform herself into someone he hardly even recognized. He had feared that even if she and her father managed to regain their family's ancestral home, she would have to sacrifice too much in the effort. He had feared for her humanity.

But seeing the look of fear and disgust on her face, seeing the way she regarded Torgan, Enly was reassured. He fully expected that her father would send this one-eyed merchant away. It was bad enough that they had to rely on Mettai magic in this war. But to use the white-hair plague as a weapon was unthinkable. Enly wasn't even sure he thought it possible. Fayonne seemed certain that the merchant was lying, and while Enly didn't regard her as the most reliable source of information, in this case he was inclined to agree with her. He'd never heard of any magic—Qirsi or Mettai—being able to create an illness of this sort. He couldn't begin to imagine the evil that would conceive of such a thing. But whether or not this curse was real, Enly wanted no part of the merchant or his basket.

He couldn't have been more surprised when the marshal said, after several moments' reflection, "We'll need to discuss this further. For now, Torgan, you'll ride with the army."

"Father?" Tirnya said, as if scarcely believing what she'd heard.

Jenoe glowered at her. "We'll discuss this later, *Captain*." He wheeled his horse away from the rest. "I want these men moving again," he called over his shoulder.

Tirnya glanced at Enly, her expression grim. But she didn't say anything more, and after a moment she steered her mount after Jenoe's.

"You heard him," Hendrid said. "Let's get these men moving."

"Make war on a demon," Gries muttered, "and you'll become a demon yourself."

It was an old expression, dating to the earliest years of the Blood Wars.

"That may be the only way to win," the captain added.

Enly looked at him. "I'm not sure victory is worth it."

Gries raised an eyebrow. "Careful, Enly. Talk like that can get a man hanged."

"You disagree?"

Fairlea's lord heir gave a faint smile, though the look in his eyes remained deadly serious. "I never said that."

They fed him, which for the moment was all Torgan really cared about. They would use his scrap of Mettai basket, or they wouldn't. They'd offer him protection until this damn war ended, or they'd send him on his way, leaving him to fend for himself and avoid the Fal'Borna as best he could. For now he'd done what he could to convince these soldiers to accept his aid. The rest was up to the marshal and his captains, and Torgan couldn't bring himself to care what they decided to do.

He was exhausted and cold and hungrier than he could ever remember being. It had taken him the better part of a day to find Trey again after his encounter with Jasha's ghost. And then it had taken another half day to convince the horse to let him approach, much less ride. Not that Torgan could blame the beast. Those wraiths had left him shaken, too. He couldn't sleep for several days after.

With the moons waxing again, he tried to travel by night, but he was starting to grow weak with hunger, and suddenly his blanket and overshirt seemed no match for the cold. Progress came slowly; every unexpected sound made him jump, made his heart race. He couldn't say with any certainty which he feared more: the Fal'Borna or Jasha and his fellow shades.

Now, though, the Fal'Borna couldn't reach him, at least not without first overpowering several thousand of Stelpana's finest warriors. And despite the dread that gripped him whenever the sun set, he knew that the wraiths couldn't haunt him again, either. Not until the last night of next year's Memory Moon. If he lived that long.

He hadn't been looking for the Eandi army. He didn't know for certain where they had crossed the Silverwater or which way they would head once they were in Fal'Borna land, though he could have guessed that they would march toward the Horn. He wasn't even entirely certain that the rumors of their approach were true. He had been trying to sleep in a shallow hollow when he heard them. At first he'd trembled with fear, convinced that a Fal'Borna army had come, and that they would find him at any moment. When he realized that he was hearing his own people rather than white-hairs, his relief was so profound that he nearly wept.

He didn't wish to let on just how scared and desperate for their protection he was. Nor did he want to give them cause to doubt his version of what happened to Jasha. So he silently thanked the gods for this singular stroke of good fortune and behaved as though he had been searching for the army.

And he ate. Dried meat, hard cheese, stale bread. It was hardly the meal he had imagined again and again over the past several nights, as he tried to ignore the ache in his hollow belly. But it was better than air and water. After he had eaten his fill—he remembered being able to eat more than this; where had his appetite gone?—he began to feel more like himself. He also sensed the kernel of an idea forming in his mind, one that took him far beyond a bit of protection and a meal or two. One that might well put him on the path to regaining the prosperity he had lost.

Since hearing that an army of Eandi warriors intended to attack the Fal'Borna, Torgan had wondered what their leaders could have been thinking. The Fal'Borna were savage warriors and skilled sorcerers. No one knew better than he how merciless they could be with their enemies. And no one with any knowledge of the Blood Wars could doubt that they were more than a match for whatever army the sovereignties sent across the Silverwater.

Or were they? He'd seen the devastation at S'Vralna. He knew what this plague had done to the mighty Fal'Borna. The leaders of the Eandi must have known this as well. They were counting on the fact that the white-hairs were weak, their numbers depleted, their cities ruined. The Fal'Borna were no longer the formidable enemy they once had been.

There was hope for this invasion. And though Torgan had

been intent on reaching the wash and the safety of Eandi lands, he now saw that the opportunity for the armies of Stelpana was also an opportunity for him. If this army could retake the Horn, they would reestablish an Eandi presence on the plain for the first time in more than a hundred years. The new Eandi outposts would need goods; they would need trade. They would need a merchant with knowledge of the Qirsi to help them provision themselves. They would need him.

Yes, there were risks. But he'd overcome worse in the past several turns. He'd escaped the Fal'Borna who held him prisoner, and more to the point, he'd thrown off his own cowardice. He still feared death, but he also feared living out the rest of his days as a pauper. He'd made plenty of enemies during his more prosperous days; many of them would delight in seeing him broken and humiliated. Regaining his wealth in Tordjanne or Stelpana or any of the other Eandi realms wouldn't be easy.

But as the first merchant in a new Deraqor, he'd be in a position to make a fortune. And traveling with this army, he'd be safer than he would be trying to complete the journey to Stelpana on his own.

As the idea took form in his mind, he became conscious of the men around him. He watched the marshal and the captains who rode with him, trying to determine which of them was most likely to help him.

He also watched the Mettai woman who had as much as called him a liar. He entertained no hope of winning her support, but he wanted to know what he was up against. And it became clear to him almost immediately that she was no threat at all. She and her people walked in the van, alongside the captains and Stelpana's bowmen. But in all other ways the Mettai clearly were outcasts in this army. They didn't trust the Eandi, and they knew that they themselves were mistrusted.

That left him with one obvious enemy.

"Excuse me," he said to one of the soldiers marching beside him. "Can you tell me who that woman is riding with the marshal?"

"Tha's Tirnya Onjaef," the man said, in a voice that told Torgan that she was a woman of some renown. "She's th' marshal's daughter."

That much he had gathered.

"And she's a captain in his army?"

The man nodded. "Didn' think much o' her a' first. Bu' she's bett'r 'n most. An' she's good with a sword, too. Nearly beat old Enly hisself in this year's tournament."

Torgan nodded. "I see. And Enly is?"

The soldier pointed at another of the captains, a trim, dark-haired man. "Enly Tolm. He's—"

"Ah!" Torgan said. "The lord governor's son."

"Tha's right."

"What else can you tell me about the Onjaef girl?"

The man narrowed his eyes. "Wha'chya wan' t' know?"

Torgan forced a smile. "Forgive me. I don't mean to seem disrespectful. I'm curious, that's all. It's not often that one encounters a woman like that leading an army to battle."

"She is a beauty, ain' she?" the man agreed. "There's some wha' says tha' she an' Enly are a pair, if ya knows wha' I mean."

"Really?" Torgan said. "Is it true?"

The soldier shrugged. "Don' know. Don' really care. Long as they leads us right, th' rest don' matter t' me."

Torgan asked the man a few more questions, but though the soldier talked for the better part of an hour, he learned precious little about Tirnya Onjaef. They called her the Falcon, just as they had once called her father the Eagle. She had lost the Qalsyn battle tournament in the final match three years running. And each time she had been beaten by Enly. That did strike Torgan as useful information, though he wasn't yet certain how to use it.

After a while, he thanked the man and increased Trey's pace enough to pull ahead of him. He rode alone for the rest of the day, and when the army halted for the night and began to make camp, he did his best to stay out of everyone's way. He lingered near the marshal and at one point even caught the man's eye. But though the marshal nodded to him, he didn't approach or give Torgan any indication that he wished to resume their conversation.

That was all right with Torgan. This was much like making a sale in the marketplace. He had something that the marshal might well want at some point. But if Torgan pushed too hard or seemed too anxious for the marshal to use it, he'd never close the deal. Better to wait for the man to come to him.

If he still had his wares and belongings with him he would have pulled out his flask of Qosantian whiskey and approached the captains. He'd never yet known a soldier to turn down a sip of the Qosantian brew, and over the years he'd found that it could loosen even the tightest of tongues. But he had nothing to offer these men or the marshal's daughter, and he wasn't sure what kind of reception he'd get if he tried to inject himself into their conversation. None of them seemed to give a thought to approaching him.

He sat beside a small fire at the fringe of the camp, savoring the full feeling in his belly while Trey grazed nearby. He listened to the quiet hum of the campground, catching snatches of distant conversation and laughter, or verses of battle songs sung slightly out of tune. And he waited. He felt reasonably sure that he wouldn't have to wait long.

She didn't like the merchant. Not at all. She couldn't say why; she just didn't trust him. Even now, sitting with the other captains, she could feel his one eye on them, on her. He kept a respectful distance, but he intruded with his furtive glances. He made her skin crawl.

Most of all, she was repulsed by his suggestion that they use the plague to attack the Fal'Borna. And she was deeply disturbed by her father's willingness to consider the notion.

All along she had been the one who had pushed Jenoe— the invasion had been her idea, as had the alliance with the Mettai. But in the past several days her father had changed. The Jenoe she knew would never have allowed his men to kill enemy warriors as they slept. He would have rejected out of hand Torgan Plye's offer of help. Leading this army had changed him.

Tirnya could hardly blame him. She had lost two men in a skirmish with road brigands and it had taken every bit of her courage and composure to face the parents of one of them. Jenoe had lost hundreds of men the last time they faced the Fal'Borna, and they had yet to encounter a white-hair force as large as their own army. She could hardly imagine the burden he carried.

She knew only that with each day that passed her father seemed more like a stranger to her, and that she herself was to blame. Her idea, her fault.

"You look troubled."

She looked up from the fire. Gries had come to sit beside her. Several of the other captains had left them, probably to go sleep. Enly sat opposite her, speaking in low tones with Stri and one of the captains from Waterstone.

"I'm all right," she said, smiling weakly.

"I see." Clearly Gries didn't believe her.

She brushed a strand of hair from her forehead and exhaled heavily. "It's the merchant," she told him. "I wish my father had sent him away."

"You must have known that he wouldn't."

Tirnya shrugged.

"If what he's saying about that basket he carries is true, he's offering us a powerful weapon. More powerful even than the wolves and eagles of the Mettai."

"So you think we should use it," she said, her voice flat.

Out of the corner of her eye, she noticed that Enly was watching them, but she tried to ignore him.

"I don't want to," he said. "I sense that you don't, either. But we can't simply refuse. We don't know yet what's waiting for us at the Horn. We don't even know what we'll have to face at the next sept. We have to consider every possible weapon we have at our disposal."

"Not this one," she said without thinking.

"Is using the plague that different from what we've already done?"

"It is if we can't keep it from killing children."

"I don't think it kills children," Gries said. "Remember the first sept we found. Most of the adults had died—the survivors were mostly children who hadn't yet come into their power."

"Yes," Tirnya said, turning to face him. "Nearly all the survivors were children, but not all the children survived. They did at the second sept, because we made sure of it."

He offered a small shrug, as if conceding the point.

"You think I'm being soft," she said, straightening. "You think that I argue this way because I'm a woman."

Gries actually laughed. "You're putting words in my mouth."

Tirnya blushed, and was thankful for the darkness. "I'm sorry. I do that sometimes. My father hates it."

"No need to apologize. And I don't think you're being soft."

She looked at him doubtfully.

He laughed again. She liked the way he laughed. It was full-throated without being too loud, and it sounded genuine, unforced.

"All right," he said. "I don't think you're being soft because you're a woman. Different people respond to these things in different ways." He grinned. "How's that?"

"Better," she said, smiling in turn.

She glanced across the fire again. Enly and Stri were gone, as were most of the others.

"It's getting late," Tirnya said, starting to stand.

Suddenly he was holding her hand, his grip gentle but insistent. His fingers felt warm and slightly rough, though in a comforting sort of way.

"It's not that late," he said quietly.

She slowly sat back down.

"What will you do if you win this war, Tirnya?" he asked, holding her gaze.

She swallowed. "My father and I will have a great deal to do. We intend to make this plain an Eandi stronghold again. We want to return Deraqor and Silvralna to the glory of their early history. That will take work. It'll take years."

"It sounds like a hard life," Gries said. "Lonely as well."

"It might be," she said, trying to sound sure of herself. He was still holding her hand and she found herself staring at their fingers. "But it's something that he and I have pledged ourselves to do, for our people and for their children."

Actually, Tirnya wasn't quite sure where all this was coming from. She and her father had said little about what would come after the war. Prior to leaving Qalsyn, all of their planning had been for the march into Fal'Borna land and the battles that would ensue. Her father remained utterly focused on their next encounter with the Qirsi. She wasn't sure he had given any thought to what would happen once they recaptured the Horn. They hadn't really talked about the lives they would lead there.

"And is there no room in that future for anything more?" the Fairlea captain asked.

Abruptly Tirnya was trembling and she didn't know why. "I . . . I'm not sure. That's such a long way off."

He inclined his head slightly. "I suppose it is." He reached forward with his free hand and touched her chin gently, forcing her to meet his gaze again. "But I'd ask you to consider whether you don't deserve to be happy as well. You say that you do this for your people and their children. What about you, Tirnya? What about your children?"

She couldn't speak. She merely gazed back at him, scared by what he was saying, unwilling to get up and walk away.

After a moment, Gries leaned forward ever so slowly, his face drawing near to hers. She leaned away just a bit and he hesitated. But she didn't say anything to stop him, and her gaze kept flicking from his dark eyes to his lips. He leaned forward again and brushed her lips with his own. Once, then again.

Tirnya closed her eyes, her lips parted, her pulse racing like a river in flood.

He kissed her. No brushing of lips this time, but a full kiss. His lips were surprisingly soft and he caressed her cheek with a finger.

After a moment, Tirnya pulled away.

"This is a bad idea," she whispered, her eyes still closed, her chest rising and falling with each breath.

"You think so?" he whispered back. He brushed his lips against her cheek. "I thought it was rather brilliant myself."

She giggled, but her hands were shaking and she felt cold.

"I can't do this now, Gries. Maybe . . . I don't know. There may come a time. But not now, not in the middle of this war."

He kissed her again, and she let him.

"You're sure?" he asked in a husky voice.

"No," she said.

He leaned back, smiling. "I didn't expect that."

She felt her cheeks coloring again. "Neither did I, actually."

"So . . . ?"

"I need some time to think," she said. "I don't . . ." She trailed off, shaking her head, unsure of what she intended to say.

He held a finger to her lips. "I think I understand." He leaned forward again and kissed her brow. Then he stood. "Good night, Captain Onjaef."

She smiled. "Good night, Captain Ballidyne."

Tirnya watched him walk away and took a long, deep breath. After a moment she glanced around, half expecting to see that Enly was watching her. He wasn't.

But the merchant was, his one good eye glinting in the firelight. Tirnya shuddered.

Chapter 17

h e slept terribly, awakened again and again by imagined noises or chased from his slumber by dark visions. At one point he dreamed that he and his men were surrounded by hordes of Qirsi, all of them carrying brightly colored flames in their hands, all of them singing battle songs and laughing at the pitifully small army he commanded.

Awakening from that dream, Enly promptly fell asleep again and stepped into a new one. This time he saw only Tirnya and Gries. They were lying together on the plain, naked, their bodies entwined. At first they were oblivious to him, concerned only with the rhythm of their movements. But as Gries's thrusts grew ever more urgent, Tirnya looked over at Enly and laughed.

This time when Enly awoke it was to a damp, grey dawn, and he was in as foul a mood as he could remember.

He'd walked away from the fire early enough the previous night that he hadn't actually seen Gries and Tirnya go off together to the captain's sleeping roll or to hers. But after his conversation the day before with Fairlea's lord heir, after watching them exchange glances throughout the evening, and seeing them sitting side by side speaking in lowered voices, Enly had little doubt that the two had spent the night together.

"So be it," he muttered to himself. "He can have her, and good riddance."

Brave words. Would that it were so easy.

He'd as much as pushed Gries into her arms, and for the life of him he couldn't imagine why he'd done it. Except that he'd had no choice. He couldn't have claimed that she was his, because Tirnya would have been quick to announce to the entire world that she wasn't. He could almost hear his father laughing at him, mocking him for wasting his thoughts on a girl who hadn't shared his bed for more than a year. Maisaak would have told him that the sick feeling in his gut was exactly what he deserved for allowing himself to become infatuated with an Onjaef.

Enly couldn't help thinking that he had put the idea of Gries in Tirnya's head the very day Qalsyn's army met up with the soldiers of Fairlea. He'd gone on and on about how much he hated the man; he'd warned her away from him. Tirnya looked for ways to infuriate him; he should have realized that nothing could have made Gries more attractive to her.

"Idiot!" he whispered, rubbing a hand over his face. He threw off his damp blankets, knelt, and rolled up the blankets and his sleeping roll. Then he stood and carried them to where he'd left Nallaj, his bay. Most of his men were already awake and they called greetings to him as he walked past.

When he reached the horses, Tirnya was there. Naturally.

He faltered at the sight of her, but recovered quickly, walking past her to recover his saddle.

He said nothing to her as he saddled his horse. She didn't speak either, and he preferred it that way. For about a minute.

He glanced at her a couple of times as he tied his sleeping roll in place. She appeared to be ignoring him.

"Good morning," he finally said.

She looked up, her expression mild. "Good morning." Her hair was tied back and a few wisps fell over her face. She looked beautiful, as always.

Great.

"Late night?" he asked.

She shrugged. "Not particularly." Then, as an afterthought, "You?"

He let out a short, harsh laugh. "Hardly."

Tirnya frowned and gave him an odd look before turning her attention back to her saddle.

Enly cast about for something else to say, something that might help him figure out just what had happened between her and Gries the night before. But nothing came to him, and he decided he'd be best off walking away in silence.

"Damn!" she said, still struggling with her saddle.

"What's the matter?"

"I can't get the cinch to fasten."

He walked over to where she was standing and squatted down to examine the buckle and leather.

"There's your problem," he said after a moment, pointing to a twist in the leather just at the point where it passed through the metal buckle. He struggled with it for several moments before finally untwisting the strap. He stood. "It should be all right now."

"Thanks," she said, barely meeting his gaze.

"I thought I'd find the two of you together."

Enly and Tirnya turned at the same time.

The merchant, Torgan Plye, was there, a smile on his face, his one good eye gazing at the two of them.

"I hope I'm not interrupting anything," he said, in a tone that gave the lie to his words.

Enly and Tirnya had grown up together. Even as children, raised by fathers who hated each other, they had seen each other in the Qalsyn marketplace and in the boxes at the Harvest Tournament. And in all these years, he'd never known her to be afraid of anything or anyone. It was one of the reasons he had fallen in love with her. But at the sight of this hulking merchant, with his scarred face and unctuous smile, she edged closer to him. At any other time, he would have enjoyed this, but he had to admit that the man made him uncomfortable, too.

"What do you want?" Enly asked him, making no effort to sound welcoming.

"Forgive the intrusion, Captain," Torgan said. "I merely wish to have a word with you and Captain Onjaef."

Tirnya eyed him warily. "About what?"

"You made it quite plain to your father and to me that you

didn't want me riding with your army," Torgan said. "I think I can even understand why. This plague is . . ." He shook his head. "It's a nasty business. I know that. I can see why you wouldn't want to use it, even against an enemy as dangerous as the Fal'Borna."

"But you're going to try to convince us to use it anyway, aren't you?" Enly said.

Torgan regarded him with an amused expression. "Yes," he said, chuckling. "Yes, I am."

Tirnya turned her back on him to adjust her saddle. "You're wasting your breath."

"You haven't given me a chance to waste anything, Captain. At least hear me out before you dismiss what I have to say."

Tirnya faced him again. "Why should I? What you're talking about is cruel and evil and . . . and unworthy of a soldier of Stelpana."

The merchant gazed back at her placidly. "Tell me, Captain, how do you intend to take back D'Raqor?" He said the name with a Fal'Borna inflection, seeming to know how much this would bother her. "Defeating septs is one thing, but taking a fortified city from the Fal'Borna is quite another."

"We'll lay siege to it, as armies do. We may draw upon the magic of the Mettai who march with us, but that's different."

"I agree," Torgan said. "It is different. And do you intend to take S'Vralna the same way?"

"Yes, of course."

The man nodded. "I see."

"Is there a point to this?" Tirnya asked.

"What would you say if I told you that S'Vralna is already in ruins, that taking it back will be as simple as marching through the city gates and claiming it for Stelpana?"

Tirnya gaped at him, her face pallid in the grey morning light. "Silvralna's in ruins? You've seen it?"

"Yes. I was there. Most of the white-hairs who lived there

are dead. The vast majority of those who survived are children." A small smile crossed his lips and was gone. "The second largest city on the Horn, and you'll reclaim it without losing a single man. Surely you see the value of that."

"But you say that the city is ruined."

Torgan inclined his head, conceding the point. "The damage was extensive."

"I don't want that to happen to Deraqor."

"A siege will damage the city, too. And if you lay siege to D'Raqor but hold back in your attacks for fear of harming her, you'll never stand a chance."

Tirnya made no answer. She just stared at him for a moment longer before turning back to her mount.

Torgan faced Enly. "You know I'm right. Both of you do. You may not like the thought of using this plague as a weapon, but the fact of the matter is you already have. You wouldn't be out here, marching on the Horn, if the plague hadn't ravaged the land. Isn't that so?"

Enly couldn't deny it. This invasion had been Tirnya's idea, and as the merchant surmised, she had seen in the plague and its spread across the plain all the justification she needed. So had Jenoe, and Enly's father, the lord governor.

"Well, think about it," Torgan said, when neither of them answered. "I'm not so foolish as to believe that soldiers like you will put much stock in what a merchant has to say about warfare. But you have to decide whether you truly wish to win this war. You may not like my methods, but I can assure you of victory. I don't think even your Mettai allies can do that."

He smiled faintly, nodded to Enly, and walked away.

Tirnya glanced back and, seeing that Torgan had left them, exhaled slowly. "I don't like him," she said with quiet intensity.

"You hide it well."

She gave Enly a sour look. "I suppose *you* like him."

"Actually I don't. And before you even suggest it, I don't agree with him about using the plague, either."

"Really?"

"Really. But he raises a good point. We're already taking advantage of the plague. How much worse would it be to use it as he suggests?"

She shook her head. "It's different. Don't ask me how, because I can't explain it. I just know that it is."

"What will your father do?" Enly asked.

"I don't know. He . . . he hasn't been himself in recent days. After losing all those men to the white-hairs' fire magic . . ." She shook her head again. "Before that, I think he would have sent the merchant away without speaking to him."

Enly wasn't as sure of this as she seemed to be, but he kept his thoughts to himself.

Their eyes met, and for an awkward moment they stood gazing at each other in silence.

He looked away first. "I should see to my men," he said. "I'm sure your father will want to be moving soon." He took hold of his mount's reins and started to lead the beast away.

"Enly, wait."

He turned to face her. Her brow was creased, and she looked like she was about to say something. Then she smiled weakly and gave one more quick shake of her head.

"It was nothing."

He didn't believe her, but he didn't force the matter. He merely nodded and walked away with Nallaj trailing behind him.

Before he had gone far, he heard someone calling to him. At first he couldn't see who it was, and he didn't recognize the voice. After a moment, though, he spotted Mander, Fayonne's son, striding toward him, waving a hand over his head.

The young man stopped in front of him, slightly winded and frowning. He was an odd-looking man, with angular features and a long, narrow face. His skin looked pale in the silvery light. With his black hair hanging limply to his shoulders and his dark eyes peering out from beneath his brow, he had the look of an overgrown waif.

"Your men didn't know where you were," he said. "And they didn't seem inclined to help me find you."

That didn't surprise Enly at all. Like most of the soldiers in Jenoe's army, his men didn't like the idea of relying on magic in this war, and they wanted nothing to do with the Mettai. They would have done all they could to keep the man away from their captain.

"I'm sorry for that," Enly said. "You've found me now. What can I do for you?"

The young Mettai glanced around, as if suddenly conscious of all the men surrounding them, readying themselves for the day's march.

"Is there somewhere else—?"

"Forgive me," Enly said, his patience running thin, "but there's not. No one's listening to us, and I haven't time to leave the camp. What is it you want?"

Mander frowned. "My m—" He stopped, licked his lips, then started again. "The eldest wanted me to speak with you. She doesn't trust this merchant who rides with us."

That seemed a common feeling, but Enly kept this to himself.

"She also doesn't believe the white-hair plague came from our people," Mander went on. "She doesn't think it's possible."

"Really?" Enly asked. "After seeing what your magic can do, I have to disagree. Sleeping spells? Giant wolves and eagles? The shield you conjured to stop the Fal'Borna's fire? I have little doubt that the Mettai witch Torgan mentioned could conjure a plague if she wanted to."

"You don't know enough about my people or our magic to say that," the young Mettai told him. "We do, and I'm telling you it's not possible."

Enly had no desire to prolong their conversation by arguing with the man. "What is it you want me to do, Mander?"

"We don't trust this man," the Mettai said again.

"I understand that, but there's really nothing I can—"

"The marshal trusts you. He listens to you. If you were to tell him—"

"Tell him what?" Enly said, cutting him off. "The eldest doesn't want to believe that the plague could have come from Mettai magic, so you need to send away this man who may hold the key to victory in the palm of his hand?" He laughed harshly. "Jenoe wouldn't listen to me, and I wouldn't blame him."

Mander ran a hand through his long hair, looking troubled and beyond his depth. "Your men hate us already," he said with quiet intensity. "They regard us as demons. With the merchant saying these things about us it'll only get worse."

Enly shrugged. "I'm sorry."

"You say that the merchant has a way to win the war? He carries a weapon?"

He felt the color rising in his cheeks. Jenoe hadn't told them to keep this information from the Mettai, but Torgan had spoken to the marshal and his captains in confidence. Enly couldn't imagine that Jenoe would be pleased with him for letting this slip.

"It's not a weapon so much as . . . as information."

Mander eyed him skeptically. "Information about Mettai magic?"

"Information about the plague," Enly said. "I really can't tell you more than that. I shouldn't have said as much as I have."

"He's lying to you," Mander said. "He can't be trusted. Can't you see that?"

"Is there anything else?" Enly asked him.

Mander looked like he did want to say more. His dark eyes smoldered and he rubbed the scars on the back of his hand as if they pained him. But after a moment he shook his head and stomped off, back toward the rest of the Mettai.

Enly watched the man walk away until Nallaj snorted impatiently.

"Yes, all right," Enly muttered. "He's right, you know." He stroked his horse's nose. "We'd be better off without the merchant. For that matter, we'd be better off without the Mettai as well." He looked at his mount and grinned. "In fact, I think I'd like to be back in Qalsyn about now, enjoying an ale at the Swift Water and flirting with anyone other than Tirnya."

Nallaj placidly stared back at him, as if reminding him that he'd chosen to march with the Onjaefs in the first place.

"Right."

He heard one of Jenoe's men calling the army to muster and he swung himself into his saddle. If anything, his mood had grown even worse than it had been when he woke.

As Torgan had wrested control over his life back from the Fal'Borna and everyone else who had tried to bend him to their purposes over the past several turns, he had also rediscovered the powers of observation that once made him such a successful merchant. Not long ago, he had been able to discern a rival merchant's weaknesses with little more than a glance. That had been his gift. Within seconds of beginning a negotiation he knew how it would end. And nearly every time, he used this knowledge to turn a tidy profit.

The stakes were different now. He was trading in blood rather than gold; he concerned himself not with profit but with his own survival. In other ways, however, the game remained much the same.

And right now, he was losing. With each day that passed he thought it increasingly likely that Marshal Onjaef would send him away without using his scrap of cursed basket against the white-hairs. He'd cautioned himself to remain patient, but after his encounter with the Onjaef woman and Qalsyn's lord heir, he didn't believe he could afford to wait any longer.

He felt reasonably sure that the problem and its possible solution lay with Tirnya. If he could convince her, he could turn the marshal. But he no longer thought that he could change her mind, at least not on his own. For whatever reason, she didn't like or trust him. That was clear.

But he thought it equally clear that she had other matters on her mind. Any fool could see that Maisaak's son was in love with her, and from what Torgan had observed the night before, it seemed obvious that Enly had a rival in Gries Ballidyne. Enly and the woman were too much alike; if Torgan couldn't convince her, he wouldn't convince the lord heir either.

Gries, on the other hand, struck the merchant as being a perfect ally. Those who knew the Ballidynes spoke often of their ambition and their daring. The fact that Gries would make a play for the woman in the middle of a war confirmed what Torgan had already known: Here was a man Torgan could understand, a man who thought in terms of risk and profit. Yes, Tirnya Onjaef was beautiful. But more to the point, if Gries could win her from Enly, he and his house would profit handsomely. She came from a powerful, wealthy family. And if this invasion succeeded in ending the Onjaef's exile, such a marriage would prove even more advantageous to the Ballidynes.

He would have liked to seek out Fairlea's captain immediately after leaving Enly and Tirnya, but he could see that the soldiers and their commanders were preparing for the day's march, and this was not a conversation he wanted to rush. Instead, he saddled Trey and, when the army of Stelpana mustered into columns, positioned himself a short distance behind the captains. A short time later they resumed their march westward, and for some time Torgan rode alone in silence.

He watched Gries closely. The captain appeared to be in good spirits as he chatted amiably with some of the captains under his command. He also kept his eye on both Tirnya, who rode with her father, and Enly, who appeared to ride alone. But it seemed to Torgan that Gries glanced at the woman now and again, as if unable to stop himself. Torgan didn't approach the man at first. He didn't wish to appear too eager, nor did he want to begin their conversation by interrupting Gries's interaction with his men.

But late in the morning Jenoe signaled for a brief halt by one of the many rills that cut through the plain. Gries dismounted and took a long drink of water and Torgan did the same, though he continued to keep his distance, positioning himself upstream of Fairlea's lord heir. One of the men with whom Gries had been riding lingered near the captain. Otherwise Torgan might have approached him then. A moment later, though, this other Fairlea captain returned to his mount, leaving Gries alone.

Scanning the area to make certain that no one else was near, Torgan stood. As he did, he purposely knocked his hat off his head and into the water. Immediately the current took it, and sped it downstream toward the captain.

"Damn!" Torgan said, stumbling after his hat along the stream bank.

Gries looked up, saw the hat floating toward him, and snatched it out of the water. He straightened and, when Torgan reached him, handed the soaked hat back to the merchant.

"There you go," the captain said with a grin.

"Thank you, Captain. It may not look like much to you, but I've had this hat a long time. I wouldn't have wanted to lose it."

"I'm sure," Gries said, his tone courteous. He started to turn away.

"There's a story behind it," Torgan said, shaking as much of the water out of the hat as he could and returning it to his head. "If you'd like to hear it."

Gries stopped, seeming to weigh whether to make his escape or agree to listen to Torgan's tale.

"This hat actually comes from your city."

Gries looked genuinely surprised. "Does it really?"

"Indulge an old man, Captain. Let me tell you how I came by it. I promise you won't be sorry."

The captain chuckled. "Very well, Mister Plye. Tell me your story."

Before Torgan could begin, one of Jenoe's men called for the soldiers to muster in once more. The timing couldn't have been better.

"Can I ride with you?" the merchant asked.

"Of course."

"The tale of this hat begins with a game of dice," Torgan told him when they were riding again. "I was in the marketplace in Fairlea, and had spent the entire day making sales and trades. This was many years back and I wasn't as successful as I am—" He broke off, his cheeks coloring. "As I later became."

Gries said nothing and had the good grace to keep his gaze fixed on the horizon.

"None of the men I was playing against had much more gold than I did," he went on after a moment. "And soon those of us who were less fortunate had to place our bets in currencies other than gold. I bet cloth and blades and, yes, even baskets." He glanced at the captain, who was watching him now. "One of the other players tried to bet this hat, and when those of us with a stake in that particular throw questioned its value, he told us that he had taken the hat in a knife fight with none other than Widlyn Crane."

Gries's eyes widened. "Widlyn Crane?" he repeated, incredulous. "The Scauper himself?"

"The very same," Torgan said, grinning. "As you probably know, Crane died in a knife fight in Yorl. He was drunk, and fell to a man who couldn't possibly have bested him had he been sober. This was the man. We let him bet the hat, and I won the roll."

Gries regarded him doubtfully.

The merchant's smile broadened. "You don't believe me."

"Not really, no."

"I don't blame you." Torgan took off the hat, handed it to

the captain, and pointed to the letters scratched into the leather at the back. They read, "W. Crane."

"Blood and bone!" the captain whispered. "Widlyn Crane."

"One and the same." Torgan smiled again. It was indeed a true story, except that he won the hat in Redcliff along the Aelean Coast and not in Gries's city of Fairlea. But now that the captain had seen Crane's name etched into the hat, he would never think to question the rest.

Gries handed the hat back to Torgan, shaking his head. "Well, I have to admit, Torgan: I didn't think your tale would amount to much. I apologize for doubting you."

Torgan put the hat back on and waved off the captain's apology. "If I'd been in your position, I wouldn't have expected much either," he said. "Look at me. It's hard to believe that just a few turns ago I was the wealthiest merchant in the Southlands."

Gries looked him up and down quickly, a slight frown on his face. "You'll be trading again before long," he said bracingly.

The merchant didn't respond, and for several moments the two of them rode in silence. Torgan could feel the captain growing increasingly uncomfortable, which suited his needs. Eventually he'd try to force the conversation along, and with any luck he'd give Torgan some sort of opening to talk about his scrap of basket.

Sooner than the merchant would have expected, Gries said, "You seek revenge against the Fal'Borna, don't you?"

"What do you mean?"

"This basket you carry, or whatever it is. You want to avenge the loss of your wealth and the time you spent in captivity. Perhaps even the life of the other merchant you mentioned when we first found you. He died at the hands of the white-hairs, didn't he?"

"He died while still their prisoner, yes. But I'm not sure that it's revenge I'm after."

Gries raised an eyebrow. "No?"

Torgan shook his head. "It doesn't matter. The marshal won't use the plague against them."

"You don't know that."

He didn't want to anger the man. Not exactly. It had to be done with care. "Actually, I do. I spoke with his captains this morning. They made it clear that they didn't like the idea. Not at all."

"Which captains?" Gries asked, his eyes narrowing.

"Well, his daughter, for one. I get the feeling that she doesn't like me, and that she has no intention of allowing her father to use the plague. And she was with the lord heir at the time. He didn't seem to like the idea, either."

"Enly, you mean?"

"Is that his name?"

Gries nodded, glancing at the other lord heir. "Yes." He faced Torgan again. "What did they tell you?"

"It wasn't as much what they told me as how they spoke to me. As I say, I don't think they like me very much."

"Perhaps it's the plague they don't like," Gries said.

"You don't like the idea, either, do you?"

The captain opened his mouth, then closed it again. "I haven't decided yet," he finally answered.

"Then let me ask you what I asked them. What would you say if I told you that your army could take back S'Vralna without losing a single man? All you'll have to do is walk through the shattered gates of the city and reclaim it for Stelpana."

"You sound very confident, Torgan. I can't imagine it will be that easy, even if the plague does all that you say it will."

"But you're wrong," Torgan told him. "The city has already been destroyed by the plague. It's yours for the taking. I'm not suggesting that you use the basket I carry against S'Vralna. I'm telling you that the city is already defeated."

Gries gaped at him. "You're certain of this?"

"I've been there. I've seen it with my own eye." He grinned, knowing that the man would think him ghoulish, and not really caring. He could see from the captain's expression that he had reached him.

"D'Raqor can be taken the same way. This plague is no trifle. It's the most powerful weapon you'll ever wield." He gave the man a sly look and, acting on instinct once more, said, "Tell me, Captain: What has it been like relying on the magic of these Mettai who march with you?"

Fairlea's lord heir eyed him briefly, then smiled and shook his head again. "I've heard tales about you, Torgan. Some of them from my father; others from merchants I've met in the marketplace of my city. But only now do I realize how skilled a negotiator you must have been when you still drove your cart."

"I intend to drive a cart again, Captain."

"Of course you do." He sighed, and looked over at Tirnya, who still rode beside her father. "As you seem to have surmised, the Mettai have proven somewhat less valuable as allies than I might have hoped. Their magic has its limits, and at times it appears that they can't control the spells they cast."

"That must be frustrating for the marshal."

"It is," Gries said. "It's bad enough losing men to the Fal'Borna. But losing men to the creatures conjured by the Mettai is nearly too much to take. I believe Jenoe regrets the alliance he forged with them."

Torgan thought about saying more, but held his tongue. He thought it likely that Gries would take their conversation where it needed to go.

"Can this plague be controlled?" he asked after a brief silence.

"No," Torgan told him. "It's like a wild beast. And it unleashes the white-hairs' magic. That's how it kills them. They expend their power until they die. They bleed to death, but they bleed magic."

Gries appeared to shudder. "So Sivralna . . ."

"It lies in ruins," Torgan said. "Its gates and walls are shattered, as are many of its buildings."

"Jenoe won't like that," the captain said, frowning.

"I don't imagine. But you have to ask yourselves, what will a siege do to D'Raqor, and how successful can that siege be if your soldiers are concerned with preserving this building or that one?"

Gries appeared to weigh this.

"Don't get me wrong, Captain. This plague is an ugly business. But it only strikes at the white-hairs. You and I are immune. I doubt the Mettai can say that about the spells they've cast on your behalf."

The man nodded vaguely. He was eyeing Tirnya Onjaef again.

"She doesn't like the idea," Torgan said.

Gries looked at him sharply.

The merchant nodded gravely. "You know she doesn't. But you need to ask yourself if that's reason enough to oppose it as well."

"You overstep your bounds, merchant!" Gries said. "You're speaking of matters that you know nothing about."

Torgan smiled. "Then ignore what I've said and forgive my presumption."

"You said that Enly opposes your idea as well?" the captain asked, as if he hadn't heard Torgan's apology.

For a third time, the merchant was forced to rely on nothing more than his intuition. The day before, a soldier had told him that there were whispers in Qalsyn of a romance between Enly and Tirnya. But last night he had seen Gries and the woman share an intimate moment. She had appeared to welcome his kiss. Enly and Gries were both heirs to governorships. Both were good-looking, confident, perhaps prone to arrogance. He would have been shocked had either Enly or Gries regarded the other as anything more or less than a rival. He was guessing, of course. But he trusted his insights here just as he did in the marketplace. And so he played on that rivalry.

"He seemed to," Torgan said. "They were together, so I can't say if he was speaking his mind or merely echoing what she had told me."

Gries nodded, his eyes still fixed on the woman. "That sounds like Enly. He . . . he dotes on her. There's no other way to say it."

"She is quite beautiful," Torgan said, as if that excused Enly's failings.

Gries glanced at him disapprovingly. "Of course she is. But that's not the point. Winning Tirnya's heart is only half the battle. I need to win Jenoe's approval as well."

Again, Torgan said nothing.

"Are you certain that this scrap of basket you carry will sicken the Fal'Borna?" Gries asked him eventually. "If this were to fail—"

Torgan shook his head. "It won't fail. I've used it before. If we can spread it over enough of the city, it will do just what it's supposed to."

The captain stared at him for several moments. "What did you say?" he finally asked.

Torgan frowned. "I've used it—"

"Not that part. Something about spreading it over the city."

"Yes. It's a small scrap of basket, and we need to find a way to expose as many of the white-hairs to it as possible."

The man grinned. "We have a way. And I think we can convince the marshal to use it."

Chapter 18

+‡+

E'MENUA'S SEPT, CENTRAL PLAIN

They had retreated to the privacy of their z'kal early in the evening. Grinsa had nothing more to say to E'Menua or Q'Daer, or even to Besh and Sirj. Probably he should have gone to see the Mettai one last time, if for no other reason than to assure them that he would do all he could to win their freedom when he returned from battle. But such assurances would have been hollow, and both men deserved better from him.

More to the point, he had grown weary of putting the needs of others ahead of his own concerns. This one night, he chose to be selfish.

Once more, he and Cresenne were being forced apart. Once more, they had no guarantee that they both would survive to be reunited. They sought refuge in each other's arms from their fears and their despair. Grinsa wanted to promise her that he would return, that once this war was over they would find a new home where they'd be safe, where Bryntelle could grow up in peace. But that promise would have been empty as well.

At one point during the evening, still breathless and flushed with spent passion, Cresenne looked up at him, her pale eyes shining in the dim light of their fire, and said, "Next time, I get to choose where we live."

Grinsa had laughed and kissed her. But a moment later she was crying, clinging to him. He searched for something to say that might ease her mind, but the words wouldn't come. In the end he merely held her until her sobbing ceased and she fell asleep.

Some time later they were awakened by the sound of someone tapping on the outside of their shelter. Grinsa opened his eyes and sat up quickly, as did Cresenne. It was still dark, and the embers of their fire glowed dully.

"Forelander," a voice called softly from outside.

Grinsa and Cresenne shared a look. Then Grinsa stood and pulled on his britches.

"Forelander?" said the voice again.

"That sounds like the n'qlae," Cresenne whispered.

Grinsa pushed aside the flap of rilda skin that covered the z'kal's entrance. Cresenne was right. D'Pera stood outside the shelter, her white hair gleaming in the light of the moons. Even in the dim light, he could see the apprehension etched in her face.

"What's happened, N'Qlae?"

"It's E'Menua. He was speaking with another a'laq, Weaver to Weaver. I'm not certain what happened, but he's . . . something's not right. He told me to get you."

That, of all things, caught him by surprise.

"He wants me to come?" Grinsa asked.

D'Pera nodded.

"Very well," Grinsa told her. "Give me just a moment."

He ducked back into the shelter and began to dress.

"What is it?" Cresenne asked, glancing at Bryntelle, who hadn't awakened.

"I'm not sure. Something's happened to E'Menua. He wants to speak with me."

Cresenne frowned. "I don't like the sound of that."

"Neither do I. But I don't think that D'Pera would have a hand in actually harming me. I'll be all right."

She nodded, though she appeared to shiver as well. Grinsa forced a smile, then left the shelter and followed D'Pera back to the a'laq's z'kal.

The n'qlae didn't say anything, but she walked quickly, a rilda skin pulled tight around her shoulders to ward off the chill night air. When they reached the shelter she shared with E'Menua, she pulled aside the flap covering the entrance and motioned Grinsa inside.

A fire burned brightly in the middle of the z'kal. The a'laq sat on the far side of it, wrapped in a blanket, his face damp with sweat, as if he had a fever. He even seemed to be trembling slightly.

"A'Laq?" Grinsa said, stepping closer to him.

"Sit down, Forelander," E'Menua said. His voice sounded strong.

Grinsa lowered himself to the ground.

"I have been speaking with other a'laqs," E'Menua began. "We'll be joining some on the plain in the next few days. Others have already led their warriors toward the Horn to meet the dark-eye army." He picked up a skin that had been lying beside him and took a long drink. "One of the a'laqs I thought would be heading north hadn't met up with the others yet. So I reached for him. His name is J'Sor; his sept is west of here." He paused again, shaking his head.

"When I entered his dreams, it was . . . it was like stepping into a fire. I could see him—he was surrounded by flame. He seemed to be in agony. I'm not sure if he could hear me or see me."

"The plague," Grinsa said quietly.

E'Menua nodded. "It took me several moments to understand what was happening, but eventually I assumed as much."

"I've seen it," Grinsa told him. "I stepped into Q'Daer's dreams when he was sick. I remember it being just as you described."

"I tried to heal him," the a'laq said. "I tried everything I could think of to defeat his fever, but it was as if the flames eluded me. I could no more put them out than I could teach him to fly."

Grinsa nodded, smiling slightly.

The a'laq narrowed his eyes. "You know what I'm going to say, don't you?"

"Isn't that why you called me here?"

E'Menua lowered his gaze so that he was staring into the fire. "I should be dead, or at least dying."

"Yes, you should. So should this man, J'Sor. But both of you are going to live long enough to fight the Eandi, aren't you?"

"After a few moments it was as if the flames around him started to recede on their own. Nothing I did worked. I know that. But I healed him just the same."

"You didn't. Besh did. The same spell that kept you from getting ill purged the plague from J'Sor's body."

E'Menua looked up again, meeting his gaze. "I've already said that they're free to leave their z'kal," he said, with just a hint of his usual bluster. "They're guests in my sept. That's what I said today, before you questioned them about their magic."

"You need to do more than that," Grinsa said. "You know

now that they've been telling the truth, and that I have as well."

The a'laq shook his head, growing more agitated by the moment. "Nothing has changed. These two men may have acted in good faith, but their people are marching against us. I can't have warriors riding to war questioning whether the men they're fighting are truly their enemies."

"You also can't have these men put to death. You put those lies in Besh's mouth, and unless you tell the truth, no one else will believe that they're innocent."

"I'm not going to execute them, Forelander. Whatever you may think of me, I'm not that cruel."

"And what if you don't survive the war, A'Laq? I believe that you won't put them to death now, knowing what you do. But unless you tell the truth about them, your successor might."

E'Menua stared back at him, frowning as if he hadn't anticipated this line of argument.

"Why did you call for me, A'Laq?" Grinsa asked. "I know that Besh and Sirj were telling the truth about their spell. So what happened to you tonight doesn't surprise me. You knew it wouldn't. And yet you summoned me here in the middle of the night. Why?"

"I'm not sure," E'Menua admitted. "I was . . . After seeing J'Sor that way, and then seeing the fires die out . . . I didn't know what to do."

"Have you told your wife about what happened?" Grinsa asked.

"Not yet."

"You should. And you should tell Q'Daer, too. You've named him as your successor—others heard you do so. He should know the truth."

E'Menua continued to stare at him, and for a moment Grinsa thought he would refuse. But then the a'laq nodded.

"Yes, all right. I'll tell them both. But for now I don't want the others to know. You understand?"

"Not entirely," Grinsa said. "But I'll honor your wishes."

The a'laq nodded. Grinsa stood, intending to leave. Before he could, E'Menua spoke his name.

"Did you have them put the spell on me?" the a'laq asked. "The Mettai, I mean. Is that why I'm immune now?"

"No," Grinsa said, shaking his head. "They didn't have to do anything. As I told you, the spell they created to fight the plague was as contagious as Lici's curse itself. Q'Daer passed it to you when he spoke to you in your dreams, before we returned to the sept."

He nearly added that he could have passed it to the a'laq as well, during their first confrontation after Grinsa's return, when they battled for control of E'Menua's magic. That contact would have been enough to make the a'laq immune to the Mettai plague. But he didn't believe that any good would come from mentioning that incident.

"Of course," the a'laq said, in a breathless whisper. "I should have remembered."

"Good night, A'Laq."

"Yes," E'Menua said. "I . . . thank you for . . . for coming so late."

Grinsa nodded and left the z'kal. D'Pera stood alone in the darkness, gazing up at the moons. She turned at the sound of his footfalls.

"Is he all right?" she asked.

"Yes, he is. He has things to tell you."

The n'qlae nodded, looking past him toward the shelter. "A Fal'Borna warrior does everything he can to protect his a'laq," she said, her voice low. "It's our way."

"I'll do what I can to keep him safe, N'Qlae."

She shifted her gaze, meeting his. "You and he—"

"I've sworn to fight for the Fal'Borna. I understand what that means." He smiled faintly. "It's late, and I'd like to sleep a few more hours before we ride."

"Yes, all right," she said. "Good night, Forelander."

Grinsa stepped past her and walked back to his shelter,

knowing that he had little hope of falling back asleep. He entered the z'kal as quietly as he could, undressed, and slipped under the blankets beside Cresenne.

"What was that all about?" she asked in a whisper, sounding very much awake.

He briefly related his conversation with E'Menua.

"So he knows that Besh and Sirj were telling the truth," she said when he was done, "but he refuses to admit as much to his people."

"That's basically right."

"And he felt compelled to tell you this in the middle of the night just before you're to follow him into battle."

"I think he was truly frightened by what happened. And I think he didn't know what to make of the fact that he was still alive. Even when he was using his magic to keep Besh from telling the truth, I don't think he believed that the Mettai spell could really work."

"I'm not sure that justifies any of what he's done," she said.

Grinsa was inclined to agree with her, but to his surprise and relief, he already felt himself getting sleepy. Sooner than he had expected, he fell back asleep.

Dawn came far too early, and before long Grinsa was dressed and outside the z'kal with Cresenne, who held a sleepy and fussy Bryntelle in her arms. He had expected that he would need to get his horse from the sept's paddock, but when he stepped out into the morning air, the bay was already saddled and waiting for him. Apparently preparing one's mount for war was one more thing the Fal'Borna didn't expect a Weaver to do for himself.

The other Weavers and their warriors were gathering at the eastern edge of the sept. Grinsa started in that direction, but after only a stride or two, he realized that Cresenne wasn't with him. He turned and saw that she still stood beside the shelter. Her eyes were dry, but she looked pale and sad in the grey light.

"You're not coming with me," he said.

Cresenne shook her head. "I don't want to say good-bye to you with everyone else there. And I don't want to be anywhere near E'Menua right now. I'm sorry."

He walked back to where she stood and kissed her. "I understand," he said. He kissed Bryntelle on the forehead, but she merely fussed at him.

"She doesn't know what she's doing," Cresenne said.

"I know."

They stood for a moment, their eyes locked.

Grinsa brushed a strand of hair away from her cheek. "I don't know what to say."

"Just come back."

"This is the last time—"

She held a finger to his lips, stopping him. "Don't," she said. She kissed him softly. "The one thing I've learned this past year is that we can't know what's going to happen. Just come back to me."

"All right. I love you."

That brought a smile to her lips. "We love you, too."

He turned and left them there, his chest aching.

When he reached the warriors and Weavers, he saw that he was the last to arrive. E'Menua was already sitting his horse, marking Grinsa's approach. L'Norr and Q'Daer were on either side of him, stony-faced. Most of the other Fal'Borna riders turned to look at Grinsa, some of them looking resentful, others merely curious. Grinsa expected the a'laq to comment on his late arrival, but E'Menua merely nodded once and, without a word, turned his mount and led his warriors away from the sept.

Several women and children had come to see the army off, but they didn't cry or cheer, or do any of the other things Eandi families in the Forelands might have done as their husbands or fathers marched to war. They stared after the men and then, one family at a time, turned and walked back into the sept, seemingly intent on their normal chores.

As the sun appeared on the eastern horizon, huge and

golden, the men struck out northward. Grinsa would have liked to ride alone, at the back of the company, but before long Q'Daer dropped back to join him.

"You should be riding with the a'laq," said the young Weaver in a low voice.

Grinsa had expected this. He just nodded, and followed wordlessly as Q'Daer led him forward.

Theirs was a small company, especially compared to the armies Grinsa had seen during the war against the renegade Weaver in the Forelands. There were perhaps a hundred fifty Fal'Borna riders. No more. Some looked barely old enough to wield magic; others appeared too old for the rigors of battle. But all of them carried spears as well as the blades on their belts, and he sensed that all of them wielded at least one magic that would serve them well in this war: shaping, language of beasts, mists and winds, fire, and even healing.

Upon reaching the front of the company, Grinsa took a position beside Q'Daer, as far from the a'laq as he could manage.

Again, E'Menua said nothing to him, and that was all right with Grinsa. He didn't feel like speaking to anyone.

The Fal'Borna were skilled horsemen, and their mounts were as impressive as any Grinsa had seen. They rode at a good pace, and when they stopped to rest at midday, he estimated that the company had covered nearly three leagues.

While some of the men ate a small meal or drank from waterskins, Grinsa stood off on his own, scanning the eastern horizon. He wasn't sure what he expected to see. He hadn't heard anything to indicate that the Eandi army had made its way this far into Fal'Borna land, but he felt tense. The last time he'd ridden to war, he had nearly died. His disfigured shoulder throbbed with the memory.

"What are you looking for?" asked a familiar voice.

He glanced to the side. Q'Daer and L'Norr had joined him. He shrugged, facing forward again.

"I don't know," he said. "Does the a'laq have any idea how far the Eandi are from here?"

"Leagues, Forelander," Q'Daer said. "Relax. Eat something. Fal'Borna riders have been sent forward to meet the dark-eyes. We might not get to fight at all."

Grinsa nodded, remembering that E'Menua had mentioned this the night before. He looked at Q'Daer again. "You sound disappointed."

"It couldn't be helped. We got sick and so we were late returning to the sept with the Mettai. But I would have liked to be part of that first assault."

Grinsa couldn't help thinking that Q'Daer sounded terribly young, like someone who had never actually seen war. But he kept this to himself.

"So we'll be meeting others?" he asked after a few moments, more to keep the conversation moving than anything else.

"Yes," Q'Daer told him. "There are at least seven a'laqs coming to join us. We'll meet them at F'Qira's Rill, to the west of S'Vralna. Even if the dark-eyes defeat the first army, they won't get past us."

Grinsa nodded but said nothing, drawing a frown from the young Weaver.

"You don't approve of that plan?" Q'Daer asked.

"It's not my place to approve or disapprove. I just hope that it won't come to that. I'd rather not fight at all."

"The dark-eyes started this war!" the man said, his voice rising. "You can't think that we should do nothing, that we should simply lay down our blades and give them the plain!"

Grinsa sighed, wishing he'd kept his mouth shut. "I never said that, Q'Daer. All I said was that I don't want to fight. I fought in a war before leaving the Forelands. A series of wars, really. Thousands died. I have no interest in being part of more carnage. And if you had any idea of what war is really like, you'd feel the same way."

He knew that he should have kept that last part to himself, but at that moment he couldn't help himself. Before the young Weaver could answer, Grinsa turned and led his horse away. He'd been apart from Cresenne and Bryntelle for less than half a day, and already he missed them both. For a moment he had to resist an urge to leap onto his horse, ride back to the sept, and carry them both away, leaving behind the Fal'Borna and their war.

Instead, when E'Menua called for the riders to resume their journey a few moments later, he swung himself onto his mount and took his place with the other Weavers, assiduously avoiding Q'Daer's gaze.

For the rest of that day and all through the next, E'Menua's warriors maintained their swift pace across the plain. They saw no sign of the Eandi, or, for that matter, of any other Fal'Borna riders. The skies remained clear, but a cold wind blew out of the north, and clouds darkened the northern horizon.

Grinsa kept to himself. Warriors brought him food and drink, as they did for the other Weavers, but none of them said more to him than courtesy required. Q'Daer and L'Norr ignored him, and though Grinsa noticed E'Menua watching him on more than one occasion, the a'laq left him alone, too. For his part, Grinsa made no effort to speak with any of them.

Late in the morning of their third day on the plain, as they rode on that same northerly line, Grinsa spotted thin plumes of smoke rising from the grasses ahead of them. He glanced at the a'laq and his Weavers, but though all of them appeared to have spotted the smoke, none of them seemed alarmed.

At least not at first.

As they drew nearer to the source of those plumes, Grinsa saw what appeared to be a large camp of warriors and horses. They were spread over a broad area, but the camp looked sparse.

"There should be more of them," E'Menua said in a tight voice. "How can there be so few?"

No one had to say a word. They all knew the answer.

They rode on and soon entered the camp, drawing the stares of nearly every man there. Looking from face to face,

Grinsa sensed with his magic that several of the Fal'Borna who had gathered on the plain were Weavers. But in all, even with E'Menua's warriors, there couldn't have been more than four hundred Fal'Borna in the camp.

When the renegade Weaver in the Forelands had faced the combined might of the Eandi courts, he had commanded an army smaller than this one, and he had been only one Weaver. Still he had nearly prevailed. But Grinsa thought it likely that the Eandi of the Southlands were better prepared to fight against Qirsi magic than his Eandi allies in the Forelands had been. And he had no idea what the presence of the Mettai might mean when it came time to do battle.

Clearly, though, E'Menua was dismayed by what he saw.

"Where is H'Loryn?" he said, dismounting and scanning the camp. "And O'Tal. I want to speak with him, too."

After a moment two men emerged from the crowd that had begun to gather around the a'laq and his Weavers. Many of the Fal'Borna had been eyeing Grinsa warily, noting, no doubt, that he looked nothing like them. They parted to let the two men E'Menua had summoned step forward, but they didn't take their eyes off of the Forelander.

"We're here, E'Menua," one of the men said, his voice tinged with annoyance.

Grinsa realized that he recognized this man. He was one of the a'laqs he had spoken to while spreading Besh's spell across the plain. The man was younger than E'Menua, probably closer in age to Grinsa. He was also taller than the a'laq, with a leaner build. His eyes were a soft yellow, and like so many of the warriors there, he wore his hair pulled back from his face. Grinsa didn't know the other man, but he sensed immediately that he was also a Weaver. He assumed that he was an a'laq as well. This second man looked to be closer in age to E'Menua, whom he also resembled in stature and build. He had pale eyes and a round face that might have been friendly had he smiled.

"These are all the men you brought with you?" E'Menua demanded.

The younger of the two men glanced past E'Menua to those who had arrived with him. "I brought no fewer than you did. H'Loryn's sept has always been smaller than ours. You know this."

"We need more warriors," E'Menua said, as if the man had been arguing to the contrary.

The man named O'Tal shrugged. "I agree. But I can't conjure them out of the air." His eyes flicked toward Grinsa for just an instant. "Can you, E'Menua?"

The a'laq scowled at him before turning to H'Loryn. "Have you heard anything from the others?"

The second Weaver shook his head. "Nothing new from the ones who rode forward. We're still waiting for J'Sor and his warriors."

E'Menua shook his head. "I don't think J'Sor will be coming. Not for a few more days."

"Why not?" O'Tal asked.

"The plague struck his sept."

Both men blanched, and murmurs rippled through the mass of warriors standing around them.

O'Tal glanced at Grinsa a second time. "You're certain of this?"

"Yes," E'Menua said.

O'Tal kept his gaze fixed on Grinsa. "You walked in my dreams, and you made me immune to the plague. At least you claimed to. Didn't you do the same for J'Sor?"

"No, A'Laq," Grinsa said. "I tried to reach as many septs as I could, but I began with septs near the Horn, to the south toward the Ofirean, and to the east. That's where I believe the danger was greatest. I hadn't yet gotten to those septs in the west."

"You know this man?" H'Loryn asked, looking from O'Tal to Grinsa.

The young a'laq nodded. "He came to me a few nights ago. He told me that E'Menua had sent him to pass on a . . . some magic that would make us all immune to the plague."

H'Loryn's eyes widened. "What?"

"I'm sorry, A'Laq," Grinsa said, addressing the older man. "I didn't get to your sept, either. You must live in the west."

H'Loryn nodded. "Yes, I do." He gave a slight frown. "Who are you?"

"My name is Grinsa jal Arriet. I come from the Forelands and I now live in E'Menua's sept."

"The Forelands," the a'laq repeated. "Well, that explains your accent and your appearance. But why would you come here?"

"We have other matters to discuss," E'Menua broke in. "We need to make plans for what we'll do if other septs don't join us here. And I want to hear anything you can tell me about S'Bahn's men and the others who have ridden to the Horn to face the dark-eyes."

H'Loryn eyed Grinsa for another moment, but then faced E'Menua. "Yes, of course, E'Menua. You're right."

For once, Grinsa was grateful for E'Menua's impatience. He had no desire to explain his past to any of these men. And he, too, was curious about the men E'Menua had mentioned. S'Bahn, he remembered, was the father of B'Vril, the leader of the company he and Q'Daer had encountered while still journeying back to the sept with Besh and Sirj.

E'Menua instructed his a'jeis and their warriors to make camp beside the other two armies. As they carried out his orders, he began to ask questions of the two other a'laqs. How many warriors had ridden forward to meet the Eandi army? Which a'laqs were leading them? How many Weavers did they have?

He didn't appear particularly pleased with any of their answers, but O'Tal and H'Loryn gave every indication that they thought the Fal'Borna army formidable enough to take on the invaders.

"They hadn't found the dark-eyes yet?" E'Menua asked, still looking unhappy.

O'Tal shook his head. "Not the last time I spoke with P'Rhil. But that was two nights ago."

"We should reach for him again tonight," E'Menua said.

"I intend to," O'Tal told him.

The tension between the two men was palpable. Clearly E'Menua thought of himself as the leader of these Fal'Borna. It seemed just as clear that O'Tal saw himself the same way. In the Forelands, rival dukes would have taken the measure of one another based upon the power, influence, and wealth of their houses. From what Grinsa had learned of the Fal'Borna, it seemed that septs judged their rivals by how many Weavers they had. If that was the case here, Grinsa's presence by E'Menua's side couldn't have been welcomed by O'Tal or his warriors.

"Well," H'Loryn said, clearly desperate to ease what had become an uncomfortable situation, "I suppose that means we have nothing to do but wait."

O'Tal and E'Menua continued to eye each other, like combatants at the outset of a battle tournament.

"We spotted some rilda earlier today," said one of the other Weavers. "Stragglers that haven't gone south yet. We could have a hunt."

H'Loryn's face brightened. "Excellent!" he said. "We'll feast tonight to celebrate the coming together of three great armies." He looked hopefully at the other two a'laqs, neither of whom appeared to take much notice of him. "O'Tal?" the older man said, a plea in his voice.

"Yes, all right," O'Tal answered. He turned away from E'Menua, a brittle smile on his lips. "A hunt sounds like an excellent idea."

H'Loryn looked so relieved it was almost comical. "Good. We'll get started right away. You and your warriors will be joining us, won't you, E'Menua?"

The a'laq's smile could have curdled milk. "Of course we will."

"I'll stay behind and keep an eye on the camp," Grinsa said. "I don't think I'd be of much use on a hunt."

"Have you ever hunted rilda, Forelander?" O'Tal asked, though it seemed to Grinsa that he already knew the answer.

"No, I haven't."

"Then perhaps you should join us. A Fal'Borna can't truly be considered a warrior until he's hunted on the plain."

He heard the challenge in O'Tal's words, and his first reaction was to refuse. He wanted no part of the man's feud with E'Menua, and he had no interest in initiating a feud of his own. But seeing the way the other Fal'Borna were looking at him, including Q'Daer and L'Norr, Grinsa began to realize that there was more at stake here than O'Tal's challenge. Most of these men didn't know him; many of those from E'Menua's sept still didn't trust him. Yet they were about to go into battle with him. Reluctant as he was to be part of this war, he knew that he needed to have the trust of the men who would be fighting beside him, whose magic he would be wielding as a weapon.

"All right," Grinsa said, looking O'Tal in the eye. "But you'll have to show me what to do."

The young a'laq looked surprised. "Yes, of course."

Q'Daer caught Grinsa's eye and nodded, a rare smile on his face. E'Menua didn't look quite so pleased.

They gave him a spear and then a large group rode southward away from the camp. It had quickly become something more than a hunt. It was a rite of passage for Grinsa, and also a diversion for the young warriors. Grinsa felt himself growing nervous and excited. He hadn't done much hunting since he was a boy growing up on the Caerissan Steppe near Eardley in the Forelands, but he still remembered fondly the hunts of his childhood.

"How is it you wound up with E'Menua?"

He turned to find that O'Tal had pulled abreast of him on his dappled grey.

"His was the first sept we found," Grinsa said, choosing his words with care.

The man's eyebrows went up. "We?"

"I came to the Southlands with my wife and my daughter."

"I see. Is your wife a Weaver, too?"

"No," Grinsa said flatly.

A small smile flickered on the man's face and then vanished. "I'd imagine that's been difficult for you both."

Grinsa regarded the man briefly, trying to determine if he was mocking their difficulties. But he saw no sign of this.

"Actually, it has been," he admitted. "But I think E'Menua has come to accept that Cresenne is my wife."

"Really?" O'Tal asked with obvious surprise. "One day you'll have to explain to me how you convinced him."

Grinsa grinned, deciding in that moment that he liked O'Tal.

"You and E'Menua don't get along, do you?" he asked.

"E'Menua is a strong leader," O'Tal said immediately. "His sept has many Weavers." He glanced at Grinsa slyly. "More even than I knew."

"I'm not sure that answers my question."

"Do you like him?" O'Tal asked.

Grinsa hesitated, then gave a short laugh. "Forget that I asked."

O'Tal smiled, but quickly grew serious again. "You've managed to win a measure of his trust, and you seem like a man who can take care of himself, so I won't presume to offer counsel where none is needed. But E'Menua is a hard man, and a clever one. Watch yourself."

"I have been," Grinsa said. "But I appreciate the warning."

A shout went up from some of the men who had ridden ahead. Both of them scanned the plain. After a moment, O'Tal pointed toward the southwest.

"There!" he said, sounding eager. "It's a small herd, but it will do."

Grinsa's first thought was that a large herd of rilda must have been a wonder to behold. There had to be at least a hundred of the animals in this "small herd." They had been grazing, but seeing the horsemen they had broken away. They looked like the antelope Grinsa had seen in the southern Forelands, but they were bigger, with sleek coats of short tan fur and white markings on their flanks and heads. Their eyes were large and dark, and many of the animals had short, pale antlers.

"What do we do?" Grinsa asked, his pulse quickening at the sight of the creatures.

O'Tal spurred his mount to a gallop. "We ride!" he called over his shoulder.

Grinsa followed, pleased to find that the horse he had bought in Yorl when he and Cresenne first arrived in the Southlands was able to keep pace with the stallions of the Fal'Borna. He was suddenly conscious of the spear he still carried in his right hand, and of the sweat on his palm.

As swift as the Fal'Borna were, the rilda were faster. They appeared to move as one, turning first one way and then the other in perfect unison, sunlight flashing on their silken flanks and then darkening again as they swerved once more.

"We can't catch them!" Grinsa shouted over the rush of wind in his ears.

O'Tal looked at him, grinning. "Watch!" he said.

Almost as soon as the young a'laq said this, a second group of riders appeared, as if out of nowhere. The rilda were forced to reverse course, so that abruptly they were headed straight for Grinsa and the other warriors.

Grinsa wasn't certain that his situation had improved much. He'd never killed an animal while on horseback, and he'd never seen a creature as fast as these rilda.

"Now what?" he called.

"The easiest way is from behind," O'Tal said. "Choose an animal, ride at it from an angle, and strike when you're close."

Right. Because it was certain to be just that easy.

The herd had turned again, angling away from Grinsa and the others while still being pursued by the second set of riders. As Grinsa watched, a young Fal'Borna did exactly what O'Tal had described. He charged at the herd, and at the last moment appeared to choose one rilda. Turning as that animal approached, he positioned himself just behind and to the left of it. Then, leaning to the right, he lifted his spear and threw it. His weapon struck the rilda in the back of the neck, just above its shoulders. The animal went down in a heap, and the warrior triumphantly raised a hand over his head.

A second Fal'Borna rider had already started his run at an animal. This one took a different approach, angling toward the herd from the front and forcing several of the rilda to peel away from the rest of the group. Dropping down low so that he hung from his saddle, this warrior threw his spear into the chest of one of the rilda. This animal fell immediately as well.

"That's how it's done," O'Tal called to him, still smiling.

"That's how it's done by a Fal'Borna," Grinsa said. "Couldn't I just use language of beasts?"

O'Tal's expression grew deadly serious. "Fal'Borna law forbids the use of magic against the rilda. Kebb forbids it."

Kebb: the god of beasts.

Grinsa nodded. "Forgive me. I meant it as a joke."

O'Tal smiled again. "Apology accepted. Now go! Hunt!"

Swallowing hard, Grinsa turned his mount so that he angled toward the herd as the first hunter had done. The rilda turned again, so that they were headed toward him, and he had to adjust his line. His horse was starting to labor—Grinsa couldn't remember ever riding this fast—and he knew he'd only have the one chance. There seemed to be rilda and horses and Fal'Borna all around him. It was as chaotic as any battle he could remember from his war with the renegade Weaver. But soon enough he had positioned himself just behind a doe. He raised himself up in his saddle, drew back his spear, and threw.

He saw the spear hit the animal, saw the rilda stumble, but then he was too far past. He tried to wheel his mount around, was nearly rammed by several rilda, and came dangerously close to falling out of his saddle. When at last he righted himself, he saw the animal he had struck. It was alive still, struggling to climb to its feet. The spear was embedded in its shoulder, and blood stained its golden brown coat.

Grinsa winced at the sight. "Damn!"

He started back toward the creature, but before he reached it, O'Tal rode up to it and halted. He looked down on the rilda for a moment. Then he hefted his spear and plunged it into the rilda's neck. The animal spasmed and was still.

"Thank you," Grinsa said, stopping beside the doe.

"You did well," O'Tal told him.

Grinsa laughed mirthlessly. "Right."

"For your first hunt? The first hunt you'd ever even seen? You did well."

Grinsa inclined his head, acknowledging the compliment. "Again, my thanks."

"It's too bad you chose a doe," O'Tal said. "Most Fal'Borna men would have chosen a buck for their first kill."

"Why?"

"The bucks have . . . certain delicacies that are given to a warrior at the feast after his first hunt."

Grinsa's laugh this time was sincere. "You should have told me earlier."

"You're right," O'Tal said. "I should have." He dismounted. "Come on. Let's get her back to camp."

With O'Tal's help, Grinsa lifted the rilda onto his horse in front of the saddle, and tied it in place. By the time they were done, most of the rilda herd had moved on. The Fal'Borna had killed nearly two dozen of the animals; they'd eat well this night.

As Grinsa was riding back to the camp, Q'Daer joined him. He carried a rilda as well, a large buck.

"I saw you hunt," the young Weaver said. "You did well for a Forelander."

"Thank you," Grinsa said, assuming that he had meant this as praise. "I'm sorry: I missed your kill."

Q'Daer waved off the apology. "It wasn't my first; it won't be my last." He paused. Then, "I noticed that you were riding with O'Tal."

Something in his tone told Grinsa that he'd erred. Too late, it occurred to him that he hadn't seen E'Menua on the hunt.

"Is that a problem?" he asked.

"Tell the a'laq you didn't know you were supposed to hunt with me. He'll understand that."

Grinsa nodded. But his mood, which had finally improved after several days of missing his family, began to darken again. He'd grown weary of having to worry about offending E'Menua at every turn.

"Thank you," he said, his voice low.

"E'Menua will expect you to ride to battle with him. He's your a'laq, and you're his Weaver."

I'm no one's Weaver, he wanted to say. *Except Cresenne's.* But he kept this to himself. "I know," he told the man. "I've pledged to fight beside E'Menua. That's what I'll do."

Q'Daer nodded once. "Good." He spurred his mount forward.

Grinsa watched him ride ahead before looking down at the rilda he'd killed. "Tried to kill," he corrected in a whisper.

He shook his head and took a long breath. For just a few moments he'd felt more like a true Fal'Borna than he ever had before, than he'd ever thought possible.

Chapter 19

UPPER CENTRAL PLAIN

After speaking with Gries about his scrap of basket, Torgan hardly saw the man for the better part of a day. He had thought that he and the captain had come to some sort of agreement as they rode together, but Gries spent that evening with his men, leaving Torgan on his own. The next morning Fairlea's lord heir took his place at the head of the

Stelpana army, leaving Torgan with little choice but to ride alone. Gries nodded to Torgan as he rode past the merchant, but he offered no greeting and gave no sign that he wanted Torgan to join him. The other captains, Tirnya and Enly in particular, had made it clear that they wanted nothing to do with him; the soldiers of Stelpana were on foot and seemed no more inclined than their commanders to welcome Torgan as a marching companion; and Torgan had no interest in riding alongside the Mettai.

Instead, as they made their way westward, Torgan merely sat astride Trey, shivering within his riding cloak, cursing Gries and the rest of the soldiers. For a brief moment Torgan had managed to convince himself that he might actually profit from this invasion. He had even found some satisfaction in knowing that the piece of cursed basket he carried would help Stelpana's army defeat the white-hairs. He remained eager to strike back at the Fal'Borna for all they had done to him, and Gries had made it sound like he would have that opportunity.

Now Torgan wondered if the captain had been humoring him. His misgivings only increased when shortly after midday, as the army rested and ate, he spotted Gries speaking with the Mettai woman who had as much as called Torgan a liar the day he joined the company. The woman didn't look pleased about whatever it was Gries was telling her, which gave Torgan some small hope. But after Gries left her, he didn't approach the merchant. In all likelihood, whatever the captain discussed with the Mettai woman had nothing to do with Torgan. Soon Jenoe had them all on the move again. Torgan seethed.

Late in the day the army came within sight of a broad, swift river. The marshal and his captains halted briefly and huddled together at the head of the company, though they didn't dismount. Torgan could see them speaking, but of course couldn't hear a thing they said. He guessed that they were trying to determine exactly where they were, and Torgan could have told them. They had reached the Thraedes River. S'Vralna lay only a short distance to the south. If Gries intended to use the basket, they'd have to act soon.

After a few moments, the marshal and captains rode on, and the army followed. But they stopped on the eastern bank of the river and made camp there for the night. Still Gries kept his distance, and Torgan cursed him in silence.

"I'll leave them come morning," he muttered to himself, chewing on a tough piece of salted meat and washing it down with cold river water. If they weren't smart enough to use the basket and win, he wasn't going to ride with them to his doom.

Darkness fell and clouds began to cover the sky. Torgan sat beside a fire built for him by a few of the Fairlea soldiers, who apparently had heard snippets of his story about Widlyn Crane. He showed them the hat and answered a few questions about the man from whom he'd won it—Was he big? Had Torgan ever seen him fight? Was it possible he was lying about how he'd gotten the hat?—before they left him alone again.

He was about to pull out his sleeping roll and blankets when he heard footsteps behind him. Turning, he saw Fairlea's lord heir step into the firelight, a grin on his handsome face.

"Well, that proved a bit harder than I thought it would," the captain said, sitting on the grass and helping himself to a pull of water from Torgan's skin.

Torgan glared at him. "What are you talking about?"

"What do you think I'm talking about?" Gries asked, his brow creased, though a faint smile remained on his lips.

The merchant shook his head, feeling his face redden.

"Do you even remember what we discussed yesterday, Torgan?"

"Of course I do! But then you didn't say anything more to me, and I . . . I thought that you . . . that maybe you'd changed your mind."

Gries's frown deepened. "What did the Fal'Borna do to you?"

"What are you talking about?"

"The Torgan Plye I know would have understood that these things take time. If I came to you looking for A'Vahl woodwork, you wouldn't just have it there waiting for me. You'd be the first to tell me that if you want the best goods, you need to be patient." He shrugged. "Alliances of the sort we're after are no different. We can't rush this. And it can't seem to the marshal that you and I have been working together. At least not immediately." He glanced around them. "That's why I circled around the camp to get to your fire. I told my men to build it for you here. I didn't want any of the others to see us together."

"You told your . . . ?" Torgan broke off, shaking his head slowly. "I don't understand. What alliances? What is it you've been doing?"

"I've been trying to convince the eldest that she needs to work with us on this."

"The eldest," Torgan repeated, still confused. "Who are you—?"

He stopped, his mouth agape. The eldest. Finally he understood.

"You're trying to get the Mettai to help us?"

"Yes! I thought I made that clear to you yesterday."

Torgan shook his head. "No. You just said that you'd figured out a way to expose as many Fal'Borna as possible to the plague, and then you rode away."

"I thought it would be clear," Gries said. "We need magic to do this, Torgan. And the eldest has agreed to help us."

"But the eldest hates me."

Gries nodded. "Yes, she does. I didn't realize quite how much until I spoke with her earlier today. But she's agreed to help us."

Torgan wasn't certain how he felt about this. He'd never really liked the Mettai. Even when he traveled to the villages around the Companion Lakes, trading for baskets and blankets and the fine pelts sold by Mettai trappers, he did his best to be on his way before nightfall. He distrusted magic of any sort, be it the strange powers of the Qirsi or the blood conjurings of the Mettai. He understood that by using the poisoned basket to sicken the Fal'Borna, he was relying on Mettai magic. Somehow, though, the fact that they'd need the help of the Mettai to spread the plague bothered him.

"You don't look pleased, Torgan," Gries said, narrowing his eyes.

He shook his head. "No, I am. I just . . ." He stopped, shook his head again. "Never mind."

"Good." Gries stood and stepped beyond the firelight for a moment. "She's coming," he said, returning to where he'd been sitting. "I think she's got her son with her."

The two of them sat in silence for several moments, until at last two Mettai appeared in the firelight. One of them was the old woman, whose dark eyes found Torgan immediately. She had a narrow face and short white hair that made her look like a half-starved child, despite the lines around her eyes and mouth. The young man with her had a harder look. His features were sharp, and his dark, stringy hair made his face look even longer than it was. He was short, but wiry looking. If Torgan had passed this man on a lonely stretch of road while driving a cart filled with goods, he would have kept his knife within reach.

Gries stood to greet them, casting a look at Torgan that all but commanded the merchant to do the same. After a moment's hesitation, Torgan climbed to his feet.

"Thank you for coming, Eldest," Gries said. He indicated the merchant with an open hand. "I believe you've met Torgan Plye."

"I still don't believe that the plague was created by Mettai magic," she said to Torgan. "You may believe that blood magic is evil, but my people have long refused to do such dark conjurings."

"Eldest—" Gries began.

She turned, leveling a rigid, bony finger at the man. "I know what you'd say, Captain. These are extraordinary times. The magic we've done on the marshal's behalf are wartime spells. Most Mettai don't know how to do this magic, and even if they did, they'd refuse."

"I saw the woman who created this plague," Torgan said, drawing the gazes of the two Mettai and Gries. "I told you as much the first day we spoke. I also met two Mettai who came from her village. They acknowledged what she'd done. They were trying to stop her plague from spreading."

"What village was this?" the eldest asked.

"I don't remember." But even as Torgan said this, he recalled something he'd overheard the night he escaped the Fal'Borna, the night he killed Jasha. "You don't have to believe me," he went on after a moment. "You have the power to prove me right."

"What do you mean?" the young man asked. "What power?"

"There's a spell your kind do," Torgan said. "It can make magic visible. Isn't that right?"

The eldest and her son shared a look. After a moment, the woman faced Torgan again. "You have the basket here?" she asked.

The merchant smiled thinly and walked to where Trey was tethered. "It's not a full basket," he called over his shoulder, as he dug into his travel sack, searching for the scrap of half-burned osiers. He found it, pulled it out, and carried it back to the fire.

He held it out for the others to see. It barely covered the palm of his hand.

"That's it?" Gries asked, clearly disappointed. "That's going to help us destroy the Fal'Borna?"

Torgan nodded. "Yes, that's it. And yes, it will help you win this war."

He was watching the woman, who stepped forward, her eyes fixed on the osiers.

"That is Mettai work," she said, her voice low. "Even in the darkness I can see that much. Look at that weave."

"They were some of the finest baskets I've ever seen," the merchant said. "Whatever her intent, she was obviously talented."

After another moment, the woman looked up into Torgan's eyes. "To answer your question from before, yes, there is such a spell. It would allow us to see the magic on it. I'd be able to tell if it's a Mettai conjuring."

"And the spell won't weaken the magic in that basket?" Gries asked.

"Not at all," she said.

Gries hesitated, clearly beyond his depth. Torgan smiled, taking some satisfaction in seeing the brash captain humbled, at least for the moment.

"Well, all right then," Gries said. "Go ahead."

The eldest nodded and pulled her knife free. She stooped to pick up some earth. Then she cut the back of her hand, gathered some blood on the blade of her weapon, and mixed it with the dirt.

"Blood to earth," she said, her voice dropping. "Life to power, power to thought, magic revealed."

With the last word she tossed the mud toward Torgan's outstretched hand. The moment she let go of the mixture of blood and earth, it changed, becoming so fine, like mist from a cascade, that Torgan could barely see it in the dim light. He felt it on his hand though, cool and damp. And at the same time, he saw it flare like Qirsi fire. It was so bright that he had to look away, and it took his eyes several moments to recover. When at last he looked at the basket again, he saw that it had changed. It was glowing now; it almost looked like it was on fire. But this was no ordinary flame. It was a malevolent green, as if the fire itself were diseased.

"Blood and bone," Gries whispered.

The eldest's son inhaled sharply through his teeth. Torgan couldn't feel that green fire burning on his hand, but still he had to resist an urge to fling the basket away.

"Well?" he asked shakily, looking at the two Mettai.

The woman almost seemed to flinch away from the flame. But she nodded and said, "Yes, that's Mettai magic. You can tell by the fire. The power of the Qirsi would look more like it was glowing rather than burning." She appeared to shudder. "I never thought I'd see a blood conjuring so . . . wicked."

"Can you spread it?" Gries asked her, seeming to ignore the last comment.

"What?" the young Mettai man said, turning to look at the captain. When he realized that Gries was speaking to his mother, the Mettai faced her. "What is he talking about?"

The eldest glanced at her son. "We'll discuss this later." Looking at Gries, she straightened, then nodded. "Yes, I believe that we can help you with this."

"Mama—"

"Later!" she said sharply.

The young man pressed his lips in a tight line, his gaze sliding toward Torgan's fire.

"It would be a difficult conjuring," she went on after a moment. "I'd first want to reduce that piece of basket to something akin to dust. Then, with the second part of the spell, we'd send it to the Fal'Borna, as you've seen us do with the finding and sleeping spells."

"And the magic that's on it now would still work?" Torgan asked.

"It should. We'd do nothing to weaken it. We'd just make it possible to reach more of the Fal'Borna than it could otherwise."

Gries nodded. "That's exactly what we want. How near to them would you have to be for this magic to work?"

The eldest shrugged. "As near as we've been when we used these other magics."

Gries nodded. "And how long does it take for the plague to kill them?" he asked Torgan.

"I don't know, exactly. It takes several hours before they show signs of being ill. And then they lose control over their magic. As I've already told you, that's what kills them ultimately."

"We'd need to be far away by then," the captain said, as much to himself as to the rest of them. "If we're still close by, they might unleash their power on us."

"We can attack and then retreat," Torgan said. "Let them believe that their magic drove us off, or that we didn't like the way the battle was going."

Gries frowned at him, almost as if he resented the merchant's attempt to come up with a strategy for battle. "Thank you, Torgan. The marshal and I will work out the details."

Torgan made no effort to conceal his surprise. "So you've spoken to him about all of this?"

The captain's cheeks appeared to redden, though it was hard to tell in the firelight. "Not yet, no," he said. "But I will." He faced the Mettai woman again. "Thank you, Eldest. We'll speak of this again soon. I'd imagine we'll save Torgan's scrap of basket for D'Raqor. But it's possible that Marshal Jenoe will have different ideas."

"All right," she said. She looked once more at the green flame burning in the palm of Torgan's hand before starting back toward the Mettai camp. Her son followed.

"Wait!" Torgan said, stopping her. "Are you just going to leave it looking like this?"

"It won't harm you," the woman said.

"No. But it . . . I don't want everyone to know I have it. And . . ." He licked his lips. "I don't like the way it looks."

The eldest regarded him with disdain, but after a moment she walked back to where he stood, picked up more dirt, cut her hand again, and mixed the earth with her blood.

"Blood to earth," she said with obvious impatience. "Earth to power, power to thought, magic concealed."

Once more, she threw the mud over his hand, this time turning away even as it became that same delicate mist and settled over the scrap of cursed basket. Torgan felt it cold on his hand and saw with relief that the green fire died away instantly.

He looked up, intending to thank the woman, but she and her son were already gone.

"They're strange, even for Mettai," Gries said.

Torgan had to agree, but he was concerned with other matters. "You're sure the marshal will agree to this?" he asked.

"I'm not certain of anything," Gries told him. "But we have a chance to take D'Raqor—the prize that he and his daughter want most of all—without losing a single man. He'd be mad not to do this."

"What about Tirnya? And Enly?"

Gries shook his head. "Enly doesn't matter. This is Jenoe's decision. And I'll make sure he gets it right. As for Tirnya, she'll be so glad to have D'Raqor that she won't care how we won it."

Torgan wasn't so sure.

have you stopped to think what the curse might do with this bit of magic you're contemplating?" Mander asked from behind her as they walked back to where the other Mettai were sleeping.

Fayonne didn't look at him. She wished she hadn't asked her son to come with her to speak with Captain Ballidyne and the merchant. Yes, the curse was real. It still haunted them, even out here. She was willing to concede that much. But what did he expect her to do? Abandon magic completely?

"Did you even mention to them that it might not work? Or worse, that it might kill their own men?"

"It's a white-hair plague," Fayonne said, her voice toneless. "It won't kill the soldiers, or us."

"You don't know that. You don't know what the curse will do to it. It could make all of—"

"That's enough!" she said, whirling on him.

He halted and staggered back away from her, his eyes wide.

"None of our magic is immune to the curse!" she said. "We both know that! So any spell we use will carry consequences. Eagles, wolves, poison—all of them are threats to us. This spell isn't, at least not the same way. It could deliver D'Raqor to the marshal and end the war. Will the curse do something to the spell? Of course it will. But that's a risk I'll take."

Mander nodded, looking frightened of her.

Fayonne made herself smile. "It's good that you worry about these things," she said. "You'll lead our people well when I'm gone. But you can't always let your concern for others get in the way of what has to be done. Sometimes we have to come first. Do you understand?"

"Yes, Mama."

She turned and started walking again. Mander fell in beside her.

"Who would have made a spell like that?" he asked after some time.

"I don't know," Fayonne said. "I've been wondering the same thing."

That flame had been as evil looking as anything Fayonne had ever seen in a conjuring. It seemed to emit pure malice. If she hadn't known better, she would have thought that another Mettai village had declared war against the white-hairs just as hers had done.

"The merchant said it was an old woman," she said eventually. "He was right about the rest, so I'll trust his word on this, too. But I wouldn't have thought there were more than a handful of Mettai who could have conjured such a plague. I wonder why she did it."

Mander said nothing. Fayonne sensed that he was still hurt by her outburst, but she could think of nothing to say that might make him feel better. And she had more pressing concerns.

"The captain wants us to keep this quiet for now," she said. "He hasn't spoken of it with Marshal Onjaef, and he's not certain that the marshal or his captains are ready to go so far."

"All right," Mander said softly.

"He'll have to decide soon," she told him. "We're close to S'Vralna and it won't be long before we reach D'Raqor. He'll make up his mind in the next day or two. I'm sure of it."

Mander might have nodded; she wasn't certain.

They walked the rest of the way in silence and before long had unrolled their blankets and were settling down to sleep. Fayonne felt exhausted, as she did after every march. She was too old to be out here on the plain with the Snows coming on. But on this night sleep didn't come easily. A north wind was rising, and the air smelled like snow. She lay awake for a long time trying to think of ways the curse might make the spell she was contemplating go wrong. But none of the possibilities she considered seemed too terrible, and this actually frightened her. The truth was, the curse never affected magic the way she and her people anticipated. It was almost always worse.

She fell at last into a deep slumber, and though she knew that she dreamed of terrible, bloody battles, she could remember nothing specific when she woke to the first faint glimmerings of dawn.

The Eandi soldiers had started to stir, and even at a distance Fayonne sensed both their excitement and their trepidation. She well understood what they must have been thinking. The armies had reached the Thraedes. Beyond it lay the Horn; to the south lay Sivralna. This war was about to begin in earnest.

It was a chill morning, and that north wind had grown stronger. A light snow fell upon them, clinging to the grass and dampening Fayonne's hair. The eldest wasn't certain where Jenoe intended to lead them from here, but she didn't relish the idea of braving those swirling waters. She folded away her blankets and walked to the Eandi camp. She sensed that Mander was watching her, perhaps waiting for her to ask him to join her. She didn't.

The marshal stood with his captains, surveying the river, his face still puffy with sleep, his expression grim. Seeing her approach, he nodded a greeting, but at first he didn't say anything.

"If we go straight on, we leave ourselves open to an attack from the rear," the marshal from Waterstone said, seeming to continue a conversation that Fayonne hadn't heard.

"I tend to agree," Jenoe said. "Deraqor is the prize, but we can't risk ignoring Sivralna. And I don't wish to cross the river if we'll just have to find a way back across eventually."

Sivralna? Fayonne cast a quick look at Captain Ballidyne, but he had his eyes trained on the ground in front of him, his lips pursed. He had told her of Sivralna's destruction, which the merchant had described for him in detail, but apparently he had yet to share this information with the marshal.

"So then we're to march on Sivralna?" asked Enly Tolm, his gaze flicking toward the marshal's daughter.

"I think so," Jenoe told him. "I believe that's the safest course. Ready the men." He turned to Fayonne. "We could encounter the Fal'Borna at any time, Eldest. I want you and your people marching at the head of the army again. And I'd like you to give some thought to how we might take the city when we reach Sivralna."

"S'Vralna is yours already," came a voice from behind Fayonne.

All of them turned. The merchant was lumbering in their direction through the falling snow, his one good eye flitting from one face to the next.

"You can cross the river north of here," he went on. "That will save us all a day on foot, maybe more."

"What are you talking about, Torgan?" the marshal demanded. He regarded the man with manifest distaste. Then he cast a quick look at his daughter as if chastising her for allowing the merchant to come near him.

"You didn't tell him?" the merchant asked Gries.

The captain glared back at him, a warning in his dark eyes.

Torgan turned to Enly and then Tirnya. "You didn't, either?"

Jenoe seemed to be growing angrier by the moment. "Tell me what?"

"S'Vralna is destroyed, Marshal," the merchant said. "I've been there. It was struck by the white-hair plague. The city lies in ruin and most of its people are dead. Taking it will be as simple as riding through the gates. You'd be wasting your time marching south from here."

"You're certain of this?" Jenoe asked.

"Yes. That's why I'm convinced that—"

Torgan stopped, and Fayonne had seen why. Gries had caught his eye and given a slight shake of his head.

"Convinced that what, Torgan?" Jenoe asked.

"That the Relics Bridge is your best route across the river," the merchant said.

Fayonne was certain that he'd intended to say something else; probably he was going to mention the cursed basket.

Jenoe eyed him briefly, seemingly trying to decide whether the merchant was an annoyance or an asset. "Do I understand you correctly? You're saying that we should bypass Sivralna, that it's already defeated. And that this Relics Bridge offers us the quickest path to Deraqor."

"That's right." Torgan looked around, appearing to mark their position in relation to the mountains that were barely visible on the northern horizon. "The nearest span would be White Bridge, which lies south of here, maybe two leagues. But Relics Bridge is the broader span, and it's to the north. Five leagues. No more. That'll be the easier crossing for an army this size."

"And all of you knew about this?" Jenoe asked, looking at Tirnya, Enly, and Gries.

For several moments none of them answered.

"I asked a question," the marshal said, his voice hardening.

"Torgan mentioned it to us," Enly said.

Gries took a breath. "And to me."

"I see." Jenoe turned back to the merchant. "Why would you choose to speak of this with my captains, but not with me?"

Torgan looked at Enly and the marshal's daughter, but his gaze came to rest on Gries. Fairlea's lord heir stared back at him, but didn't say anything.

"Answer me, Torgan! I want to know what's going on here."

"I've been waiting for your decision, Marshal. I want to know if you're going to use the plague against the Fal'Borna. You've refused to speak with me, and you've seemed content to let me wonder what you'll eventually decide to do. So I went to the captains, hoping they'd help me convince you."

"And you thought that telling them this tale about Sivralna would do that."

Torgan's face reddened. "It's no tale! It's the truth! If you want to waste two or three days marching down there, go ahead! You'll find exactly what I've told you! They were destroyed by the plague! Twice, actually. The survivors returned to their city, and when they found some of these baskets, half burned and buried in the rubble, they got sick. For all I know there's nothing left of the walls or gates or buildings. It might just be a pile of rock now."

Fayonne thought that Jenoe might argue further, but he seemed to hear the truth in Torgan's words. Just as she did.

"Why would you keep this from me?" the marshal asked Tirnya. "Don't you think I should have been told?"

"I'm sorry, Father. I thought that if you simply heard this—if you thought that we could take the city without losing a man—you'd use the plague as a weapon to take back Deraqor. But I hoped that if you actually saw Sivralna lying in ruins it would show you how dangerous this plague could be."

"This was your thinking as well?" he asked Enly.

Qalsyn's lord heir nodded.

Jenoe turned to Gries. "And yours?"

Gries didn't hesitate for long, but it seemed to be enough for Tirnya to discern the truth.

"You wanted him to use it," she said.

"Of course he did," Torgan broke in before the Fairlea captain could answer.

"Torgan—" Gries began.

But the merchant cut him off. "They're being fools! We both know it!" He faced Jenoe again. "The Mettai can help us with this. They have a way of spreading the plague over the entire city. I could only reach a few white-hairs with this basket. But with their magic, they can reach every one of them."

"You knew of this, too?" Jenoe asked, fixing Fayonne with a hard glare.

The eldest straightened. "Captain Ballidyne asked for my help," she said. "All I did was tell him what our magic was capable of doing."

Jenoe shook his head. "So let me see if I understand this. My daughter, and the lord heir of Qalsyn, both of them captains in my army, knew that Sivralna had been destroyed and failed to tell me, in the hope that my shock at seeing the damage would keep me from using a weapon I hadn't even decided to use. And the lord heir of Fairlea, also a captain under my command, has conspired with this merchant and the eldest to use that weapon without my consent. Is that about right?"

"No, Marshal," Gries said. "I didn't conspire to do anything. I spoke with them both. I tried to determine if we could in fact spread this plague to the Fal'Borna. But I never would have done anything without your approval. You have my word on that."

"I'm not sure what your word is worth right now, Captain," Jenoe told him. "But I'll consider what you've said."

The Fairlea captain's cheeks colored, but he nodded.

Jenoe turned to Fayonne. "You and I will speak later, Eldest," he said, with more courtesy than he'd shown to the captain.

"You're not going to use it, are you?" Torgan said.

They all looked at him, the captains wearing angry expressions, the marshal looking proud to the point of haughtiness.

"This was never your decision to make, Torgan," Jenoe said.

"Without the plague, you'll lose this war," Torgan said. "They'll shatter your army and run you down as you retreat. Without me, you're doomed."

"I want you gone," Jenoe told him. "I want you to get on

your horse and ride away from here, and I never want to see your face again."

The merchant regarded them all with disgust. "This is why we lost the Blood Wars. We're weak. We're not willing to do what's necessary to win, and so we lose, again and again. You'll be no different." He shook his head and gave a harsh laugh. "Very well, Marshal. I'll leave. Good riddance to you all."

He turned on his heel and started to walk away. But before he'd gone far, he stopped again, staring eastward.

An instant later, Fayonne heard it, too: voices shouting at the edge of the camp. The sound was growing by the minute, and there was a note of panic in every voice she heard. Men were running toward them, shouting for the marshal.

The first to reach them was a young man with black hair and dark eyes. He was out of breath, and his face, damp with melted snow, looked pale except for red spots high on each cheek.

"What's happened, Crow?" the marshal's daughter asked.

"There's a white-hair army," he said, looking back and forth between the woman and her father. "It's headed this way. They're on horseback an' they're close."

"How many?" Jenoe asked.

"Hundr'ds," the man said. "Maybe a thousand."

The marshal looked as if he'd been kicked in the stomach. "Damn," he whispered. "And we're backed up against this river." He looked at the captains. "Muster your men," he said, his voice suddenly crisp. "There's nothing to do but fight." He turned to Fayonne. "Eldest, we'll need every bit of magic you can give us."

She nodded. "You'll have it, Marshal." And she ran to find Mander.

Chapter 20

+-I-+

In mere moments, all was tumult in the army camp. Soldiers ran in every direction, gathering their weapons and mustering into their units. The two marshals and their captains shouted for the archers and tried to arrange the men into some semblance of a formation.

Tirnya's men had been among the first to come together, thanks in large part to the efforts of Oliban and her other lead riders. Tirnya herself had remained close to her father, dispatching soldiers to relay his orders to commanders throughout the army. But the Qirsi were almost upon them, and she needed to take her men to the right flank of the army, where Jenoe had already positioned Stri and Enly.

"You should go, Tirnya," her father said.

"Yes, all right." Her heart hammered in her chest, and she was sweating, despite the cold. Their other battles against the Fal'Borna had gone relatively well, but if there really were a thousand sorcerers in this army . . .

"Tirnya!"

"I'm sorry, Father. About before, I mean."

For just an instant, his expression softened. "We'll talk about this after the battle is over. I promise. Now go."

She nodded, gazing at him for one more moment. Then she turned and ran to where her soldiers awaited her.

Most of her soldiers, even those not trained as archers, had sheathed their blades and taken up bows. Tirnya's father, along with Hendrid Crish and the captains and lead riders left their horses tethered where they were, knowing that the animals would be susceptible to the Fal'Borna's language of beasts magic. They had been on foot for the other battles as well, but Tirnya hadn't yet grown used to this. She preferred to be on her horse, where she had a view of the entire battlefield.

She moved to the front of her company, near where Enly and Stri stood with their men, and not that far from her father, who had positioned himself at the center. The eldest and her people were with him, as was Hendrid. The grass had grown slick with the snowfall. If it came to close fighting, the footing would be treacherous.

Tirnya could now see the Qirsi clearly. They were on horseback, their white hair damp and limp, giving them a ghoulish look. Tirnya couldn't help thinking that Crow had understated the size of their force. There had to be more than a thousand of them, and she assumed that they had enough Weavers to destroy her father's army.

They weren't yet within range of the bowmen, but it seemed that they had halted. With a sudden rush of fear Tirnya realized that they had no intention of coming closer.

"Their magic can reach us from there," she said. And then, before Oliban could ask her what she'd said, she shouted the same thing to her father.

Jenoe nodded and said something to the eldest. Immediately all of the Mettai pulled their knives free and bent as one to grab handfuls of dirt. An instant later, Tirnya heard them mumbling their spells and then the creatures began to appear. Eagles first, then wolves, then more eagles. After a time, something new: giant serpents that flew from the hands of the Mettai as the eagles and wolves did, but landed low on the ground and slithered away with unnatural speed. The Mettai kept grabbing more dirt and drawing more blood, and the creatures continued to materialize until there was an army of them. This time, at least for now, the creatures seemed intent on the white-hairs.

The eagles soared toward the Qirsi army, keeping pace with the wolves that loped below them. Before any of the animals could reach the Fal'Borna lines, however, they began to fall. It was as strange and terrifying a sight as Tirnya had ever seen. The eagles seemed to be swatted out of the sky like overgrown flies smote by some great, unseen hand. One moment the wolves were running with effortless grace, and the next they collapsed in heaps, as if those same hands had crushed them. Tirnya could hear the yelps of the animals, the piercing shrieks of the birds. They were creatures of magic—moments before they hadn't even existed—and yet, watching them die, she felt hot tears on her cheeks.

And still the Mettai conjured more of them.

The serpents proved more difficult for the white-hairs to kill, perhaps because they remained so low to the ground and thus were harder to see. Whatever the reason, several of them reached the Qirsi lines, lashing out with curved fangs at the legs of the Fal'Borna's mounts. The horses went down, taking their riders with them. And instantly the serpents struck at the white-hairs.

Screams of men and horses filled the air, mingling with the cries of the eagles and wolves to create a horrible din. Fayonne shouted something to her people and suddenly all of them were conjuring the giant snakes.

Tirnya knew little about Mettai magic, but Fayonne and her people had been conjuring for several minutes now without rest, and she doubted that they could keep this up for much longer.

Looking at the white-hairs again, she saw that the grasses in front of the Qirsi had begun to blacken. A pale yellow fire rushed toward the Stelpana army, fanning out as it went, melting away the snow and then searing the grass. Tirnya could see serpents writhing in the flames, but she could also see that the fire wasn't intended just for the snakes. Fayonne appeared to understand this as well. She called to the other Mettai, who stooped once more for handfuls of earth. The fire swept swiftly across the plain, killing snakes and wolves, and filling the air with a dark, choking smoke. The Mettai barely had time to speak their spells and throw the mixture of dirt and mud. Torrents of water flew from their hands, dousing most of the flames and sending a great cloud of steam into the morning air.

Where their conjured water failed to stop the white-hairs' magic, Eandi soldiers were enveloped in flame, including several men in Enly's company and Stri's. Many of them screamed, thrashing wildly, desperate to extinguish the fires on their clothing and hair. Others succumbed to the flames before they could do anything at all.

Several eagles still circled over the Qirsi riders, but in mere moments they had been destroyed by the white-hairs' shaping power. For all the conjuring that the Mettai had done, they had precious little to show for it. The blood wolves, eagles, and serpents were dead, only a handful of Qirsi warriors had been unhorsed and killed, and a greater number of Eandi had died. The Mettai could begin their conjuring again, but even from a distance Tirnya could see how exhausted the eldest looked. She could only imagine how much the Mettai's hands ached.

Yet they began to conjure again anyway. Serpents, wolves, eagles. They created more of the beasts and sent them forth. And in doing so, they saved their lives and those of countless Eandi, including Tirnya's father.

The wolves and snakes were halfway to the Qirsi lines when the pulse of magic hit them. The way their bodies crumpled, there could be no doubt that it had come from the Fal'Borna shapers. It seemed clear as well that it was aimed not at the animals but at the Stelpana army. The eldest shouted something to her people, and at the same time dropped to her knees. She grabbed for dirt, rubbed it on the back of her bloodied hand, and, mumbling once more, flung it in front of her. The other Mettai did the same.

The clods of bloody earth became large, flat surfaces of rock that coalesced into a near-seamless wall. And as quickly as they appeared, they were shattered by that same wave of shaping power. Where the magic hit the rock, it seemed to dissipate. None of the Mettai were hurt by the shaping power, and only a few of the Eandi standing beside them fell, although those who did howled in agony.

But their cries were lost amid the screams of those near the center of the army who had been standing beyond the Mettai's protection. There the devastation was overwhelming. Literally hundreds of men collapsed to the ground. The sound of their bones snapping made Tirnya's stomach heave. If the Mettai hadn't managed to erect their wall, most of the army would have been lost. As it was, that single pulse of magic took a third of Jenoe's force.

To Tirnya's great relief, her father appeared to be all right. But they wouldn't be safe for long. More than ever, she understood why the Eandi had fared so poorly in the latter years of the Blood Wars. And at last she realized that this invasion was a mistake, just as Enly and her father had warned it would be.

"Eldest!" she heard her father shout over the continuing cries of the wounded. "Whatever magic you have left, use it! We can't take another assault."

Fayonne stared back at him. After a moment, she nodded.

"No!" her son said, his voice carrying as well.

The eldest eyed her son. Then she raised her blade over her head and called to the other Mettai, "We've spoken of this spell. We know how to do it. This is the time."

"I won't do it!" Mander said, even as his mother picked up more dirt and cut herself yet again.

Fayonne looked up at him and spoke, and though Tirnya couldn't hear her, she could see what the woman said. "Then don't."

The Mettai spoke as one in low voices and then threw their spells. This time the mud turned to that same silvery mist Tirnya had seen them conjure so many times before, and soared over the plain toward the Fal'Borna army.

An instant later the Mettai conjured another set of walls, though Tirnya didn't understand why until she saw the stone fracture again. More Eandi soldiers died, but again the Mettai conjuring saved countless lives.

Tirnya heard a cry go up from the Qirsi lines and then

saw the grasses near the Fal'Borna flattened as if by a hard wind. She assumed that the white-hairs were trying to slow the advance of the Mettai's spell. It didn't work.

She heard more cries, saw Fal'Borna grabbing at their throats. And then the Qirsi began to topple off their horses. After another moment, even the horses started to fall. She'd seen how the Mettai sleeping spell worked. This was different. There was something . . . sinister about how those men and animals collapsed to the ground. Within moments, there wasn't a single white-hair warrior or horse remaining upright. Not one.

Usually she would have expected to hear a roar of triumph from an army that saw its foe vanquished so. But most of the Eandi soldiers merely stared at the prone bodies of the Qirsi. Aside from the low rustle of the wind, and the moans and sobs of wounded men, Tirnya heard nothing at all.

Tirnya looked at the eldest again. She stood with her arms hanging at her side, her bloodied knife still in one hand, dark earth clinging to the other. She looked utterly spent, and there was a haunted look on her face. Her son stood beside her, obviously horrified.

"Report!" Tirnya's father called, his voice ragged.

Tirnya started toward her father, walking slowly. She felt weary, though she hadn't done anything more than stand there and watch.

After a moment she realized that Enly was walking beside her. She glanced at him, and their eyes met briefly. Then she looked away.

As they approached Jenoe and the Mettai, Tirnya heard the eldest's son say, "That spell should never have been used again! It was forbidden centuries ago! And for us in particular—!"

"That's enough, Mander!" the eldest said.

"What spell did you use on them?" Jenoe asked, sounding as if he didn't want to hear the answer. "Are they asleep?"

"No," Fayonne said. "It was a poison spell. The Fal'Borna are dead."

Jenoe took a long breath and nodded. "Then at least we don't have to go and kill them."

"I didn't know Mettai magic could do that," Gries said, staring at the bodies of the Fal'Borna.

"It's a spell from long ago," Fayonne told him, damp hair clinging to her brow. "I wouldn't have used it if we hadn't been desperate."

One of Hendrid's captains approached them, his face deathly pale, one of his arms hanging limply at his side. He stopped in front of Waterstone's marshal and saluted. Tirnya saw that there were tears on his face.

"Report, Verin."

"We're still counting the dead, Marshal. The last . . ." He swallowed. "The last I heard it was five hundred."

Hendrid closed his eyes briefly and rubbed a hand over his beard. "Blood and bone." He looked at his captain again. "How many wounded?"

"I don't know, Marshal," Verin said. "Hundreds."

Hendrid sighed and nodded. "I see you're one of them. I want you to get that arm splinted. And keep me informed. I'll want a final count."

"Yes, Marshal."

"Now are you ready to listen to me?"

They all turned. Torgan Plye stood nearby, holding the reins to his horse.

For a moment Tirnya thought her father would pull his sword free and run the man through. His eyes blazed and his hands appeared to be trembling. He opened his mouth to speak— probably to remind the merchant that he'd been banished.

But at that moment, a series of odd, strangled cries rose from the far left flank of the army. Turning to look that way, Tirnya saw several Eandi soldiers grabbing at their necks much as the Qirsi had done, and falling to the ground.

"Gods save us all!" Mander said, his voice barely more than a whisper.

Jenoe had a frown on his face. "What's—?"

"It can't be!" Fayonne said, her face ashen.

"Of course it can!" Mander told her, his tone harsh. He turned to Tirnya's father. "The poison spell is coming this way! It might be the wind or . . . or something else. But we all have to get away from here as quickly as possible!"

"Blood and bone!" Jenoe still looked confused, as if unsure of what to make of this Mettai magic, which always seemed to turn against them. But he didn't waste time. "Signal a retreat!" he shouted to his captains. "South, along the river!"

"What about the horses?" Tirnya asked him.

He looked toward the far end of the camp again. Tirnya did the same. Men were dying by the moment, and others were already starting to flee. "Quickly, Tirnya! Untether them. If they follow, they'll be saved, but don't delay if they linger. I'd rather lose horses than soldiers." *And I don't want to risk losing you.*

He didn't have to say this last. She read it in his eyes.

"I'll go with you," Enly said.

She didn't object. Together they ran back to where the marshals, captains, and lead riders had left their horses. The animals were still there, all of them alive. Tirnya could hear orders being given above the tumult of death cries and shouting. She and Enly worked wordlessly and in moments had all of the animals untied. Enly started slapping the animals on the haunches and shouting for them to run. Some did. Others bolted short distances before stopping again.

A few ran the wrong way, back toward where the poison spell had killed soldiers. They hadn't gone far—not far at all—before several of them began to thrash violently. In moments they had collapsed to the ground, their flanks heaving. And then they were still.

"Come on!" Enly called. "It's getting close!"

He was running again and Tirnya sprinted after him. She could see their horses. Thirus, her sorrel, was just ahead of Enly's bay. They both shifted directions slightly to intercept the animals. For all they knew, they couldn't outrun the poison, but perhaps they could outride it.

She whistled for Thirus, and immediately the animal

stopped and turned toward her. Enly's horse halted at the sound of his whistle. They reached the animals and swung themselves onto their backs.

"What about the others?" Tirnya asked, breathless, her eyes scanning the mass of soldiers for her father.

"There's nothing we can do for them," Enly said. "If we try to bring your father's horse to him, or do the same for any of the others, we risk slowing ourselves down too much." He eyed the army briefly, apprehension in his pale eyes. "They're moving, and most of the horses are moving. That's the best we can hope for."

She nodded. She could see Jenoe now. He was near the head of the army. He would run several paces, then pause to urge his men on and mark their progress before running farther himself. Men at the back of the column continued to fall, so that the army appeared to leave a trail of broken bodies in its wake. But the number of those afflicted seemed to be decreasing. Perhaps they could outrun it.

"We need to ride, Tirnya. We've done what we can."

She knew he was right. When Enly spurred his mount to a canter, she did the same with Thirus.

They rode for more than a league, stopping periodically to mark the progress of those on foot. The army kept up a swift pace, marching as if another Fal'Borna army pursued them. Tirnya could see her father leading the soldiers, and Stri beside him. She also spotted Gries, Hendrid Crish, and many of the captains. She lamented the loss of every life, of course, but she couldn't help but be relieved to see that most of those who led the army had survived. She noticed that the Mettai were near her father, too. Most of them seemed to have made it. Some of the horses had lagged behind until Tirnya finally lost sight of them. But many of the animals had followed her and Enly.

At last, as Enly and Tirnya waited once more for the army to catch up with them, she saw her father raise a hand, indicating to the soldiers behind him that they should halt. Enly and Tirnya rode back to join them.

"I want a count made of survivors!" Jenoe was shouting as they reached him. "Every captain should make a count of his or her lead riders, and then every lead rider should make a count of the men under his or her command. Quickly! I want to know how many we've lost." He turned to Tirnya and Enly. "That goes for the two of you, as well."

"Of course, Father."

"How many horses did we lose?"

"We're not sure," Enly answered. "I'm hoping some of the stragglers will find us eventually. But right now we've got maybe half the number we started with."

Jenoe nodded, though he looked disgusted. Turning to Fayonne, he said, "How did this happen? I find it hard to believe that the Mettai of old would have been valued as allies had every one of their spells killed Eandi as well as Qirsi."

"It must have been the wind, Marshal," the eldest told him.

"Mother."

All of them looked at Mander, but before the young Mettai could say more, Fayonne shot him a look that could have kindled wet wood.

"You should see to your men, Marshal," the old woman said. "I want to make certain that all of my people are all right."

Jenoe eyed her and Mander for several moments. "Yes, of course," he said at last. "But we're not done here, Eldest. I have questions, and I'm going to expect answers."

She hesitated, then nodded.

"Go," Jenoe said to Tirnya and Enly. "Check on your companies and then come back here."

Tirnya and Enly exchanged glances and then went in search of their men.

Tirnya found Oliban, Crow, Qagan, and her other lead riders in a small cluster not far from where she'd been speaking with her father. Oliban spotted her first and said something to the others, who turned to greet her. None of them appeared hurt or any the worse for their brush with the Mettai spell. But their expressions were bleak, and Tirnya felt her heart begin to pound.

"Report," she said as she approached them, her mouth suddenly dry. She looked around, feeling panic rise in her chest. "Where's Dyn?"

"He's with th' others, Capt'n," Oliban said. "He wasn' hurt."

"Good. But we lost men, didn't we?"

"Not many compared with th' others," Oliban told her. "Eighteen, t' be exact. Most o' them were lost in th' mess as we retreated from th' battlefield. By th' time we knew they were missin' . . ." He stopped, shaking his head. "We were lucky we didn' lose more. There are companies from Waterstone and Fairlea tha' were wiped out entirely. And Enly's and Stri's men didn' fare too well."

Eighteen men. It could have been so much worse. They'd been lucky to be near the Mettai when the Fal'Borna attacked with their shaping power, and far from the flank when the poison began to drift back over the men of Stelpana.

"What happened to the other Qalsyn units?" she asked.

"Th' white-hairs got 'em," Crow said. "The shapers. Some weren' dead, bu' there was nothin' we could do t' help 'em once tha' spell started killin' th' Waterstone army."

Oliban looked briefly at the other lead riders before meeting Tirnya's gaze again. "Capt'n, tha' Mettai magic . . . Is i' really worth this?"

Not long ago, a few days perhaps, she would have been angered by the question. But not after today. Somehow the poison spell had changed everything. Killing the Fal'Borna as they slept had appalled her, and fighting off the great magical wolves had been a trial for all of them. But they'd been as defenseless as the white-hairs against the Mettai's poison. The spell killed indiscriminately. It was worse than Fal'Borna magic, and Tirnya hadn't believed she'd ever think that about anything.

"I don't know," she told him. "I thought so before, but I'm

not sure now. I'll speak with my father and Marshal Crish and the other captains," she said. "We'll need to decide what to do next."

Oliban appeared surprised by her candor. "All righ', Capt'n."

She started to walk away, but stopped after only a couple of strides and faced her riders once more. "I'm glad all of you are all right," she said. Then she grinned. "Even you, Crow."

The men laughed.

"Thank you, Capt'n," Oliban said.

She nodded to them and went to find her father.

She and Enly were the last two captains to report to the marshals. The others stood by silently as Jenoe and Hendrid spoke in low voices. Tirnya noticed that several of the Fairlea and Waterstone captains weren't there, including the man who had fallen in the Silverwater and been rescued by Gries so many days back. Gries was there, but Tirnya avoided his gaze, remembering how angry she had been with him just a few hours before.

Thinking of this, she looked around for the merchant. He stood with his horse a good distance away from the army and its leaders.

"How are your men?" Jenoe asked Enly and Tirnya.

"I lost eighteen," Tirnya told him.

"You were lucky," Enly said dully. "I lost forty-six, including four of my riders."

She looked at him. "I'm so sorry, Enly."

"Eighteen and forty-six," Jenoe repeated. "The army of Qalsyn was fortunate. We lost fewer than two hundred. Waterstone lost more than six hundred. Fairlea nearly four hundred." He rubbed a hand over his face. "More than a thousand men. Add that to the hundreds who died at the last sept we fought and we've lost more than a third of our army, and we're still not to Deraqor."

"I hesitate to bring this up again, Marshal," Gries said. "But perhaps we should reconsider Torgan's offer."

"Yes, I noticed that he's still here," Jenoe said, making no effort to hide his annoyance. "Was that your doing, Captain?"

Gries shook his head. "No, Marshal. The Fal'Borna attacked before he could leave, and I think he followed us when the poison spell reached our lines."

"I ordered him away from here," Jenoe said. "I haven't changed my mind."

"He can help us defeat Deraqor. We wouldn't need wolves or eagles or poison."

"You'd still need our magic."

All of them turned. Mander and Fayonne were walking toward them, the young man in the lead, his mother trailing behind him looking pale and small.

"Yes, Mander, we would," Jenoe said. "Is that a problem?"

"I believe it is, Marshal," the young Mettai said.

His mother looked at him, narrowing her eyes. But she remained silent, and after a moment dropped her gaze again.

Jenoe frowned. "I don't understand."

"No," the man said. "I'm sure you don't." He took a breath. "Perhaps you've noticed that our spells often don't work quite the way they're supposed to. The wolves turn on our people, or the eagles turn on each other, or the poison kills those it was supposed to help."

"What of it?" Jenoe asked, ice in his voice.

"Perhaps you also noticed that the land around our village was blighted," he went on, seeming to ignore the question. "Or that our people weren't as prosperous as other Mettai you encountered in your travels."

"What is this about?" Tirnya's father demanded. He looked at Fayonne. "Eldest? What is it he's trying to tell us?"

Fayonne opened her mouth, as if intending to reply. But she closed it again and looked away.

"Our people have been cursed," Mander said.

Jenoe stared at him. "*Cursed*?"

"Yes. By other Mettai. It's been over a century now. I

won't bother you with the details of why they did it, but they had their reasons, and some would insist to this day that our people deserved their fate."

"A curse," Jenoe said, his voice low. "What does this curse do?"

"Just what you've seen, Marshal. It ruins our land, it robs us of our prosperity, and it twists our magic in ways we can't anticipate."

"And you didn't think to tell us this before marching with us to war?" Enly asked.

"Would you have offered us this alliance?" Fayonne asked him.

"Of course not!"

"That's why we didn't tell you," she said.

Enly started to object, as did Jenoe, Gries, and several others, Tirnya among them. But the eldest raised a finger, silencing all of them.

"I thought it possible that by leaving Lifarsa, we would also leave the curse behind, particularly once we were past the Silverwater. And since I knew we wouldn't conjure on your behalf until we were clear of the wash, I thought there was some chance that you'd never need to know of the curse."

"It seems you were wrong," Jenoe said in a hard voice.

The eldest's mouth twitched. "Yes, I was. But as a leader who is risking all to regain his people's homeland, I'd think that you'd understand, Marshal. My people have been suffering under this curse for a hundred years. You presented me with an opportunity to start over, to leave our afflicted land and build a new life. I would have been mad to turn you down, or to say anything that would jeopardize that chance. Surely you understand that."

For a long time Jenoe didn't answer. Tirnya had spent most of her life gauging her father's moods by subtle changes in his expression or the sound of his voice. But for the life of her she couldn't tell in those moments what he was thinking.

"I do understand it," he finally said. "But you have to understand that I can't allow this to continue." He looked at Tirnya. "You know what we have to do, don't you?"

She nodded, surprised by how calm she felt. Yes, she'd fought long and hard to convince her father and Qalsyn's lord governor to let this invasion go forward. But she'd already seen and done enough during this war to make her balk at the prospect of additional battles.

"We have to stop relying on Mettai magic," she said. "And that means that we have to head home."

"But we've come so far!" Fayonne said. "We're on the Horn. Sivralna is already defeated. All that remains is Deraqor!"

Gries stepped forward, so that he stood just in front of Tirnya's father. "I have to agree with the eldest, Marshal," he said quietly. "One city remains. And if we use Torgan's basket, we can take it without risking the lives of any more of our men."

"You haven't been listening!" Mander said. "The only way that basket can help you defeat all of Deraqor is if you use our magic to spread it over the city. And with this curse, we have no guarantee that it won't lead to another disaster."

"And I've already told you, Captain," Jenoe said, and this time there could be no doubt as to his thoughts, or his mood. "More than once as I remember it. I will not be using the merchant's basket. I want nothing to do with the man, and I don't want him anywhere near my army."

Gries's face colored. "Yes, Marshal."

Jenoe held the man's gaze for another moment before facing Hendrid.

Waterstone's marshal, though usually a formidable man, looked broken. His shoulders were hunched and there was a dusting of snow on his uniform. His face was ashen.

"Marshal, your soldiers have suffered greatly today," Jenoe said, his voice softening. "What is it you'd have me do?"

Hendrid shook his head. "I don't have the stomach for another battle, Jenoe. It's time I took the few men I have left and returned to Waterstone."

Jenoe nodded and turned to Stri, Enly, and his other captains. "What do the rest of you say?"

"Without the magic of the Mettai, we can't win," Stri answered. He hesitated, his glance flicking toward Fayonne. "And I no longer trust the magic of the Mettai."

"I agree," Enly said. "I believe continuing this war would be too dangerous."

"And you're all right with this decision?" Jenoe asked, facing Tirnya again. "I know how much you wanted to take back Deraqor."

"Yes, I did," Tirnya said. "But the cost of this magic is too high. And His Lordship made it clear that we weren't to go on without the Mettai."

Jenoe smiled, looking as proud of her in that moment as he had the day she almost bloodied Enly in the Harvest Tournament a few turns before.

"All right then," he said, raising his voice so that all could hear. "We start back now. Muster your men into their companies. I want our march back toward the Silverwater to be orderly and disciplined. We're still in Fal'Borna land, and we may still face more battles before we reach the wash. I want to be on our way within the hour."

"What about us, Marshal?" Fayonne asked.

Tirnya's father regarded the woman soberly. "I hope you and your people will march with us, Eldest. You may need our protection along the way. And though I may regret this before all is done, we might well need yours."

Chapter 21

The freedoms E'Menua granted Besh and Sirj just before he led his warriors out of the sept did much to improve the spirits of both Mettai men. It bothered Besh that the a'laq had not actually spoken to them again before leaving and that the man had said nothing about their future beyond the end of this war. But Besh had faith in Grinsa, and that faith had been bolstered by the fact that he and Sirj were no longer prisoners in their shelter.

The two Mettai had spent the first several evenings after the warriors' departure with Grinsa's wife and their beautiful daughter. She spent her days working with the Fal'Borna women in their tanning circle. But late on that first day, when her work was through, she retrieved her child from the girls who cared for the sept's young children, and walked to Besh and Sirj's shelter.

"I understand you're free to leave your z'kal now," she said, after they had greeted her.

"Yes," Besh said, exchanging glances with Sirj. "I believe we have your husband to thank."

"Probably," she said. "I was wondering if you'd like to eat your meals with Bryntelle and me. The Fal'Borna give us food now, because Grinsa's a Weaver. And I'd enjoy the company."

"We'd enjoy that as well," Besh said.

He and Sirj followed her to the shelter she usually shared with Grinsa, where they ate a small meal and chatted deep into the evening.

Cresenne appeared to enjoy their company, and being around the woman and her child was a balm for Besh's heart. He'd been away from Elica, his daughter, for too long, and he missed his grandchildren, Mihas, Annze, and Cam, terribly.

In many ways, Cresenne reminded him of Elica. She was strong, with a sharp wit and a keen mind. Even her laugh was similar to Elica's, low and strong, as if it came from her heart.

He and Sirj ate with her again the following night. Sirj was quiet during their evenings with the woman, though he, too, seemed to enjoy himself. Still, Besh could only imagine how much the man missed Elica and their children, and he wondered if being with Cresenne and the baby brought him some comfort or made him feel even worse.

On this third day, as the sun started its slow descent in the west and they waited for Cresenne to come to their shelter again, Besh asked Sirj if the two of them should have their supper alone that night.

"Why?" Sirj asked, clearly puzzled by the suggestion.

Besh shrugged. "I thought that maybe . . ." He stopped, frowning slightly. "I don't know if it's hard for you to be with Cresenne and Bryntelle. If it makes being apart from Elica and the children even worse."

"Nothing could make that worse than it already is," Sirj said in a low voice, staring off across the sept.

Besh put his hand on the man's shoulder. "No," he said. "I don't suppose it could."

"I like going," Sirj said. "She's a good woman. She and Grinsa . . . they belong together."

For a moment Besh thought that Sirj would say more. But he didn't and Besh didn't see any need to belabor the point. When Cresenne appeared in the distance a short time later, he raised a hand in greeting and when she neared, he and Sirj stood to greet her.

They didn't talk about much as they walked back to her z'kal. Besh asked her about what work she had done that day, but she didn't have much to say. She seemed quieter than usual, though her daughter was chattering enough for all of them. Since the first night they had supped together, the girl had taken a special interest in Sirj. Cresenne said that she thought that it was Sirj's dark, wild hair and beard, which were so different from the white hair of the Qirsi and even from Besh's grey. She didn't think that the babe had ever seen anyone who looked like the young Mettai.

Whatever the reason, the girl peered at Sirj as they walked, her pale eyes as wide as they could be, a faint smile on her perfect little mouth.

After a few moments of this, Cresenne said, "Would you like to hold her?"

Sirj looked at the woman, a slightly panicked expression on his face.

"Hold her?"

"You have children, right?" she said. "You've held babies before."

Besh fought hard to keep from laughing.

Cresenne stopped walking and held out her daughter for Sirj to take. He hesitated a moment and then took the child in his arms. She let out a delighted squeal and immediately grabbed hold of his beard with both hands.

"Bryntelle!" Cresenne said, laughing.

"It's all right," Sirj said, looking up from Bryntelle's face. "It doesn't hurt. At least not much." He grinned, but there were tears in his eyes.

"All right," Cresenne said. She glanced at Besh, her expression pained.

They walked on, and had nearly reached Cresenne's shelter when the woman abruptly halted.

"Damn," she said under her breath.

Looking in the same direction she was, Besh saw the n'qlae standing in front of the shelter, her arms crossed over her chest.

"What do you think she wants?" Besh asked in a whisper.

Cresenne shook her head, her lips in a tight line. "I don't know. But she and her husband don't seem to like any of us very much. Better let me do the talking."

He nodded. Cresenne took the baby back from Sirj and they walked on.

"Good evening, N'Qlae," Cresenne said, stopping in front of the woman.

The n'qlae nodded to Cresenne and then, after hesitating for just a moment, nodded to the two Mettai as well.

"Is something wrong?" Cresenne asked. "Has something happened?"

"I've had no word from the a'laq, if that's what you mean."

Cresenne appeared to relax somewhat. "Then what can I do for you?"

"I've noticed that the three of you sup together each night," the woman said.

"What of it?" Cresenne demanded, her voice hardening. "Is that why you've come? You think we're plotting against your sept? I would have thought that after the a'laq's dream the other night you'd know better." She shook her head. "You and your people will never trust me, will you? Just as you'll never trust these men, though they've saved your life and that of every person in this sept."

Besh had some idea of how the Fal'Borna honored their a'laqs and n'qlaes, and he feared that Cresenne had pushed the woman too far. But the n'qlae's expression hardly changed, except for a vague smile that touched the corners of her mouth.

"Are you through?" she asked.

Cresenne blushed. Abruptly she seemed unwilling to look the woman in the eye. "Yes."

"I've noticed that the three of you sup together each evening, and I was wondering if you would join me tonight in my z'kal. The food would be little different from what you've been eating. And like you," the n'qlae said, looking at Cresenne, "I'm without my man right now. I grow tired of supping alone every night."

There was a lengthy silence. Sirj caught Besh's eye and raised his eyebrows. The n'qlae was smiling again.

"I owe you an apology, N'Qlae," Cresenne said at last.

"Yes, I believe you do. But I also believe that settles an old debt. We won't speak of it again."

"Thank you, N'Qlae."

"Come along then," the n'qlae said after another brief silence. "I'm hungry, and it's too cold to be standing out here doing nothing."

They followed the woman back to her shelter. A fire already burned within, and there were several bowls of food arrayed on the far side of the shelter. Some of it was similar to the food Besh and Sirj had eaten with Cresenne in recent nights: smoked rilda meat, boiled roots, and flat bread. But there were also dishes that Besh didn't recognize, including some sort of dried fruit that smelled wonderfully sweet.

They sat by the fire and the n'qlae began to pass the bowls around, urging her guests to take as much as they wanted.

As the bowls made their way around the circle, the n'qlae pulled out a small flask, unstoppered it, and poured a small amount of golden liquid into four cups.

"What is that?" Sirj asked.

The woman grinned. "Sweetgrass whiskey," she said. "Usually I only drink it with E'Menua. But you're guests, and I've been thinking about it all day."

She passed a cup to each of them.

When Cresenne took hers, Bryntelle reached for it and looked down into the cup.

"She wants some, too, eh?" the n'qlae said, and laughed.

Besh sniffed at the cup and was entranced. It smelled like sweet clover and honey and wine all mixed together. "What did you say this was?" he asked in amazement.

"Sweetgrass whiskey," the n'qlae said. "It's the one thing we Fal'Borna won't trade with the Eandi or even with another Qirsi clan. Our people make it here on the plain and only a few know how it's done. We have to trade for it with other septs, because no one in this sept can make it. We rarely share it with outsiders. Few who aren't from our clan have even tasted it."

"You honor us, N'Qlae," Besh said.

She waved off the remark. "I wanted some, and I didn't want to drink it alone." She winced. "I didn't mean that as it sounded."

Besh smiled. "I think I understand."

Sirj lifted his cup to his lips, but before he could drink, the n'qlae raised a finger.

"Slowly," she warned. "It's very strong."

Sirj nodded, took a sip, and nearly choked.

Cresenne was the next to try it, and though she managed not to cough or spit it out, her eyes widened and her cheeks flushed. Bryntelle tried to grab hold of the cup, but Cresenne held it beyond her reach.

"You next, Mettai," the n'qlae said to Besh, a friendly smile on her face.

Besh took a sip and made a face that he imagined must have been very similar to Cresenne's. The whiskey was pleasantly sweet, but the flavor was nearly lost in the burning sensation on his tongue and throat.

The n'qlae nodded approvingly and then sipped from her cup. She swallowed and inhaled deeply through her teeth, but otherwise seemed unaffected.

"I think I need to try that again," Sirj said. He took another sip and this time had no trouble with it.

They began to eat, taking occasional sips of the whiskey throughout the meal. While they ate, the n'qlae asked Besh and Sirj about Kirayde, their village, and the lands surrounding it. As usual, Sirj deferred to Besh most of the time, leaving the old man to answer. He chose his words with care, though he sensed no dark intent in her questions. The n'qlae seemed most interested in the animals that the Mettai trapped in the Companion Lakes area, and after some time Besh finally turned to Sirj, who knew far more about trapping than Besh ever had.

At first Sirj spoke reluctantly, his eyes fixed on the fire and his voice low. But after a time he became more animated.

Eventually, the n'qlae seemed to run out of questions and it grew quiet in the shelter. Besh had finished his food and his whiskey, and he felt both full and slightly light-headed. Bryntelle had fallen asleep in her mother's lap, and Cresenne appeared weary as well.

"It's getting late," the n'qlae said, climbing to her feet. She grinned. "And if the whiskey hasn't made you tired yet, it will."

The others stood as well, Sirj taking Bryntelle for a moment as Cresenne got up. They stepped out into the night, and immediately Besh shivered. The sky was clear and a cold wind blew from the north. Both moons hung low in the eastern sky, casting long pale shadows across the sept.

"Thank you for inviting us to your z'kal, N'Qlae," Cresenne said. "And thank you as well for allowing us to taste the sweetgrass whiskey. It was wonderful."

The n'qlae nodded. "You're welcome." She turned to Besh and Sirj. "You may not know this, but you saved my husband's life a few nights ago."

Besh frowned. "What?"

"A Weaver can walk in the dreams of other Qirsi. That's how the a'laq of one sept speaks to other a'laqs elsewhere on the plain."

The old man nodded. "This I knew from Grinsa."

"The night before he left, E'Menua entered the dreams of an a'laq who was sick with the plague. He should have fallen ill himself, but he was immune. And the spell you conjured spread to the other Weaver and cured him, too."

Besh wasn't sure what to say. This explained the freedoms he and Sirj had enjoyed in recent days. But a part of him wondered why the woman had waited so long to tell him all of this.

"Anyway," the n'qlae went on after a moment, "I wanted to thank you for saving him. For saving all of us."

"You're welcome," Besh said.

She nodded and started to duck back into her shelter.

Before she could, however, someone called to her by her title. She straightened and turned, searching the darkness. After a few seconds a warrior appeared. He was an older man, broad in the shoulders and chest, but also thick in the middle. Nearly all the younger warriors had ridden to war with the a'laq. The men who were left were either old, like this man, or just barely of age to wield magic. The man stopped in front of the n'qlae and bowed to her.

"What's the matter, I'Yir?" the woman asked.

The man eyed Cresenne and the Mettai as if unsure of whether he could speak freely in front of them.

"It's all right," the n'qlae said. "Tell me."

"We're not sure what it is, N'Qlae," the warrior said. "G'Hirran and I—we were on patrol—and we thought we heard horses to the west of camp. That was earlier, and when we didn't hear anything more we decided we'd been imagining it. But just now we heard it again, and this time we're sure."

"Horses?" the n'qlae said, clearly unnerved. "You're certain?"

"Yes, N'Qlae," the man answered.

"What does this mean?" Besh asked.

The n'qlae stared westward into the darkness, as if trying to see what the warriors had heard. "I don't know. The Eandi army is largely on foot. They wouldn't send horsemen, and I don't think they'd approach a sept by night. But the J'Balanar would."

"The J'Balanar are the ones who have markings on their faces, right?" Cresenne asked.

The n'qlae nodded, still gazing into the gloom. "Yes."

"They'd attack when we're at war with the Eandi?"

At that, the Fal'Borna woman faced her, smiling slightly. "You said 'we.' Are you Fal'Borna now?"

"I'm Qirsi," Cresenne said, "just as I always have been."

"The answer is, yes, they would. The Fal'Borna and the J'Balanar have been rivals for centuries, and though we fought together during the Blood Wars, they probably want to take advantage of our weakness, just as the dark-eyes have done."

"They can't think they'd hold this land," Cresenne said.

"No. They'll take horses, food, any goods that they can trade. And they'll take children to sell as slaves."

Cresenne appeared to clutch her child a little more tightly, but to her credit, her voice remained even as she asked, "So, what can we do?"

"It will be a large raiding party," the n'qlae said. "Forty strong, at least. The J'Balanar never come with fewer than that. And they'll have two or three Weavers with them. Chances are they'll take positions to the west and east of the sept and attack from both sides at once."

"You've dealt with these people before," Besh said.

"As I told you, we've been rivals for a long time. E'Menua goes on hunts every year. He makes certain I know what to do in case of an attack." She raked a hand through her long white hair. "But usually he leaves me with at least one other Weaver. I don't think he believed the J'Balanar would be so treacherous as to raid our lands when we were at war with the Eandi."

"We only have a few warriors," Cresenne said.

"You're a warrior. Your friend F'Solya is a warrior. Every woman in this camp is a warrior. That's the way of the Fal'Borna."

Cresenne nodded, looking white as a ghost.

"I suppose, then, that we're warriors as well," Besh said, drawing a smile from the n'qlae. "What would you like us to do?"

"What can you do?"

The old man grinned as he pulled his knife free. "I won't be much good to you in a fight," he said. "But I can conjure. I'm very good at that."

"Why aren't they attacking now?" Cresenne asked.

"They must be getting in position. But as long as it's dark, we have the advantage. We know our sept; they don't. They'll attack at first light, thinking that we'll be unprepared."

"We could use language of beasts to frighten their horses," Cresenne said. "Show them that we know they're out there."

"Yes, we could," the n'qlae said. "I just don't know if that's the best way to handle this."

"What if we were to wake everyone and lead them out of

the sept?" Besh asked. "They'd attack in the morning and find no one here."

The n'qlae seemed to consider this for several moments before shaking her head. "I don't like the idea of abandoning the sept, and I'm not sure we could get far enough away tonight. They would still be able to see us come morning, and they'd simply ride us down."

"Can you fight them?" Sirj asked. "There are more than forty women in the sept. We'd outnumber them."

"The number of Weavers matters more," the n'qlae said. "They'll be able to attack with several magics at once, and I'll only be able to block one of them." Her brow furrowed in concentration. "No, we need to think of something that will forestall their attack. If it comes to a fight, we'll lose."

"The a'laq was afraid of the creatures we could conjure," Sirj said, looking at Besh.

The n'qlae bristled. "The a'laq fears nothing."

"Perhaps fear wasn't the right word," Besh said. "But he wanted to know what creatures we could call forth with our magic. He seemed most . . . most concerned with the creatures of legend that our people can summon."

The n'qlae stared at him. "You can conjure such things?"

"There may be those among us who can. I know that the Mettai of old—those who fought in the Blood Wars—could call forth demons and creatures of myth."

"But can *you*?" Cresenne asked.

Besh shrugged. "I've never tried. I'm not sure I know the spells."

Clearly he had the n'qlae's attention now. "What about other creatures?" she asked. "Real creatures? Can you conjure those?"

He nodded. "Yes. Wolves, wild dogs, highland lions, bears. I've used hornets against . . . enemies. They work quite well."

The n'qlae shook her head. "Fire magic," she said. "A Weaver with access to fire would have little trouble against a swarm. And shaping would work against these other animals you've mentioned." She shook her head a second time. "We'd need something more difficult to fight, something that would surprise them so much that they wouldn't know what magic to use."

They stood there in silence for several moments, all of them seemingly lost in thought. And then Sirj began to laugh.

They looked at him.

"What are you laughing at?" Besh asked.

At first Sirj didn't answer. He was laughing still, but now his brow was creased in thought.

"You say that fire magic would protect them against a swarm," he finally said, looking at the n'qlae. "How would that work?"

The woman gave a small shrug. "They'd see the swarm coming and they'd use fire to burn it out of the air. It would be fairly simple really. Even if we use the hornets now, in the dark, they'll hear them and they'll be able to direct fire at them."

"So they'd need to see it," Sirj said.

"Well, yes, of course."

"What is it you're thinking?" Besh asked.

Sirj laughed again. "You'll think I'm mad."

Besh grinned. "I've thought that before."

"Quickly!" the n'qlae said, clearly annoyed by how amused both men seemed. "What is this about?"

"Ants," Sirj said, facing the woman. "Armies of biting ants. By the time the J'Balanar understand what we've done, it will be too late for them to do anything about it without burning themselves."

The n'qlae appeared unconvinced. "Ants," she repeated.

Sirj nodded.

"Can you make enough of them?" Cresenne asked.

"Absolutely," Besh said. "The harder part will be getting them to the J'Balanar. For this to work, we'd have to do it before they mount their horses, but as long as it's dark we can't see where to send them."

"Then we'll just send them west for now," the n'qlae said. "We know that at least some of the J'Balanar are there. Maybe if this works, the others will give themselves away."

"We should be ready to strike at them," Cresenne said. "We should wake the others, and when Sirj's ants stir up the J'Balanar, we should attack. They'll be distracted, even the Weavers."

The n'qlae gave her a hard look, but then nodded. "Yes, all right." She turned to the warrior. "Wake every adult, but do it quietly. Have the children remain in the z'kals, and have at least one older child with the younger ones. Quickly, I'Yir."

The man nodded, bowed, and hurried off.

"It would be helpful to know just where they are," Sirj said, scanning the dark plain beyond the sept.

Besh nodded. "It would be. But there might be a way to do it without knowing. It would be more complicated, but we can direct the magic at the Qirsi. We just have to make certain that there are no Fal'Borna in front of us when we do."

"How soon can you do this?" the n'qlae asked.

"I need some time to work out the spell. Not long. A few moments. I'll let you know when I'm ready."

The woman took a breath. "Yes, all right."

She appeared tense, even afraid, although no more so than Besh felt. He trusted that she would lead her people well. It was up to Sirj and him to give the Fal'Borna a chance. The two men walked a short distance from Cresenne and the n'qlae.

"How do we do this?" Sirj asked quietly.

"The ants are easy," Besh said. "It's the rest of the spell I need to work out." Mettai magic worked best when the elements were recited in groups of four. This spell would be too complicated to be accomplished with four elements, which meant that he needed eight, or perhaps twelve.

"We need to send them in a mist," Sirj said. "They can only become ants when they reach the Qirsi. Otherwise this will never work."

"I agree."

He heard whispers and light footsteps coming from the shelters around him. The Fal'Borna were stirring, preparing for this battle. Before long they'd be ready for his magic.

"Blood to earth," he muttered, practicing the spell, the words empty of magic without his blood. "Life to power, power to thought, earth to mist, mist to magic . . ."

Sirj was watching him, waiting. Seeming to realize that Besh had faltered, he frowned. "Three more elements."

"I know," Besh said. "But I'm not sure how to finish it. That's the hard part—getting the incantation right."

Sirj repeated the spell as Besh had spoken it, trailing off at the same point.

Besh scoured his brain, searching for the right words for the spell, knowing that he was close. He wished that he hadn't tried any of that sweetgrass whiskey. His mind felt sluggish, and he knew that he wouldn't have a second chance to get the spell right if he failed the first time. Still, nothing came to him, and he began to grow frustrated.

"She's coming," Sirj whispered.

Besh looked up to see the n'qlae walking toward him, followed by Cresenne, who no longer held her child.

He drew himself up, preparing to tell the n'qlae that this magic couldn't be rushed.

"We hear horses moving again," the woman said before he could speak. "I fear the J'Balanar have noticed all the activity in our sept. We need to act now."

"Is it possible they'll move on?" Sirj asked. "Perhaps find another settlement?"

She shook her head. "I don't think so. It's more likely that they're taking up new positions, or that they're preparing to attack before dawn. Are you ready?" she asked Besh.

What choice did he have? "Yes," he said.

Sirj shot him a look, but Besh kept his eyes on the n'qlae.

"Good," she said. "We are as well." She started to make her way toward the south end of the sept, leaving Besh and the others with little choice but to follow. "They seemed to be moving in this direction," she said as they walked.

"All of them?" Besh asked.

She slowed. "I'm not sure."

Besh halted, and began to retrace their steps. "We should start in the west, since that's where they were."

The others looked like they might come with him, but Besh held up a hand to stop them. "Just Sirj and me. We'll try to stay out of sight. You keep going to the other side of the sept. Let them believe that we think they've gone there."

The n'qlae nodded and started south once more.

Sirj and Besh went back to the west end of the settlement, taking care to keep low to the ground, lest the J'Balanar were watching.

"Have you figured out the spell yet?" Sirj asked in a hoarse whisper.

"No, not yet. But it'll come to me."

Sirj looked at him. "When?"

"Soon, I hope."

They crept past the last of the shelters, and pulled their knives free. Besh reached for a handful of dirt and cut his hand, catching the blood on the flat of his blade. He mixed the blood and dirt and then closed his eyes.

"Blood to earth, life to power, power to thought, earth to mist, mist to magic, magic to Qirsi . . ." He trailed off again. He only paused for an instant, but that was long enough. He even managed a smile. Why limit the spell to the warriors, when he could disrupt the J'Balanar's plans so much more? "Magic to horses, mist to ants."

He let the magic fly from his hand.

"You heard?" he said, looking at Sirj.

Judging from the grin on the man's face, he had. He chanted the same spell and threw the blood and earth in the same direction.

Already Besh could hear men muttering in the distance. They weren't directly in front of him, but it seemed that the spell had found its way to the Qirsi just the same. A horse whinnied, and then another.

"Come on," Besh said.

They ran back into the sept and to the southern edge, where the n'qlae and her warriors were waiting for them.

"It sounds as though your spell is working," the n'qlae said.

Besh smiled. "Yes, it does." Sirj had already grabbed more dirt and was cutting his hand. Besh did the same, and the two of them spoke the spell in unison before throwing it into the night. Once again, it didn't take long for them to hear voices rising in surprise and anger.

"You attacked their horses?" the n'qlae demanded, sounding displeased.

Besh knew that he should have anticipated this. The Fal'Borna were fiercely protective of their own animals, and were said to be as merciful with their enemies' horses as they were merciless with the enemies themselves.

"The animals are in no danger, N'Qlae," he said. "They'll have some discomfort, but that's all."

"We need to strike at them now, N'Qlae," Cresenne broke in.

The woman didn't appear mollified, but after a moment she nodded to Cresenne, and said in a soft voice, "Language of beasts."

Besh saw several of the Fal'Borna nod in response, but otherwise he couldn't tell what was happening. An instant later, however, he heard the sound of galloping horses and more angry shouts from the J'Balanar.

"Those of you with language of beasts go to the west end of the sept and send away the horses of the men there," the n'qlae said. She looked at some of her other warriors. "Shapers."

This time the sound that followed made Besh's stomach turn. He'd been attacked with shaping power; he knew how much it hurt to have the bone in his leg shattered by magic. The muffled cracks and screams of pain that rent the night brought back those memories far too vividly.

The n'qlae turned to look at several other Fal'Borna, and then at Cresenne. "Fire."

The flame seemed to rise from the ground, like an orange mist. But it fanned out quickly, lighting the night. Besh could see the J'Balanar now. Most of them were sprawled on the ground. Some were still upright, but were vainly trying to outrun the n'qlae's fire. They never had a chance. It swept over them like floodwaters, and when it had passed, all on the plain was still.

They could hear more shouts coming from the west, and the n'qlae wasted no time.

"Follow me!" she called, sprinting in that direction. Besh, Sirj, and the other Qirsi did as she commanded.

Before they could reach that end of the sept, however, they saw a second wave of fire. This one was headed toward the sept.

"Damn!" the n'qlae said. She halted, closed her eyes, and held out her hands.

Besh was running beside Cresenne and now he saw her stumble, right herself, and stop, swaying slightly.

Another wave of fire formed, sailed over the shelters that were still in front of them, and then swooped down to meet the J'Balanar's magic. The two walls of fire crashed together a short distance from the sept, lighting the night as if the sun itself had fallen to earth. But the enemy's flame was stopped.

The n'qlae started running again, shouting "Shapers!" as she went. Perhaps a dozen of the Fal'Borna women ran after her. The others followed, too. And before they made it past the last of the shelters another wall of fire was headed at them from the J'Balanar.

The n'qlae called on those with fire magic once more and sent another flame to meet that of the enemy. The two bursts of fire magic met farther from the sept this time, but the effect was much the same as it had been last time: brilliant and violent. He could see the J'Balanar beyond the conflagration, the dark markings around their eyes stark against their pale skin.

"Shapers!" the n'qlae said again, even before the fires had faded.

Silence, and then that terrible snapping sound, and the howls of agony.

"Why haven't they attacked us that way?" Sirj asked of no one in particular.

"I think they must have sent their shapers to the south end of the sept," Cresenne said, her voice low. "They're dead already."

"Fire!" the n'qlae said, a note of triumph in her voice.

Already another flame was forming out on the plain, but this one was small and weak—a far cry from the attacks that had come earlier. The n'qlae's answering fire dwarfed that of the J'Balanar. It rushed toward what remained of the raiders, smothering that small flame and abruptly cutting off the low moans and cries of those who had been wounded.

Silence descended on the plain, broken only by the wind, the dry crackle of burning grass, and the crying of a young child from one of the z'kals.

The n'qlae turned to all of them, the smile on her face harsh and exultant. "The night is ours!" she said.

A cheer went up from the Fal'Borna.

The n'qlae approached Besh, Sirj, and Cresenne. "The three of you fought well! The a'laq will hear of what you did tonight." She looked around at her fellow Fal'Borna. "These three fought as Fal'Borna! It'll soon be dawn and I say we should feast on the morrow and all day to honor them as new members of our clan! What say you?"

Again the Fal'Borna shouted their approval.

The n'qlae nodded, still smiling. "So be it!" She looked at Cresenne and the two Mettai. "You have our thanks. We'll see to the young ones and then gather the dead," she said, raising her voice again.

She walked away, followed by the women and those few men who were still in the sept.

Watching her go, Besh felt sick to his stomach. He had done what he had to—and he would have done it again if it meant saving Sirj and himself, and Cresenne and her child. But this had been his first battle, and though he and Sirj hadn't killed anyone, they'd had a hand in the deaths of dozens.

"Are you all right?" Cresenne asked him, seeming to read his thoughts.

"Yes, thank you."

"You saved us all," she said. "Both of you did. The a'laq is sure to free you now, no matter what happens."

Besh nodded, but neither he nor Sirj said anything.

"I need to check on Bryntelle," the woman said, backing away from them, clearly anxious to find her daughter.

"Of course. Go." Besh made himself smile, though it faded as soon as she turned her back on them and hurried away.

"We're warriors now," Besh said, as they watched the woman disappear into the night. "First Lici made me a killer, and now I'm a warrior."

"What did you expect would happen when we cast that spell?" Sirj asked.

"I didn't think about it."

Sirj turned to look at him. "Well, I did. If we'd lost, the J'Balanar would have killed us both, and that woman, and her baby. Maybe I should feel guilty, but I don't. You promised Elica that you'd keep me alive, and you did that. Again. So, unless you regret it, I'd suggest you stop feeling sorry for yourself and instead thank the gods that we're still alive to tell Mihas and Annze and Cam the story of this night."

"You're right," Besh said.

The younger man seemed surprised by this. After a moment he nodded once and then walked away.

Besh remained where he was, staring out over the plain, watching as the last of the small grass fires burned themselves out. He wanted to weep, but he didn't allow himself that release. Cresenne and Sirj were right: People were going to die this night no matter what. Better the J'Balanar raiders than them.

But a part of him couldn't help wishing that he'd never left Kirayde.

Chapter 22

After the hunt, the warriors and their a'laqs enjoyed a feast of all the rilda that Grinsa and the other hunters had killed. Grinsa made a point of sitting with E'Menua, Q'Daer, L'Norr, and the warriors from E'Menua's sept, though he would have preferred to sup with O'Tal and his men. He also apologized to E'Menua for hunting with O'Tal rather than with Q'Daer.

"I didn't realize I was expected to hunt with the men from our sept, A'Laq," he said as they ate. "O'Tal invited me to hunt and I thought it would be all right if I hunted with him. I meant no offense."

E'Menua still appeared to be sulking, but he waved off Grinsa's apology. "It doesn't matter," he said. "I wasn't offended."

Grinsa wasn't sure he believed this, but he kept his doubts to himself. "You and O'Tal are rivals," he said instead.

The a'laq's eyes narrowed, giving his face a feral look. "Is that what he told you?"

"I just gathered as much from the way the two of you spoke to each other."

Again E'Menua dismissed the comment with a wave of his hand. "I care little about him one way or another. He's a pup. A few years from now he might be a worthy rival to me, but for now he doesn't have enough hunts under his belt or Weavers in his sept to be of consequence."

For several moments they ate, saying nothing. The rilda was delicious—the best meat he'd ever had. He still hoped to leave the Fal'Borna and make a life for himself and his family somewhere else in the Southlands, but he couldn't deny that he would miss rilda meat. Dried and salted, or fresh like this, he couldn't imagine growing tired of it.

"Q'Daer says you hunted well," E'Menua said, finally breaking the silence.

Grinsa glanced past the a'laq to the young Weaver, who sat beside E'Menua on the a'laq's right. He was chewing and grinning back at Grinsa. "Q'Daer is being generous, A'Laq. I brought down the doe I was hunting, but another hunter had to kill her for me."

"You brought her down while you were riding?" E'Menua asked.

"Yes."

"And you didn't fall from your horse?"

Grinsa smiled in spite of himself, remembering how close he had come to being unhorsed. "No, I didn't fall, though I almost did."

The a'laq nodded. "For a stranger to these lands on his first hunt, that's nothing to be ashamed of."

It might well have been the kindest thing E'Menua had ever said to him.

"Thank you, A'Laq."

They lapsed into silence once more. E'Menua ate but seemed distracted, his gaze continually sweeping over the gathering. Grinsa knew that he'd been unhappy when he and his army first joined O'Tal's and H'Loryn's. E'Menua had expected there to be more warriors and Weavers at this meeting place—six or seven septs' worth. But no new a'laqs had joined them. They had perhaps four hundred warriors to face an Eandi army that some had said consisted of ten times that many men.

"Do you think they're coming?" Grinsa finally asked him, drawing E'Menua's gaze. "The other a'laqs you were expecting, I mean."

"I don't know," the man said, lowering his voice. "It may be that others suffered J'Sor's fate, but had no one to cure them. Or it may be that they're on their way and will be here in the next day or two. I hope to hear from P'Rhil or S'Bahn tonight. I want to know where they are and whether they've found the dark-eye army yet. It may be that we won't need other septs to finish the war. But we won't know until we hear from those who rode north."

They finished eating their meal, though Grinsa could have stopped far earlier and been sated. He was glad that they probably wouldn't have to battle the Eandi come morning, because with all that the men had eaten, he couldn't imagine any of them would be in much condition to fight. E'Menua rose and suggested that all of them get some sleep, and then he went off to do just that.

Grinsa thought about staying awake so that he could walk in Cresenne's dreams and speak with her, but he really had nothing to tell her, and he knew that contacting her in this way left her exhausted the following morning. He found his sleeping roll and blankets, laid them out on the cold ground, and was soon asleep.

He awoke early the next morning to grey skies and a light snow. After stowing his blankets and roll, he went in search of the a'laq, certain that E'Menua would have expected no less of him. He found the a'laq speaking with Q'Daer, L'Norr, and the other two sept leaders. E'Menua seemed in a darker mood than he had been in the night before and barely acknowledged Grinsa as the Forelander joined their small circle.

"They probably haven't fought the Eandi yet," H'Loryn was saying. "As soon as they do, they'll reach for one of us. You know they will."

E'Menua nodded vaguely but said nothing.

"You think they've fought them already and lost," O'Tal said.

"I don't know what to think," E'Menua said. "I only got here yesterday, so you know better than I do how many warriors and Weavers they had, and how soon they thought they'd reach the Horn. I . . ." He shrugged. "I have a bad feeling. That's all."

"Maybe we should head to the Horn now, then," Grinsa said.

The others looked at him, their expressions revealing little other than surprise at the fact that he had spoken.

After a brief, uncomfortable silence, H'Loryn said, "We're supposed to wait here for warriors from other septs."

"Yes, I know, A'Laq," Grinsa answered, trying to keep his tone respectful. "But won't any army, even one this size, do more good reaching the Horn in a timely way than a larger force would if they arrived too late?"

O'Tal and E'Menua shared a look. For once they appeared to be in agreement.

"He raises a good point, H'Loryn," O'Tal said.

E'Menua added, "We can reach for the Weavers who are supposed to join us here, and tell them where we've gone. But I'd feel better knowing that we're doing something, even if it is just riding north."

H'Loryn looked scared, as if he didn't wish to admit the possibility that something had gone wrong with the army that had already ridden to the Horn. But at last he nodded his agreement. "Yes, all right."

E'Menua looked at his Weavers, including Grinsa. "Ready the men. I don't want to linger here any longer than we have to."

"Yes, A'Laq," Q'Daer said.

Grinsa started to follow the younger Weavers, but E'Menua caught his eye. "Thank you," he said.

The Forelander merely nodded, and hurried after the others.

It was a small force, and the Fal'Borna warriors responded to orders with alacrity. It seemed only moments before the men were astride their horses, thundering northward. They rode hard throughout the day, pausing only long enough to eat and drink a bit and keep their horses fresh.

By the time they camped for the night, Grinsa was stiff and sore and wearier than he had been at any time since leaving the Forelands. He ate a small supper, the feast of the night before seeming a distant memory, and then lay down to sleep. Many in the army camp remained active, but Grinsa fell asleep almost at once.

He was awakened some time later when someone gently shook his shoulder.

"Forelander. Forelander, wake up."

Grinsa opened his eyes. It was dark still, though a fire burned low nearby. E'Menua squatted beside him, his tapered face in shadow.

"What is it?" Grinsa asked, sitting up and trying to clear his head. "What's the matter?"

"I need you to do something for me," the a'laq said. "I need you to reach to the north with your magic and tell me if you sense anyone."

"Anyone?"

The man hesitated for an instant. "An army," he said. "Do you sense the Fal'Borna army?"

"Why me?" Grinsa asked, rubbing a hand across his eyes. "Why not Q'Daer or one of the other a'laqs?"

"Because I think you've done this more than they have. I think you've done it more than I have, and I'm . . . I'm concerned." He faltered again. "Please."

"All right," Grinsa said. "Where am I looking?"

"North. On or near the Horn. There should be an army of eight hundred or nine hundred Fal'Borna warriors."

Grinsa felt the blood drain from his face. "And you don't sense any of them?"

E'Menua shook his head. "No."

Grinsa closed his eyes and reached forth with his magic, much as he had done when he spoke to the a'laqs and passed Besh's spell to them. He sensed S'Vralna first. There were Qirsi living there still, but very few. The plague had taken its toll. Farther north, he sensed D'Raqor, a city of several thousand Fal'Borna, and he sensed a few smaller septs as well, beyond D'Raqor. But there was no army here. When he reached forth in this way he could see the magic of a Qirsi with his mind, as if it were a candle burning in darkness. An army that size would have appeared as a bright blaze in the night. But he saw nothing. *Demons and fire.*

He opened his eyes again and looked at the a'laq.

"Anything?" the man asked.

"No," Grinsa said. "Either the army isn't near the Horn, or every man who rode to meet the Eandi is dead."

"That's what I think, too," E'Menua told him.

He stood. Grinsa threw off his blankets and climbed to his feet as well.

"I was looking for P'Rhil or S'Bahn," E'Menua said. "Both of them should have been there with their warriors. But like you, I couldn't find them. There was no sign of them at all."

"What do we do?" Grinsa asked.

The a'laq exhaled heavily. "We have to tell H'Loryn and O'Tal."

"Do you want me with you?"

"Yes," E'Menua said. "O'Tal will want to know that I'm not mistaken or lying."

E'Menua woke one of his warriors and sent the man to find the other two a'laqs. Then Grinsa and he woke Q'Daer and L'Norr. Before long the six of them were standing together around a fire. The sky above them was dark with clouds, and snowflakes fell on them and hissed in the small blaze.

"The army has been wiped out," E'Menua told them.

O'Tal looked incredulous. "What?"

H'Loryn shook his head. "Impossible."

"I just reached for them," E'Menua said. "Not only couldn't I find any of the Weavers, I couldn't even find their men. None of them. I had Grinsa try. He couldn't find them, either."

"I don't believe it," O'Tal said.

"Try it yourself."

The young a'laq closed his eyes for several moments, his brow creased in concentration. He stood that way for what seemed a long time, until at last he opened his eyes again, looking stricken.

"Blood and bone," he whispered.

"It's true then?" H'Loryn said, a tremor in his voice.

"Could they have gone somewhere else?" Grinsa asked, ignoring him for the moment. "Somewhere we haven't thought to look?"

O'Tal shook his head. "It's only been a few days. Where else could they have gone?"

"Is it possible they went south instead of north?"

"No," O'Tal said. "We saw them ride off. They went north, and they wouldn't have turned around without letting us know."

"But how could they all be dead?" H'Loryn asked. "Even if the Eandi had managed to defeat them somehow, some would have escaped. There might be wounded, or prisoners. But you're saying that there's no one at all?"

"The Mettai," E'Menua said. "It has to have been some spell of the Mettai."

Grinsa had to agree. H'Loryn was right: If it had been a normal battle, there would have been survivors. But if it was magic, as E'Menua suggested, that could explain how every last man had been lost.

"So what do we do?" H'Loryn asked.

"We continue north, and we fight," O'Tal said, staring at the old man as if daring him to disagree.

E'Menua nodded his approval. "That's right. We'll find a way to defeat the Mettai, and then we'll crush the dark-eye army."

"Yes, of course," H'Loryn said, as if willing himself to be brave. "My warriors will be ready to ride when you give the word, E'Menua."

E'Menua looked grim but determined. "Good. We've still a few hours until dawn. I'm going to try to sleep. The rest of you should, too."

The others turned and started back toward the warmth of their sleeping rolls. Grinsa had every intention of doing the same, but the a'laq spoke his name quietly, stopping him. Q'Daer halted as well, eyeing both Grinsa and E'Menua.

"Go," the a'laq told him. "I just need to speak with the Forelander for a moment."

Q'Daer frowned, but after a moment he left them.

"This would be a good time to tell me all that you learned from the Mettai about their magic," E'Menua said when they were alone. "I had no idea they were capable of anything like this. I don't think any of my people did."

"I'm not sure Besh and Sirj did, either," Grinsa said.

"You'll tell me what they told you?" E'Menua asked.

"Yes, of course. To be honest with you, Besh and I spent most of our time talking about the creatures they could conjure. That was what you were most concerned about, and the idea that they can conjure beasts of any sort still amazes me."

The a'laq scowled at this.

"I'm just being honest, A'Laq. Our magic, which can do so much, can't do anything like that."

"What's your point?" E'Menua demanded.

"That all of us were so concerned with dragons and demons, creyvnals and blood wolves, that those were the only spells we considered. Besh mentioned something to me, though—I didn't make much of it at the time, and neither did he. But it could explain what's happened to the other army."

E'Menua looked genuinely alarmed. "Demons and dragons don't explain it?"

"Not really, no. Even they might leave survivors. But Besh spoke of magic that could kill hundreds at a time. A poison spell, he called it. He didn't tell me how it works, and so I wouldn't know how to stop it, except . . ." He took a breath. "Except to try to kill every Mettai in the Eandi army."

"We intended to do that anyway," E'Menua said. "You don't know of any defense against this poison spell?"

Grinsa started to say that he didn't, but then stopped himself, recalling his own experience with Mettai magic. That terrible night when he nearly died from Lici's plague, Besh tried several spells on him, and each one fell over him like a cool mist. It seemed that even a spell that didn't lead to the creation of a fox or hornets or a creyvnal had to take some physical form.

"Forelander?"

"Fire magic," Grinsa said.

"What?"

"Mettai conjure with earth and blood, which means that all their spells have some form, some substance. They're not just thought, like ours are. It may be that they can be burned away. That is, if we see them coming."

The a'laq nodded slowly. "Yes. That makes sense." He looked Grinsa in the eye. "Well done." He started away. "Get some sleep, Forelander. We'll be fighting before long."

Grinsa returned to his sleeping roll, but he was wide awake. Again he considered reaching for Cresenne. But she would ask him questions about the war, which inevitably would lead to what had befallen the other army. The last thing he wanted to do was frighten her.

He lay down and pulled his blankets up to his chin. Snow-flakes fell on his face and melted, running over his cheeks and into his hair like tears. After a few moments of this, he pulled the blanket over his head and eventually fell asleep again.

Morning came quickly, and soon the Fal'Borna were riding again. It seemed that word of the other Fal'Borna army's fate had spread through the ranks of the warriors. Only the day before, the men had joked and sang as they rode. Now they made not a sound. Grinsa saw fear in their faces, but also the same iron resolve he'd seen in E'Menua the previous night.

Q'Daer and L'Norr rode next to Grinsa, but they didn't speak to each other or to him. The young Weavers scanned the horizon continually, as if both were eager to be the first to spot the Eandi army. Snow fell intermittently throughout the day. At times it was so heavy that Grinsa could hardly see. At other times it stopped completely and the sun shone through breaks in the clouds, making the light layer of snow on the plain sparkle brilliantly.

They came to the Thraedes late in the day and followed it northward, past the point where the K'Sahd joined its flow. They'd reached the Horn; it was just to the west, across the river. But still the riders saw no sign of the Eandi, and when they stopped for the night, the mood in the camp was somber.

It was a cold night, and though it stopped snowing and the skies cleared, a harsh, frigid wind blew out of the north, making it hard to sleep.

With first light they were up and moving again, and before long they found what they'd been seeking.

Q'Daer was the first to notice, and he rose in his saddle to point, a cry on his lips. Snow still covered the ground, but ahead of them a wide swath of grass had been trampled, leaving it dark compared with the rest of the landscape.

Grinsa and the Fal'Borna riders stopped at the edge of the tracks, and the a'laqs and Weavers dismounted to take a closer look. The tracks must have been made by the Eandi. When Grinsa and the others had reached forth with their magic two nights before, there hadn't been nearly enough Qirsi in the area to disturb the land in this way. Add to this the fact that most of the prints they could make out had been made by humans and not horses, and it seemed clear that a vast Eandi army had passed this way on foot.

But Grinsa was struck by the route they seemed to have taken.

"They came from the north," Q'Daer said, sounding as confused as Grinsa felt. "They followed the river. And then they . . . they turned to the east."

"That's how it looks to me, too," said O'Tal.

E'Menua stared at the tracks, rubbing a hand over his mouth. "It makes no sense. They defeated our army and made it to the river. Why would they turn away from the Horn?"

"Could it be a trick?" H'Loryn asked.

Q'Daer appeared to weigh this. "Perhaps," he said. "A path this wide, made by so many men. With so much of the snow trampled, it's hard to read. I suppose it's possible that they doubled back." He turned to scan the riverbank. "But I see no sign that they crossed the river, at least not near here."

"Then we'll assume that they've turned east," E'Menua

said. "We'll follow these tracks as far as they lead us. They're still fairly fresh, and with so many of them on foot, we should catch them before long."

"What if they're retreating?"

Every one of them turned to look at Grinsa.

"Why would they retreat?" O'Tal asked, looking puzzled. "We know from last night that our army has been destroyed. There's nothing to keep them from crossing into the Horn. They'd have no reason to turn back now."

"We don't know how many men they lost," Grinsa answered. He gestured at the trampled ground. "This could have been done by four thousand men. It also could have been done by half that number or fewer. Maybe they defeated the Fal'Borna army, but lost so many that they decided that they couldn't go on."

"What does it matter?" E'Menua asked irritably.

"If they're retreating, we should let them go," Grinsa said. "Particularly if the Mettai have magic that can destroy an entire Qirsi army."

H'Loryn raised an eyebrow and glanced at the other two a'laqs, a hopeful look on his face.

O'Tal caught Grinsa's eye, and shook his head slightly. But it was too late.

"Let them go?" E'Menua said, his voice rising. "*Let them go!* They invaded our land! They killed hundreds of our warriors! Who knows how many septs they attacked? And you want to let them go?"

"Forgive me, A'Laq," Grinsa said. He felt weak for apologizing, but he knew that he'd been mistaken to speak of retreat in front of everyone. He would have been better off first approaching E'Menua in private. Or better still, O'Tal. Too late for that now.

For his part, E'Menua didn't seem to hear his apology.

"I thought that you finally understood what it meant to be Fal'Borna!" the a'laq was saying. "I thought you were becoming one of us, at long last." He spat on the ground at Grinsa's feet. "Clearly I was wrong."

The a'laq turned away without another word, walked back to his horse, and swung himself onto the animal's back.

"We follow them east!" he said fiercely, glaring at all of them.

He wheeled his horse away and spurred the beast to a gallop, leaving the rest no choice but to follow.

"I'm sorry," Grinsa said to no one in particular. "This war has already been costly. I just thought perhaps we should consider letting it end. I meant no offense."

None of the others would so much as look at him, except H'Loryn, who seemed even more disappointed than Grinsa felt, and O'Tal, who shook his head ruefully and said, "You should have known better. You've lived among the Fal'Borna for a few turns now. You should have known what he'd say."

O'Tal didn't seem angry with him, as E'Menua had. But he and H'Loryn followed the others, so that Grinsa was left there alone. He climbed back onto his horse and rode after them, knowing he'd been a fool to say what he had.

The a'laq set a grueling pace. It almost seemed that E'Menua wished to punish his entire army for what Grinsa had suggested. They pushed their mounts throughout the day, barely resting. Grinsa had rejoined the other Weavers at the head of the army, though still none of them spoke to him or even acknowledged him. His back and legs ached, and he longed for nightfall so that he could sleep.

The trail left by the Eandi army stretched out before them. It seemed the invaders were still headed due east, toward the Silverwater and the safety of their homeland. Even as the snow began to melt, making the enemy's tracks less apparent, other signs of their passage became more obvious. The grass had been flattened; scraps of food—rinds of cheese, crusts of bread, and bits of dried meat—littered their path. The riders could even see where men had strayed from their course to relieve themselves. There could be little doubt at this point: The Eandi were leaving Fal'Borna land, and it appeared they were in a hurry to do so.

Just let them go! Grinsa wanted to scream. *This war is over! Return to your parents, your wives, your children!*

But he said nothing, and he rode with the rest of them.

They spotted the rearguard first, perhaps two dozen soldiers, all on horseback. The men were too far ahead for Grinsa and the others to reach with magic, though that didn't stop E'Menua from trying. He used language of beasts first, and when that failed, shaping power. But the Eandi riders had seen the Fal'Borna and were galloping away, no doubt to warn their commanders that the Qirsi riders were coming.

E'Menua signaled a stop, and while the warriors rested, the a'laqs and Weavers gathered to discuss what they should do next. They made room in their circle for Grinsa, but otherwise he might as well have been invisible.

"We're going to do this quickly," E'Menua told them. "I don't want to give them any time to prepare. Our first attacks will be directed at the Mettai. Shaping, fire, even mind-bending if you can manage it. I don't need to tell you that they're the greatest danger. Once they're dead, we can turn our attention to the rest of their army."

"Forgive me, A'Laq," Grinsa said. "But don't you think the other Fal'Borna army will have tried the same thing?"

E'Menua stared straight ahead, still refusing to look at him.

"What of it?" he asked after a moment, his voice as tight as a bowstring.

"I think we need to ask ourselves why they failed and what we can do to overcome whatever attacks the Mettai throw at us."

For a moment no one spoke, and Grinsa wondered if the rest intended to keep on ignoring him.

But then O'Tal cleared his throat and said, "The Forelander makes a valid point. P'Rhil would have done all he could to destroy the Mettai first, and clearly he wasn't able to."

E'Menua's face reddened. Grinsa was sure he was going to dismiss what they were saying as cowardly or foolish. But the a'laq surprised him.

"Perhaps they're able to strike too quickly," he said. At last he faced Grinsa. "Do we know how close the Mettai need to be for their magic to work?"

"No, A'Laq," Grinsa said. "At least I don't know. But what we discussed the other day remains true. Fire magic might work against any spells they try to use against us. And shaping should work against any creatures they conjure."

E'Menua appeared to think about this for several moments. "All right, then. Forelander, I want you watching for any attacks that can be destroyed with fire magic. I'll give you fifty men who wield that power; that should be plenty. That's all you're to do. The rest of us will fight off whatever they conjure—we have plenty of shapers in this army."

Grinsa nodded. "All right."

"What about language of beasts?" H'Loryn asked. "Won't that work on the creatures they send against us?"

"I don't think so," Grinsa said. "From what I know of Mettai magic, their creatures could be immune to that power."

"And how is it that you know so much about the Mettai?" O'Tal asked him.

Grinsa didn't need E'Menua's small head shake to tell him that they had strayed into dangerous territory. "I haven't been in the Southlands long," he said, "but I've journeyed here a good deal. And in the course of those travels I've met many people, including some who are Mettai."

O'Tal frowned, clearly not satisfied by this answer. But before he could say more, E'Menua gave the order to resume riding. Moments later they were galloping after the Eandi, the drumming of their horses' hooves seeming to make the ground tremble. Grinsa wasn't sure how far they'd have to ride before they encountered the invaders. The rearguard could have been two leagues behind the army, or one mile behind it. As it turned out, the distance might have been even less than that.

Grinsa and the Fal'Borna topped a small rise, and found themselves facing an army of at least two thousand men, possibly more. Archers were positioned at the front of the force, spread in a wide arc, no doubt to make it harder for the Qirsi to raise a wind against their volleys of arrows. The Mettai stood near the center of the army. There didn't appear to be many of them, but Grinsa was sure there were enough to kill every Fal'Borna rider in E'Menua's force.

But the army itself was the least of his concerns. The expanse of grass between the Qirsi army and the Eandi was already teeming with creatures that made Grinsa's blood turn cold. There were serpents, as long as a peddler's cart and as thick around as a horse's neck. Great wolves, nearly as large as the horses ridden by the Fal'Borna, loped toward the Qirsi army. Enormous eagles circled overhead, their wings so broad they seemed to blot out the sun, their talons as long and sharp as daggers.

E'Menua signaled a halt, and for a few moments Grinsa and the others simply stared at the scene before them. Several of the younger warriors appeared stricken with terror.

"These creatures are nothing," E'Menua said at last, contempt in his voice. He looked back at his riders, a harsh grin on his face. "They think they can frighten us with big dogs and a few snakes?" He faced forward again and shouted, "Shapers!"

The eagles were closest, and so they were the a'laq's first target. Grinsa felt the pulse of magic as E'Menua sent it forth. But still, he wasn't prepared for the deafening shrieks that came from the giant birds above them. A moment before they had been as graceful and terrible as any creatures Grinsa had ever seen. Now, their wings broken and flailing, their backs arched in agony, they tumbled to the earth, landing in great heaps on the plain.

"Shapers again!" E'Menua called.

This time the a'laq directed their magic forward instead of up. An instant later, the lead wolves let out loud yelps of pain and crumpled to the ground. Grinsa could see the Mettai conjuring more birds and more wolves, but clearly the creatures could be defeated with shaping magic.

"The snakes!" Q'Daer shouted.

Grinsa saw them, too. It seemed they were too low to have been hit by the shaping magic that killed the wolves. They were disturbingly fast and had nearly reached the Qirsi lines.

His eyes wide, E'Menua shouted, "Fire!"

The a'laq aimed the flame low, and made it spread like low waves over sand. It blackened the grass and slammed into the snakes, so that they twisted and writhed on the charred ground.

Again, these horrors called forth by the Mettai couldn't withstand the Fal'Borna's magic. But Grinsa couldn't help noticing that E'Menua and the other Weavers had yet to direct an attack at the Eandi. It was all they could do to defend themselves against the Mettai attacks.

Even as he formed the thought, he saw the Mettai conjuring again. And this time, rather than calling forth more wolves or eagles or snakes, the blood and earth that flew from their hands changed into something that looked almost like sand. Except that it didn't billow in the wind and fall to the ground. Instead, it spread across the sky and soared toward the Qirsi riders so swiftly that Grinsa felt panic grip his heart.

"Fire!" he shouted. Reaching for the magic of the Fal'Borna around him, he sent forth a wall of flame that shimmered and danced over the plain even as it broadened to consume the spell of the Mettai sorcerers. And when the two met, the fire flared like lightning in the Growing turns, so that every person on that battlefield threw up a hand to shield his or her eyes.

"What was that?" E'Menua called to him.

Grinsa shook his head. "I don't know."

The a'laq surveyed the battlefield, his expression far more sober than it had been a few moments before. Already the Mettai were creating more of their blood animals, and Grinsa could see the Eandi archers creeping forward, trying to put themselves within range of the Fal'Borna. It seemed E'Menua saw this, too.

"O'Tal!" the a'laq called. "You take the snakes. Use fire on them—that seems to work best. H'Loryn, I need you to raise a wind. Keep it swirling. Don't let those archers reach us."

"Yes, all right," H'Loryn said in return.

"I'll keep using shaping on the eagles and wolves," E'Menua went on. "The Forelander will fight off their other spells. Q'Daer and L'Norr," he said, dropping his voice slightly. "I want the two of you to gather twenty warriors from our sept and try to use shaping magic against the Mettai. You might need to get closer to them, and I'm not sure how you should do that. That's up to you. But until the Mettai are defeated, we can't win. You understand?"

"Yes, A'Laq," the two men said in unison.

"Good. Now go."

There was much about E'Menua that Grinsa didn't like or even respect, but he couldn't find fault with the a'laq's battlefield strategy. He tried to keep one eye on the Mettai, so that he could guard against their next spell, but he also watched as Q'Daer and L'Norr wheeled their horses away and waved to several of their riders to join them. As he did this, Q'Daer glanced back at Grinsa and for just a moment their eyes met. Grinsa nodded to him, and the young Weaver gave a fierce grin. It wasn't surprising, really. It seemed to Grinsa that the man had been itching for battle since the day they met. Here it was at last.

"Fire!" O'Tal yelled.

And E'Menua followed that almost immediately with another call of "Shapers!"

Grinsa's gaze snapped forward again. Another line of snakes was getting close. Two dozen wolves trotted just behind them. Already a number of eagles were tumbling out of the sky, their great beaks open, their death cries making E'Menua's warriors cringe. He felt H'Loryn's wind rising. He saw the Mettai conjuring another of their strange mists, and he reached for the fire magic of the men behind him.

He hadn't started to tire yet, but no Qirsi, not even a Weaver, could wield his power forever. He wondered how long the Mettai could conjure.

Chapter 23

There was little for Tirnya to do but watch and wait for something terrible to happen. If Mander had been telling them the truth about his people's magic and the curse that had been put on his village, something was bound to go wrong in this battle. The eagles, wolves, and snakes would turn on the soldiers of Stelpana. One of the Mettai spells would work against the Eandi instead of the white-hairs. The plague would return and strike at her father's army.

The eldest and her people had already tried their sleeping spell against this second wave of Fal'Borna riders. Tirnya had heard her father calling for the spell, and Tirnya's first thought had been that it would fly back at them as the poison spell had by the river. She could imagine the soldiers around her falling asleep; and she could imagine as well the Fal'Borna riders moving among their still bodies, killing them as they slept, as Tirnya and her men had done in that sept they'd encountered early on. It was as if the gods were punishing her people for starting this new Blood War. It was like a waking nightmare.

When a wall of Qirsi fire appeared and burned the Mettai spell out of the sky, Tirnya actually cried out, fearing that this was the curse again, that the dazzling blaze overhead would rain down upon them and kill them all.

When it didn't, and when the Mettai recovered from their shock at what had been done to their spell, it all started again. More wolves, more eagles, more serpents.

We're leaving! Tirnya wanted to scream at the white-hairs. *Why can't you just leave us alone and let us go home?*

But she knew the answer. They were Fal'Borna; her people were Eandi. And this was a new Blood War. She'd started it, and she should have known better than to think that it could end so easily. If white-hairs had crossed the Silverwater into Stelpana, killed thousands of her people, and then retreated, she wouldn't have been willing to let them go. She would have wanted vengeance. She would have wanted to see every one of those invaders killed. The army of Stelpana would be lucky to make it back across the wash.

"How much longer can you keep this up, Eldest?" her father called to Fayonne.

The Mettai woman didn't take her eyes off the Qirsi lines. The back of her left hand was bloody and raw, though Tirnya had yet to see her give any indication that she was in pain. "As long as we need to to stay alive," she answered. "I have a lot of blood in my veins, Marshal."

Tirnya had come to believe that she'd been wrong to suggest the alliance with the Mettai, but she couldn't deny that she admired this woman.

"Do you want us to try the poison spell?" Fayonne asked a moment later.

Jenoe looked over at Tirnya, a question in his eyes. She shook her head.

"Not yet," he said. "Try the sleep spell again."

Fayonne nodded and said something to her people that Tirnya couldn't hear. A moment later they again threw handfuls of blood and dirt at the Fal'Borna. As before, these balls of mud transformed themselves immediately into streaks of silvery mist.

And once again, the spells hadn't made it halfway across the expanse of plain separating the two armies when they were met by a wave of fire. The magic flared so brightly, it seemed like the sun had exploded above them. When Tirnya could see again, the white-hairs were still awake, still fighting.

"Damn!" the eldest said, her fists clenched, blood oozing from her many cuts.

Tirnya felt the wind freshen against her face, though moments before it had been blowing from the other direction.

An instant later it had shifted again, and was blowing from her left, and then from the right.

"They've noticed the archers."

Tirnya turned at the sound of the voice. Enly was beside her, his brow furrowed, his gaze sweeping over the battle plain. After a moment, she nodded.

"Do you think we should let them use the poison spell?" she asked.

"No," he said, without hesitation. "It could kill us all. Even the sleep spell is risky. If it puts all of us to sleep, the Fal'Borna might wake up first, and then we're dead."

"Have you mentioned that to my father?"

He grimaced, though he might have been trying to smile. "Your father hasn't been so fond of me recently. I haven't said much of anything to him."

"You have to tell him this, Enly. He keeps telling the eldest to try that sleeping spell. You have to make him stop."

He looked over at her father with uncertainty.

"Never mind," she said. "I'll talk to him."

"No," Enly said. "I will."

He took a breath and started walking toward the marshal.

Tirnya didn't know much about Mettai magic, and she knew even less about what it meant to be put under a curse. The day before, listening to the eldest's son talk about how his people had suffered because of the spell cast by their Mettai rivals, she had barely grasped all that he was telling them. She had thought about it a good deal in the past day, and had been struck again and again by how awful it would be to feel such malevolence from the very land on which they lived. But even worse than that would be the knowledge that their magic, the single thing that defined them as a people, couldn't be trusted.

Tirnya was a skilled swordswoman. She had tried to imagine what it would be like to lose faith in her blade, to worry that every tactic she tried in the ring might end up helping her opponent. The unpredictability of it all: That was what she would have found the most unnerving. Never knowing when the curse would next strike.

It seemed that this was the worst part of it for the Mettai as well.

They'd been conjuring beasts out of earth and blood for some time now, and all of these magical creatures had advanced on the Fal'Borna. There was no reason to expect that the Mettai's next conjurings would be any different. No reason except the curse.

Fayonne and the other Mettai gathered more blood on their blades, and mixed it with the dark soil of the plain. The mud flew from their hands, as it had countless times already on this day, and it twisted and writhed and grew into wolves, snakes, and eagles. But this time, the animals turned on the Eandi. Several of the wolves lunged for the nearest of the Mettai. Tirnya saw one beast leap at a Mettai and close its jaws on the poor man's throat. He was probably dead before he hit the ground.

Several of the eagles soared up into the sky, wheeled sharply overhead, and then dove at the nearest soldiers, who happened to be men from Gries's company. One of the birds rose into the air again with a man clutched in each talon. Both soldiers were screaming, fighting to get free. Another bird merely pounced on a soldier and with its huge beak tore into the man. Tirnya turned away rather than watch.

"Archers!" Jenoe hollered. "We need archers here now! Eldest, do something!"

Fayonne stared at the creatures, clearly appalled.

Snakes were rampaging through the Eandi lines, striking as if at random, leaving a trail of bloodied, lifeless forms in their wake. One snake actually struck at a wolf, just as the great animal sprang at it. For several moments the two creatures fought viciously, rolling over each other, the wolf snarling, the serpent hissing horribly. Then the wolf let out a yelp and was still. The snake untangled itself from the creature and slithered toward a knot of soldiers.

Everywhere Tirnya looked, soldiers, their swords looking pitifully small, tried to fight off the animals of the Mettai. Men screamed in agony. Archers fired their arrows at the eagles, though they had little effect on birds so large.

The Mettai threw another spell into the air, and this time several of the eagles went rigid and then fell to the ground. Dozens of soldiers were crushed.

"Tirnya!"

Enly's voice.

She turned just in time. One of the snakes was slinking toward her, its mouth open to reveal long, gleaming fangs. She pulled her sword free, and then her dagger as well, and she lowered herself into a fighter's crouch.

As the creature struck at her she dove to the side, rolled, and came up with weapons held ready. Already the snake was rearing back to strike again. She dove a second time, angling away to distance herself from the creature. Not that it helped much. Gods, these serpents were fast!

She lashed out at the creature with her sword, but it snapped its head back out of the way before striking at her again. Once more Tirnya dove away, and as she came up she saw that the snake had anticipated her dive and roll and was already readying itself for another strike. She tried to wrench her body out of the way, but knew that she'd fail this time. The serpent was too quick for her, for anyone.

But just as the snake began to strike, it suddenly twisted to the side, its tail thrashing violently. An arrow had embedded itself in the side of the snake's powerful neck.

Tirnya looked to see where the arrow had come from, and saw an archer standing beside Enly.

"Finish him!" Enly shouted to her.

Of course. She leaped forward, raising her sword, and she hammered at the beast as hard as she could, catching it just below where the arrow had struck. Dark blood spouted from the wound, and the beast flailed about even more desperately. She struck at it again, and the serpent gave one last mighty heave and was still.

Tirnya stared at it. She was breathless. Her pulse pounded. Blood dripped from her sword. Finally, she wiped the sword clean on the grass and turned to face Enly again.

He was staring back at her, looking pale. But he nodded to her and even managed a thin smile. By then, though, Tirnya was already looking past him, her eyes widening, her mouth opening to shout a warning. Not that it would do any good. The snake she had killed might have been fast, but the eagle hurtling downward toward her father, its talons outstretched, its enormous beak open wide, was like a dark blur in the bright sky.

Their defenses against the great beasts conjured by the Mettai seemed to be holding. Grinsa remained vigilant for any sign that the Eandi sorcerers were going to try another of their spells, but he also watched as E'Menua, O'Tal, and the others kept the snakes and wolves and eagles at bay. Already the plain was littered with the bodies of those animals that had been killed, yet still more of the beasts advanced on them.

When the Fal'Borna saw that some of the animals had turned against the Eandi army, they cheered and began to sing a war song Grinsa had never heard before. Still he watched the sky, but he could also see that the Mettai were now more concerned with their own creatures than with the Qirsi army.

"This is the time to attack!" E'Menua shouted, looking first at Grinsa and then at the other two a'laqs. "We can finish them now!"

He was probably right, but Grinsa wasn't sure he wanted to see thousands slaughtered on the plain. He kept silent.

"Well?" E'Menua said, his voice rising further.

"Yes, all right!" O'Tal called back, even as he scanned the charred grasses for more of the snakes.

"I want shapers and fire wielders together!" E'Menua called, swiveling in his saddle to look behind him. "Shapers will ride with me; those with fire go with O'Tal." The a'laq looked over at Grinsa. "Stay with O'Tal. Use the fire against any spells that they send our way."

"All right," Grinsa said, still watching the Eandi.

One of the eagles that had been attacking the men of Stelpana wheeled away from the Eandi army, gliding over the battle plain. Several arrows jutted from its belly and chest, and when it flapped its wings it appeared to labor mightily. As it approached, one of the other eagles turned to intercept it.

Grinsa glanced at the a'laqs, but they were speaking to one another.

The second eagle circled once over the wounded bird, and then, with a sharp cry, it abruptly pulled in its wings and swooped toward it, raking its talons across the first bird's back. The wounded eagle let out a sharp scream, and when the second bird dove at it again, it flipped over in midair and met the assault with its own outstretched claws. The two eagles grabbed hold of one another, each tearing at the other with its beak, both of them flailing with their great wings, desperate to stay aloft.

By now their struggles had carried them closer to the Fal'Borna army, so that they were almost directly overhead.

"The wolves!"

Grinsa tore his eyes away from the birds in time to see that another line of blood wolves had almost reached the Qirsi army.

"A'Laq!" he called, not caring just then which of the three men heard him.

E'Menua reacted first. "Shapers!" he bellowed.

The pulse of shaping magic slammed into the wolves just as they reached the Fal'Borna, knocking their broken bodies backward and to the ground.

Another scream from the eagles drew their gazes toward the sky. The wounded bird seemed to be clinging to its foe. There was blood on its neck and breast, and one of its wings hung limply from its body, while the other beat fitfully and weakly against the breast of the second bird.

They continued to grapple with each other for another

moment. Then the second bird released the first, letting it drop to the earth. Most of the Fal'Borna riders on the ground below had already started scrambling to get out from beneath the giant eagles, but not all of them made it. Several men and horses were crushed by the dying creature; others were sent sprawling by the impact.

And by the time the Qirsi and their leaders had recovered enough to take stock of what was happening, the snakes were almost upon them. A wave of serpents reached the riders all at once, some of them striking at men who had fallen to the ground, others going for the legs of horses.

One of them sank its fangs into the haunch of E'Menua's mount. The animal bucked ferociously, sending the a'laq flying. He landed hard on his side, rolled once, and was still.

Without bothering to reach for the power of any of the Qirsi around him, Grinsa crushed the snake's head with shaping magic. But E'Menua had landed near another of the serpents, and before Grinsa could do anything, this second beast struck at the a'laq, drawing blood from his side.

Grinsa killed this snake as well, though he knew that it was too late. Feeling sick to his stomach, he leaped down off his mount, killed a third snake that was slithering toward him, and then sprinted toward the a'laq.

A wolf lunged for him and he set the beast on fire with a thought, barely even breaking stride. Snakes and eagles and blood wolves were all around him, as if this were some terror visited upon him in his sleep. But he left it for the other Fal'Borna to fight them off.

He dropped to his knees beside the a'laq, laid his hands upon the wound from the serpent, and began to pour his healing magic into the man. The wound itself was nothing. But the venom nearly overwhelmed him. It was as cold as death and as bitter as tansy. Already it had spread through E'Menua's body, seeping into the man's heart.

"Don't," E'Menua said weakly. His eyes fluttered open and with a great effort he turned his head to look at Grinsa. He made a feeble attempt to push the Forelander's hands away. "Save your strength," he said. "I'm dead already. Fight the dark-eyes. Guard the others."

"I'm sorry, A'Laq," Grinsa said, his chest aching. He'd never liked E'Menua, any more than the man had liked him, but he'd come to respect him, and he knew that his death would be a terrible blow to all the people of his sept. "I should have kept you safe."

"I should have done that for myself." E'Menua stiffened, squeezing his eyes shut and gritting his teeth. "Gods!" he gasped. After a moment the spasm appeared to pass. "You need to protect the rest," he said, barely strong enough to make his voice heard.

"I will, A'Laq. You have my word."

"And D'Pera. I love her. Tell her."

"You have my word on that, too."

E'Menua moved his head slightly, as if trying to nod. "You're a difficult man," he whispered. "But your word is good with me."

His body went rigid again, and this time he remained still.

Grinsa closed his eyes for just an instant. "Damn," he muttered.

He climbed to his feet and looked around him. A pair of Fal'Borna stood a short distance away, and several dead wolves and snakes lay nearby. He recognized the men as warriors from E'Menua's sept.

"You were protecting us?" Grinsa asked.

One of the men nodded, his eyes fixed on the body of the a'laq. "Is he dead?" the man asked.

"Yes. I'm sorry. The venom from that snake was too powerful. I couldn't save him."

The man swallowed, then nodded again. There appeared to be tears in his eyes, but Grinsa couldn't be certain because the man turned and quickly walked away. The other warrior remained there, still looking at E'Menua.

"I think there was another a'laq once, when I was a boy," he said. "But I don't remember."

"Q'Daer will lead us well," Grinsa said. "He's a good man, a strong man."

The warrior nodded at this, and then he, too, walked away.

Grinsa could see that Qirsi warriors were still fighting off the Mettai's creatures, and at least a dozen of the great eagles still circled over the battle plain. Looking below them, he saw that Q'Daer and his small company had halted and were staring back at the Fal'Borna lines. The young Weaver might have been trying to spot his a'laq amid the obvious tumult in their ranks.

A moment later, Q'Daer faced forward once more. Grinsa watched him and his men, though from this distance it was hard to tell what they were doing. Then it became obvious. The Mettai were no longer all together at the front of the Eandi lines. But several of them stood in a cluster, and now every one of them in this group collapsed to the ground, as if they had been smitten by some great unseen fist. A cheer went up from Q'Daer's men and was echoed by those warriors closer to Grinsa.

Almost immediately, the Forelander saw another, smaller group of Mettai reach for their blades and for handfuls of dirt. He knew what they were going to do and he shouted, "Fire!"

But he could also see from the trajectory of their spell that he'd be helpless to stop it. He threw a ball of flame at the shimmering mist, but it had already started to settle over Q'Daer and the others. He roared the young Weaver's name, and then watched the man fall to the ground.

Only spun to see what had put that horrified expression on Tirnya's face, and felt the breath leave his body in a rush, as if he had been punched in the stomach. The eagle plummeting toward Jenoe looked to be the size of a small house. A house with talons like dagger blades and a beak that could swallow a horse whole.

Arrows jutted from its body in every direction, and more were hitting it even as it dove. But they wouldn't be enough to stop the creature. Tirnya was screaming to her father and now Enly did, too, even as he pulled out his sword and started sprinting toward the marshal. It was hard to hear anything above the tumult of all that was happening around them, but at last Jenoe seemed to grasp the danger. Not that there was much he could do about it.

The marshal began to run, peering back over his shoulder to see what the great bird was doing. The eagle adjusted its course with little more than a flick of its tail and the subtle shift of a wing. Even as Enly continued his desperate run, he was startled to note how much this creature of magic had in common with the normal eagles he had seen in the foothills of the Aelind Range. He also saw that Jenoe's attempt to escape had bought them both another moment or two. Enly never would have made it otherwise.

Just as the eagle reached out to grab the marshal in its claws, Enly caught up with Jenoe and shoved him to the side, out of reach of the eagle. An instant later the bird's talon closed, not around Jenoe, but around Enly, tearing a gasp from his chest.

The creature's grip was as strong as iron; he felt a rib break, and then another. One of the claws punctured his back just below the shoulder. The pain blinded him, stole his breath, and nearly made him pass out. It was a miracle beyond reckoning that he managed to hold on to his sword.

The bird started to rise, its wings pounding the air, its hold on Enly tightening even more. He felt and heard another rib crack. He knew he couldn't allow the beast to get too far off the ground, and so he drew back his blade, the pain in his side and back making his stomach heave, and he hacked at the talon that held him.

The bird let out a deafening cry.

Enly hacked at the foot again, and then a third time. Then he stabbed at the bird's leg with the point of his weapon.

The eagle shook him; it clutched him even tighter, crying out again. Enly stabbed at its leg a second time and then a third. The eagle bent its head down and for one terrifying moment Enly thought that it would tear into him with its beak, right there in midair. Instead it tried to take hold of him with the other talon. He hacked at this one, too, with as much force as he could muster.

The talon gripping him opened and he started to slip from the eagle's grasp. He rolled, and let out a howl of pain as the flesh below his shoulder tore away. The eagle grabbed at him with the other talon, but only managed to knock him out of reach.

It was only then, as he started to fall, that Enly realized how high he already was. He'd thought that he'd kept the eagle from taking him too far, but he was wrong. This was like falling from one of the towers on his father's palace.

He was spinning, tumbling. It seemed to take forever. And as he saw the ground coming to meet him, he thought, *I'm dead.*

Chapter 24

◆‡◆

They were farmers and trappers, wheelwrights and smiths. They had lived their lives under the Curse of Rheyle, coaxing livings from a stingy, blighted land. They weren't wealthy or powerful, but they were her people. They had left families behind in Lifarsa, men and women, boys and girls who prayed every night for their safe return to the village.

And now more than two dozen of them were lost, crushed as if by the war goddess herself. It had happened in an instant, without warning. That was the power of Qirsi magic. No blood, no earth, no spell. Just a thought, and in an instant more than a score were dead. If Fayonne and Mander had been standing with the others, they would have died as well. Being eldest didn't impart to her any special powers—she was no Qirsi Weaver. She would have been as helpless as the rest. But she was the leader of these people, and she felt their deaths in her heart in ways no one else on this plain could imagine.

And when she heard the cheer go up from that small party of Fal'Borna that had ridden forward on the left side of the battle plain, she knew that they were responsible.

It was a rash choice, especially after what had happened by the river in their encounter with the last Fal'Borna army. Fayonne didn't care. These white-hairs had killed her people, and now they were celebrating.

She bent down and grabbed a handful of earth, then held it over her head for just an instant.

"Blades!" she called to the Mettai who were still with her. "The poison spell!"

"Mother, no!" Mander said, whirling to face her.

"You heard me!" she said, ignoring him.

The others stared at her. A few of them exchanged troubled looks.

"You saw what they did!" she said, her voice carrying over the din of battle. "You saw how many of our people fell. And now you can hear the white-hairs cheering. We'll be next, unless we stop them, unless we avenge those we lost."

Mander strode to where she was standing and planted himself right in front of her. "Mother, you can't—!"

It happened so fast that she didn't realize she'd slapped him until he raised his hand to his cheek. She saw the imprint of her hand forming there, red and stark on his pale skin. Fayonne felt her own face coloring, but she didn't apologize.

"Blades!" she said again, stepping around him and cutting her hand.

She caught the blood on her knife, mixed it with the dirt she held, and began to recite the poison spell. Some of the others merely stood there, watching her. She didn't need them. Enough of the others were speaking the spell with her to take care of that small company of Qirsi.

"Mother, you can't do this!" Mander said from behind her, his voice tight with rage and humiliation.

She glanced back at him. "I have to do it."

"But the curse—"

"The curse is not absolute!" she said. "I know what happened last time, but you know that it's not that predictable." The eldest actually laughed, though she sounded slightly mad to her own ears. "I wish that it was so predictable! Our people would have overcome it generations ago."

"There will be a cost!" Mander said.

Fayonne nodded. "Perhaps. But there must be a cost for the Fal'Borna as well."

She faced forward again, spoke the spell once more from start to finish as the others completed reciting it, and sent the deadly silvery mist at the Qirsi.

The effect was immediate and absolute. The white-hairs who had been gloating over the deaths of her people moments before now clawed at their throats and toppled off their horses. Their animals fell, too, which was unfortunate but unavoidable.

Seeing the Fal'Borna die, Fayonne knew a moment of satisfaction, though it was fleeting. When it had passed, she felt terror take hold of her heart, like a cold, taloned hand. *There will be a cost.*

Suddenly she was aware of the tumult that surrounded her: The attacks of the wolves and snakes and eagles, the Qirsi wind that swirled around them, the moans and cries of the wounded.

She scanned the Eandi army for the marshal and, unable to find him, felt another wave of fear crash over her. She wasn't overly fond of the man, but she trusted him far more than she did any of the other leaders of this army.

To her relief, she spotted him after a moment. He was stiffly climbing to his feet, looking around as if dazed. And then he looked up, his mouth falling open.

Fayonne raised her eyes as well.

One of the magical eagles was beating its wings above him, struggling to keep aloft. It had been struck by so many arrows she found it hard to believe that it could still fly. But more remarkable, it held a soldier in one of its clawed feet.

He was struggling to break free; Fayonne could see his sword flashing as he struck at the bird's foot repeatedly.

A voice reached her. A woman's voice. Captain Onjaef.

"Enly!" she cried out over and over.

"Gods!" Mander said. "It's Captain Tolm."

No sooner had he spoken the words than the eagle let the man drop.

It hadn't seemed such a long way—other eagles were circling far higher than this one. But it seemed to take Enly forever to fall. Fayonne felt rooted to the earth. She couldn't bring herself to move. It seemed none of them could, until he smashed into the ground.

Fayonne didn't think she'd ever forget that sound, or the scream that came from Tirnya when he hit.

Then all of them were running: Tirnya, Jenoe, Mander and Fayonne, and a dozen other soldiers the eldest barely noticed. Jenoe reached the captain first, but Tirnya pushed past all of them and fell to her knees beside the man, tears streaming down her face.

Fayonne felt certain that Enly was already dead. He had to be after that fall. He lay on his side. His shoulder and back were a bloody mess, and blood oozed from his nose and ear. His legs were splayed at odd angles—she could only assume that the bones were shattered in a dozen places. But his chest rose and fell, each breath sounding wet and labored. After a moment, his eyes fluttered open and, though they looked dull and lifeless, he seemed to recognize Tirnya.

"Your father?" he whispered.

She was sobbing, but she nodded. "He's here; he's all right. You saved him."

"Don't tell my father," he said. A faint smile touched his lips, but then he began to cough and he winced, closing his eyes.

"We need a healer," Tirnya said. And then she shouted it. "*We need a healer!*"

"Tirnya," Jenoe said, and shook his head. "There's nothing a healer can do."

"There has to be!"

Fayonne had never cared for the woman, but her heart ached for her nevertheless.

"There has to be!" Tirnya said again.

She looked up at Fayonne, their eyes locking.

With Q'Daer's name still on his lips, Grinsa sprinted to his mount, intending to ride to the young Weaver and his men. Perhaps . . . He didn't complete the thought. He had to see for himself.

Before he could get on the horse, however, the animal reared, kicking out with its front hooves. Grinsa jumped back, then turned a quick circle. Someone had made the horse do that with language of beasts. Having used that magic many times himself, he was certain of it.

O'Tal was staring at him, still sitting his mount a short distance away.

"You did that!" Grinsa shouted.

"Yes. And I'll do it again if you try to ride to Q'Daer."

The Forelander glared at him for another moment before turning back to his mount and trying to climb into his saddle again. He used his own magic to keep the animal calm, but with O'Tal wielding his power, too, the horse remained jumpy.

"Damnit!" Grinsa faced the a'laq again, his fists clenched.

"I don't know what that spell was," O'Tal said. "But it killed them in an instant. And I'm not letting you or anyone else get near them."

Grinsa opened his mouth to argue, but then stopped, a vision of Cresenne and Bryntelle flashing through his mind. What would Cresenne have wanted him to do? If this was one of the spells Besh had described for him, there was nothing to be done for Q'Daer. O'Tal might well have saved his life.

He closed his eyes and took a long, shuddering breath. He felt as though a spear had pierced his heart.

O'Tal steered his mount to where Grinsa stood.

"You and Q'Daer were close," he said.

Grinsa actually laughed, though his eyes stung. "No," he said. "That's the funny thing. We fought all the time."

"I have a brother. We fight all the time, too."

The Forelander nodded, unable to put a word to his emotions.

"We have to end this, A'Laq," he said.

"We're trying."

Grinsa looked up at him. "No. I don't mean we have to win it. I mean we have to end it." He gestured at the dead beasts around them, the eagles circling above, the Eandi soldiers fighting off wolves in the distance. "This is madness. The Eandi were in retreat. Let them go. End this now."

O'Tal's expression hardened and he looked away. Grinsa was sure he'd refuse.

"That's not the Fal'Borna way," the man said with quiet intensity.

"It can be today. H'Loryn won't fight you. E'Menua would have, and Q'Daer, too. But they're gone. You lead us now, and you have to stop this battle before it spreads. Too many—"

"Enough!" O'Tal was eyeing him again, his jaw set. He looked out over the battle plain. After a few moments he raised himself up in his saddle and shouted, "Fal'Borna riders! Return to me now!"

L'Norr and his men were the farthest away, and at first they didn't appear to have heard him. But O'Tal called for them again, and this time L'Norr turned to look back at the a'laq. Seeing that others were gathering around O'Tal, he and his company started back, too. Grinsa could see him scanning the plain as he rode, no doubt looking for Q'Daer.

"If one of the dark-eyes takes so much as a step toward our lines," O'Tal said, his voice low and hard, "I'm going to signal an advance again, and we'll kill every last one of them."

"I wouldn't expect anything different, A'Laq," Grinsa said.

The man nodded, though he still looked unsure of his decision.

"What's happening?" H'Loryn asked as he steered his mount toward them. "Why have you called us back?"

O'Tal glanced at Grinsa before facing the other a'laq. "E'Menua is dead. Q'Daer and his company are dead. The Forelander believes it's time to end this war, and I agree with him. The dark-eyes were retreating. We're going to let them go."

H'Loryn looked from one of them to the other, as if not quite believing what he had heard. "I think that's a wise choice, O'Tal," he finally said.

O'Tal didn't answer. He looked out over the plain once more, seeming to mark L'Norr's approach. "He's young to be a'laq." He faced Grinsa again. "Have you considered—?"

"No," Grinsa said. "The sept is his."

"Where's my a'laq?" L'Norr said as he drew near. He scanned the faces of those gathering around O'Tal, his gaze coming to rest at last on Grinsa. "Where's Q'Daer?"

Grinsa walked to where the young Weaver had halted his mount. "The a'laq is dead, killed by one of the Mettai snakes. And Q'Daer and his company are lost as well."

L'Norr merely stared down at him.

"You lead our sept now, A'Laq."

The man shook his head. "I'm not . . . I can't."

"Of course you can," O'Tal said. "You must. There's no one else."

L'Norr cast a look at Grinsa, a question in his pale eyes. But Grinsa shook his head.

"Yes, all right," L'Norr said quietly.

"H'Loryn and I have decided that this war must end," O'Tal said. "But you're a'laq of your sept now, the leader of your men. And you've lost two Weavers today. If you say we should fight on, that's what we'll do."

L'Norr stared back at him, clearly unnerved. He glanced at Grinsa, but only for an instant. Then he began to look around, as if taking in the carnage that surrounded them. Finally he gazed out in the direction Q'Daer had led his men. Facing

O'Tal again, he shook his head. "I want vengeance," he said. "I want to see every one of the dark-eyes dead."

O'Tal frowned, but recovered quickly and nodded. "Very well."

L'Norr looked down at Grinsa. "Aren't you going to argue? Aren't you going to tell me that I'm being reckless and foolish?"

"No," Grinsa said. "I understand how you feel. I think it's likely that E'Menua would have made the same choice."

L'Norr nodded. "I agree. It's the Fal'Borna way."

"That doesn't make it right," O'Tal said.

They all looked at him.

"We may be able to destroy them," he went on, directing his words at L'Norr. "Or they may destroy us, just as they did Q'Daer's company and P'Rhil's warriors. For some reason, the dark-eyes were already in retreat, even though they had prevailed in a battle with the first army we sent to meet them." He stared across the battlefield at the Eandi. "I have a family that I want to see again. I have no stomach for this war, and I have no confidence that we can defeat this enemy. We should let them go, and live to defend our land another day."

"Is that what you believe, too, A'Laq?" L'Norr asked H'Loryn.

The older man nodded.

"And you?" he asked Grinsa.

"I think you know the answer to that."

L'Norr eyed them all for several moments, until finally his body seemed to sag slightly. "Yes, all right," he said, his voice falling low. "We'll let them go."

Grinsa exhaled, and exchanged a look with O'Tal. He nodded to the man, careful not to let L'Norr see. O'Tal nodded in return.

L'Norr steered his mount away from the others, and Grinsa stared after him, trying to imagine what the young Weaver must have been thinking and feeling just then. For his part, though, Grinsa thought that he would make a good a'laq.

You have to save him!" Tirnya said, desperate now, her vision clouded by tears, her throat aching.

"I can't," the eldest said. She actually took a step back, as if afraid of what Tirnya was suggesting.

"You have that magic!" Tirnya said. "I know you do!"

Fayonne shook her head. "I don't think our magic can save him. His injuries . . . He's too far gone."

"No!" Tirnya cried. She looked down at Enly's broken body. "He's alive still! You can do this!"

"Tirnya," Enly whispered. "Let me go. There's nothing she can do."

"I don't believe that!" She stared up at the eldest again. "And you don't, either. You know you can do this."

The eldest's eyes flitted from Enly's face to Tirnya's to Jenoe's, making her look like a cornered animal. "I don't know what the curse will do to any healing spell I use. I could try to heal him and wind up killing him."

Tirnya shook her head. "It doesn't matter. As you said yourself, he's dying already. At least he'd have a chance. Please," she said, her voice breaking on the word.

"The curse could do other things. It could . . ." Fayonne shook her head. "The risk is too great."

"Then I'll do it."

Tirnya looked up into Mander's face. "Thank you," she whispered.

"No!" Fayonne said. "I won't allow it!"

"I don't need your permission, Mama. And I won't just let him die. We conjured those eagles. This is our fault."

"Not ours! The curse did this!"

"Yes," Mander said. "The curse. Our curse." He knelt beside Enly and pulled out his knife. Looking at Tirnya, he said, "I don't know if I can save him. But I'll try."

"Thank you," she said again.

Fayonne dropped to her knees on the other side of Enly and stared intently at her son. "You can't do this, Mander! It's too dangerous!"

He smiled thinly. "I have to do it. That's what you said before, isn't it? Well, I have to do this."

The eldest blinked once, then sat back on her heels.

Mander took a handful of dirt, cut his hand, and mixed the blood and soil. "Blood to earth, life to power, power to thought, power to life."

He didn't release the mud, as Tirnya had seen the Mettai do with other spells. Instead, he merely held his hand over Enly's body and closed his eyes. For what felt to Tirnya like an eternity, everything on the plain seemed to stand still. Enly barely moved, except to draw breath. No one around them spoke. It even seemed that the fighting had stopped. At one point Mander opened his hand, and to Tirnya's amazement it was empty, completely clean. She saw not a trace of the earth and blood that had been there before. But he picked up more dirt, cut himself again, and repeated the spell, and in a moment he was healing Enly once more.

There was sweat on the young Mettai's brow, and his skin had turned ashen. His hand even appeared to be trembling. Still, he didn't stop. After some time Enly's color began to improve, as if Bian's grip on his heart had loosened. His face, which had been grey, now had a pinkish tinge. He looked pale still, but Tirnya could definitely see improvement.

"Mander?" Fayonne said, sounding frightened.

He raised a finger on his other hand, as if to silence her. "Not yet," he said, his voice hoarse. "I'm not done yet."

He continued to heal Enly in silence, pausing once more a short time later to cut himself yet again. Then he resumed his conjuring.

Soon after, Enly's eyes opened and he looked up at the Mettai man. "Thank you," he said in a weak whisper.

Mander smiled faintly, but he didn't open his eyes or speak. He looked terrible.

At last, he opened his hand, glanced down at it as if to convince himself that it was empty, and then let it drop heavily to his side.

"By the gods," Jenoe said, looking at Enly the way he

might have regarded a ghost. "I thought you were dead for sure."

"I'm not sure I wasn't," Enly said.

Tirnya's tears had started to fall again, though this time she couldn't keep from smiling.

"Thank you," he said to her, staring up into her eyes.

She swallowed, frightened by how full her heart felt just then. "I just wanted another chance to beat you in the Harvest Tournament. I wasn't going to let you get out of a rematch so easily."

He grinned, turning to Mander. "Thank you as . . ." He trailed off, his smile fading.

Tirnya looked at the young Mettai and gasped.

His eyes had rolled back into his head, and his face was the same color Enly's had been a short while before.

"Mander?" Fayonne said. "*Mander?*"

The man swayed for a moment and then toppled over onto his side.

"Mander!" the eldest screamed.

His mouth moved, but Tirnya couldn't hear what he said.

"What?" his mother said, bending closer to him, panic in her eyes. "What was that?"

"I told you there would be a cost," he said, his voice as soft as a Growing breeze.

"No!" the eldest sobbed. "*No! Mander!*"

But he didn't move again.

Some of the other Mettai led the eldest away. She was sobbing still, and though Tirnya was grateful beyond words for Enly's life, she grieved for the woman and her lost son.

Eventually Enly found the strength to sit up and drink some water, but he remained weak, his movements stiff. As it became clear to all of them that he really was going to survive, they began to realize just how many others had been lost. Scores of Stelpana's soldiers had been killed, and countless others lay wounded on the bloodied grass. The carcasses of the Mettai's creatures were scattered everywhere, but it seemed to Tirnya that none of the beasts remained alive.

Jenoe had ordered his archers back into position, but he stood near where Tirnya still knelt beside Enly, gazing across the plain at the Qirsi.

"What is it they're doing?" he muttered.

Tirnya laid a hand gently on Enly's arm before standing and walking over to her father. The Fal'Borna, she saw, had re-formed their lines. But they gave no indication that they intended to attack.

Gries joined them, looking as puzzled as Jenoe.

"Could they be waiting for us to start fighting again?" Tirnya asked her father.

"I never would have believed that they'd do such a thing," the Fairlea captain said before Jenoe could answer. "But I think they are."

At that moment, four men rode forth from the white-hair lines. They bore no spears, and they halted halfway between the two armies.

"A parley?" Jenoe asked.

Gries shrugged.

"Get Hendrid," the marshal said. "The four of us will speak with them."

"What if it's a ruse?" Gries asked.

"Then I suppose we'll be killed."

Gries raised an eyebrow, and went to find Waterstone's marshal.

The two of them returned a short while later with their horses as well as Jenoe's and Tirnya's.

"You think this is wise?" Jenoe asked, taking the reins from Gries.

"They're on horses," Gries said. "I believe it puts us at a disadvantage to face them on foot."

Jenoe looked at Tirnya.

She nodded, taking a breath. "I agree."

"So do I, actually," Jenoe said. He looked at Hendrid, who nodded in return.

They swung themselves onto their mounts and rode out to meet the enemy, halting a short distance from them and eyeing them warily. Three of the men who waited for them were clearly Fal'Borna. They were stout and broad, with golden-hued skin and long hair worn tied back. The fourth man appeared to Tirnya to be from another clan. His skin was as pale as bone and he was taller than the others, though just as broad. Actually, she'd never seen a Qirsi like him, and she found herself continually glancing his way.

The three Fal'Borna were of different ages. One of the men appeared old for a Qirsi, and the other terribly young. But it was the third man who spoke, breaking a lengthy silence.

"By all rights, you and your army should be dead by now," he said, his voice as deep and cold as ocean waters. "Those of your kind who trespass on our lands rarely live to see their homeland again."

Jenoe smiled thinly. "I've seen no evidence yet that you're capable of killing us. So perhaps you should skip the idle threats and tell us what you want."

The Fal'Borna narrowed his eyes. "Without your Mettai friends, you're nothing."

"And with them we're more than you can handle. So I'll ask you again, what do you want?"

"You were leaving before we caught up with you," the pale stranger said. "Isn't that so?"

Tirnya's father regarded him with genuine surprise. "I've never heard such an accent before. What clan are you from?"

"I'm from the Forelands," the man said. "But I ride with the Fal'Borna, and I'll die with them if I have to."

Jenoe stared at him for another moment before nodding slowly. "Yes," he said. "We were leaving. We've come to see that we were wrong to start this war, and we wish to return to Stelpana. As you've seen, though, we're willing to fight if you force the matter."

"We won't," said the Fal'Borna man. "If you leave now, we'll allow you safe passage out of our lands. Raise a weapon against us again, and we'll unleash the full might of our magic."

"What about other armies we might encounter between here and the Silverwater?"

"I can speak to other a'laqs—Weavers have that ability. I'll tell them to let you pass. But they'll be just as unforgiving if you break your word."

Tirnya thought that her father would reply in kind with a threat of his own, but he seemed to think better of it.

"All right," he said. "We'll need time to care for our wounded, but you have my word as commander of this army that as long as we aren't attacked, we'll do nothing to harm any of your people."

"Done," the Fal'Borna said. He glanced at his companions, wheeled his horse away, and started back toward his army. The other men followed, though the Forelander hesitated just a moment, as if he wanted to say something more. Instead, he simply rode away with the others.

"I never thought I'd see this day," Hendrid said, watching them go. "The Fal'Borna agreeing to a truce; who'd have thought it possible?"

"Not me," Jenoe said. "Let's do what we have to and be on our way before they change their minds."

Chapter 25

❖❧❖

There were many other wounded in the Eandi army besides Enly, and though none of them was as badly hurt as the lord heir had been, many of them were in terrible shape. Not long after Tirnya, Gries, and the two marshals returned from their parley with the Fal'Borna, one of the

Mettai, a man Tirnya had never spoken to before, approached Jenoe. He was slight and shorter than Tirnya, and he had dark hair and dark eyes, like so many of the Mettai.

"Excuse me, Marshal," he said. "But if you need healing for your warriors, we can help you."

Jenoe smiled, though he looked puzzled. "Thank you . . ."

"Barjen, sir."

"Thank you, Barjen. Tell me, where is the eldest?"

The man shook his head. "She grieves for her son, and she has asked me to speak for our people in her place."

"What about the curse?" Tirnya asked.

"We'll use care when we heal your men," Barjen said. "Mander saved a man who should have died. It's not surprising that the curse took him. We won't be so bold, and if a spell does go wrong, the cost shouldn't be as great."

Tirnya's father appeared to weigh this for a few moments. "Very well. We appreciate your offer, Barjen. We have many wounded and not much time to get them ready for the journey back home. So however many of them you can heal, we'd be most grateful."

"Then we'll get started right away."

The army had its own healers as well, men trained in the use of salves, tonics, and poultices, and for the rest of the day everyone in Jenoe's force focused their energies on aiding those who had been wounded. The Mettai used their magic on those whose injuries were most serious, while Stelpana's healers tended to the rest.

Tirnya did what she could to help the healers who had marched from Qalsyn, preferring to keep her distance from the Mettai, though because of distaste for their magic or fear of the curse she couldn't say. She also avoided Enly. The mere thought of him roiled her emotions in ways she couldn't quite comprehend, and she needed time to sort out her feelings. She thought him arrogant and insufferable, and though there had been a time when she was attracted to him despite his many faults, that was long ago.

At least, this is what she had been telling herself for the

past several hours. But she would never forget the panic that gripped her when she saw him fall from the talons of that eagle. Her heart had quailed at the thought of his death, of having to live the rest of her days without him. Half the time he made her want to tear out her hair. They bickered constantly, disagreed about almost everything. But she'd known him nearly all her life.

That's what it was! They'd been . . . well, yes, friends . . . for so long that she couldn't imagine not having him around. He was as familiar to her as her parents. This made sense to her. She even nodded to herself, drawing an odd look from the healer she was assisting at the moment.

He was like a brother. Anyone would have been terrified of losing a brother.

But with that thought came a memory, unbidden and unwelcome. Her vivid recollections of the passion they had shared, the taste of his skin, the feel of his lips on her neck and breasts, gave the lie to the idea that he had ever been anything akin to a brother to her.

"Captain."

She started, spilling some of the tonic the healer had asked her to hold for him.

He glared at her and she winced. "I'm sorry. Do you need me to get more for you?"

The man forced himself to smile, as if remembering that he was speaking to the daughter of Jenoe Onjaef. "No. Thank you. You must be . . . You've had a long day. Perhaps you should rest."

"Yes, all right," she said, knowing a dismissal when she heard one.

She placed the vessel carefully on the ground beside the healer and walked away, taking care once more to steer clear of Enly. Without intending to, she walked right into the Fairlea army and had nearly made it all the way to where Gries was giving orders to his men before she realized her error.

Tirnya and Gries had barely spoken since the night they kissed, the night Gries made it clear to Tirnya that he wished to spend the rest of his life with her. So much had happened since then. They'd fought battles with the white-hairs, Gries had tried to convince her father to use Torgan's piece of basket, Enly had nearly died.

She really wasn't sure how she felt about Fairlea's lord heir—what was it with her and lord heirs? Not wishing to face him right now, she turned quickly and started back toward the Qalsyn camp.

"Tirnya!"

She forced a smile onto her face and turned. Gries was striding toward her, his golden hair dancing in the wind, the late-day sun shining in his dark eyes. Gods, he was handsome.

"Were you looking for me?" he asked.

"Um . . . not really. I was just . . . I was wandering."

He gave a little frown. "Oh. All right. How's Enly?"

She glanced back over her shoulder, as if she could see Enly from there. "I think he's doing well. He's tired. The Mettai tell us it'll be days before he can walk again. I'm not even sure he can ride."

"Still, it's remarkable that he's alive at all."

Tirnya nodded. "Yes, it is."

They stood for a moment in awkward silence. She avoided looking at him, but she could feel him watching her.

"You're angry with me," he finally said. "You think I was wrong to speak to Torgan and to tell your father we should use the plague."

She shook her head. "That's not . . . That doesn't matter anymore."

He reached out and gently took hold of her hand. She made herself meet his gaze.

"Have you given more thought to what we talked about the other night?" he asked.

"There's hardly been time."

He gave her what had to be the most beautiful smile she'd ever seen on a man. "Then will you give it more thought now?"

She exhaled, closing her eyes briefly. "Gries, I . . ." She shook her head, looking away again.

The smile on his face changed, grew more forced. She might even have seen a touch of bitterness in his eyes. "I think I understand."

"You do?"

He released her hand and laughed. "You don't even know your own heart, do you?"

"What?"

"You and Enly deserve each other. You're both so certain that you don't care about the other, when it's plain to the rest of us that you're both being fools."

Tirnya opened her mouth, closed it again.

"I've left you speechless, have I?"

"You have no right . . . Enly and I are . . . You know nothing about me!"

"Forgive me, Tirnya," Gries said, smiling again. "But I do think that you and Enly are pretending there's nothing between you when in fact there is. And I think that I've had enough of playing that game with you." He regarded her for another moment, then shook his head and walked away.

Tirnya watched him go, feeling that she was in a haze. Eventually she returned to her father's camp, where she found Jenoe staring across the battle plain at the Fal'Borna, who had made camp within sight of the army of Stelpana.

"Is everything all right, Father?"

He started. Facing her, he offered a wan smile and nodded. "I think so. They haven't done anything to indicate that they've reconsidered. How's Enly?"

"Why does everyone assume that I've been checking up on Enly? I'll have you know that I haven't seen him in a couple of hours now."

Jenoe merely raised an eyebrow.

"Sorry, Father," she said sheepishly.

He said nothing, though he did appear to be suppressing a smile.

"What has you so amused?" Tirnya asked crossly.

"Nothing," her father said, raising his hands to calm her. "Nothing at all."

"Father?"

He shrugged, a small grin on his face. "I just think your mother would be amused to know that you've got two lord heirs falling over themselves trying to get you to notice them. She's always been afraid that serving in my army would keep you from marrying well. That doesn't seem to be the case at all."

Her cheeks burned, but she had to smile. "How is it you know all this?"

"I'm not that old, Tirnya. And where my daughter is concerned, I miss nothing."

"So what should I do?"

He shook his head and kissed her brow. "That, I can't say. You know your heart. Or at least you ought to."

"Gries says that I don't."

He started to say something, then stopped himself.

"Tell me," she said.

Jenoe hesitated. "I think Gries wishes that you didn't. But he knows better, and deep down, so do you."

They started back toward Stelpana the following morning, under the watchful eyes of the Fal'Borna. A haze of smoke hung over the battle plain from the pyres the Qirsi had built the night before for their dead. Enly had spent a restless night, kept from sleep by the stench of burning bodies and the pain in his limbs and ribs. He felt too weary for this journey, but he knew that he had no choice. Every part of his body ached. He trusted that the eldest's son had done all he could to heal his broken bones and bruised organs, but he was sure that had the man still been alive he would have counseled rest. By all rights Enly should have been dead. He feared that he was asking too much of his battered body to travel so soon.

Jenoe set an easy pace, no doubt concerned for Enly and the other wounded, but any movement at all was too much.

His men had fashioned a litter for him, and he lay on it stiffly, gasping at every bump, every jolt. His lead riders took turns checking on him. Aldir even rode beside him for a while, trying to make conversation, until Enly gently but firmly informed the man that he didn't wish to speak with anyone.

"O' course, Capt'n," Aldir said. "Let us know if'n ya need anythin'." With that he rode ahead, joining the other riders.

Immediately Enly felt badly for sending the man away. But he couldn't bring himself to call Aldir back. He remained alone, staring back at foot soldiers who steadfastly avoided his gaze, and watching the day slip by. He assumed that Gries and Tirnya were together, but the one advantage of not being on his horse was that he couldn't look for them.

Tirnya had saved him. He was certain of it. And even at the time, barely alive, in more agony than he had ever thought possible, he had noticed how she wept for him, how she begged the eldest and then Mander to save him. Fool that he was, he allowed himself to believe that she did this because she loved him.

He knew better now. He had been dying; she didn't want him dead. Even in the midst of their worst moments, she had never wanted him dead. Probably the thought of his death frightened her.

The first time they stopped to rest, Enly stayed on his litter. As uncomfortable as he was, he thought it would be infinitely worse to have to climb off of it and then back on. He sipped a bit of water and chewed gingerly on a piece of cheese. Even his face hurt.

When they halted again later in the day, he did get up, not because he felt any better, but because he could no longer resist the urge to look for Tirnya. He spotted Gries first, and much to his surprise, Tirnya wasn't with the man. She was with her father and Stri. He refused to believe that this meant anything, but it did lift his spirits.

Soon they were moving again and, perhaps mercifully, the pain made Enly forget about anything else.

Late in the day, Barjen joined him and asked him how he

felt. When Enly told him, the Mettai nodded as if he had expected this.

"That will pass eventually," the man said. "But it could take half a turn or more. Your injuries were severe." He faltered briefly, but then went on. "With injuries like yours, there's only so much our magic can do."

Enly felt as if someone had poured cold water down his back. "What do you mean?" But he knew. Actually he'd been expecting this. He'd come too close to dying for there to be no lasting effect.

"You might not be able to . . . to do things that you used to. I've heard soldiers speaking of your skill with a sword. You might not be the swordsman you once were. You might not be able to move as nimbly or as fast."

He swallowed, nodded. "Thank you for telling me."

"Of course. Should I leave you?"

Enly shook his head, but didn't say anything at first. Something had been gnawing at him for the past day, and he didn't know quite how to put into words what was on his mind.

"I didn't mean for the eldest's son to do what he did," he finally said, knowing that this didn't sound right. "Neither did Captain Onjaef. We didn't know what the curse would do."

"We know that," Barjen said. "None of us knew, except perhaps Mander. He seemed to understand."

"I'm sorry."

"Don't be," Barjen said. "Live well. Make his sacrifice mean something. That's all any of us can ask of you."

"How is the eldest?"

The Mettai shook his head. "Not well."

He started to walk away, but Enly called him back.

"Forgive me for asking," he said, "but yesterday, when you healed the others, did anything . . . did anything go wrong?"

"No," Barjen said. "Not a thing. It probably means nothing. But there are a few among us who wonder if by embracing the curse as he did, Mander finally broke it."

"Is that possible?"

"I don't know," the man told him. "I suppose we'll find out."

"I hope those of you who believe this are right," Enly said.

"Thank you." The man smiled and walked away.

Enly took a long, slow breath. *With injuries like yours, there's only so much our magic can do.* He'd be lame for the rest of his life. That's what the man was telling him.

"Damn," Enly said quietly. He felt tears welling and he willed them away. He could still be a soldier, and someday he'd still be lord governor. He refused to give in to self-pity. He stared back at the foot soldiers with his head held high. But inside, his heart ached. Tirnya would never settle for a broken man.

A short time later, they halted for the night. Enly's men built him a fire and laid out his sleeping roll and blankets. He ate a small supper and then lay down, grateful to be still and warm.

He had almost dozed off when he heard footsteps nearby. Opening his eyes, he saw Tirnya standing over him.

"Hello," he said guardedly.

"Hello." She stood there for a moment, clearly feeling awkward. At last she sat down on the grass beside his fire, a few fourspans from where he lay. "How are you feeling?" she asked.

"Lousy."

She frowned.

"Oh, I'm sorry. I thought you wanted an honest answer." He forced a smile. "I feel great, never better."

Her frown deepened and she stood again. "I'm sorry you're not well. I'll leave you alone." She turned to leave.

He cursed under his breath. "Tirnya, wait!" He tried to sit up, winced, and collapsed onto his back.

She had stopped and faced him again, and now she looked down at him, her brow furrowed with concern.

"Do you want me to get a healer?"

"No," Enly said. "I want you to sit and talk to me."

"You're sure?"

"Yes."

She sat again, closer to him this time.

"It's been a long day," he said.

"You're still in a lot of pain."

He nodded. "But Barjen says that's to be expected." He turned his head toward the fire so that he wouldn't have to see her face. Best just to get it over with. "He also said that I might not heal entirely. I'll be . . . I'll be lame."

She said nothing. After a few moments of silence he chanced a look at her. She was chewing her lip, staring at the fire as well.

"I'm sorry," she said.

"Don't be. I shouldn't even be alive. I wouldn't be if it wasn't for you." He made himself grin. "I suppose this means you'll have a clear shot at the crystal dagger next year."

A sly smile crept over her face. "I was thinking along similar lines," she said. "This makes things easier in a way."

He stared at her, stung by her words. "That's quite a thing to say!"

"Oh, hush!" Tirnya said. "I didn't mean it that way. I was simply pointing out the obvious. Only one person from any family is allowed in the tournament, and you and I would have fought day and night over which one of us would enter."

"What are you—?" Realization crashed over him like an ocean wave. "What are you saying?" he asked, his grin genuine this time.

"Figure it out for yourself." She leaned over and kissed him gently on the lips. "Sleep," she whispered. "You need rest."

He nodded, unable to speak.

She stood and started to walk away. Then she stopped and walked back to him. "Was there anything else Barjen said you wouldn't be able to do?" she asked coyly, a hand on her hip.

He felt his cheeks redden. "No," he said. "Nothing else."

"Good," she said, turning and starting away again. "Because that would have been a problem."

Enly laughed. It made his ribs ache, but he couldn't have cared less.

Chapter 26

They watched in silence as the Eandi army marched away from the plain. Grinsa stood with L'Norr, H'Loryn, and O'Tal, fearing that at any moment one of the Fal'Borna, or perhaps one of the Eandi, would decide that ending this war was a mistake. He sensed that L'Norr regretted acquiescing to the rest, and he actually found himself keeping a light hold on his own magic, just in case he had to stop the young Weaver from striking at the retreating soldiers.

As it happened, his precautions proved unnecessary, and before long the Eandi had vanished from view, leaving the Fal'Borna army alone on the plain. The air was turning cold again, and dark clouds loomed in the west. Grinsa caught the scent of snow riding the wind.

L'Norr stared eastward longer than the rest, but at last he turned to Grinsa and said, "Tell the a'jeis I want to be riding within the hour. We have a long journey back to the sept."

"Yes, A'Laq," Grinsa said.

L'Norr steered his mount away from the others.

"You're his only Weaver now," O'Tal said, watching the young man ride off.

"He has D'Pera," Grinsa said. "And her daughter shows signs of being a Weaver."

"How long have you lived among the Fal'Borna, Forelander?"

Grinsa hesitated, knowing what the man was going to say. "Long enough to know that an a'laq cares far more about the number of men who are Weavers."

O'Tal nodded. "D'Pera will be able to help him as he learns what it means to be a'laq, but she's not a warrior. And

U'Vara will probably be his n'qlae before long. But his sept has lost two Weavers. He needs you now more than ever."

He might as well have said, *He'll never let you leave now.* That was how Grinsa heard his words. He'd been hoping that with the end of the war he and Cresenne would be able to get away from the plain, to make a life elsewhere for themselves and Bryntelle. He still believed that they could leave now—L'Norr and D'Pera wouldn't be strong enough to keep them there against their will. But there could be no denying that L'Norr would want him to stay.

"It's too bad, really," O'Tal said. "If E'Menua had lived, I would have asked you to come and live in my sept."

Grinsa looked at him. "What?"

"You didn't seem to like E'Menua very much, and he didn't seem fond of you. And I think you and I could be good friends."

"I think so, too, A'Laq," Grinsa said, smiling. "Thank you for saying so."

"Would you consider it?"

The Forelander looked away.

"You can speak honestly with me."

Grinsa rubbed a hand over his face and looked at the man once more. "It's not that I wouldn't be honored to be part of your sept. But I'm not sure that the plain is the right place for my family and me."

O'Tal seemed to consider this for a few moments. If he was angry or insulted, he showed no sign of it. "Where is the right place, then?" he asked eventually.

"I don't know yet. But I should find the a'jeis, as my a'laq asked me to. Please excuse me."

He found the warriors together not far from where he'd been talking to O'Tal, and told them that their a'laq wished to be riding soon. They listened to him in silence, eyeing him warily, but they moved quickly to follow his orders, and within the hour the warriors of E'Menua's sept were ready to follow their new a'laq home.

It seemed that the Fal'Borna were not given to long good-byes. H'Loryn wished Grinsa and L'Norr well, but was more concerned with readying his own men for their ride home. O'Tal was similarly distracted, and he and L'Norr barely acknowledged each other. It seemed that O'Tal's rivalry with E'Menua would not soon be forgotten. He smiled warmly at Grinsa, though. When L'Norr was out of earshot O'Tal said, "If you decide to stay on the plain, let me know. I'd like to hunt with you again. Next time we'll get you a buck."

Grinsa laughed. "Thank you, A'Laq. I'd like that, too."

He rejoined L'Norr and the rest of E'Menua's warriors, and soon they were riding southward back toward the sept.

Their journey home was uneventful. Grinsa had expected that L'Norr would wish to speak with him, but the young Weaver kept to himself, speaking to Grinsa only when he wanted him to convey orders to the other riders. That first night after the Eandi marched away from the battle plain, Grinsa reached out with his magic to speak with Cresenne. He told her about the battle that had been fought and the loss of E'Menua and Q'Daer. Mostly he simply held her and asked about Bryntelle.

As he was about to leave her dream to let her sleep, he remembered to ask how Besh and Sirj were faring.

"They're doing well," she said brightly. "They're heroes."

"They're what?"

And as he listened in stunned silence, Cresenne told him of the sept's battle against the J'Balanar. When she had finished her tale, Grinsa couldn't think of anything to say. He just stood before her, shaking his head, muttering, "Amazing, just amazing."

As he and the Fal'Borna riders drew closer to the sept, Grinsa began to wonder if L'Norr had spoken with D'Pera to let her know that E'Menua had been killed. Grinsa and Cresenne had agreed that it probably wasn't her place to convey such tidings to the n'qlae. But he didn't know what the new a'laq intended to do about this. On the fifth night of their journey back to the sept, he finally decided that as L'Norr's lone Weaver, it was up to him to raise the question.

As usual, L'Norr sat by a small fire, apart from the other warriors. When Grinsa drew near to where L'Norr sat, he called to him by title.

"Yes, what is it?" L'Norr asked, not bothering to look at him.

Grinsa didn't answer until he had reached the fire. "Forgive me, A'Laq. But I was wondering . . ." He faltered. "I was wondering if you had heard of the raid on our sept."

L'Norr gaped at him. "A raid?"

Grinsa nodded and briefly related what Cresenne had told him about their skirmish with the J'Balanar, taking care to include all that Besh and Sirj had done to protect the sept.

When he'd finished, L'Norr shook his head. "The J'Balanar have no shame. They've always been cowards." He said nothing about the Mettai. Grinsa didn't either; he had a far more difficult matter to discuss with the man.

"I take it then," he said, "that you haven't yet spoken with the n'qlae, to . . . to tell her of E'Menua's fate."

For some time L'Norr didn't answer, and Grinsa wondered if he had angered the man. But finally L'Norr rubbed a hand over his face and shook his head. "I don't know how to tell her." He looked up at Grinsa. "Perhaps you should do it for me. Do you have experience with such things?"

"I could do it for you. But I didn't know if this was something that . . ."

"That an a'laq is supposed to do for himself?" L'Norr said, finishing Grinsa's thought.

"Yes."

L'Norr nodded slowly, gazing into his fire again. "She's been my n'qlae for nearly as long as I can remember. And now I have to tell her that her husband is dead, and I'm a'laq of the sept. Yes, it's something I have to do. I just don't know how."

"She's strong, A'Laq. She's Fal'Borna. She knew that this might happen."

"You're right. I'll speak with her tonight." He didn't look at Grinsa again.

After a few moments of silence, Grinsa said, "Thank you, A'Laq," and walked away.

The following morning, as they prepared to ride, L'Norr caught Grinsa's eye and nodded once. They didn't speak of their conversation again.

The riders reached the sept two days later. Though they hadn't been gone long, Grinsa's reunion with Cresenne and Bryntelle was sweeter even than it had been when he had returned to the sept with Q'Daer, Besh, and Sirj. Warriors were welcomed home by parents and wives and children, and L'Norr was received as the sept's new a'laq without question.

E'Menua, Q'Daer, and the other warriors who had been killed were honored with song and silence, and that night L'Norr was honored with a somber feast. Grinsa and Cresenne attended, as they were expected to do, though they wanted only to be alone together.

Besh and Sirj, on the other hand, were told courteously but firmly that they were not welcome at the feast. D'Pera sat alone, though Grinsa noticed that throughout the evening her people approached her singly or in pairs and spoke to her quietly. Eventually Grinsa and Cresenne did the same.

It felt awkward to offer his condolences; D'Pera knew all too well that Grinsa and E'Menua hadn't liked each other. But she greeted them graciously.

"We're sorry for your loss, N'Qlae," Grinsa said, as they stood before her. "The a'laq loved you very much. He told me to tell you so."

"You were with him when he died?" Her voice was steady, but tears shone in her eyes.

"I tried to heal him, but there was poison in his blood. I couldn't fight it."

"But you tried. Thank you for that." She hesitated. "You were right about the Mettai. Your wife has told you how they saved us?"

Grinsa nodded, noting to himself that this once she didn't falter at the word "wife."

"Yes, she told me."

"That's twice that they saved us—that all of you saved us. You have our gratitude."

Grinsa wanted to ask if that meant they would let Besh and Sirj leave the sept, but he thought that was a discussion best left for another day. He and Cresenne bowed to the n'qlae and returned to where they had been sitting.

The feast seemed destined to go on through much of the night, but eventually Grinsa and Cresenne left on the pretense of needing to put Bryntelle to bed. Judging from the way Cresenne's friend F'Solya looked at them, though, they weren't fooling anyone.

Back in their z'kal, they put their daughter in her small bed before undressing and slipping under their blankets. After that, Grinsa lost track of the time, caring only for the taste of Cresenne's lips and the soft warmth of her skin.

Later, as they lay together, their desire sated at least for a time, Cresenne said, "So what now?"

Grinsa was running his hands through her hair, and he laughed. "What did you have in mind?"

She propped herself up on one elbow. "I'm serious, Grinsa. Where do we go from here? I don't want to stay with the Fal'Borna, but I don't know where we should go next."

"Neither do I," he said, turning serious. "We can't leave here until we know that Besh and Sirj are safely away from the sept. But after that . . ." He shrugged.

"We should head west," she said. "North and west. I don't want to go near the J'Balanar, but I want to get away from here."

"All right," he said. He felt the kernel of an idea forming, but he didn't know if it was even possible, and he wasn't ready to say anything that might get Cresenne's hopes up.

"What are you thinking?" she asked.

"That I'll go anywhere you want me to," he said, which was true.

She smiled and kissed him. "Good."

Grinsa waited a few days before seeking an audience with the new a'laq. As the lone male Weaver in the sept, he spent a good deal of time alone outside L'Norr's z'kal, but the young Weaver said little to him, and at least at first, Grinsa was reluctant to intrude on the A'Laq's solitude.

But Grinsa had also spoken several times with Besh and Sirj. Now that the war had ended, both of them were eager to be on their way back to their home village.

"We helped them fight off the J'Balanar raiders," Sirj said with quiet intensity. "They should be willing to let us go."

"I'll do what I can," Grinsa told him.

That same day, he went to see L'Norr in his z'kal.

It was warm and dark within, and it smelled of smoke and cooking meat.

"Forgive the intrusion, A'Laq," Grinsa said.

"It's all right," the man said, motioning for him to sit. "Let me see if I can tell you why you've come. You want to know if I intend to let the Mettai leave."

Grinsa smiled and nodded. "That's part of it, yes."

L'Norr grimaced. "I don't want to. That probably doesn't surprise you. The Mettai killed Q'Daer. Their serpent killed E'Menua. But I understand that these two helped fight off the J'Balanar, and that their magic actually did protect us from the plague." He paused, eyeing Grinsa. "D'Pera has done as you asked. She's convinced me to let them go."

"I'm grateful for that, A'Laq, but you should know that I didn't ask her to speak with you. She did this on her own."

L'Norr appeared genuinely surprised by this. "Really?"

"I swear it."

The man seemed to weigh this briefly. "Well, regardless, the Mettai can leave whenever they're ready. I'll trust you to let them know."

"Thank you, A'Laq."

The man regarded him expectantly. "You indicated there was more."

Grinsa nodded but said nothing, suddenly unsure of how to proceed.

L'Norr watched him for several moments, and then abruptly his eyes widened and the color fled his cheeks. "You want to leave, too."

"Yes, A'Laq."

The young Weaver looked away. "Damn," he said.

"I know that—"

"You'd be leaving me with no Weavers aside from D'Pera."

"U'Vara will be a Weaver."

To Grinsa's surprise, the color rushed back into L'Norr's face, so that it turned bright crimson.

"I know that," the a'laq said. "But I'd have no warriors who could weave."

"We can't stay here, A'Laq. I respect the Fal'Borna— truly I do—but this isn't the life Cresenne and I want for ourselves or for our daughter."

L'Norr wouldn't look at him. "So long as you're with us, you'll never want for anything. You'll be part of the most powerful clan in all the Southlands."

"I thank you for that."

"But it doesn't change your mind."

Grinsa took a breath. "No, A'Laq, it doesn't."

"I see." His eyes flicked toward Grinsa for just an instant, but then he looked away again. "I won't keep you here against your will, but I would ask you to take a few more days and think about this."

"Of course, A'Laq." Grinsa stood. "Thank you."

Before Grinsa could leave, L'Norr asked, "Where would you go?"

Grinsa shook his head. "We don't know yet."

Even after Grinsa had told him twice, Besh couldn't quite believe that he had heard the Forelander correctly.

"They really will let us go?" he said. "Whenever we want?"

Grinsa and Cresenne were both smiling. Even their baby had a huge grin on her pale, beautiful face.

"Whenever you want," Grinsa told him.

"First light," Sirj said. "I want to leave in the morning."

It was cold and it had begun to snow. Besh had no doubt that the journey home would be difficult and long. But he was every bit as eager to be leaving as Sirj.

"Yes," he agreed. "First light."

"Will you be coming with us?" Sirj asked the Forelander and his wife.

The two Qirsi shared a look and then Grinsa shook his head. "No, I'm afraid not. I don't know yet where we're going, but we've been in the sovereignties, and they weren't at all welcoming."

"No," Besh said. "I don't suppose they were."

"I believe I can prevail upon the Fal'Borna to give you food and horses," Grinsa said. "Cresenne and I can even give you some gold if you need it."

"We don't," Besh said. "But thank you. We'd welcome the food and horses, though."

Grinsa and Cresenne left them for a time, saying that they wanted to give Besh and Sirj a chance to gather their belongings. In truth, though, the Mettai had precious little with them. They put their clothes in their travel sacks, and they were done.

They had been granted the freedom to go anywhere in the sept, but they rarely took advantage of this, preferring to remain near their shelter, where they felt most comfortable. On this day, however, Besh insisted that they go to see the n'qlae. Sirj seemed reluctant, but he followed anyway, as Besh knew he would. Sirj felt responsible for him, and would want to make sure that Besh was safe.

The n'qlae was in her z'kal, and she greeted the men with little warmth.

"We'll be leaving tomorrow," Besh told her. "We simply wanted to thank you for helping as you did."

"I'm not sure I did very much," the woman said. "But you're welcome."

"We're sorry for the loss of the a'laq."

The n'qlae nodded, but said nothing.

"We're sorry as well for the death of the other Weaver, Q'Daer."

"He was closest to L'Norr, the new a'laq," the woman said. "I think you'd be best off staying away from him. He won't be interested in your sympathy."

Besh nodded, thinking that it had been a mistake to come speak with the woman. "Very well. Thank you, N'Qlae."

The two Mettai left her shelter and returned to their own. Neither of them said a word.

They ate their evening meal with Grinsa, Cresenne, and Bryntelle, and for once their conversation with the Forelanders didn't linger on matters of war or their captivity or even the Fal'Borna. They exchanged stories about their homelands and their families. They talked about magic. And they tried to ignore the fact that come the morning they would say goodbye and never see one another again. They stayed with Grinsa and Cresenne late into the night, lowering their voices after Bryntelle fell asleep. But still, the evening ended too soon.

The following morning Besh and Sirj awoke with first light and, upon emerging from their shelter, found a young Fal'Borna warrior waiting for them in the cold morning air. Two horses stood beside the man, each laden with a pair of leather sacks filled with dried rilda meat, smoked cheese, and hard bread. Besh thanked the man, who just nodded and left them.

As the warrior strode away, Grinsa and Cresenne arrived from a different direction.

"Is everything all right?" Grinsa asked, staring after the Fal'Borna.

"Yes," Besh said. "Horses, food—this is all that we were hoping for."

Grinsa frowned, glancing around the sept. "The a'laq hasn't come."

Besh smiled ruefully. "No, but I didn't expect him."

"You saved the life of every man and woman here. You deserve more."

"We're Mettai," Besh said, as if that should have explained everything.

Grinsa shook his head, looking like he might say more. But Cresenne placed a slender hand on his shoulder, and that seemed to calm him.

He stepped forward and gathered Sirj in a warm embrace. "You're a good man," the Forelander said. "May the gods grant you and your family a long, happy life together."

Sirj thumped him on the back. "Thank you, Grinsa. May they help you and yours find a home where you can be safe and live out your years in peace."

Grinsa stepped back, and Cresenne gave Sirj a light kiss on the cheek. "Thank you for saving my husband," she said.

Sirj laughed. "I think he returned the favor more than once."

Grinsa faced Besh, smiling sadly. "You still have F'Ghara's necklace?" he asked. "You might need it if you encounter any Fal'Borna on the way back."

Besh patted his pocket. "I have it. But we'll try to avoid any septs just the same."

"Probably wise," Grinsa said. He regarded Besh for several moments. "I wish we'd had more time," he said. "I think I could have learned much from you."

"Thank you," Besh said. "I wonder if you would do me the honor of exchanging blades with me."

The Forelander looked puzzled.

"It's an old Mettai tradition," Besh told him. "A gesture of friendship and respect."

He pulled out his knife and offered it to Grinsa. After a moment, Grinsa took it. Then he pulled out his own blade and handed it to Besh.

"You honor me," Grinsa said.

Besh smiled. "That was my intention."

They embraced like brothers, and to Besh's surprise he found himself blinking back tears.

"Be well, Besh," Grinsa whispered. "May the rest of your days be filled with joy."

"And yours, Grinsa."

Besh released the man and turned to Cresenne. "Take care of him," he said. "He seems to spend much of his time taking care of others."

She smiled. "You've noticed that, have you?" She kissed Besh as she had Sirj. "I'll do my best. And who will take care of you?"

Besh smiled in turn. "Sirj will. And his wife, my daughter. And their children. I go home to a good life. You needn't worry about me."

"Good," Cresenne said. "Then I won't. I'll just thank you for all you did for us—and for the Southlands—and leave it at that."

Besh nodded, his eyes stinging again. He turned quickly to Sirj. "Let's be on our way," he said. "We've a long journey." He paused, looking at the Forelanders one last time. Then he climbed onto his horse and led Sirj out of the sept and onto the plain.

For a long time the two Mettai rode in silence, as a cold wind swirled around them. Besh had expected to feel cold and miserable throughout this ride back to Kirayde, and he thought it likely that there would be times when he would. But for this morning at least, his relief at being away from the Fal'Borna and on his way home was enough to keep him warm.

"Do you think they're all right?" Sirj asked suddenly.

"Who?"

"Elica and the children."

Besh could picture them all in his mind—Elica, strong and long-limbed, her dark hair framing her face; Mihas, Annze, and Cam laughing at some joke one of them had told, their dark eyes dancing. And beside them all, he saw his beloved Ema, dead these many years, but still a presence in his heart and his memories. She looked at him now and smiled, as if to reassure him. To reassure them both.

"Yes," he said. "They're fine."

Sirj cast a look his way. Clearly he wanted to believe what Besh had said, but was afraid to. "How can you be so sure?" he asked.

Besh grinned. "Call it the intuition of an old man. They're well, and they can't wait to welcome us home."

Chapter 27

◆╫◆

EASTERN PLAIN, SOUTH OF THE COMPANION LAKES,
CELEBRATION MOON WANING

U 'Selle had never thought that she would ride to war as the leader of her people. She could hardly think of men like S'Doryn, T'Noth, and T'Kaar as warriors, and she didn't think of herself as an a'laq who could lead men into battle. But with an Eandi army on the march in Fal'Borna lands, and with so many septs ravaged by the Mettai plague, even people in villages as remote as Lowna had been called to arms.

She was old and frail, but she was a Weaver, and she could still ride. She had spoken with other a'laqs, who had told her that a large Fal'Borna army was on its way to face the Eandi, and a second was forming in case that one failed. She and her people were to ride south, along the Silverwater, to make certain that no Eandi reinforcements entered the clan lands from Stelpana.

They rode to N'Kiel's Span, a short journey of four days, and they made camp by the wash. There they waited, watching for any sign of Eandi soldiers. U'Selle had expected that the journey would be a hardship, but she found it exhilarating instead. The cough that would eventually kill her seemed to subside, leaving her feeling stronger and more alive than she had in some time.

S'Doryn rode with her, as did the brothers, T'Noth and T'Kaar. Despite their grim task they spoke of many things and spent a good deal of their time laughing. U'Selle never would have thought that riding to war could be such fun. Perhaps this was why men of the Southlands did it so often. So long as there were no battles to be fought, she thought she could continue to enjoy herself.

And so she was deeply relieved when, just three nights after their arrival at the span, an a'laq named O'Tal entered her dreams to tell her that the fighting had ended, and that she and her people could return home.

"The Eandi army is marching your way," he said. "But we've given them leave to cross the plain back to their home. If you see them, you should allow them to cross the wash."

"We will, A'Laq," she said. "Thank you for letting me know. How did the battles go? Were we victorious?"

"There were losses on both sides," he told her. "This was a war of magic. We should be grateful that it didn't last long."

He told her no more than that, and she found his reticence unsettling.

U'Selle informed her people the following morning that they would be heading back to Lowna. Most of the men seemed pleased, though confused. As they began to break camp and prepare for the short ride home, S'Doryn approached her.

"So we've won?" he asked. "Just like that?"

She regarded him briefly, then started walking back to where she'd tethered her horse, knowing that he would follow. "I don't know exactly what happened," she said quietly. "It sounds as though the battle was . . . inconclusive. The Eandi are leaving, so clearly they didn't win. But when I gave O'Tal a chance to say that we had won, he refused. When was the last time a Fal'Borna warrior did that?"

"What did he say?"

"That it was a war of magic, and that we should be glad it's over." U'Selle made herself smile. "Go. Saddle your horse. The sooner we leave, the sooner you'll see N'Tevva and your girls again."

He smiled at that. But before he could say anything, a cry went up from the far side of the camp. The two of them shared a look and then hurried in that direction. By the time they reached the western end of the camp, several of the men had gathered there and were watching a lone rider approach on horseback.

It appeared to be a large man, and U'Selle thought it likely that he hadn't spotted the army yet. He was close enough that she could hear him singing to himself—he sang poorly and loudly. Their camp was near a cluster of trees, which might have explained how the man could have missed them, though U'Selle thought it odd. Perhaps he didn't see well.

A moment later, he did see them. Suddenly he reined his horse to a halt. After a moment's indecision, he turned southward and spurred his animal to a gallop.

"After him!" U'Selle said. "I want to know who he is."

In moments several of the men, including T'Noth, were on their mounts thundering after the stranger. U'Selle and S'Doryn returned to their horses, saddled them, and followed. By the time they caught up with the others, they had surrounded the man.

He was Eandi; a big, heavy brute of a man with a scarred face and only one good eye. His hair was the color of storm clouds and unkempt. His clothing was tattered and travel-stained. His mount, on the other hand, was an impressive beast. It might even have been a Fal'Borna horse.

The other riders parted when U'Selle and S'Doryn reached them, allowing the two of them to face the man.

"Who are you?" the man demanded. "I've asked them but they won't tell me."

U'Selle raised an eyebrow. "Perhaps that's because you're an Eandi on Fal'Borna land, and that's a question for us to ask you."

The man scowled at her.

"I'm a merchant. I'm headed back into Stelpana."

"A merchant?" she repeated doubtfully. "Where are your wares, merchant?"

The man licked his lips, his one good eye darting from face to face, as if seeking a friend, or searching for a weakness in their circle.

"I lost them," he said at last. "I . . . had a dispute with one of your a'laqs. He took my wares and my cart."

"But he gave you a horse?" S'Doryn asked. He sounded skeptical, too.

"What's your name?" U'Selle asked the man.

He didn't answer. After a moment's hesitation he reached into his pocket and pulled out something that looked like a burnt piece of cloth or parchment.

"Don't come near me!" the man said with such menace that U'Selle nearly laughed out loud. "I don't want to hurt you, but I will if you give me no other choice."

"You'll hurt us with that?" S'Doryn asked.

"Yes. You can laugh all you like. But I can destroy you all with this. I'm nearly home. I just need to get across the wash. And you're going to let me, because if you don't you'll all die."

Several of the men were chuckling now, but T'Noth wasn't, and neither was U'Selle. Looking more closely at the thing in the man's hand, she saw that it wasn't parchment after all. And it appeared too stiff to be cloth. An instant later it hit her like a fist.

"What is that you're holding?" she asked in a hard voice. But she knew.

"You know of the plague," the man said, looking her in the eye, his back straight. "The one conjured by the Mettai."

"We know of it," U'Selle said.

"This is a piece of cursed basket. It still carries that Mettai magic, and if you come near me you'll be sickened. All of you will be. I've seen what this plague can do, and trust me, you want no part of it."

S'Doryn glared at the man, murder in his pale eyes. "We've seen what it can do, too, you bastard. You dare to use that plague as a weapon?"

"I will if I must. It's up to you. Let me go, and you'll be spared. Try to stop me, and you'll die a terrible death."

"No," U'Selle said.

The man stared at her. "What do you mean, no?"

She smiled harshly. "I mean no, you won't be making any of us sick. Not with that."

"You think you can stop me?"

"I know we can," she said. "Apparently you haven't heard that there's a second Mettai spell. It's spread across the plain nearly as quickly as that first one did. It makes us immune to the plague."

The man's hand holding the scrap of basket dropped a bit, but then he raised it again. "I don't believe you. There is no such spell."

"There is," she said. "It was conjured by two Mettai on the Central Plain. It saved the lives of men who had been sick with the plague and it made them immune. One of those men walked in my dreams as Weavers can and passed the spell on to me. I've passed it on to all the people in my village. So that basket you hold is no more dangerous to me than a blade of grass."

And to make the point, she glanced at the scrap of basket and used her magic to make it burst into flame. The merchant let out a small cry and dropped it. It fell to the ground and continued to burn, as the merchant watched helplessly.

"This man who came to you," he said, his voice barely audible. "Tell me about him."

"He was a Forelander, living now in—"

"E'Menua's sept," the man finished for her.

"You know him."

The merchant nodded. "I thought he was dead."

"You were wrong," U'Selle said. "Now, merchant, tell me your name, so that when other a'laqs ask me, I'll be able to tell them who it was we killed."

The man sighed, seeming more weary than scared. "My name is Torgan Plye."

U'Selle's eyes widened. "You're Torgan Plye?"

He nodded.

"You're the one who spread the plague in the first place."

"Actually," he said, "I wasn't. At least not intentionally." A bitter smile flitted across his homely face. "I don't suppose that matters much, does it?"

"No," U'Selle said coldly. "You were declared an enemy of the Fal'Borna a long time ago. And today you threatened to kill us with a plague that has already devastated our land. You've earned this death. Get down off your horse."

The merchant dismounted and looked around the circle, shaking his head slowly. "I knew you white-hair bastards would be the death of me. This morning I started thinking that I might actually make it to the wash, but even then I knew. One way or another, you were going to find a way to kill me."

"It seems you were right," U'Selle said evenly. "Do you have anything else you wish to say?"

He frowned. "I hope you all rot."

U'Selle nodded once. "And I hope that Bian is as merciful as you deserve, Torgan Plye."

She reached for her shaping magic and snapped the man's neck. He collapsed to the ground and was still, his one good eye still open, staring up into the sky.

"Leave him for the dogs and crows," U'Selle said loudly. "It's time we were headed home."

The others stared at the man's body for a moment or two before slowly riding back to the camp. Only T'Noth, S'Doryn, T'Kaar, and U'Selle remained.

"I wonder if the spell would have worked," T'Noth said.

U'Selle looked at him. "You mean the one that made us immune?"

The young man nodded.

"I believe it would have," she said. "But I'm just as glad that we didn't have to find out." U'Selle turned to S'Doryn. "The Forelander told me that the old Mettai witch was killed by the two men who made this new spell. And now Torgan's dead, too. When we return to Lowna, you can tell Jynna that all this is finally over."

S'Doryn smiled sadly. "I could tell her that," he said. "And I will if she asks. But usually she doesn't like to talk about it, and I can hardly blame her."

U'Selle reached out and patted his shoulder. "I think she and Vettala are lucky to have you."

"Funny," the man said. "N'Tevva and I feel that way about them."

The four of them wheeled their horses away from the broken body of the Eandi merchant and returned to their camp. Within the hour, they were riding back to their home by the Companion Lakes.

Epilogue

◆—┼—◆

Grinsa, Cresenne, and Bryntelle left the sept only a few days after the departure of the two Mettai. L'Norr and D'Pera spoke to them at length in the days before, trying to convince them to stay, but both Grinsa and Cresenne had long since made up their minds to leave the Central Plain.

They rode north and west on the horses they had first purchased in Yorl, their very first day in the Southlands. They skirted the Fallow Downs, wishing to avoid the J'Balanar, and entered the Berylline Forest. There they encountered the woodland clans—the A'Vahl and the M'Saaren. They had heard other Southlands Qirsi speak of both peoples, and had been prepared to find that the A'Vahl were difficult and arrogant. After the Fal'Borna, they seemed anything but.

They found an A'Vahl settlement along the eastern banks of the river named for the clan. They were welcomed there, of course, because Grinsa was a Weaver, and even among the less warlike clans of the Southlands, Weavers were sought after. They stayed among the A'Vahl for nearly half a turn, learning the ways of the clan, and enjoying their wonderful food, which included a dazzling array of roots and greens, fruits and nuts, and some of the finest venison either Grinsa or Cresenne had ever tasted. They were shown how the A'Vahl shaped wood into bowls and furniture and musical instruments that they traded with peddlers from throughout the land. To his surprise, Grinsa discovered that he had a certain talent for woodwork, just as Cresenne had found during their turns with the Fal'Borna that she had a penchant for tanning.

It was curiosity, more than anything else, that made them leave. They liked the A'Vahl and both of them believed that they might have made a life for themselves there. But they had heard much about the M'Saaren, and so they crossed the A'Vahl River and journeyed south, until they found a large M'Saaren settlement called Sh'Rette. Once more they were welcomed into the village, and once more they were impressed with what they found there.

In many ways the M'Saaren and A'Vahl were alike, and it seemed that whatever rivalry existed between the two clans had been exaggerated by those Qirsi who lived outside the woodland. Grinsa and Cresenne remembered being told as much by D'Chul, a M'Saaren lutenist they had met when they first entered the clanlands. They ate similar foods, did similarly marvelous things with the various woods growing in the forest, and were equally friendly to strangers.

Again, Grisna and Cresenne could have remained in the village for a long time and been very happy. As it happened, they stayed with the M'Saaren for longer than they had been with the A'Vahl, though mostly because Bryntelle came down with a bad fever while they were there, and they wanted to wait until she recovered fully before moving on.

But move on they did. In the end, Cresenne realized that she missed the open skies of the plain. As much as she liked living with the woodland people, she found the woodland itself dark and oppressive.

As the waxing of the Fire Moon—Eilidh's Moon in the Forelands—began, they left the Berylline Forest and made their way into D'Krad land. They found K'Hosh, a small fishing village along the coast of the Gulf of T'Saan, where the people were desperate for a Weaver to help them recover from an outbreak of Murnia's pox. They were given a small house that had belonged to K'Hosh's healer, who died in the outbreak. It sat on the outskirts of the settlement right along the rocky shoreline, and Cresenne and Bryntelle remained there while Grinsa tended to the villagers. The D'Krad weren't as friendly as the woodland clanfolk had been. They were wary of strangers and nearly as abrupt in their manners as the Fal'Borna. But when Grinsa healed their sick, including several children, the villagers warmed to him and his family.

By this time, though, Grinsa and Cresenne had made their decision. One day, after the outbreak of pox had passed, they made their way down to the small port below the village, and Grinsa gave a message to a sea captain who was heading north.

Their missive had a long way to go. They remained in the house by the coast, enjoying the first days of the Planting and the return of warmer winds. Bryntelle learned to walk and began to speak, much to the delight of both her parents. Cresenne and Grinsa both worked a small garden plot by their modest home, and Grinsa learned enough about fishing to provide their supper on most nights.

They made their way to port every half turn or so, seeking the captain they had entrusted with their message, but for a long time they saw nothing of the man. The Planting gave way to the Growing. Warm damp winds and great violent storms swept across the gulf. Their garden grew. Ships managed to make port, and the small village bustled with fishermen and merchants. But it wasn't until the middle of the Growing, what people in the Southlands called the Sky Moon, that the captain returned with a message for Grinsa and Cresenne.

It said just what they had hoped it would.

"Are you sure you want to do this?" Grinsa asked Cresenne as they stood outside their house, watching the sun descend over the gulf and the distant island of Senkora.

She took a breath and nodded, looking both excited and apprehensive. "I think so."

"It means a long voyage."

Cresenne had suffered greatly on their sea voyage to the Southlands a year before.

Her expression soured, as if his words had triggered a memory of those days. "I know," she said. "But there's nothing to be done about that. The western waters are supposed to be calmer than those in the east."

"All right then," Grinsa said, pleased that they had a plan at last.

Bryntelle was playing in the garden, pulling a petal from each flower, filling her hands with color. He called her over and she tottered to where they were standing.

"How's my Bryn-Bryn?" he asked, scooping the girl into his arms.

"Good," she said. She held out her hands to show him all the petals. "Wook what I find."

"They're very pretty," Grinsa said. "Mama and I have been talking, and we're wondering how you'd feel about going on a ride on a boat."

"A weaw boat?" she asked breathlessly, her pale eyes growing wide.

"A real boat. We'd be on it for some time, and at the end of the trip we'd have a new place to live."

"I wike this pwace."

"I know you do, sweetie. But this new place will be nice, too. And we'll still be by the water."

"And we go on a weaw boat?"

He grinned. "Yes."

She shrugged, then nodded. "Aww wight."

Grinsa turned to Cresenne, who was smiling as well. "All right," he said. "Looks like we're going."

Two days later, they made their way down to the docks, paid the captain one half the cost of their passage, and stepped onto a good-sized merchant ship called *Golden Tern*.

The captain was an Eandi man from Braedon in the Forelands, and though he seemed to have no particular affection for people of the sorcerer race, neither did he seem as hostile toward Qirsi as were most Eandi of the Southlands. He took their gold, welcomed them onto the ship, and proceeded to ignore them for most of the journey. Grinsa and Cresenne didn't mind at all.

The journey north went better than Grinsa could have hoped. Cresenne had been right: The western waters were calmer, and the only storm that might have endangered the ship struck while they were in port in the city of Rawson, in Braedon. Grinsa, Cresenne, and Bryntelle spent the night in the city, before returning to the ship the next morning. The skies already had begun to clear again, and the ship set sail a short time later on smooth waters.

Still, by the time the *Golden Tern* had navigated around the Braedon Peninsula and into the Strait of Wantrae, they had been on the ship for more than a turn, and were ready to disembark. Seeing Curgh Castle perched atop the cliffs of the Eibithar coast, Grinsa and Cresenne couldn't have been happier or more relieved. Even Bryntelle, who loved the ship and had become a favorite of the *Golden Tern*'s sailors, seemed ready to step back on dry land.

They docked at sunset and were met at the Curgh pier by only two people, which was how it had to be. There were those in Curgh and elsewhere who would have wanted Cresenne imprisoned for things she had done long ago, when the conspiracy of the rogue Weaver first began to spread across the Forelands. And there were those who would have wanted all three of them put to death simply because Grinsa was a Weaver.

One of those who met them was a slender, pretty Qirsi woman with long white hair that she wore in twin braids. Her eyes were paler than Grinsa's but similar enough to his in shape that a person looking for the resemblance might have guessed, correctly, that she was Grinsa's sister.

The other was a young Eandi noble with dark blue eyes, wheat-colored hair, and a face that might have been handsome were it not for a lattice of deep scars.

Both the woman and the nobleman smiled broadly as they watched Grinsa, Cresenne, and Bryntelle approach. They embraced the travelers and then, while Keziah, Grinsa's sister, fussed over her niece, who regarded her with a puzzled smile, Tavis, the young duke of Curgh, took Grinsa aside.

"Your house is waiting for you," he said. "It's on a remote promontory overlooking the strait. It's close enough to the castle that I can keep an eye on you, but far enough from anything else that no one should stumble across it. I'm sure you'll all be safe there."

Grinsa smiled, gripping the young man's shoulder. "Thank you, my lord."

Tavis scowled, giving his scarred face a fearsome look. "Don't call me that!"

"What am I supposed to call you?"

"You're supposed to use my name, of course."

Grinsa nodded, still smiling. "Very well, my lord."

The duke shook his head, and walked over to Cresenne and Keziah.

"We're most grateful to you, my lord," Cresenne said, sounding terribly formal. Theirs had never been an easy relationship. Tavis bore his scars in part because of things she had done for the conspiracy.

But Tavis smiled and took her hand. "You're to call me Tavis, too."

"All right," she said. "Tavis."

Bryntelle looked up at the duke's scarred face, and for a moment Grinsa feared that she'd shy away from the man. But she merely smiled and said, "I'm Bwyntewwe. Who ah you?"

"I'm Tavis," the duke said, squatting down beside her. "And I knew you when you were too small to walk or talk."

Her eyes widened. "You did?"

He nodded.

"I'm gonna wiv in a new house," she told him.

"Yes, you are," Tavis said. "And I'm going to make certain that you and your parents are always very happy there."

The duke paid the ship's captain the balance of what he was owed. Then the five of them started up the lane away from the pier, toward Curgh city and the promontory where Grinsa, Cresenne, and Bryntelle would spend the rest of their days.

Tavis led the way. Keziah carried Bryntelle in front of her on her horse. Grinsa and Cresenne followed them, riding side by side.

Grinsa stared up at the great castle of Curgh, which was shrouded in shadow and framed against an indigo sky. He hadn't thought that he'd ever see this city again. He hadn't thought he'd ever get to see his sister holding Bryntelle, or his friend the duke growing into his title. They'd been away from the Forelands for less than a year, but it felt like far longer. Leaving these shores for the Southlands had seemed like the right decision at the time. But only now did he feel that he and his family were where they belonged.

"Are you all right?" Cresenne asked him.

"Yes," he said, smiling at her and reaching out a hand. "Are you?"

She took his hand in hers and nodded. "Yes," she said. "It's good to be home."

TOR

Award-winning authors
Compelling stories

Please join us at the website
below for more information
about this author and other great
Tor selections, and to sign up for
our monthly newsletter!